OF ASHES AND DUST

Ron Roman

OF ASHES AND DUST

Addison & Highsmith

Addison & Highsmith Publishers

Las Vegas ◊ Chicago ◊ Palm Beach

Published in the United States of America by
Histria Books
7181 N. Hualapai Way, Ste. 130-86
Las Vegas, NV 89166 USA
HistriaBooks.com

Addison & Highsmith is an imprint of Histria Books dedicated to outstanding works of fiction. Titles published under the imprints of Histria Books are distributed worldwide.

Library of Congress Control Number: 2022943679

ISBN 978-1-59211-178-7 (hardcover)
ISBN 978-1-59211-426-9 (softbound)
ISBN 978-1-59211-240-1 (eBook)

Dedicated to veterans everywhere who have marched to orders from above even when the heart has begged otherwise.

"I have set before you life and death, the blessing and the curse; therefore, choose life, that both you and your descendants may live."

— Book of Deuteronomy

Chapter 1

I looked at the screen, and — behold — there appeared a huge mushroom-like cloud, the likeness of which I had never seen, other than like those in photographs from my history book when I was a kid back in high school so long ago.

I'm not a timid man. Never have been. Decorated veteran of the Vietnam conflict, but this, this juggernaut was like nothing you could ever imagine. Gargantuan in its breadth, even more so in what it did to your inner psyche: exploding from its epicenter, then enveloping your soul, your very being, and then, almost snakelike, worming its way into your consciousness in a way that seared memory. You could never forget it — in a sense, not even beyond death — a product not so much of man's hatred of others, but, rather, of himself.

And death and the seemingly eternal darkness are what it brought to us, the survivors, the forgotten ones, like the memories I have — and always will — of gazing up into night blackness in Vietnam, trying to configure the constellations in some sickening attempt to keep grips on my sanity, wondering when Charlie and assorted Viet Cong would slither out from predawn jungle hideaways and slit our throats. But this one was IT; this was the one that spread out its tentacles everywhere. So, it is with this faraway, half-dreamlike memory, somehow burned indelibly into the forefront of my brain, that I look back at our own mammoth denial and self-delusion presaging the nightmare of living hell come riding to earth. How I survived it all, I don't know. Or have I? That is, I'm here, physically, but some parts of me, maybe most of me, are dead. Dead. Dead. Dead. Forever. I don't know what part of me left over I want to share. This is the story of survival, consummate survival. This is the story, constructed from my own meticulous diary, of those who looked over the edge, saw the past, present, and future in one glance, and tried to carry on, our egos shattered as well as the American society to which we had wedded our hopes and dreams for a better world for ourselves, our kids, and our kids' kids. Somehow, we survived to the best of the ability God saw fit to bestow upon us.

I was already well into feeling middle-aged, fresh out from a prestigious grad-uate school nestled in my native New England hills and with another degree in tow, this time in the humanities, and not much else. With a newly-splintered mar-riage and the overall post-Cold War economy again heating up, yet with no job prospects for me within the walls of academe, my future looked dim and just plain tedious. Damn depressing. Until I met Mark Mercotti.

Soldier sphinx. Steady of hand and pony of tail, Mark had done time in 'Nam, was about my age, and like myself had gotten himself decorations pinned to his tit and nightmares pitted into his head. Recipient of the Silver Star. He had been a member of the First Cavalry Division in 'Nam and again, like me for a brief time previously, had done a stint with the most fucked-up unit in the US Army — the Eighth US Army in Korea. Not that Mark totally disliked Army life; he had been an outstanding field-grade officer with about fifteen years in service. Yet, when it came down to the long haul, as careers go, at fifteen years or so, he'd said he had had enough. Mark's last long-term assignment had been in military intelligence. Something to do with aerial phenomena.

***

"How ya doin', buddy?" A throaty, masculine voice that sounded like Mark's burst forth from my right. Nursing a rum and Coke as I steadied myself on my stool at the local pub, I caught a glimpse of a hulking figure lumbering toward me. There he was: tall, clean-shaven with a strong, chiseled profile, well over two hundred solid pounds, and looking like he had somehow been stuffed into his mauve out-of-style leisure suit. He wore his still-luxuriant, jet-black hair in a short ponytail and a single tiny gold earring in his left ear. Unusual, I thought, for an ex-military officer. Somebody still stuck in the 70s. "What'd you say the name of this place was?"

"Central Cafe."

"Central Cafe? Ah, yeah; that's it. Didn't have much trouble finding it. Not in a town this size at any rate."

"Good. Sit down."

"Thanks."

"What are you drinking?"

"Uh, make it a Budweiser," he nodded to the bartender.

"No Buds available today, Bud. How about a Miller?"

"Uh — no, I prefer Budweiser. In that case, give me a seltzer water."

Yes, he fit my very first impression: soldier of steady habits. "So, what's up?" I asked pensively. The rum and Coke went down easily.

"Well, remember what we started talking about back on that hike in the Berkshire Mountains last month? The time we went out to Mount — "

A sudden commotion silently erupted to our left. It involved a young couple sitting diagonally across the counter — a boyfriend-girlfriend squabble. Couldn't have been more than a couple of years out of high school. Then for some unexplained reason, other faces focused upon all four of us at the counter.

"Look, let's sit in that booth over there," Mark said, one tone above a whisper. "I really wouldn't want this to get out to anybody else. Besides, the damn smell's killing me." The place was starting to get musty.

Not knowing what to make of this sudden confession, other than the fact that military intelligence had made him semi-paranoid, I grabbed my drink, and we walked over and sat down. The place, a plain no-frills eatery in my hometown's swanky downtown district, was fast filling up with a lunchtime crowd. Yodeling cowboy lyrics from a nearby jukebox began to fill the air, and it was getting hot and stuffy.

"Look, guy," he said earnestly, leaning over on his elbows, "I know you may think this a bit much, but I really gotta keep this stuff low, low-key, see?"

"Yeah, sure. Have to do what you have to do, Mark. So, what's the story?"

He paused, freed his hands, and refocused his glasses, sliding down his nose from the noonday humidity, then looked at me intensely. "OK, where the hell was I?"

"'Bout not letting this stuff out because — "

"Yeah, that was it." He leaned back, as if to study my reaction and have room still to notice his surroundings. "Well," he paused, narrowing his eyes, "it all started out in the deserts of east New Mexico in '47. July, first week to be exact. I know what kind of stickler you are for details." He smirked.

"Wait a minute, Mark! Why are you telling me this? Why me?"

"Well, Bill, you'll know when the time comes. Trust me."

I'll never forget the way he paused, as if his revelation held some secret significance.

He focused on my face again, as if to see some hidden fear, some secret misgiving. "We — ah, I mean Army Air Corps — recovered some kind of airborne craft, initially described as a sort of flying disk. Crashed in the deserts about sixty — or was it eighty?— miles northwest of Roswell, outside some shitkicker place called Corona. There was a rancher first on the scene. Military intelligence had to get him to keep his mouth shut! We couldn't afford to have this stuff get out!"

"Wait a minute! You're talking about that alleged flying saucer crash at Corona, aren't you? There've been shows on it, documentaries, on TV."

"'Alleged,' Billy Boy?"

"Now wait a minute — "

Everybody looked again toward the counter. The squabbling kids had started up again. The girl's boyfriend, or whatever he was, looked back our way. Steve, the bartender, standing behind them, had a look of resignation on his face, as if he had been through this with them before.

"What the fuck you looking at?" the guy yelled at us.

I got really scared, hoping he meant Mark. Though not much more than a high school kid, he looked formidable in his dirty gray, tight-fitting muscle shirt. The kind of shirt some guys his age wear to show off. Looked like some college football tackle.

"I said, what the fuck are you looking at, Four Eyes?" I guessed he was referring to Mark's rather thick glasses. I breathed a sigh of relief. "I'm talkin' to you!"

"Honey, please…." moaned the girl.

"Shut up!" He rammed her into the next bar stool. Hard. Then got off his. I don't remember exactly what happened next; I was trying to keep my mind off the ever-increasing heat. I think Mark was already on his feet; it all happened so damned quick. I do remember Mark standing momentarily just off to the right, the much-maligned glasses sitting contentedly on our table. Then it looked like the kid had second thoughts. Didn't matter. The kid had moved too close. Mark let him have it — an open hand thrust right to the throat followed by a lightning-fast headlock. The kid squealed like a little pig. Some women screamed. Everyone backed off. There was a loud thud. Mark had rammed the kid's head into the counter, knocking him semi-conscious. He staggered. Mark grabbed him by his ear.

"Next time, son, pay attention to what comes out of the mouth." Mark repositioned him on his stool. The kid slumped over, his meaty arms dangling from his sides, a rivulet of blood trickling down his neck, a tiny puddle beginning to form next to his stool. The cowboy on the jukebox finally stopped his yodeling.

The kid's girl had been standing there all along, taking it all in, too stupefied by the violence, by the speed, for any reaction. Or maybe she was just plain glad somebody had finally shut his big, fat mouth. Secretly, I think she liked it. I don't know. Never inquired. Never said a word to her. It's a funny thing, violence. Show it on TV, and people pay little attention; see it live, and they get sick. Most of them, at least. Unless you get too numbed by it all … like in 'Nam.

Folks were still glaring at us. Steve motioned for us to leave. We didn't hang around for a second request. It appeared that Steve was familiar with this kind of scene with these kids or whomever. Besides, I was recently back in town — no need to get reacquainted with the police this way.

"Geez, you plugged him good. Damn, Mark, thought you were going to kill that kid."

An early spring breeze blowing through the door felt cool on my arms.

Mark positioned his glasses as we made our way out onto the sidewalk and into the hot overhead sun. "Don't worry. If I'd wanted to hurt him, they'd be calling for the town coroner right now instead of giving him that wet towel."

We lingered awhile on the sidewalk. I thought maybe the cops would be there any moment. Wedgemont Police Station was but only a block away. I gave Mark some stupid excuse that I had to get home — pay the landlady and work on some dissertation on epistemology and Molière, or something like that — and would call him later that evening. Fact was, maybe I wasn't as inured to violence as I'd thought.

"OK, Billy Boy. Gimme a call later, huh?" He straightened out his collar, eyeing me oddly. "Hey, you're not upset that I –"

"Naw! You kidding? Who, me?"

"Oh, all right. That's good. Later."

I watched him as he walked toward the parking lot behind the pub, pausing for a moment to peer into the pub window to check out the kid. It really was time for me to go home, yet I headed for the library to check out a few things about UFOs. What Mark had said thus far was reminiscent of things I heard when I was in uniform myself. Things I couldn't quite put my finger on, yet, like some half-foggy memory that refused to fade, jabbed at the brain.

As I look back, nothing else that afternoon was memorable save some library newspaper stories hollering about our national currency sliding long-term against foreign ones. Again. Yeah, as if that mattered to me at the time. No full-time job. Nothing.

A few days later, I was returning from the Veterans Administration to see my counselor and the unemployment office to see if I qualified for food stamps when I got a call from Mark.

"Billy Boy! What's doin'? Hey! You don't mind if I call you 'Billy Boy,' do ya?"

I said I didn't.

"Got some documents pertaining to what we've been talking about I thought you might like to have a look at."

"You mean about aerial phenomena, pie plates in the sky?"

"Whoa, buddy. Remember what I told you about being 'low-key'?"

At first, I didn't; then it hit me. And as I was getting increasingly depressed over my dour-looking employment prospects, and I half-wanted to end the conversation quickly, something about Mark, and something about this aerial phenomenon shit, began to take on a steadily increasing sense of immediacy. I hadn't realized it then, but I had an all-too-real dream about UFOs in Vietnam. At least, I think I did.

"No ... Yeah ... Wouldn't know anything about it, really; it wasn't my business...."

I would meet him that weekend.

The day broke clear and crisp. I woke up to find myself in a sweat, sounds of screaming and goddamned helicopters exploding in my head. Mark was over to the house earlier than agreed upon. I had hardly finished shaving and he was already at the door, again in that mauve leisure suit. Christ, hadn't he something else to wear? He scanned the neighborhood, nervous-like.

We small-talked about sports and nothingness, the kind of things men say when they're still too unsure of each other and of themselves. I guess I'm not good at small talk. That's what my ex-wife used to say, right after we'd return home from something social. Bloody bitch. I felt a bit awkward and sensed the same in Mark. Perhaps it had to do with our earlier incident. I don't know. I yearned for a smoke but decided against it. I knew Mark didn't like tobacco smoke. But it was my own home for Chrissakes, even if it was rented in what was obviously the poorest section of town. I had to quit anyway.

He laid his briefcase on the kitchen table and shuffled some papers rather clumsily. One or two dropped to the floor. He knelt, kind of covering them up as if he didn't want me to see them. Not yet.

"OK, remember, for now, this stuff's between you and I."

How I hated it when college-educated guys said, "between you and I."

"Let's have a look."

He picked up the papers and laid out on the table what appeared to be several poorly reproduced photostatic copies of official government documents, beginning with headings like "Top Secret/ORCON" and "Project Such-and-Such" followed by "Proword" and "OPR." One was titled something to the effect of "For the President's Eyes Only." Mark pushed up his sleeves. I browsed through the copies.

"It all started right after World War II," he said. "Like I was saying back at the pub, in 1947 in New Mexico. Some put it — "

"Some what?"

"Some of the earlier researchers put it as early as '43 during the war itself, during a tryout of a little-known top-secret project called Rainbow having to do with invisibility and teleportation of warships. The Navy was overseeing it. In fact, Einstein played a pivotal role, although it looks like he tried to hide it. And you thought the Manhattan Project was secret?"

"Go on." I put down the papers.

"The Navy was working with Einstein's Unified Field Theory, trying to put it to practical wartime use. As it happened, it's reported that they did actually teleport a warship from the Navy dockyards in Norfolk to — and this is where it sounds really crazy — to another dimension or something. Don't ask me exactly where. Anyways, it was gone for about thirty minutes. It was reported the guys on board, think it was forty-two, saw spirits, alien beings, and UFOs, and the experience made them crazy. One sailor went public with it. At least tried to. The Navy shut him down and has disavowed knowledge of the incident ever since. Believe it or not, Hollywood did a movie on essentially the basic facts I've given you."

"So, so why isn't it known? I mean, why hasn't somebody come out with the story definitively?"

"That's it! You see, the government can't. Can't let it out. It'd cause too much of a panic, as lame as that sounds, and you gotta realize the whole thing, UFOs and all, is being investigated from a weapons research development point of view. Besides, it's all so bizarre that who'd believe it at face value anyhow?"

I had been so absorbed that it was only at that moment that I became aware of my next-door neighbor's dog barking. "And what about UFOs?"

"They're called AVCs or Alien Visitation Crafts within intel. Anyhow, that was next, in '47. First time we ever got hard-core physical evidence. I'm telling you...." He composed himself. "Couple of them crashed in New Mexico, like I said. The one by Corona carried four aliens. Dr. Bronk, one of twelve original investigators appointed to an ultra-secret presidential panel to report to Truman — the panel was called Majestic-12 — nicknamed them EBE, for Extraterrestrial Biological Entities, until a better term could be agreed upon. Bronk was the one who did the first autopsies. The panel was headed by Dr. Vannevar Bush, one of the country's preeminent scientists at the time. Ever hear of him?"

I said I wasn't sure.

"Doesn't surprise me. He wasn't internationally known like Einstein. Incidentally, evidence points to the probability that the panel continues today."

I glanced at a couple of the documents. Mark pointed out one referring to the MJ-12 panel. "You said there were 'a couple of them.' What happened to the other?"

"That's mentioned here too someplace. Anyways, the crash was about one hundred and fifty miles from Corona, west. In good condition."

"You mean occupants?"

"No, the craft."

"Any of them ever survive?"

"Yes."

"What happened?"

"Another crash occurred in '49. There was one survivor, EBE-1. He died in 1952."

"Died in 1952? And just how the hell was this all kept secret?"

"You have to understand this was — is — considered 'Above Top Secret.' He was kept — I believe it was at Los Alamos. I'd have to go back and check on details. It's all pretty confusing."

"That's an understatement."

"Naval Intelligence Support has primary field operational responsibility; from there information is funneled to the Director of the CIA, whose job it is to coordinate with MJ-12 and the president directly. The president might not even be fully appraised of what's going on."

He meant 'apprised.'

"How do you mean, 'not fully appraised'?"

"I mean, even the president doesn't have the highest security clearance. You were in intel. Thought you might have known that."

I told him I didn't, though I had heard rumors to that effect. My head began to hurt.

"My own gut feeling is that presidents, ever since Kennedy, are not being kept appraised of all details, like many of us believed they should be."

"What makes you think that?"

"Gut feeling."

I had the distinct impression Mark knew more than he was letting on. I knew instinctively by now not to push too hard. "OK. Between you and me, where does that leave it all now?"

He repeated my question. "Well...." He tugged at his shirt collar, loosening it as if the revelations were making him squirm. "It means that the whole thing is the biggest secret in history."

Obviously, I thought.

"It means that soon it'll be too late."

"Too late? Too late for what?"

He eyed me. Coolly. "Too late for most of us. Too late for just about every unlucky bastard on the planet, 'cept maybe those who go underground."

"What the f — " I caught myself. Since 'Nam, I had picked up the tempting habit of ubiquitous cursing. I was trying to stop. I was even told by a female colleague that I had said 'fuck' once quite casually in formal company, at an official academic function at that. I was surprised. Academics have to watch what comes out of their mouths, either in class or official events.

This sudden eruption of emotion appeared to delight him. It was as if he were waiting for some display of intense feelings about all this. He leaned back on his heels, making his stature loom even larger. I realized what had caused my headache. His damn aftershave lotion. Bad enough he had to wear that same silly suit. He folded his arms across his chest, enhancing his already considerable aura of authority.

"What the heck are you talking about?" I was excited.

A wan smile eased across his face; then, almost as suddenly, his manner changed from earnestness to passive engagement. "Really," he said, "we'd better end it. You've had about all you can absorb for one day."

"Wait a minute. Tell me everything!" I leaned toward him. He stood his ground.

"No, big fella. That's it for today. Besides, now it's my time to run. The other stuff entails religion and evolution. Too much to get into now."

I persisted. I forgot that he couldn't be swayed. He shook his head. I had to know what he knew. He nodded toward the papers. "Go ahead," he said, "have another look. Quick." I devoured the documents ravenously. I sat down to steady myself. I couldn't read fast enough. He began to fidget.

"Can I keep them? Just to have a look overnight?"

I guess I must have looked too eager, something of a fool. He didn't have to say no. It was in his eyes. This time I wouldn't ask twice. He knew he had me where he wanted me.

***

Over the next several days, I thought of our encounter. Constantly. We stayed in touch sporadically. In a sense, that was fine by me. I had too many piddling details to attend to, like those involving my ex-wife, though I craved the answers to what he had titillated me with. Then while playing with Buckie, my neighbor's big, long-haired mongrel, it dawned on me. Mark said that I had been in Intelligence. This was true, albeit for a short time. I'd never told him that. Or at least I didn't remember doing so. I wondered aloud at times how he knew. I felt it was I who was starting to look over shoulders. Events of the previous days steamrolled into my mind.

Job hunting was not going well. I was starting to get scared. Bills were beginning to pile up, and resources starting to slim down. After surviving Vietnam, I thought nothing would ever bother me again. I was wrong. My life was playing itself out like a script already read. Apply to this college department, harangue the department secretary on my status, and then more often than not, get some shitass this-position-is-not-to-materialize-after-all-due-to-unexpected- financial-exigencies answer. I constantly had to remind myself I wasn't seeking work at Harvard.

It was getting late in the spring and, as academic jobs go, time to get a bit desperate. The good thing was I hadn't heard from my ex-wife in quite some time. When we'd been in high school, Sheila had been the girl in all the guys' wet dreams. Fresh off a Norman Rockwell canvas. Now I hoped she had moved out of the area. She hadn't been bothering me for money. What a relief. It wasn't to last long. She'd lasso me when I least expected it. It was early Sunday morning. My phone rang.

"William, why in hell haven't you been in touch, goddammit? Why?"

"Uh, I don't — "

"Dammit! You know you're supposed to. What the hell's going on with you, anyway?"

"I, uh, d — didn't even thought — "

"'Didn't even thought'? 'Didn't even thought'? What the fuck kind of English is that? English teacher, eh?" She laughed.

"Now, wait a minute. Calm down. Payment's on its way," I lied. "It'll be there in the blink of an eye."

"In the blink of an eye and your ass! If I haven't heard from you by the end of next week...." She let her voice trail off. There was a pause. Then she yelled, "You know what the hell you have to do! I know you're lying, not by what you say, but by what you don't."

I said nothing and just sat there in a fool's fog.

"William, William, you playing games with me again?" She shrieked in ever-louder shrillness. "Speak to me, damn you! You're always so damn indecisive!"

I assured her I was not playing games.

"And when you start working in September, I want to know where it is! What solid prospects have you had since March?"

"Several."

"'Several'? Where?"

"You know, several — "

"No, I don't know!" She sarcastically emphasized "don't."

"Several down South and up North. Two-bit junior colleges and religious-affiliated institutions."

She uttered something like, "Uhm." That always meant she didn't believe me. I wanted to smash down the phone. Another period of silence. "Did that Yale seminar lead anywhere, the one where you were supposed to give your paper on e-piss-ta-me-jee — I can't even say it." She meant epistemology.

"The Yale seminar?" I didn't correct her; it wasn't at Yale. It wouldn't have mattered to you if it had been at Idiots Anonymous, I thought to myself. "Yeah, that went off OK." She laughed hilariously.

"William?"

"Yes?"

"You're such a stupid fuck! With all the education you've got, you'd think by now, why, you'd think by now — ah, forget it.... When you going to settle down and get a real job, the kind that a man can help support his wife and kids with, if we were to have any?"

I hung up the phone. Maybe I was a 'stupid fuck.' All I knew at that moment was I had had enough.

I wasn't doing anything in the way of dating since the breakup. Didn't socialize much. For all the punishment she dished out, I was still secretly half-yearning for reconciliation. I knew it'd never work. No matter how hard I tried. Sometimes a thing just dies out between a man and a woman. Or maybe they never had it, only thought they had — created the whole damned thing in their heads and transferred it between their legs. Or was it the other way around? I was scared of dating again. Besides, the girls — or "women," as they insist upon — I met in grad school or at work were not my type. Fat or looked half-lesbian. Sheila? Sheila was gorgeous — at least on the outside.

There was this girl I had taken "Modern Interpretations of Feminist Literature" with. Julie. I thought of her — a lot. Great body. Only one in the whole bloody program. I'd dial her number. Got it when everybody in class exchanged them to 'keep in touch,' although we all knew we never would. After the first ring, I'd slam down the receiver. I wasn't good at this. Socially constipated. Strange, but I wasn't like that when I'd been in the Army. Must have been because I was then in Asia or something, women there having fewer expectations.

I was staying in touch with Mark by volition and with Sheila by decree. Mark assured me he was willing to go over additional details of his UFO disclosures.

***

The days continued to slide by. As the temperature increased, so did my anxiety. Still no full-time job prospects. That would mean I'd have to continue working part-time at the local university and at whatever two-bit jobs I could line up. Spring cleanup of senior citizens' homes in town and the like. Damned hard work, but the pay was good and out of the sight of the tax man.

I did get a call from, of all people, Julie. She was going to suggest that we go out for dinner; I just knew it. Instead, she asked me to make a donation to the Little League team she was coaching. I couldn't think straight or fast enough on my feet. I knew she wouldn't call again. I had to propose something — fast. We agreed to keep in touch. That was the best I could manage.

Then one day, I got an e-mail from a college dean up in New Hampshire. I had just about given up on securing a fall position. This looked good, though it had the '-t' in 'Watson' misspelled with a '-d.' Couldn't even get my damned name straight. It said my phone had been out of order or was malfunctioning, and would I please contact them ASAP, collect, about an interview? I was already imagining all sorts of things when I realized I had better calm down. Perhaps I would interview only to make their predetermined candidate look legitimate. I had experienced this before. I thought of giving Mark a call, asking him if he'd like to accompany me on the trip; he was a computer salesman, and I was sure he'd be able to take time off. And, after all, he did say he wanted to fill me in on the UFO questions I still had running around in my head. But just as quickly, my thoughts ran to Julie. I'd rather have her company, for this trip at any rate. I vowed to ask her. I became the dreamer; she the dreamed.

We would go during the academic spring break. I knew she roomed with a girlfriend and, like me, was looking for a teaching assignment. I rehearsed the invitation over and over in my head, trying to imagine every minute detail, rebutting every possible objection she could proffer. We'd take my motorcycle. Afraid? We'd go by car. We'd stop in Boston's Chinatown for dinner. Didn't like Chinese food? No problem, we'd go elsewhere. I tried to make it sound more-than-fascinating. I finally dug up the courage.

No, she couldn't — or wouldn't?— go; thanks for asking. Period. Didn't even offer a cursory maybe-some-other-time.

That brought me back to Mark. By now, I convinced myself I'd rather have a man's company anyway. We both liked survivalist-type camping, something you could hardly do with most women, and perhaps we could turn it into a weekend trip. But first, I needed to get a date from the college.

Then Mark said he couldn't make it but thanked me for asking. I would take myself. Besides, now that meant I'd be free to take off on a dogleg if I wanted — no need to come up with a justification for anybody. I received an interview appointment for the week after the following.

While I was packing my camping gear a day or two before departure, Mark called to say that, yes, he should be able to make it after all. "I'd love for us to go to Lake Winnipesaukee," he gushed, though I told him there wouldn't be time, and then he said he'd go anyhow. We would leave first thing Friday morning; the interview was set for late afternoon, and we wouldn't return till Saturday evening or early Sunday. At least I would have company.

***

Spring came in spurts that year. Unusually steady winds were keeping summer-like temperatures from arriving early; since Vietnam, I've had an aversion to hot weather. The redolence of early lilacs hung in the air, and I couldn't get over the number of robins there were. Yellowish-orange crocuses and brilliant hyacinths at the edge of my landlady's front yard came up "bee-you-tee-ful" this spring, she said, and that we should all be grateful for God's grace, particularly right after Easter. She was an elderly, plump Puerto Rican widow with a remarkable green thumb. Everything on her small plot was budding in complementary hues of greens, reds, blues, and yellows. Even the colors of her laundry, when hung out to dry, appeared to match the surroundings. Looking back, little did I realize it then; springtime's breath was one to be treasured. It felt great to be alive.

I had my own loft over her house yet felt hemmed in nonetheless. I yearned to get away from the sterile homogeneity that came with the expanding mindless commercial development swallowing up what had been my cozy hometown of Wedgemont. I needed to get out into open countryside. The New Hampshire trip would do me good, I reflected, and might help to veer my thoughts away from Sheila and Julie. If I got the job, I felt I would take to countryside more reminiscent of traditional New England well, but I wasn't raising my expectations. Disappointment had been my only reliable companion back then.

Mark came over again earlier than expected, waking up Buckie and with her everybody else. He hadn't thrown off the soldier's habit of early rising, something I'd sloughed off years ago. He was in unusually high spirits and, in lieu of cheap aftershave, was wearing his scintillating Hollywood smile. Maria, the landlady, could never quite get over how handsome he was in her eyes, alternately swooning between "muy guapo!" and "Oh, papacito — eef I only met heem twentee jeers ahgo!" It was true; this time he looked even more "guapo." He had traded in his glasses for contact lenses; it made him look younger, less intellectual, he said. In Vietnam, he said, guys wearing glasses in combat looked like guys right out of a biology lab. Meanwhile, Maria had invited us downstairs for last-minute coffee, no doubt to gaze more at Mark than to be ladylike nice to me. I told Mark to go down without me. Perhaps if I left her alone with him for a few minutes, she would be extra nice to me when I got back.

The sun was already shining strong in the east, signaling a promising day. As we walked toward the driveway, Maria remarked how ridiculous I would look dressed in a suit and tie under my weather suit while driving the motorcycle. That reminded me of something Sheila would spit out. But I knew Maria meant no slight. I removed my tie.

Mark straddled the backseat; I got on in front. Maria waved good-bye, all the while her eyes glued to Mark. We edged our way out slowly, taking extra care not to accidentally run over Maria's beloved crocuses. With the start-up of the bike, Buckie began yelping and yomping all over again. "Joo 'ave ah save treep," Maria yelled over the crescendo of the engine as we pulled away.

The spring air felt good flowing over my body. I felt alive. Mark appeared to be enjoying himself as well.

We seemed to fly the next few hours over the highways and byways cutting through greening towns dotting the southern New England countryside, towns with names like New Britain and Manchester, Pequabeck and Wapping, names that echoed New England's lost British and Indian heritage, lost to the sprawling rot of ever-sprouting national chain stores and fast-food franchises, car washes, and faceless shopping plazas. The artificiality of it all was overwhelming.

We roared through Hartford and Worcester, arriving in Boston well before noon. "Let's lunch in Chinatown," I hollered over the engine rumble.

"All right by me, Billy Boy," Mark shot back. I considered what it would have been like if Julie had gone with me. "Probably would be complaining about damn-near everything," I thought out loud. Mark's strong grip on my hips felt good. It reminded me of the time I dragged out a big, raw-boned Polish kid from Minnesota, Army PFC Kablinski, from a bomb blast on Tran Quay Cap Street in downtown Saigon, blood oozing from his legs, just above the kneecaps, his arms squeezing me as I dragged him to safety. Years later, as I reflect upon it, it made me feel wanted, needed. I had hardly developed a man's friendship since my discharge. I missed the military camaraderie. Still, I missed a woman's hands more.

We got back on the road and headed north, crossing over into New Hampshire earlier than expected. Towns sailed by more slowly; perhaps it was the roomier countryside that made it appear so. We passed Manchester; it wouldn't be much farther. The spring air felt cooler.

Well into the New Hampshire woods, we pulled over by a deserted stream for a break. We made our way over to what almost resembled a man-made arbor. Mark began massaging his feet.

"I get a funny feeling, still, when I'm around Orientals, you know," Mark exclaimed without notice. "I don't know. Don't hate them or anything. I know they looked at it over there as their calling too. Just sometimes I feel like I can't trust them. Like they're going to come at me from behind. Know what I mean?" We were sitting on a bed of cool, moist pine needles; he looked like he was far away. Though too early in the season, what smelled like newly cut hay from a nearby farm wafted our way.

I told him I understood. Maybe more than he realized. I figured out then why he'd insisted on our being seated backs to the wall when we had stopped at the Vietnamese restaurant back in Boston. Faces there shook some not-too-distant memories for both of us.

"I mean, here the goddamn Army is telling us to call them 'gooks' and yet, when it's all over, you know, like, if you ever used that term in peacetime, they'd drum you out of the service before you could zip up your fly after taking a leak."

I knelt by the stream to rinse out my mouth.

"You know what I'm saying, Bill?" He looked at me. Hard. The kind of look I had not seen in a long time. "And you know what it was like when we got back home." He mumbled things about his return, how his sister didn't want to talk to him. He shook his head. "God bless America." We didn't say anything for a long time.

"Goddammit!" He dropped his head between his legs and cupped his ears in his hands as if he wanted to drown out the moment, the horror of yesterday, the reality of today. Cackling from a distant bird shattered the silence.

I didn't know what to do. I took a step toward him, cracking a dried tree limb, half-wanting to put my arms around him, as I did that big Polish kid, but I was too embarrassed. My own eyes had gotten a mist on them and I looked away. Anger inside me that I thought had died down was still there. Undiminished. I looked back. I couldn't tell if he was crying or not. Whatever it was, I knew then as I looked down at him, now smaller and almost pitiful, there would always be something special about that frozen-framed moment....

We rolled under a vine-covered steel archway: 'Swenson College. Est. 1947.' Again, I couldn't get the topic of UFOs out of my head. Mark and I had agreed we would talk about it over more documents when we got back. I was supposed to be focusing on the interview, for Chrissakes. The campus appeared quiet.

The interview did indeed go smoothly. Answers to questions on the applications of Burke's rhetorical pentad, recent theories of phallocentrism in feminist literature, finer distinctions of Rogerian arguments in communication analyses were all bandied about with as much ease as you could say how-do-you-do. Dean Rodgers, the bow-tied and British-accented interview committee chief, would preface every other question with "And now for your analysis, Mr. Watson?" while curling his big handlebar mustache, pausing to peer over the edge of his glasses at the other committee members in a ridiculously ingrained repertoire aimed at intimidating his subordinates while puffing up his own bloated sense of worldly importance. His appearance, prissy as it was, when coupled with his oversized bouffant hairdo held together with plenty of hair spray, gave him a surreal look, like some Sunday comic strip character come to life.

Later, I walked over to meet the college president for tea, at which time we talked about absolutely nothing, and then hurried across the spacious campus square toward the library where Mark was killing time. Rock music from the 80s was now blasting out of the second story of the nearby dormitory to my right. Some coeds were standing behind a row of tables, hawking anti-"Violence Against Women" posters in anticipation (another poster read) of some big rally later in the term.

Mark was seated in a corner, late-afternoon sunshine illuminating the book he cradled in his hands, something about alien abductions, as far as I could make out. I never inquired. As I walked toward him, out of the corner of my eye, I caught a coed behind the bookracks surreptitiously eyeing him.

"How'd it go?"

"Don't ask. Who the hell knows? You know when we pointy-heads get together. Couldn't spit out a straight answer if our lives depended on it." I laughed. "This queer, the dean, is the funniest character I met all year, Mark."

He looked upset. "What's the matter?" I had purposely kept my voice low. "I didn't say he sexually harassed me, for God's sake." I then launched into a mime. Mark laughed. "You should've seen this guy."

The ride back would go slowly. Neither one of us was in a rush to return: I to my loft, Mark to dumping computers onto underworked, overpaid candy-assed office managers, as he put it. Since I met him, Mark had maintained he was seriously considering a career change. To what I didn't know. Never asked.

We would camp out that night not far from the college. I was tired more from contemplating the interview than from going through with it or driving up; I needed a rest. Mark, too, looked forward to sleeping out under the stars. We headed westward.

At nightfall, we rumbled off into a public rest area. It was the last one on that stretch of road. The stars began to make a twinkling canopy overhead. Early-evening birds rustled all around us. It was a beautiful night. I half-wished to myself that daylight would never come. There wasn't a vehicle to be seen in the lot. We planned to bunk down here for the night, which meant I had to get to sleep early. Mark would be up at "0-6-30 hours," he was still often wont to say, as if the act of early rising wasn't military-like enough for him.

The night spring air was nippy; we didn't care. Mark stretched out and lay on his sleeping bag, not bothering to get in, as if by doing so, he would not fall asleep early and miss out on New England's early-evening springtime magic. An occasional small animal strayed too close, reminding us that the forest was not sleeping yet either. I had gotten settled after considerable fidgeting, locked my hands behind the nape of my neck, and looked up and into the heavens. Remembrances of night-patrol duty in Vietnam came flashing back. There appeared to be a million stars, starlight so bright, it was almost breathtaking.

"Ever wonder what it'd be like out there if you could go, visit for one day, one day out of eternity, and visit other worlds?" asked Mark. "And these other lives, other beings, do you think they'd be as violent, as cruel, as we can be? Kill others in the name of God and righteousness?"

I looked back at him. He lay there, smiling, the phosphorescence of moon glow reflected in his face. "Don't know. But I've thought about it. A lot." I looked back toward the sky. "You know, I used to try to figure out the constellations in 'Nam on night patrol. Thought that way, maybe I wouldn't go crazy by dawn, or at least, if Charlie got to me before then, I'd die with some kind of peace of mind."

"Did it work?"

"No ... no, I don't think so. Think I did go somewhat crazy. God knows I didn't retain any peace of mind."

"Yeah."

"Funny thing is, you know, after all the time I spent stargazing, only one I thought I could ever identify for sure was the Big Dipper. Ain't that a bitch!"

We both laughed. A shooting star streaked toward the east. Both of us lay there, mesmerized by the awesomeness and majesty of it all. It was something I found hard to put into words. Fact is, I didn't think that I would ever make it back alive to the States and that somehow, I had cheated the hands of Fate from prematurely clasping another soul. The times when I used to think about why I got back not crippled, physically at least, would hit me in the stomach, and, if I dwelled on it, it'd make me sick, so I tried not to dwell on it. All I know was that there were guys I went to Wedgemont High with who never made it back to our little hometown, other than in a body bag — if they were that lucky. There were guys killed in a manner I won't go into; there should be some dignity in death. They were no more than overgrown kids. Goddammit. A passing truck honked its horn, piercing the silence of nightfall.

True to his word, Mark was up by '0-6-30 hours,' rousing me from my slumber, his powerful hand on my shoulder. Said he didn't need a watch; he knew by the sun. I looked at mine. Sure enough, he was within ten minutes' accuracy, and I didn't give a damn. Far as I was concerned, this was vacation, and I wasn't about to answer to his form of reveille.

"C'mon, get up! What the hell you gonna do all mornin', huh? Sleep till the cows come home tonight, too?"

Half-asleep, I shot back: "Sonofabitch! Leave me alone!" and something to the effect that he "could walk back" if he liked. I'm short-tempered early in the morning, Sheila always reminded me, and I regretted the outburst almost immediately.

Mark hurriedly backed off. My eyes still drooping, I could see he was hurt, and I apologized immediately. Some time would pass before he would get over it, and

I chastised myself for being such a nasty bastard, till I heard Sheila's remonstrances ringing in my ears. Suddenly, I didn't feel so bad.

On the return leg home, he didn't say anything memorable other than "I empathize that you couldn't find any peace, especially when peering into the heavens while on night recon in 'Nam, you know?" I became more befuddled than ever.

As I roared into Wedgemont, Maria, digging in her front yard, mentioned that "some Hulie" had called and would call back. She was full of inquisitiveness as to the nature of the call. I had temporarily given out the old lady's number to the few people I knew while my home phone was being repaired, and she incessantly badgered me about "Hulie." Then, I remembered Julie had said she would call about the interview.

"Professore, why don't joo — "

"I told you, don't call me that. I'm only an adjunct, you know, part-time teacher. That's all." She appeared oblivious. I wasn't about to protest too vigorously. I liked Maria.

"Why don't joo meet my niece, Juanita, Professore? She's bery preetty, nice, ahnd, oh, Professore, kooks goood. 'Ice and beans. Chee-keen. Ahnd soo deboted. Gooz to shurch ev'ry Soonday! She — "

"OK, OK. This time, you win." I was more tired from the trip than expected and had had enough debate with the interview committee.

"Goood!" She smiled her familiar gap-toothed smile. She had been urging this upon me for several months. I wasn't about to decline anymore; I was so lonely for some feminine company, the prospect of some blind date gone awry didn't faze me any longer. Her tenacity won out. I'd seen Juanita's old college graduation photo, wedged in between a half-dozen pictures of the Virgin Mary, every time I stepped into Maria's living room with its distinctive, lingering smell of recently cooked Spanish foods. "Looks like a hot tamale," I'd said to myself the first time I saw it. Juanita looked better with every passing glance.

"Professore, I weel arrange eet eemmeediately." She wiped the dirt off her hands on her already-dirtied apron and scurried inside the house, pausing to look back and smile when she got to the porch.

***

The next several weeks dragged on. Swenson College mailed a cutesy rejection-form letter thanking me for my interest, again misspelling my name. After making another payment, I hadn't heard from Sheila. Julie inquired about my interview and said she had some unexpected problem with her parents and had to move back in with them; Maria's niece was on an extended vacation in Puerto Rico and wouldn't be back for at least three weeks. Aside from my students at the university, I only talked with Mark, Maria, and Buckie next door.

In retrospect, Mark must have been measuring me up for my "suitability" (as he later put it) to receive additional intelligence disclosures on UFOs. He no longer delayed information about evolution and religion pertaining to the topic. He stated that it had been ascertained that humankind was the product of several-to-many alien genetic (DNA) manipulations, the last occurring about five hundred years before Christ and that Christ himself was a genetic hybrid, put on Earth to teach about love and tolerance, his own birth, life, and death carefully monitored by the aliens. All the while, he showed me secret documents testifying to the seeming absurdities. As amazing as these revelations were, there was more.

There was a "Project Looking Glass" about seeing back in time, and another project, whose name escapes me, about the future. Somehow the latter project was initiated to test the Catholic Church's Lady of Fatima prophecy. Whether the project was supposed to be conclusive, I don't know. However, it did imply that Christ would make his Second Coming and the world, or more precisely our civilization, would end as the result of World War III at or shortly after the turn of the millennium. When asked about how he could have smuggled out such sensitive information, Mark was vague, only saying he still had inside contacts. Because of the disclosures, I knew he trusted me; why he had chosen to show them to me, coupled with his remarks during our Swenson trip, bothered me more now than ever.

All this was, naturally, very disturbing and, on the surface at least, if it weren't for the documents, my belief in Mark, and my own considerable recent research, I could have easily disabused myself of the whole thing. Some crackpot paranoid conspiracy theory, not much else. But hard as I tried to come up with logical explanations, I had to admit there was some subterranean, internally logical consistency to it all. I knew how the government, dating back to President Nixon and Secretary of State Kissinger, lied and left behind many of our brothers imprisoned in Southeast Asia to circumvent paying secretly agreed-upon war reparations and later tried to cover up the effects of Agent Orange so as not to pay our own veterans.

"Things are not always what they seem," Mark had once said. The remark echoed in the corridors of my mind. Everything had to be more than mere coincidence.

Chapter 2

Memorial Day weekend had come and gone. Along with summer came the chance to teach again at the university, but for students in the remedial program. Stupid shits, I thought to myself. It wasn't the appropriate attitude to maintain, I knew, but I felt that way anyway. Nothing materialized in the form of job offers, not even a single interview. I would've been in the dumps, but the UFO enigma and its resultant government cover-up absorbed me even more. It started to get a hold on me, and I found myself doing more and greater in-depth analysis of it, to the neglect of my own literary research. My conscious daytime thoughts often didn't seem to be my own anymore. All I seemed to think of were UFOs, alien contact, and the looming prophecy of doom. Coupled with still-recurrent nightmares of the war in 'Nam, I thought I might be headed over the edge, so to speak, and decided to force myself to concentrate on other things.

Summer session started up, and I was able to settle my mind somewhat. I was assigned some bonehead courses that really should have been limited to high school freshmen. I constantly had to remind myself I wasn't teaching with Miss Frances on television's old Ding Dong School.

I needed the money.

Robilas, the teddy bear-sized newly-designated department chairman, beseeched me repeatedly to allay his underlying secret fear that I might not be up to the task, as if you had to be Einstein himself to instruct this bunch of stupid shits. Throughout the spring, he had been getting on my nerves.

I was late to class again, hoping nobody noticed. Robilas caught me as I was running up the stairs toward him on the last floor of the three-storied Arts and Sciences building, making sure to block my way by jumping back onto his previous stairway step, thus effectively towering over me.

"I, I, think that you, uh, might want to take a rather, ah, open approach apropos of grades." I loved the way he emphasized "open approach" as code for any-thing-goes-so-theyreregister-this-fall. "We, uh, really don't want to lose these youngsters, Bill, if you follow what I'm, uh, saying. The dean has emphasized to all department heads how significant their contributions are to the institution, that is, uh, in terms of enrollment." He almost choked on "significant" and "contributions."

Somehow, I suspected he sensed a streak of insouciance in my mien; he wasn't about to let me violate his air of newfound authority.

"I say, Bill, we really have to respect the dean's admonitions; it is, uh, all the best for the institution in the last analysis. Owing to imminent financial exigencies, I would like to, uh, engage your cooperation in this respect, as your own lecturer position here is — may I take the liberty to remind you — contingent upon sufficient enrollment. I, uh, could have given the assignment over to Ramon, but I felt you could financially benefit from the opportunity."

Rent was overdue. I marched to class, obedient as any astute lieutenant reporting in to his company commander, bright-eyed and ever-willing to please.

The gentleman he referred to was Ramon Garcia, a Central American immigrant in the process of being appointed interim assistant professor. It was rumored he was some belated Affirmative Action appointee and Robilas' personal pick and that he had not completed his terminal degree nor much else, yet the school, especially our department, was woefully lacking in ethnic diversity. All this may or may not have been true. I always tried not to play department politics. Sheila maintained that was my problem in the first place. After 'Nam, I'd wanted to make peace with everybody, even her. Unfortunately, Garcia lived by another code.

It had started with the department office-copying machine. Late-morning sunshine poured through the solitary window behind the secretary's desk. I had grown weary of the recent sounds of outdated Muzak that the department had arranged to pipe in, the result of a squabble between two of the old-time women profs over musical "diversity," quickly leading to practically the entire department being contentiously lined up on opposite sides of this purportedly most significant of issues. I must have been in a surly mood.

Garcia was fumbling with some paper clips, trying to append them faster than anybody's fingers would allow; the more he fumbled, the heavier his breathing became. He would alternately look up at me and at the wall clock, as if he were going to be late for class. It was 10:30. It looked like he had developed some sort of twitch. He had never before appeared rushed, let alone nervous, though being employed part-time, I only met him occasionally. A couple of teaching assistants, Michelle and Pierre, and Vicki, department secretary, were the only others in the office. It was quiet. He cleared his throat in a bid for my attention.

"Excuse me, uh, how much longer do you think you'll be?" He wasn't looking my way.

I think I rattled off something slangy like "long enough to finish off this here bunch," pointing to the small stack of papers sitting nearby. I sensed that he, too, like Robilas, detected some sort of defiance. It was well-known that many full-time staff treated their part-time counterparts (though they never considered them "counterparts") with disdain, this having been a simmering bone of contention among the part-timers at union meetings. He had gotten my attention. I wasn't in the mood to be browbeaten.

"Do you think I can slide in a few? I really must be going. I have to give an examinacion," he whined with the tiniest hint of an accent. He edged closer to intimidate me, though he still wasn't quite capable of looking at me foursquare.

"Well, I'll, ah, I'll only be a moment or two longer, you know." I stammered slightly myself. It may have been childish, I knew, yet now I was determined to hold my territory.

Garcia became visibly irritated. The others in the office looked at us. "Really?" he uttered in indignation, arching his eyebrows. Finally, he stared at me forthrightly, if only for a moment. I didn't budge. He pivoted on his heels and stormed out the doorway; no doubt convinced in his head by now that he had been made something of the fool by the arrogance of a mere adjunct such as I.

I, too, walked out, forgetting about the remaining copies. Later, I regretted the idiocy of the whole thing. I revealed myself to have become as petty as so many of the other profs whom I detested so. Perhaps I had been at this gig far too long.

Then I found out what had really gotten his goat. It was about lunchtime Friday, the last day of spring final exams. A pimply-faced twerp of a sophomore, who was taking classes with both of us unbeknown to me, set me up; some will do that. He asked a question about Molière's Tartuffe. I didn't know it, but it had been on Garcia's exam, something to do with one of the play's characters, Orgon, within the context of seventeenth-century classicism. Garcia prided himself, I discovered later, on being something of a "specialist," as the term is bandied about in academe, on that era. No doubt, in fact, he was. But he had made a seemingly bland over-sight on one of his test questions. It really wasn't a big deal; anybody could have done it. I pointed out the valid answer; the kid jumped with glee since it coincided with his own and said he was off to achieve a final higher letter grade for the course. I had shown up Garcia, a senior colleague, a cardinal sin in the academic world. Worse, several profs heard about it.

Soon I would have to pay the price. Shortly after the copying machine incident, Robilas called me into his office.

"Uh, Bill, can I, may I, have a word with you? Please."

"Of course."

"You know, Bill, we really have to watch what we, uh, say, and how we act around senior members of the department." He eased himself into his oversized mahogany chair in his expansive office and locked his hands behind his head, re-sembling an oil tycoon more than a public servant at a state institution. Scores of books and papers with titles like "Paradigms of Oppression and Restraint in Para-dise Lost" and "DeLorca: A Heuristic" lined the walls. I remained at attention like some snot-nosed corporal in front of his platoon sergeant, Robilas not extending the offer for me to sit down in the remaining plain, straight-back steel chair situ-ated in the corner.

"What do you mean, 'senior members'?" I had a hunch as to what he was get-ting at but didn't let on.

"I, uh, think that you have an insight into the situation. You've been here quite some time, Bill. We must be reminded from time to time how important it is to be particularly sensitive to the, uh, sensibilities of veteran department members and new appointees." He was beginning to feel more at ease at projecting his new image of authority.

"Did somebody complain? Vicky? Pierre?" I knew that adding Pierre would unnerve him a bit; he was only a teaching assistant and not much liked by him anyway. Came to work one day sporting a pro-National Rifle Association emblem. Something for the office scuttlebutt to chew on the rest of the semester.

"No, now, Bill, I'm referring to our ability to get along with, uh, members of the faculty, including new members. It's important to make them feel at home, especially in a new country." Nobody could mistake the allusion. He changed his tone. "You're popular with the students, Bill. We'd like to have you back this fall." His emphasis on 'like' did not elude me. "In plain English, we have to be conscious of collegial comportment."

I mumbled some contrite tripe, what for in retrospect, I don't know, and slithered out of his office, stealing a couple of cans of Coke from the department's refrigerator on the way home. Fringe benefit. Didn't care if anybody saw me. Thought I might get shitcanned. I was beginning to care less.

Robilas, Garcia, 'Heuristics' — the whole damn game you had to play for what little you got out of it, essentially nothing — weighed heavily on me. I didn't want to be 'back this fall.' Already well into middle age and not getting anywhere since getting laid off from my previous tenure-track position, I was seriously considering making a move out West, out to Hollywood to work in the family business of an old Army buddy who would periodically propose the offer. Perhaps I could do some scriptwriting on the side.

***

The last week in June came. Maria came running up the stairs to my loft, waving an envelope in hand, saying that "joo have jour tahx rebate, Professore, jour mooney back froom de goov'r'mahnt. I goot mine tooday, too!"

"Yeah." I laughed. "The government is giving me my money back, eh? What money? Hardly made anything last year, for Chrissakes!" I knew the woman hadn't meant to rub it in. I could also see she was upset over my loose Jesus reference, and I quickly modified my tone. "Let me have a look at that." I ripped open the envelope. "Ha! $442.84! How d'ya like that? I'm rich." Maria beamed and clasped her hands, sharing in my sudden-found fortune.

"Tank joo Jesus!" she wailed.

The voice of Charlie, my tax preparer and long-time financial guru to my parents when they'd been alive, popped into my head. "Jesus, your adjusted gross income last year was $19,800! How in hell ja live on that? I mean, ya gotta pay bills 'n stuff. Gotta eat for Chrissakes, don't ja, Billy?" I'm sure it had been overheard by others in his office. Had Sheila been there, I could picture her bowling over with laughter.

Public reference to my recent penury was bad enough. Since the Army, nobody called me "Billy." "Billy Boy" was one thing; "Billy" was something else. I didn't like it, though I never said a word to old Charlie; he was too much of an old family friend. I kept my mouth shut.

"This'll come in handy, Maria, in part for that Fourth of July trip to western Massachusetts Mark and I are planning. Want to come along? Be with Mark, huh?"

She threw back her head and roared, thumping my chest. "Ja! Professore!" She hurried downstairs as fast as she had run up.

Mark recently said he had been "bustin' my ass with those computer candy-asses these past several months" and that he was "looking forward to rubbing elbows with folks who prefer meat and potatoes over quiche." I asked him which category I fell into. He laughed. "Sounds like a winner!" he exclaimed when I suggested when we'd leave. Lately, he had been repeating that silliest of expressions.

Always with Mark came recurrent memories of his tantalizing UFO disclosures. My own ongoing research had led me to confirm, albeit reservedly at times, most of what Mark revealed, and he was pleasantly surprised at the tenacity of my pursuit. I was as involved as ever. Friday came; we were ready.

"Preparing for the Apocalypse, Billy Boy?" Mark laughed as he stepped through my doorway and saw a multitude of camping gear piled high in the corner. My loft wasn't spacious; it looked like it was about to explode. "How'd I make it past the downstairs enchilada?" he mused. We laughed.

We were off and running to the Berkshires in Mark's brilliant purple '88 Dodge sedan.

Mark's driving talents were less than exemplary, at least in my eyes, but my own vehicles were not up to it, and I relented under his easygoing insistence that I "just kick back and enjoy the ride." We pulled out of Maria's driveway.

We hadn't driven far on Route 7, the picturesque former colonial road running latitudinally through western New England —'picturesque' at least when you got away from the incessant modern-day American sprawl that pockmarked the western Long Island Sound area, and you got to cruising in the countryside, where we started on what went wrong for us, the country, the damned world.

I noticed an "Education is America's Future" bumper sticker on the back fender of the car weaving in front of us. I started chuckling.

"What?" Mark chimed in, both hands gripping the steering wheel, looking straight ahead. He started slowing down.

I turned my head and looked out the window at the hayfields passing us by, half-talking to myself. "Funny thing is, you know, you fight for your country, or so they tell you, in some God-forsaken jungles, go to school half your life, run yourself into debt, and then — what do you get for it? Land of the Free, Home of the Brave. Christ, only country in the world where you can be a scientist who went to Harvard and find yourself unable to make a living or be in show business and grab your crotch in public in front of the world and make millions. It just doesn't make any sense anymore."

He howled with laughter. He pulled back in his seat; the exhaust from the car in front smelled noxious. "Yeah, I know how people can feel that way, especially you." He looked out the window on his side and spat, resting his elbow on the window edge, a breeze gently pushing back on the sleeve rolled up high on his muscular arm. The car ahead started weaving more erratically. "Billy Boy, whatever happened to the American Dream, huh?"

"I dunno. What did happen to it?"

"Well," he said, pausing to clear his throat as if to avoid the need to repeat himself later. "Not quite sure myself. Guess the Dream is still there. See that car ahead? The country's rolling down the road of history somewhat like that drunken driver. Kind of going here, going there, everybody just hoping and praying that they'll make it; that they won't collide with history. Yet we're hell-bent on self-destruction. You know it; I know it. We're pawns on history's chessboard."

"Think so?"

"Like I said, we both know it." He swerved to avoid hitting a squirrel darting in front of us. I settled back in my seat, throwing back my head on the headrest. The air felt even better on my neck than it did on our springtime trip to New Hampshire. I was gladder than ever to get away from the likes of twits like Robilas, Garcia, and the others, if only for a few days, though I was starting to like the classes Robilas assigned me. I must have sounded like a whiner to Mark. Nobody owes anybody a living, I silently reminded myself and dozed off.

I awoke to Mark jerking the Dodge to a standstill. A good two hours must have passed. He had pulled up to one of those little all-night diners on the outskirts of what looked like the downtown district of a small farming community. A half-dozen or so men off to our left were talking animatedly about gun control. One was eyeing Mark's pro-Second Amendment bumper sticker on the Dodge. Though cloudy, it was only late afternoon; somebody had forgotten to shut off the diner's neon sign at dawn or just hadn't bothered.

"Remember when we were shooting the breeze about that drunken driver back there?" Mark said. "Well, the fool lost control and ran himself off the road and into a ditch. Didn't want to wake you. Let's get us some grub." A vehicle, close at hand, backfired like a gun blast. Skittish as rabbits, we both jumped. Mark gave me a once-over and shook his head. We went inside.

We got to the base of the mountain range well before nightfall and started driving up a one-lane dirt mountain road. It started getting cloudier; rain threatened to dampen my middle-aged optimism, but not Mark's youthful zeal. He was determined to make the best of it, come "hell or the First Cav," he said.

"So, what do you think about what those guys were talking about back there?" Mark asked.

"What guys?"

"The farmers ... about gun control."

"What do you think?"

"I think we're headed for deep shit." He leaned behind the wheel, upper-body muscles rippling in unison with the centrifugal force resulting from the sashaying of the vehicle as we hit a stretch of bumpy road. The old Dodge held its own as we rocked our way up the half-jagged mountainside. We were getting deeper into rugged terrain, and I wondered how much longer the Dodge would hold out.

"What do you mean?"

"I mean that at the rate we're going, we won't have any guns to hold on to. Waco and the Oklahoma City bombing — whoa — !" The Dodge hit a hidden pothole; we bounced around in our seats. "After Waco and Oklahoma City, the feds have been fast orchestrating a plan to undermine our right — yours and mine — to bear arms. It's going on quietly at times, but going on." Two chipmunks up the road scurried by, chasing each other.

"I don't know. Don't see it that way. Why did those Waco whackos have to have all that stuff in the first place? They had more weapons than a battalion, for Chrissakes. Have to have some sort of gun control over fanatics."

"Don't be fooled."

I looked at our map and stuck my head out. We were coming up to Burr Pond. Over the skyline, clouds darkened; tops of fir trees swayed with the growing wind, and crows cawed over an impending storm. "What do you mean?" I said as I pulled my head in.

"Look, let me tell you something." He leaned toward me to press the point home, his face a mask of earnestness. The open mountain air felt good in my lungs. "Did you know the Bureau of Alcohol, Tobacco and Firearms — BATF — secretly was trained by Army Special Forces in defiance of DoD regulation, let alone constitutional law, in preparation for their assault in Waco? Joint Task Force Six in conjunction with Special Operations Command. And that the whole thing was being set up under the ruse of looking for drugs, methamphetamines, as a fallback if it didn't turn out as planned? And that when the president ordered the Treasury to investigate, they doctored the reports and have been covering up ever since? The congressional investigation into it was all for show."

"Take it easy, man."

"Yeah, 'take it easy' all right. Easy for you to say. Tell it to those Branch Davidian kids who got roasted alive."

Droplets from a slight drizzle began forming on the hair on my arm resting over the window edge. It felt good. I felt good. Mark was in top form. We rumbled onward.

"Bunch of kooks," I countered.

"How can you say that, Bill? Innocent kids, for Christ's sake!" he trumpeted.

"Yeah, maybe...." I let it trail off. He was not upset with me but with history, yet I didn't want to be perceived as the devil's advocate. Sheila would taunt me that way at times. Neither of us said anything for several minutes. The Dodge staggered forward.

"Hmm." I couldn't resist. "Got some more privileged documents to show me?" Another bump sent us lurching forward.

"If you want to see them."

It was getting dark, no doubt because of the density of the forest. We decided to pull off onto a tiny, deserted dirt lot. The drizzle had become light rain; we would set up camp by an inconspicuous brook that cut a swath through a greening open field resembling a forgotten pasture dotted with firs and mountain laurel brush along its edges. A tall, singular, muscular-looking pine tree in the middle of the field promised to offer protection against the growing storm. We got our gear and ran toward it.

The southern Berkshire Taconic Mountain range, now a hazy silhouette against the dwindling sunlight to the west, loomed majestically over the horizon. It was raining harder now, and thunder echoed over the mountain ridge to the north. We threw down our gear under the towering pine and started unpacking.

I was glad not to have gotten wet. Mark chided me: "What the hell you worried about some raindrops for?"

"I'm not worried."

"Then slow down, for God's sake. Never got soaked to the gills in 'Nam?"

He was right, but I didn't say anything. Sometimes during the monsoon season, we'd all but get washed away with all the trash and shit floating on by us. I thought about how soft I had become.

"Let's get the camo canopy up first."

My thoughts wandered thousands of miles away and to another lifetime....

"I said, 'Let's get this canopy up.'"

"Huh?"

"Hey, Billy Boy, you OK? You look far gone."

The crack of a thunderclap brought me back to my senses. "Yeah. I'm OK. Thanks."

We settled down to a hot, humid night. A couple of white-tailed deer and their sole fawn were barely discernible in the distance along the field's edge against the backdrop of the low mountain ridge to the east.

"You don't mind if I play the radio low for now, do you?" I asked. "Since 'Nam, sometimes I get nervous at night when it's too quiet. Can't help it." That used to drive Sheila nuts.

He didn't answer, only nodded his acquiescence and looked straight up as he lay on his back on the oversized camo tarp, chewing on a small twig he had put in his mouth. He fidgeted with the twig.

"Mark, remember when you said earlier in the year that I was in military intelligence? How'd you know that?"

He stopped fidgeting; he didn't blink. "I, well — did I say that? Don't remember."

His response caught me off-guard. I didn't expect this. I believed I had thought of all possible rejoinders, but this, simple and to the point as it was, took me unawares, and I thought about how stupid I had been. I didn't say anything. Didn't know what to say. He continued looking straight up and at the canopy overhead, now alive with the sound of raindrops. Long moments went by, passing thunder, gentle rainfall, easy music nightfall's only sounds.

"Well, what did you do in MI?" he asked nonchalantly, again not moving a muscle.

"Nothing much. Stationed with the 121st MI detachment with Eighth Army near the Korean DMZ. Just intercepted, listened, and analyzed propaganda emanating from the North. Boring stuff."

"Hmph," he grunted.

By now, I considered him a friend: he had surreptitiously revealed privileged information, yet I still sensed there was this distance — call it what you will — between us. He didn't appear eager to hear more of my response. Maybe he figured remaining silent was the best way to deflect my suspicion. I was always good at remaining silent with Sheila when it served my purpose — this irritated her no end — but with Mark, it was different. His reticence embarrassed me, and I changed the subject. "You know, the way you chew on that twig reminds me of my old man."

He rolled over on his side and faced me. The storm had all but passed. "Hmph," he grunted again. "Your 'old man,' huh? Hmph." He shook his head. His eyes narrowed. "What was yours like, Bill?"

"Oh, not a bad guy. Had our disagreements. He really hated LBJ and his boys, especially Secretary McNamara, and openly conjectured about my going to Canada when I got my draft notice — said we had distant relatives there I could initially get help from — but as father-son relationships go, when we did spend time together, it was all right, I guess. As I told you before, he was a sales rep for an international marketing association."

Mark lay listening pensively. "Your 'old man,' eh?"

"What about yours?"

"Hmph." There was a long pause. "My old man, Billy Boy? My old man, sh — there were three things my old man would say to me: 'Hello.' 'How are your grades?' — I went to a private boarding school — and 'Take care of yourself.' Then I would say to myself, 'So long, you bastard!' He never accepted me for who and what I am. That was me and my old man." He spat out the twig.

He looked out over the hump formed by our camping gear piled by our feet and in the direction the deer had been moving earlier. Where the deer had been minutes ago was now moody darkness. Though the storm passed, another was going on inside us both, and I wondered how I would sleep. Summertime crickets had begun their racket. I leaned over to turn off the radio.

"Don't," he whispered above the murmur of the music, muttering something about needing outdoor sounds to sleep. And I let it play on....

I awoke to the high-pitched barking of an angry chipmunk whose territory we had inadvertently invaded and claimed as our own the preceding night. He was plenty upset, and I momentarily wondered what it would be like if the little fellow were our size. The sun was already high in the sky, and I estimated the time to be at least half-past seven since the chrome of the purple Dodge's hubcaps was already reflecting the morning rays. Mark was gone. I figured he was out for an early-morning walkabout. I stretched and got dressed. He must have seen or heard me — how, I don't know — for a shout came out from the direction of Burr Pond.

"C'mon over!"

I fumbled to turn off the half-dead radio and ran over.

He was nude, at the edge of the pool, low-hanging fir branches slightly obscuring my view. It was hard to imagine: he was already well into middle age, yet lean and powerful as a racehorse. His muscles rippled with his every movement. I hurriedly took off my clothes, leaving on my boots for protection, and waded in. The water was colder than I expected, and I soon got out, brushing aside Mark's admonishment to "just come on in." I must have looked foolish, standing there, naked, wearing only boots. Mark stared. I floated back in time to a Saigon bar, lying on a bed in some back room with a bar girl, and I could hear her laughing when she saw the size of my puny penis. The bitch. I turned away from him.

The water sensitized my skin to the early-morning air. "Little chilly for me," I protested and quickly put on and zipped up my pants. I thought I heard voices coming from the east ridge. Though I knew the area was fairly deserted, I wondered if there might not be any stray hikers around. "Think I'll get back to camp."

We spent the rest of the weekend fishing, eating, drinking beer, and talking about what Mark insisted was the growing militia movement. Mark had additional information to divulge, "sensitive stuff," as he put it, and I was as eager as ever to be in on it, though I tried to hide this. But, try as I may, I'm sure he saw through me, and I felt even more crestfallen over my seeming inability to mask my emotions.

Not that there was anything for me to mask, but in my own way, I felt the men of the paramilitary, the people's militias, to be a group of half-paranoid backwoodsmen, and I prided myself on being above that sort of thing. Figured they never read more than a tattoo. Mark saw it differently.

We were fishing for perch in the pond. He said that the government might have been planning a takeover, with the suspension of civil liberties and confiscation of all civilian firearms, under Presidential Executive Order, under the pretext of fighting drugs and crime. And reining in the militias. When I asked him about proof, he was not as specific as he had been with the UFO phenomena. This was different, he maintained, but anecdotal and otherwise, there was evidence for it nevertheless. An Army officer that he still kept in touch with said there were huge camps out West being built and readied to round up thousands "when the word is given." That the militias were "dying out," he said, was false. Only the media made it look like that — on purpose.

It was getting cloudy again. Fishing bored me. Listening to Mark didn't. "Death is tippy-toeing on America's doorstep. Hasn't come yet, but will — and sooner than you care to think about it." We sat uncomfortably side by side on a slimy log from which we kept sliding off. Mark got a nibble and hastily reeled in a large perch. "Supper," he said with a rare smile as he hoisted up our prize, and we walked back to camp under a refreshing drizzle.

Monday the Fourth dawned; it was our last day. We hiked up the dusty mountain road a couple of miles, partly for the hell of it, partly out of creeping boredom. Mark liked fishing; to me, it was a waste of time.

We came across an old dairy farmer and several local friends out for some late-morning beers and holiday sunshine. Standing by a cattle fence and drinking, they made sure not to get too close to the electrified wire. They had been drinking for some time; a case of empty beer cans lay strewn in the mud nearby. They were mostly dressed in blue denim three-quarter-length coveralls held up by suspenders that formed an X over their backs, the kind commonly worn by farmers, especially in that part of the country. Over the din of a nearby generator pumping water in a pasture, we could overhear their raucousness as we wandered up the road.

"Can't trust not one of 'em lying bastards down in DC ..."

"Gotta stick together, gonna take away our guns an' take us over, look at Waco and Ruby Ridge ..."

"Not if we don't let 'em! ..."

"Ah! What the hell would you know? Go back with your Uncle Milt and that faggot cousin of yours ..."

"The Lord God says it's an abomination in His eyes, James, Chapter Three ..."

"Shut the fuck up with your Jesus crap! ..."

One of them, a huge, burly fellow with a massive red beard and the biggest potbelly I'd ever seen, asked if that was our "Dodge back yonder by Burr's Pond?" Mark nodded it was. He grinned. "I seen ya bumper sticker," he bellowed and quickly motioned us to "sit down a spell and sip on some suds." His huge belly quivered every time he roared. We sat down, beers in hand, and tried to make ourselves comfortable amid the crowing of strutting roosters and the bellowing of cows in the pasture. The hot summer sun beat down on us, and we drank the suds like water. Beer in hand and anger abounding, they battled on.

A towering, lanky lad, throwing furtive glances to his left and right so often, he resembled a weasel, spoke in a distinctively squeaky voice over the raucousness: "The Lord God shall not suffer a forked tongue to defile His kingdom. The Lord

God shalt punish those who have 'smirched the temple. Book of James, Chapter Three. I think." The weasel beamed, showing two missing front teeth.

"Fuck you and your goddamned Bible-quoting mouth! You want to know what the hell made this country free 'n what'll keep it free?" the potbellied one roared, single-handedly crushing and throwing his beer can at the petrified weasel. He strode across the road to a weather-beaten pickup truck with a suddenness that belied his massive stomach, leaned over the rear end, and held up a twelve-gauge shotgun.

"See this, shithead? This — 'n only this — is gonna keep you 'n your momma free, Padre asshole!" The weasel backpedaled, slipped in the mud, and fell backward and into the electrified fence, letting out a yowl. The others exploded in laughter. Things were getting out of control.

The old farmer, apparently their leader, ordered them "to jus' simmer all down, ya hear me?" He walked over and grabbed the potbelly's shotgun and gingerly put it back in the rear of the truck. "They'll be no squabbles amongst yous as long as I'm in command. Ya hear?" He glared at the potbelly. The others huddled around the near-empty beer case as if to find some secret solace from it and mumbled apologies about "getting carried away." "It's jus' that steam's startin' to boil over," one said in mixed metaphor, "and we gotta do sumpthin before them fed'ral bastards do sumpthin to us."

Mark sat there keenly, taking it all in, making mental notes. Indeed, neither of us had uttered a word. "Gotta be goin' now, brothers," he said in what sounded like a rural affectation, half-intended, I felt, to curry favor and half-intended to dissuade them from further insisting on more drink with us, while we decided on the most tactful manner by which to excuse ourselves and be on our way.

Both of us arose simultaneously from the cleanly cut tree stumps that had served as our makeshift chairs and, like twins each intuitively sensitized to the other, knew this was the opportune moment. Not that we couldn't leave anytime we wanted; it was just that as invited guests, we somehow felt we had stumbled upon a family feud in progress, the way one sometimes does with neighbors or friends, and we didn't want to embarrass them further. Besides, we had already drunk more than our fair share of their beer.

Half-giddy, we wandered back down the dirt road as quietly as we had come upon them, and before I realized it, all that remained of them were distant and fading sounds of their raucousness.

"Massachusetts Berkshire Boys' Militia?" I joked, yet I was half-serious.

"No," Mark answered softly, shaking his head, and we continued our walk down the road.

***

Classes at the university were going well, better than I expected, and summer sweltered on. Maria began to grow impatient: I should meet her "deboted" Juanita without further delay now that she had returned from Puerto Rico, for "what kind uv' mahn waits for de womahn to call heem?" she wailed. I decided I would call upon Juanita the following week, though my thoughts drifted to Julie, then willy-nilly to Sheila. The absence of women in my life was creating schizoid sexual fantasies within me, and I found myself increasingly repressing daydreams, even in class, about all sorts of crazy things I'd do with, and to, women, even to my students.

I phoned Juanita at work. I learned she was a senior CPA with a well-known law firm in a nearby city. She pretended not to have been expecting my call and further inquired as to my "intention." I reminded her of her Aunt Maria; then she said something like, "Oh — oh that. Well, so as not to disappoint anybody over whatever it was I said to Auntie Maria...." She painfully relented to see me that coming Saturday at half-past seven at a trendy Filipino restaurant in a fashionable section of the city, not far from her downtown office.

I was nervous as hell. Though Juanita may not have been an all-out "eye-popping looker," at least not judging from her photo, this would be the first woman I'd be with since Sheila. Judging from the hostile reception she'd given me over the phone, I knew less than ever what to expect, and negative thoughts ran wildly through my head. This was funny; back in Far East Asia, going out with women was no big deal. Yet here? Back here, I was nervous as a kid at his first big school dance.

"Have a hard time finding the place?" I stood up as a young Hispanic woman of about thirty made her way from the entrance and to my chair.

"Pardon me?" she groaned and glowered, then hurried by.

"Uh, excuse me. I thought you were someone else." I sat back down and looked over my shoulder sheepishly as she joined a party of four in the corner. She and the others looked back and scowled.

Not only had I mistaken someone else for Juanita, but I had also asked if she had been able to find the location, belatedly realizing it was Juanita's idea to come here in the first place. I felt like an idiot. Time on the wall clock dragged on. This place was hot, too, just like the humid Saturday night air outside, despite the loud air conditioner hovering over my head, and I tugged at my shirt collar.

It was soon 7:50; the waiter, a short, nasty Filipino with a pencil-thin mustache, kept bothering me as to when I wanted to order. It was a weekend night; they were busy, and we hadn't made reservations. There was much commotion as customers talked and walked about constantly. I didn't know whether to leave or to wait.

I was about ready to walk out or maybe later only convinced myself that I was when somebody looking like her strutted in. I had imagined all sorts of things about what she actually looked like: tall, dark, and sexy would immediately be canceled out and replaced with short, dark and fat. My thoughts played on.

"Uh, how do you do? Pleased to meet you, Juanita." I rose.

"That's OK." (She motioned for me to sit down.) "And my name's Jane." She sat down as I clumsily half-rose to help her with her coat and reposition her chair. "That's OK. I've got it, thank you." That she was nearly a half-hour late was of no consequence, evidently, and she never made any reference to it.

She was about thirty-five, a little older than I hoped, and indeed older than the "'bout tur-tee" that Maria mentioned. She was a little on the short and heavy side, with smooth, soft, light skin, lighter than I'd expected based on her photo, and her dark hair was no longer in the beehive style that had stood out so prominently atop Maria's dresser but cascaded softly around her broad shoulders. She was stylishly attired in a lavender four-buttoned, one-piece business suit with 'Fifth Avenue' written all over it.

"Your aunt has talked much about you." The waiter looked our way, and I motioned for him to stay away momentarily.

"Really?" she replied coquettishly. "What else did she say?"

"Uh, just that at Adelphi, you were a high honors graduate — "

" — highest honors."

"Uh, yes, magna cum laude — "

" — summa cum laude."

"Yeah, summa cum laude graduate at Adelpee — ah, Adelphi." I didn't even get the academic honor ranks straight, damn it. So there I was. Socially constipated. Again. I thought it best just to sit down and shut up, at least not to try to keep any obligatory conversational ball rolling. It looked like a tough night ahead.

So, the evening wore on like this, more or less. I learned that she had two small children, funded her way through school, and was divorced from her "machismo asshole of a Puerto Rican husband." She complained first about the sinigang, a kind of fish and vegetable soup, and later about the chicken adobo being undercooked, even though she had requested earlier of the waiter to "take it back to the chef to prepare it the way I instructed you!" By now, the poor fellow really did have something to be peevish about, and I tried to concentrate on my meal.

Despite my efforts, conversation kept gravitating toward the cantankerous. "Don't you think it, Will, just awful how women still can't get compensated equitably, vis-à-vis men? I mean, at Williams, Barnes, and Williams here in Stamford, there is still a woman attorney making eighty- to ninety-thousand while her male colleagues are getting at least six figures." Had she droned out "male"? Or was it my imagination?

When I responded with, "Maybe they've more seniority there, I mean at Williams, Barnes, and Williams," she denounced it as "typical male heresy," something akin to the "oppression, repression of all women — lesbian and straight, I'll remind you — by a three-thousand-year-old patriarchal system in place for...."

My mind wandered, and I wondered why in hell I was putting up with all this Modern- American-Woman-of-Today shit. Why, once you got out of Saigon and in the delta, a woman (and good-looking at that!) could be had for a carton of cigarettes for the whole bloody weekend, for Chrissakes. That goddamned Maria. I lambasted Maria, and then myself, over my twisted fate. By the time the mixed mango and papaya slices arrived, even Sheila started looking good. To top it off, she never once asked me anything about myself.

Filipino background music hung in the air; our waiter came around and slipped the check under an unused napkin closer to Jane's plate than to mine. I didn't think anything of it, but Jane felt miffed that "he would naturally try to pawn it off on me" and sniffed "just like an Asian." I suggested we leave, grabbed the bill, and headed for the cash register as the Popcorn Princess remained pouting in her seat. "At least Sheila paid for the tip when we were dating," I mumbled half-aloud and made my way for the door, the waiter now looking relieved.

***

As summer wore on a little tediously, so did my classes, and again my mind drifted to thoughts of sex, UFOs, and the people's militias. The militias had been receiving increased media attention. Mark said that "there was growing federal repression of the militias, especially out West, but here on the East Coast as well" and referred to specific legislation pending in Congress as well as on the state level. His statements lingered heavily on my mind. There had been yet another shoot-out, this time in North Carolina between BATF agents and rural folks, principally farmers calling themselves the North Carolina Christian Militia, similar to another group of the same name in South Carolina (militias were springing up like mushrooms according to Mark) that had left several dead on both sides. The Christian Militia had instigated it, the media screamed, and, indeed, some elements in Washington began hollering for a crackdown. You didn't know whom or what to believe.

On the personal side, I dreaded returning to the university in the fall, particularly after my run-in with Robilas over Garcia, both of whom I had managed to steer clear of, and I longed for the personal stability of a full-time job and marriage. Or was it that I was deluding myself all over again? With Sheila, at least I'd stayed home and out of trouble, yet now I found myself spending more time at Steve's Central Cafe downtown, gibbering with him about our days at Wedgemont High. I was graying, middle-aged, and still talking like a teenager. And not very happy with the skin I was in.

"Saw Sheila at Oasis the other night," he said in between toweling the beer mugs neatly arranged atop the counter. "She's lookin' pretty good, ya know."

I didn't say anything. Just fingered the rim of my glass.

"She's got a new boyfriend now too, ya know. Yeah, some guy workin' in man-ufacturin', some hotshot executive. Makes a mint they say." He kept on wiping down the mugs while hunched over the bar sink.

"Hmph." I wasn't about to show much excitement.

Steve continued looking at me out of the corner of his eye. "Might catch 'em runnin' aroun' town in his BMW, pitch-black one, ya know."

You trying to elicit my response? I asked silently.

"Looks like they're hoochie-kootchie, if ya askin' me."

"Yeah, well, nobody's asking you."

"Ah, c'mon, Bill. Jus' tryin' ta let ya in on what's goin' on. No need ta get huffy over it."

"Yeah, Steve, I know. Sorry."

Just then, the girl whose boyfriend's head Mark had used as a hammer walked through the entrance. Alone. She looked even more attractive than before, her hair now pulled back in a cute ponytail, and I wondered how a mere several months could make such a difference. Then, too, I feared that she might recognize me and decide to file a belated complaint with the local cops, if not against me as a prin-cipal, then as an accessory. I could hardly afford a lawyer. Yet I looked right at her.

She looked right back at me but appeared not to remember, and I wondered if the incident with her and her boyfriend hadn't been played out again elsewhere several times. Steve glanced up.

"Seen her since my friend hammered Mr. America?"

He shook his head. She sat down at the far end of a table opposite where she had sat earlier in the spring.

It was around dinnertime and, though it was usually noisy at Steve's place then, I could overhear snatches of her conversation with another woman sitting across from her. They spoke briefly about repaying some favors to somebody or other, and then the topic changed.

"Babe's brother is going out with some local bitch ... some Sheila Wetson or something, a real looker, they say ... and wouldn't you know they're talking of getting engaged! Ha! Imagine that? Little does she know about his past — "

I strained yet couldn't catch the rest of it and almost slid off the stool trying. Steve appeared oblivious to them and was waiting on customers demanding refills. I couldn't get any closer without appearing too obtrusive, and then the girl hastily got up and headed for the exit. I quickly got up and bolted after her, but Steve was just as quick in reminding me that I hadn't paid for my drinks. I discovered I had only a fifty-dollar bill and turned it over to him. By then, she was gone.

When I got home, I stealthily opened the door leading to the stairway. Maria was still simmering over how I "walked out ahn my preecious Juanita," and I wanted to lay low for several days. But unfortunately, Buckie next door heard me and started barking for my attention, and I found myself scurrying up the stairs like a frightened rat. Also, my yearly rental contract was almost up. It's tough to be poor, I reminded myself, and I wondered out loud if Maria might be tempted to raise the rent.

There was a phone message from Julie asking me to return her call, but she forgot to leave her new number or erroneously thought I knew it. Just my luck. Since the fiasco with the bitch Juanita, I thought of Julie all the more. How I'd get in touch with her, I didn't know. As I scanned my mail, I heard a shout from downstairs. It was Maria.

"Professore! Turn on jour TV! Turn on jour TV!"

"I hear you." I did what she asked. All the major networks were broadcasting live — from Pittsfield, Massachusetts.

"Hell, that's right up Route 7," I mumbled, turning up the volume and steadying myself into the worn-out chaise longue left by Maria's previous tenants.

"This is Tim Morehead of CBS News taking you to the Castigoney Ranch just north of the Pittsfield city limits. In case you've just tuned in, there's been a dramatic standoff between federal agents and heavily armed civilians, leading to a surprise confrontation. Repeat: We have a countdown to confrontation. Agents of the Bureau of Alcohol, Tobacco and Firearms' paramilitary team, aided by the FBI, are confronting a group of heavily armed civilians calling themselves the Berkshire County Patriots League — we think — and things are getting tense. We take you now to our station affiliate WWPR and Janette DePauley at the ranch house. Janette? Janette? Can you hear me?"

"Yes? Yes? Tim? Is that you?"

"Yes, Janette ... Janette, can you give us the latest?"

"Yes, Tim. I'm here in front of the Castigoney Ranch house, as you can see behind me, and from the looks of it, we have an extremely tense situation brewing that may explode into unrestrained violence with catastrophic consequences any moment now, God forbid."

"Janette, can you tell us what is at issue here? What do the — what did you say this outfit calls itself?"

"The Berkshire County Patriots League."

"Yes, the Berkshire County Patriots League."

"Well, Tim, as far as we can make out here, they are against a myriad of assaults they allege is taking place against the Constitution and their civil liberties. They — here comes one of their leaders, John Heyman, now on his way back inside. Excuse me, excuse me, John. May we have a word?"

A big, broad-shouldered black man, most likely in his fifties and wearing well-worn work clothes, lumbered toward her.

"Yeah, long as you don' edit this tape at broadcas' time."

"John, can you tell us your demands? What is it you want the government to do?"

"Hell, we jus' want 'em to live up to the law, to follow the Constitution, goddammit!"

Surprisingly, they broadcast the words. Confusion reigned as the camera angle shifted to and fro. Angry obscenities were hollered anonymously in the background.

"What do you mean by that, John?" asked Janette. "Could you be more specific?"

"Well, ah dunno how much more specific you can be. All ya gotta do is read the Constitution 'n the Bill ah Righ's."

"What are your demands, John?"

"We demand tha' guv'r'ment get off our backs. We demand tha' the DC pol'ticians stop messin' with our right to firearms. We demand tha' the mili'try — US mili'try — stop colludin' with UN troops. We demand tha' fed'ral agents stop harassin' our farmers here an' particu'ly out West — EPA, BLM, FEMA, Fish 'n

Wil'life, US Marzhalls, Fores' Service — and, yez, Janette, we demand tha' you reporters in the mainstream media tell the Lord's truth 'bout wha' happened las' month in Raleigh. Ah know, ah am from Caralina."

"What do you mean?" Janette sounded genuinely puzzled.

"Ah mean tha' y'all said the Carolinian Christian Militia fired firs'. Tha's a damned lie 'n you — at leas' your producers know it. Special Agen' in charge, Ralph Winsor, assigned to FBI Militia Wahtch Tas' Force, gave initial orders to shoot on sigh', includin' chil'ren, 'n it's been covered up by — "

Everything went haywire. A loud zzz-sound emanated from the set. I scanned other channels — same thing. The image continued. Finally, DePauley, looking even more diminutive beside big John, reappeared, this time in focus. Minus Heyman.

"We've experienced some technical difficulties, uh, I've been told. But please stand by, ladies and gentlemen. We've much more to report on this fast-breaking countdown to confrontation."

That a black man was of and for the militias, I thought intriguing. I continued to watch, alternately switching channels, and drifted off to much-needed sleep, the set still on. I awoke to find the reporter, the now exhausted-looking Ms. DePauley, informing us that "the standoff is over, thank God — for now."

Over the next several days, the media was full of stories, innumerable political pundits all spinning their versions of what had happened in western Massachusetts. New York City's flagship newspaper, in uncharacteristic language, bluntly begged the president to "crack down on these kooks"; a nationally syndicated columnist called for a more moderate, "reasonable approach, lest all our civil liberties be curtailed for the actions of a few extremists," for, she wrote of Castigoney, quoting Nelson Rockefeller from 1964, "'to extol extremism whether 'in defense of liberty' or 'in pursuit of justice' is dangerous, irresponsible, and frightening.'" Few mainstream journalists came to the defense of the militias. For the first time since the Vietnam War, I wondered where the country was headed, and public media battles over the surging militias continued to swell.

Back at my classes on campus, most of my summer students either appeared completely oblivious to what was going on or couldn't have cared less; this only reaffirmed my initial impression of these "stupid shits," and I marveled at their air of detachment. Even other faculty appeared unconcerned and rarely spoke about what was slowly escalating into a national crisis, preferring to be absorbed over morning coffee in interminably niggling arguments concerning things like "post-structuralist provisos" and "multicultural eclecticism and the post-modern Anglo-American woman." Other than Mark and a few others scattered superficially throughout my daily existence, only Maria was interested, and she to the point of paranoia.

***

At the tail end of July, one rainy Sunday morning, Maria, with her limitless energy, came bounding up the stairs upon returning from church. Buckie's damned barking had me up already, and I couldn't get back to sleep. I was still in pajamas and not in any mood to lend an ear to her ranting. I was at the breakfast table poring through documents Mark had given me and drinking Saturday night's leftover five-dollar-a-bottle watery red wine; that was all I could afford. "Nectar of the gods." I toasted myself. She didn't even bother to knock on the screen door.

"Oh, Professore, dese mileeshas. What do de wahnt weeth us? Why do de coon-froont de Amereecan goov'r'mahnt?" She was all dressed up in her Sunday finery, and I figured she wanted some so-called Anglo slant on it; except for the neighbors, she usually only spoke with Puerto Rican friends and family.

"Well, I don't know for sure, Maria. Many different kinds of militias, perhaps. In any case, nothing for you to be worried — "

"But, Professore, jou 'ave to admeet dat de hate de Spahneesh-speaking peo-ples, why de wahnt to send dem bahck to where we coome froom. I 'eard eet too-day een de shurch. Professore, whatz gooing to 'appen to uz?" She raved on.

I dragged myself up from the table, put my arm around her, and nudged her out the door, mumbling some lie that "everything works out for the best in the end, thank the Lord Jesus. You know that, Maria. Just pray to the Holy Mother." Christ, I wasn't even a churchgoer.

She smiled and made her way downstairs. And I made my way back to bed.

Chapter 3

With summer winding down, about mid-August, I received a call from Swenson College. It was the dean's office. They said their first pick, a black woman I later found out, a specialist in the Harlem Literary Renaissance and a new teacher with an even-newer Ph.D., belatedly decided to "accept an offer elsewhere," meaning she got a job at a more prestigious institution. Not that there wasn't anything wrong with Swenson, yet, in lieu of cold cash, in academe, prestige and status are everything. The offer wasn't negotiable, as much as I would have liked; it was "take it now or leave it." They didn't give me much time to think it over. Didn't need to. Beggar that I was, I couldn't be choosy. They knew it.

It meant I would be leaving Wedgemont for the first time since graduate school years ago. This time for good. Not that it really mattered; there was nothing to be all that upset about. The community had grown in the past couple of decades, though expansion had plateaued in recent years, and I maintained few long-term personal relationships, none meaningful. Perhaps it was time to go. I sometimes caught fleeting glimpses of Sheila, all lovey-dovey with her new beau, and, though my male pride would never admit to it, that cut my gut. At times I found myself trying to sleep it all off....

Over the horizon, was dawn breaking? I lay over to one side and looked out just over the windowsill of the loft. The sky was starting to light up to the east, where it touched the horizon. I hadn't realized it, but I was drenched in sweat and shaking and panting like a bitch in heat. My recurrent nightmare from 'Nam. Always in slow motion. Glimpses of the blood and the guts and the headless baby I'd cradled in my bloody arms danced before me in the recesses of my mind. Or what I thought I had left of one when I awoke. I ran for the toilet as quickly as I had run from exploding ordnance the night I'd gotten hit while on night patrol outside Loc Ninh. I went to vomit. Nothing came out. I started to laugh.

Early-autumn morning rays awoke me again a few hours later. Buckie was already barking as usual. The day had arrived to pack what few possessions I had left after Sheila and I had split. Heaven knows that will be easy, I thought while chuck-ling to myself. It was almost Labor Day and outdoors the mid-morning sun no longer quite warmed the house as it had a few days earlier. Creeping fall foliage gave an air of immediacy, an impending sense that changes were in the offing, and I had better try to get my life back on track. My car had already been sold to pay ever-mounting debt — that still left the motorcycle — and I packed so furiously that the stack of mementos I had so neatly arrayed the night before atop Maria's mahogany dresser went splattering all over the floor.

Kneeling down, I spied an old photo of Sheila and me staring back, taken shortly after the wedding, a photo I thought she, in fact, had had all along. Slowly I picked it up, being careful not to smudge it, as if by touching it now, it would somehow besmirch the memory it had captured. I knew it all didn't make any sense — nothing did anymore — yet a feeling of interminable loneliness welled up inside me. Some powerful, irresistible force held me in its tentacles. I did some-thing I had not done in a long time: I began to weep — and I remembered reading while a student that the Roman poet Ovid had once said, "Grief is satisfied and carried off by tears." I hungered still.

***

"Ja! Professore!" It was Maria seeing me off. The half-packed rental truck waited outside. She had been a delight. Yes, she was my only friend in town. We settled ourselves down in the worn-out sofa, ridiculously oversized for her minuscule liv-ing room, and small-talked over cup after cup of coffee. I realized I didn't want to leave. Abruptly, I stood up, excused myself, then, seemingly by willpower alone, forced my legs toward the door like some zombie, as if I were no longer in control of my body movement. Already I had said good-bye to Steve and old Charlie, not even close friends, and thoughts of not having anyone else in town to say the same to weighed heavily on my heart. Try as I did to shut off reflecting on the years spent in Wedgemont, I knew for the first time since Vietnam, I was scared of tomorrow.

"Oh, Professore. O-moost I forgot. Juanita's message." I tore open the enve-lope.

"Dear Bill,

Sorry if you thought me a little too assertive. Let's talk. Please call.

Jane"

I crunched the note. Maria wasn't looking. I threw it in the trash.

While walking out, she threw her arms around me and hugged me. It felt awkward. I stepped outside and knelt to pat and give a biscuit to Buckie, lying lazily in the driveway next door. We stared into each other's eyes. For the first time, I saw something of a soul within hers. I jumped in the truck.

***

Springvale, home to Swenson College since 1947, was a small, sleepy community, predominantly farmers, nestled on patches of granite and rolling hills just out of range of New Hampshire's White Mountains. Didn't even have a McDonald's. The college itself lay on the western outskirts, and the biggest thing that had happened in town since the end of WWII was when Wally "Crazyman" Wilson had burned down the town hall over a disputed property tax bill. Other than the town hall, downtown was the common on Main Street lined by roughly two dozen dreary-looking buildings, none built in the past twenty years, of which Joe's Diner across from the new town hall featured most prominently for local politics and gossip. Swenson students were well received by townsfolk, compared to most other college towns, yet given the fact that they solidly represented the 'haves' of American society, and almost all were from out of the area, there was your occasional why-don't-you-get-out-of-my-town-punk incident. With Wedgemont behind me, Springvale, which looked to the first-time visitor as if it had been plopped belatedly onto the state map like a cosmic afterthought, would be home.

Dean Rodgers officially introduced the new faculty, a woman in the Mathematics Department and me in Language and Literature, at a late September Friday night social. The president was out of state, and the dean would pounce on every opportunity to hog the college limelight, no matter how insignificant the event. By this time, I had settled down in my teaching routine and set up residence on the top floor of the home of one of the local ministers, practically within walking distance of the college. The only way I had to get around town was on my noisy motorcycle, which appeared to annoy the mild-mannered minister, incessant proselytizer that he was, and I calculated the number of paychecks it would take to put a down payment on a small apartment while in my head angrily subtracting money owed to Sheila (at long last quiet). Mark and I still met on weekends.

"Mr. Watson, please join me in my office after class." It was Dean Rodgers.

Within the hour, I was standing in an expansive, dimly-lit room surrounded by stacks of books sheathed in drab, dull-looking covers. Stacks and more stacks. There were so many; in fact, I surmised that the room housed close to the number of non-reference books the public library had downtown. Already well into the semester, I had not yet been in his office. A pungent, acrid sensation of what smelled like pipe smoke hit me as I walked in.

The dean remained seated behind a sedate, expensive-looking Tiffany desk lamp. The light obscured his face (you could barely discern an eerie silhouette), and an unwary visitor might have gotten the uncanny impression of staring at some disembodied spirit. Or did he want it that way? From atop his huge black walnut desk echoed the faint, steady tattoo of fingers drumming.

"Please sit down, Mr. Watson. I'll come right to the point. This is a small town. People are generally easygoing here, although not as easygoing as they might appear. To the newly arrived, of course."

My eyes adjusted to the light. His right hand alternately fidgeted with his bow tie and overgrown mustache. Reminiscent of the interview, he had the inveterate mannerism of peering over his glasses while he lectured you, undoubtedly cultivated from his glory days at Oxford.

"You've been seen repeatedly with a tall, dark-haired gentleman, evidently not from the area, in the consort of members from the New Hampshire Liberty Militia. Impressions are created; people's sensibilities may be, uhm, rubbed the wrong way. One wouldn't want to give off any undue impressions, would one? I know you dress and drive rather uncharacteristically for an Ivy League man. Of course, that's your business; however, we must be sensitive that Swenson has a reputation to uphold."

"Me and the gentleman — I mean, the gentleman in question and I, well, we like target shooting. That's all."

"I see."

"One wouldn't want to give an untoward impression."

"Splendid. Then I'm glad we share a complementary vision."

"Of course."

Townspeople here were a decidedly friendly bunch overall, so much so that I marveled at their initial inclination to open their arms to outsiders. I had the impression, from where I don't know, that rural people in this region of the country were standoffish. Of course, I was comparing locals' sociability with that of the gentlefolk of Wedgemont, only a few hours' drive away, many of whom I had known almost all my life, and I could see how wrongheaded I was. There, neighbors you knew for decades never much more than nodded at you in passing, no matter how friendly you tried to be; in Springvale, I already felt taken into the bosom of the community — at least by members of the New Hampshire Liberty Militia. Some said it was because of the way I eagerly volunteered to pitch in on miscellaneous petty jobs. At first, I only wanted to target shoot with them. Soon the militia became my second home.

With a few notable exceptions, the men of the militia (women were admitted as auxiliary members) were neither racist crackpots nor paranoid world-federalist conspiracy kooks. The media had been playing up the 'kook' angle much more since the shoot-out in the Carolinas, and I could see how misleading it was. Or was it because my own perspective had evolved?

All the while, Mark and I had become closer. He was like a brother I never had, and I trusted him intuitively as I had old Army buddies on nighttime recon. He kept feeding me more purloined Above Top Secret government documents on involvement with and cover-up of UFOs and assorted matters. Where he'd gotten them, he'd still not be more specific than to say 'through channels,' but I appreciated what appeared to be the continued risk he was taking, and I could see he trusted me implicitly. I devoured them all and became more convinced, though not completely. Besides, I was delving into these matters on my own more than ever.

The New Hampshire Liberty Militia, headquartered just outside Springvale, began to simmer. Several hardcore cadre saw to it. All told, we had a command roster of almost fifty. Looking at them by their day jobs, you would never ascertain their weekend one. Principals included Big Walt Patterson, a huge strapping book salesman by day at a tiny publishing house in Laconia, deputy commander by night to Commander Mike Richards, local car salesman. Richards was the new commander since Old Man 'Jimmy' Adams had more or less retired to his farm owing to old age. Under Adams, the organization had languished: Richards' astute leadership enlivened and expanded the group to make it a tight-knit force. Farmer Petey 'Boney' Hinson, who always dressed like a Bible salesman, childhood friend of Richards, was a public relations specialist, a rather pompous title given what he did. Leroy Morton, ex-Golden Gloves lightweight champion, was another hard-core 'soldier,' one of the few non-white members, as devoted as any to the cause. There were others, of course, too many to name, all dedicated to the militia's motto: By the sword we seek peace, but peace only under liberty. The sole member from academia, certainly the only one from the college, I nevertheless felt at home.

***

"Shut the damned door!" It was Petey Hinson swiveling on his stool and yelling at nobody in particular. "Freezing our asses here! Joe won't even turn on the damn heat yet. Damned near Columbus Day. Jesus Christ." A draft, cold this early in the season, blew through. Other early Sunday morning diners chimed in.

Joe, long-time proprietor of the only diner on Main Street and 'Mr. Mayor' to many town residents, steadied his ponderous weight on his makeshift stool as he stooped over to pour more steaming coffee into the big stainless-steel vat. "Hold yer britches there, Corporal." Joe knew Petey didn't like the nickname; it had stuck to him too long, though.

The aroma of freshly brewing coffee wafted through the air. Weak sunlight shone through the Venetian blinds only partly shut and projected a refracted image of Joe's beer belly in the coffee vat. The near-clamor of clanging utensils, coffee cups banging on saucers, and the airy chitchat that characterized Springvale's early-morning breakfast crowd generated the notion that this place was as good as any to be this time of day. Hell, except for church, there really wasn't any other spot in town.

"More coffee, Hon?" asked Mabel, Joe's waitress.

I nodded. I tried my best to 'rub the tired' out of my eyes, as my sister used to say when we were kids. "What's your take on this?" I said, pointing to the headline on the Manchester Free Press: "President Pleads For More Firearms Limits." Mark was sitting next to me to my left in our cramped booth.

"Yeah, I saw. Something else, too, you're not going to read there." He pulled on his gold earring.

"What?"

"Good chance he'll try to initiate something before year's end. Executive Order, perhaps, most likely presented in the guise of public safety. That way, he can skirt Congress. As usual. Good chance in conjunction with a militia confrontation somewhere, maybe coerced."

"Think so?"

"Yes, heard it through channels." He wiped his chin. A tiny dribble of egg yolk appeared on his shirt. I wiped it off. "Could get your governor involved here, too." This year wasn't an election year; however, everyone knew that in Concord, the new governor was also playing the militia card.

"In reference to what we said last week, what do you think we ought to do next?"

"Lay low — for now." Things suddenly got quiet. We looked up.

In had walked resident state trooper Sergeant Joe Hines and his deputy, Trooper Kevin Leopold — "Little Leopard" some militiamen called him. Relations between local law enforcement and the militia had been unusually good thus far, and the militia hierarchy wanted to keep it that way. On weekends you could always find several cadre at the diner, and today was no exception. Leopold strutted over, momentarily standing in front of us to get a better look at Mark and me. Mark stared at him foursquare. I stared into my scrambled eggs.

"Mornin', boys," Hines mumbled from behind his deputy. "Coffee, Mabel."

They sat down. Mark and I could make out Richards and Petey quibbling over operation tactics in the next booth.

"Need to cache some additional 'stub' ammo out at the Old Man's range. Think I can get a good discount on it … Do it, fast. Washington's pushing hard for a moratorium on production. No doubt to make a permanent ban … Sonafabitch! You don't say! Since when? … Caught it in an NRA faxed message alert…."

Didn't think much of it. Then. Everybody continued to dig in on Joe's greasy home fries, bacon, and eggs. Mark's summertime prophecy reverberated in my head: We were all fast becoming unwitting 'pawns on history's chessboard.'

***

Back at school, nothing special was happening other than the time during Halloween Homecoming when some coeds led by a feminist in the Athletic Department tried to kick out men from the department gym during certain hours because the women were being "looked at." I got along with others and even had a "new" monograph on Molière accepted by a prestigious journal. The dean and members of my department were quite impressed over my "splendidly original research," as he put it. Little did they know it was a mere hodgepodge of material lifted from my previously published work.

Nobody could accuse me of not fulfilling my academic duties, yet in my heart, they were gradually being supplanted by my militia ones. For the first time since the military, I felt I belonged, though not to anyone in particular, and certainly to no woman. It was more an organizational sense of belonging, like to my platoon, rather than your one-on-one attachment. That didn't mean I didn't desire feminine affection. It was just that I almost didn't know how to go about it anymore. In the shadows of the landscape of my memory, alternating images of Sheila, Julie, and Juanita would appear. Then one of them called.

"How do you like Swenson?"

It was Julie of all people on the phone. Never expected to hear from her after I dropped her a line and told her I'd taken Swenson's offer. She sounded sexy. I got nervous. Images started popping in my head. I squeezed the phone and tried to steady myself.

"Thought I'd keep in touch since I last met your friend and you earlier in New Haven."

Mark, Julie, and I had met at Yale in mid-August. She and I had bumped into each other at a small conference we had both attended only to network for a job. Mark had come along with me. Their talk was smooth; with her, mine was choppy. Like always.

"When are you coming down this way again?"

Didn't need any coaxing. Immediately, I mumbled something about the following weekend, right before Thanksgiving. Had to tie up a few odds and ends in Wedgemont, I reminded myself.

"Fine. Call me then."

We talked of little nothings the best I could, and I thought I finally had a date. I would ride my motorcycle from central New Hampshire to southwestern Connecticut. It would be damned cold. Didn't care. I'd stay over at Mark's place (he'd lived alone since his divorce), and I told Julie I'd call Saturday.

Friday afternoon arrived. I called and suggested we meet that night — any night. Steve's cafe had come to mind; I quickly shelved that image for something warmer, more intimate.

"No," she replied. "Something" had come up; she would only consent to Saturday or Sunday afternoon and "while you're at it, why don't you bring Mark because I really need his advice on my brother's Post-Traumatic Stress Disorder."

This hit me by surprise. I told her I could tell her everything she needed to know.

"I appreciate that, yet my brother's experience appears to approximate Mark's," she said, "and that makes a difference."

How she knew this, I didn't remember; they had mostly spoken in the context of Yale's anti-war demonstrations of the 70s. She remained cordial but adamant. We would meet Saturday afternoon in a coffee shop in Danbury....

**

"Why, hello, Will. How have you been?" I crossed the room. Julie slowly rose. She had been there a while. The table was cluttered with scattered newspapers and stale cigarette butts. She extended her hand. She looked even sexier than in summer, having let her dark blonde hair grow. It appeared to bounce off the lapels of the soft caramel-colored business suit that hugged and streamlined the contours of her athletic body. I tried to collect myself, yet nervously stubbed my toe on the chair leg when receiving her hand. I was so damned sexed-up I could barely control myself.

"I see you brought Mark." She looked straight at him and smiled. Mark nodded. Except for the three of us, the coffee shop remained almost deserted. It was chilly. An outdoor ambiance hung in the air; huge potted plants were positioned next to every one of the tiny tables and at the entrance. We all sat down. A waitress walked over and took our order.

"Teaching any phallocentric theories yet? Or only practicing them with your students?" She laughed. The allusion to our shared Feminist Literature class was unmistakable, though I think it all sailed over Mark's head. She always made me hot. I squirmed in my seat. Julie and I laughed. Mark didn't know what to do.

"What are you doing now?" I inquired. "I take it you've given up on teaching."

"Not exactly. As I said over the phone, I've taken the head public relations position with New Farms, the private school, and I coach the girls' soccer team. It'll have to do for now." She looked at Mark.

"Sounds like a winner!" he blurted out.

"Think so?" Julie said softly, arching her fingertips and leaning toward Mark on her elbows. "Why, thank you, Mark," she cooed.

Conversation gravitated toward her brother's Southeast Asia experience. She mentioned he reminded her of Mark and me, "though more you, Mark." I excused myself to go to the men's room.

When I returned, our coffee was the topic. Talk of her brother's stress disorder was over, I figured. I think they rambled on about the August Yale conference. Looking out the window, I saw it was pouring sleet, and I worried about the motorcycle trip back and meditated over my having come back. Then all I recall of Julie was the sight of her dashing toward her car in the sleet now turned to wet snow.

***

I had only been away a few months, but it's surprising how imperceptible daily environmental changes can be. When I'd gotten back from the war, it had been as if nothing had changed in Wedgemont. I remember walking downtown and meeting my then-retired high school principal. He had talked about this teacher and that as if both of us were still in his school. Even though I had decorations from hell to breakfast, I sure hadn't felt like any war hero. I'd harbored polarized feelings about what I had done. In those days, Vietnam vets kept their stories to themselves. Most still do. In the short time since I had gone to Swenson, several changes were apparent: another branch bank office over the spot where long-standing Johnnie's Restaurant had recently burned down (most Wedgemont folks had plenty of

money), a newly expanded library, and a bakery across the railroad tracks from
Steve's cafe. Steve remained too much like his old self for me, however.

"How's Maine?"

"Vermont, Steve."

"Uh-huh. Ya know, Sheila's still with our BMW boy...."

Christ. Couldn't he tweedle a different tune? After putting up with me, Sheila
was lusting after the smell of money. I guess I had been just bad news for her. It
seemed only Maria and Buckie welcomed my return.

On the national scene, things were going downhill. Fast. The stock market had
taken its customary October nosedive and hadn't bounced back. An especially ex-
citing World Series that year helped to divert attention. People were looking for
scapegoats, and for some, the militias would do. Washington was ever-eager to
oblige. Things didn't look better overseas. Fact is, they looked far worse. Markets
crashed. Territorial disputes worsened. Japan took to saber-rattling against Korea;
China lay siege to a tiny island off Taiwan; open conflict erupted between Turkey
and Greece. These conflicts were but a small fraction of the hostilities and upheav-
als that had exploded. All over the globe, the UN and Washington were helpless
to contain a slide toward anarchy. The New World Order metastasized into the
"Old World Disorder," as Mark put it. Unresolved regional conflicts began to
coalesce into an ever-growing patchwork quilt of escalating violence. A few prepared themselves; the masses buried themselves in their sports headlines. American
society kept itself glued together at the altar of celebrity worship.

***

Mid-Sunday afternoon, I left Mark's place. A storm was predicted; I needed to
return early. He hadn't brought up Julie, and I was glad. While on my motorcycle
just past Hartford, I remembered I had forgotten a few textbooks I had taken with
me to get a leg up on classes. The sun was setting when I rumbled back into Mark's
driveway. A car that looked familiar but one which I couldn't place was parked on
the edge of the driveway. I rang the doorbell. Through the transparent curtains, I
saw a woman's figure move toward the door. It was Julie.

When I arrived back at the minister's house that night, Mark called. He said
Julie meant nothing to him; indeed, he had caught her in lies about her brother's

"so-called war experiences," if, in truth, "she even had a brother." Among other things, he said when she couldn't exactly remember her brother's unit, he suggested to her it was the 'Thirty-sixth Cavalry Regiment' and that then she was sure of it. There was no 'Thirty-sixth Cav.' He had made it up, he continued, hesitating. I asked him why he didn't find her attractive. "That's my business," he said.

Shortly afterward, Julie left a puzzling message on my answering machine: "… Why, he's — he's strange." The Mystery of Mark Mercotti deepened. I didn't know him as well as I thought I did.

Chapter 4

"My name is Kimiko Tanimoto. I will be your new teaching assistant. I will try my best. Hope you be satisfied."

"Yes, I know. Rodgers — Dean Rodgers — told me. Welcome aboard."

"A broad?"

"Never mind. I mean, it's nice to have you. To help us, that is."

Kimiko was about thirty, a little older than Swenson's typical TA, and reportedly the Korean-Japanese daughter of a wealthy Osaka businessman. She was slim and tall for an Asian and one of Swenson's few international students. I was surprised that the dean had assigned her to our department; other more heavily enrolled departments went begging for help. She was undoubtedly attractive, though "no knock-out," according to Mark, and radiated an aura of demure and quiet gentleness. I had seen her around campus in the company of other international students, especially at the student campus center at the end opposite the bookstore, which served as their unofficial gathering spot, and we might have said something in passing from time to time. I adjusted a stack of mail on the department secretary's desk, mindlessly arranging the pieces. Kimiko was supposed to be doing this, for God's sake. I hadn't been used to anybody working for me.

"That's OK. I have it," she said. "Would you like cup of hot green tea? I brought it from summer trip when I came back from Osaka." I nodded. "You been Japan?"

"No, afraid not."

"Ahh, always too busy studying to travel, hmm?" She smiled, wetting her lips.

Suddenly, I remembered Sheila. "That's what some people would say."

She set two tiny cups on our table. I sat down on the department's worn-out, coffee-stained upholstery. It was late Friday afternoon and quiet. Everyone had gone for the weekend.

"How do you like me to make your tea?"

"Plain, please, thank you." I was a tad shy of becoming unglued. Apart from Maria and old Buckie, no female had deferred to me lately. "Plain's fine, thank you." I motioned for her to sit down. "What's it like for you to be here?"

"Ahh, yes. Here? It's — " Kimiko paused and gently laid her hands on her knees. "It's, it's been … nice — yes, nice." I motioned again, this time for her to drink. She cradled the teacup in both hands.

"I see. Seen much of the countryside?"

"Well, I've been to top of Mount Washington, Boston, MIT, and Harvard campus. Yes." She nodded. "Everything so much spacious. Not like back home."

"Homesick?"

"Maybe first. Not anymore." She softly blew on the cup and looked down on the table. We didn't speak. I heard the loud tick-tock of the grandfather clock at the entrance. I had hardly touched the tea. She continued to look at the table.

"Maybe you could see more sights."

"You mean you'd take me?" She looked up, yet not directly at me. "I mean to see more, see more sights?"

I wasn't thinking of it but nonetheless felt compelled to utter something silly like, "It could be considered." Still not looking at me, her face eased into a soft smile. She turned toward the window. It was snowing.

***

Morning broke dull and gray with low overcast skies. The recent cold spell had only slightly broken. Far too late for Indian summer this time in the year. Crystals of melting ice still crunched under my feet as I crossed over the campus square to meet Kimiko. I thrust my hands into my pockets.

"I hope I'd not be late." She was standing by her new Mercedes. The morning air shot out from her nostrils. She alternately blew on her hands to warm them. "We take my car, OK? Here's keys. You drive, OK?" Howling winds from the east whipped our faces.

We got in and, on Route 25 past the old granite quarry slowly headed east for Old Man Adams' barn on the flattest stretch of land outside Springvale. Stretches of still-frozen ice pockmarked the road.

"What food you say we eat this day?"

"Here, plenty of deer and bear," I answered. I hadn't a clue. Both of us remained quiet.

We pulled into the half-frozen unpaved driveway crowded with vehicles, mostly pickup trucks and one or two modified Jeeps. Mark was busy, and I didn't care to spend the holiday alone. Bringing along Kimiko to a militia-sponsored event gave me second thoughts, even if it was only a meal. A score of people, mostly men dressed in an odd mix of farmers' work clothes and military fatigues, were milling around an old hand water pump and occasionally jumping up and down to keep warm. We got out.

"Ah, here's the professor — and his new girlfriend!" Someone snorted.

"Oh, no!" Kimiko demurred. "Only my teacher." But she slipped her arm around mine anyway. I was never her teacher, yet said nothing. A couple of the women appeared to snicker. I noticed the American flag draped over the entrance to the barn, and suddenly everyone went inside.

Old Jimmy's barn, now replete with kerosene heaters and a fireplace, continued to serve as militia headquarters. You could smell the kerosene immediately. High on the walls, images of stuffed bear, moose, and deer heads flickered in the light of the burning logs and cast a dour gaze upon all who entered, testimony to Jimmy's bygone hunting prowess. Kimiko jumped back, momentarily mesmerized; Jimmy's granddaughter giggled. We inched our way to the table laden with dishes of venison, hare, moose, bear, and turkey. A huge log piled high on the crackling pyre slipped against one of the andirons and startled Kimiko; she instinctively pulled me toward her. The pungent scent of burning wood permeated the room, softening my spirit.

"I'm predictin' a crackdown on guns or ammo purchases right after New Year's." That was Petey Hinson, his voice clear amid the din of the group now settling in their seats. "Your buddy Mark even mentioned it, Will."

I didn't look up. Though Mark wasn't officially a member, let alone part of the inner circle, he was well respected by the cadre, especially the many Vietnam-era vets.

"Now hold on," said Big Walt, jabbing the air with his meaty hand. "My money's on next year, right after the elections. That way, those sons-of-bitches on Capitol Hill can make good on campaign pledges of disarmament."

Walt's wife slapped him on his forearm so hard a red welt immediately surfaced. "Watch your goddamned mouth in front of the kids, Walt!"

"Think ya both got it wrong," shot back Mike Richards. "Based on my communications with a few of the other brothers, notably in Pittsfield and West Virginia, my bet is after a triggered event."

"You mean instigated?"

"That's right, Petey."

"Shit," muttered Big Walt. Walt's wife sneered. "On what basis?"

Mike, retired from the Marine Corps with more stripes on his sleeve than a zebra, looked right at him with his usual authoritarian air. "I'll let you know, sir, during formation," he said, the salutation bespeaking his thirty-year-plus subordination to officer ranks. He remained ever-cognizant that not all in attendance were members. Talk revolved around individual political stands staked out by local politicians. That Kimiko was there appeared not to bother them, however; for the moment, I felt at ease.

"Let's have Grace," someone yelled.

"Yes, why not from the professor?" squealed one of Old Jimmy's grandchildren. "Let's eat," said another. All motion ceased except for the fire. Then every head stiffened and bowed in unison.

"Uh, I'm not, you know — " I started. Even Kimiko leaned forward and looked straight at me. I resigned myself.

"Bless us this Thanksgiving Day, our Holy Father, with the full cornucopia" — several of the children giggled — "that Thou hast bestowed upon us this year. And may the coming year's harvest be bountiful. May we remain a free people...." The last item hit a respondent chord with several of the menfolk. At one moment, their heads were lowered in supplication; at the next, they came alive as if electrified. Kimiko managed the tiniest of smiles. Maria would've been proud of me; Sheila would've roared....

***

"Whaddya in all hell doing? What's got into your head?" Fingers that felt like steel jabbed into my shoulder socket so hard they felt that they'd go through me.

"What do you mean? What the hell's got into you, Mark, anyway? Chrissakes, calm down!"

"I mean, I want to know why you'd want to piss your career away on a bitch. A slant at that!"

"Now you wait a goddamned minute. Kimiko may be a Jap, but that doesn't mean she's a slant — er — I mean, all right, she's Oriental and all that, but she's a helluva nice girl, Mark. Helluva nice girl. I gotta admit that she's all I — "

" — you know what the hell I'm talkin' about! You've got a position here, an image to maintain that goes along with it. How the hell do you think it looks when you — single, foot-loose, fancy-free prof — go 'round all over town, prancin' and dancin', with some goddamned student from his department practically half his age?" His eyes narrowed. He stepped toward me, his face inches from mine. I smelled that cheap aftershave lotion, so familiar to me by now. "What the hell's gotten into you, anyways?"

I had to admit; he had a point. Kimiko and I had been seen together like lips and teeth all over town the past several weeks. We'd become inseparable. It was true. People were beginning to talk.

"Jesus, Bill…." His voice trailed off. Maybe the emotional intensity of the moment was too much. I don't know. His usual nonchalant aplomb returned, and he stepped back and looked down the firing range at the black-and-white paper targets flapping in the wind. Powerful sounds of sporadic pistol gunshots punctuated the invigorating early-morning New Hampshire air. It was the weekend Liberty Militia handgun competition behind Old Jimmy's barn. Bitter cold as it was, every range slot was occupied. He pivoted around toward me again.

I looked straight into his eyes. "Look, I know, uh, I might've gotten carried away lately — "

" —'carried away'?"

"Well." I paused. "Look, you're not making this easy for me. What the hell do you want me to say? I haven't had any female in my life for a while 'cept Buckie and Maria. Seriously, I haven't had any woman since Sheila left me, Mark. Hasn't been easy. Whew! It hurts to admit … to admit I failed her. And now Kimiko's all I have here. All I have anywhere."

His eyes had been locked all the while on to mine. Then, all of a sudden, I realized I had never even noticed their color. Had never really looked at — let alone in — them. Sonafabitch. I didn't see any sympathy.

"Another thing is — " He yanked up his shirt zipper for more protection against the intensifying wind, cupped and blew on his hands, then rammed them into the side pockets of his ski parka. Shouts rang out in the distance. It was Larry. He had scored consecutive bull's-eyes, and you could always count on him to let all of Springvale know it. Though the sounds came from opposite ends of the range, they almost drowned out Mark.

"Thing is also some people here don't take kindly to you two arm-in-arm. Not talkin' 'bout you and Kimiko as from the college, but as her being an Asian, Japanese, out here with you in these woods."

"Now listen here. I don't give a damn what people think about her nationality. That's none of their damned business. And if anybody says anything? You tell them I said so!" He stared back at me. It was a cold, empty stare. "Can't you understand, Mark? She's all I got here. She's with me."

Guess we both got carried away. That a woman would get between Mark and me, I never would've guessed. And I found myself wondering why he seemed so perturbed by her presence.

By then, shooting had ceased. An argument about the suitability of long arms over handguns for the militia was escalating into a quarrel at one end while an ever-loud Larry was getting out of hand at the other. The wind changed course. A cloud of gun smoke hit us. One could be overwhelmed by the distinctive smell of concentrated gun smoke unless one had experienced it before. Mark said it would always take him back to Vietnam no matter how hard he tried for it not to. Old Jimmy swore rifles and handguns would create different smoke, not to mention different problems with laws and logistics at the range. In Vietnam, we had the new M-16s and some guys, the communist AK-47s (thought more reliable, especially in mud and monsoons); here, we had handguns. But "guns are guns," Petey Hinson would argue; one would kill you as quickly as another, and for me, the issue of long arms versus handguns didn't much matter. A halo of gun smoke had drifted over to envelop Mark, and for a moment, he had a far-gone look.

"Yeah! J'ya see that? Lookadat! Goddamned near another bull's eye. That bull's eye could be a nigger's eyes. Whoowee! Ha! Better yet, some nigger federal agent. Right in his nigger eyes. Nigger balls. Or through his goddamned big, thick nigger lips. Nigger fish lips." It was Larry again.

"Would you tone it down?" someone said.

"No, how about just knocking it the hell off, Larry?" shouted another.

The stainless-steel finish to Larry's Kahr MK .40 pistol reflected the strengthening rays of the morning sun, and he clutched it tenaciously in his small right hand as he confronted his detractors. After Jimmy had relinquished leadership, the command took special care to weed out racists, kooks, and hotheads. Already there had been run-ins between Larry and our few non-Caucasian members, particularly Leroy Morton.

Larry was one weed that kept coming back.

"Whaddya, some fucking nigger lovers?" Larry squinted his eyes and sneered. "Don't ya think we have 'nough already in Concord? Washington? Huh? You know how they're taking over — financed by the damned kikes in Washington and New York — and, next thing before ya know it, they'll be here grabbing our guns, humpin' and pumpin' our wives and daughters, and making a mockery of that there." (He aimed the MK .40 at the American flag over Jimmy's barn, barely visible from our vantage point, the allusion understood by all.) Loud, biting winds, whipping across the flat, snowy stretches of Jimmy's farm, added to the acrimony of his outburst. He wasn't backing down.

The regulars were all there, save Leroy, gone to a New York boxing match. Petey snickered; Walt grunted; Mike rolled his eyes; the rest all looked like they'd rather be someplace else. By then, even Mark looked almost perturbed. Larry and what few sympathizers he appeared to have couldn't be ignored any longer. Something had to be done; something had to be decided; he had stepped out of the march one time too many. Suddenly, sensing he had again violated some semblance of military-turned-civilian protocol, Larry reversed himself and started walking away in an apparent bid to defuse the situation. Mike, evidently feeling a need to say something as incumbent militia leader, blocked his path.

"How many times you going to screw up, Larry? We've been over all this before. We can't have division in the ranks. And you, sir, are continuing to divide us. And I — we — will not tolerate it."

Larry fiddled with the MK .40. He looked like a boot camp trainee getting chewed out for the umpteenth time, not able to look at his drill sergeant, and he alternately stared up at the thin clouds over the horizon, then down at the shells scattered over the ground.

"You understand me, soldier?" On the surface, it may have sounded silly, but Mike's tone was serious.

Larry still wouldn't — or couldn't — respond. He stood stupidly as the object of our attention, all eyes glued on him front, straight, and center — and on the still-loaded MK .40, now being squeezed so hard in his shaking hand, you half-expected it to go off. In a perverse sort of way, I felt he liked it. Made him feel something of a soldier, if only on the weekend, one who could walk away from the battlefield Monday morning. Later I found out he had never been in the service.

"Well?" Mike said in a less strident tone.

Larry remained staring into the sky, unblinking, then finally, and only for an instant, lowered his head, looked into Richards' eyes, glanced down, and shuffled his feet. He relaxed his grip on the pistol. The worst looked to be over for now and none too soon for everybody, especially Mike; he didn't relish this part of leadership, necessary as it was.

Later, Mark and a few of the others said they sensed this about Richards, yet the thorn was still in the foot. A member would nonetheless have to be dealt with administratively. Mike Richards was not a man given to punishing others. Earlier in life as a Marine Corps senior non-com, he was used to officers meting out official punishment; now it was his turn to command. Not that he wasn't apt and able as militia commander and well respected, too, but in this respect, one could see his new boots would never fit. He would remain our leader, however, till treachery overtook him.

Mark's heated admonition about Kimiko proved prophetic the very next day. Final exams were finished; Swenson was closed for the holidays, though Kimiko would stay in the international grad student dorm over the intersession. She and I were at Joe's Diner for lunch. There were few customers, but typically some were occasionally vulgar; this day was no exception. I felt decidedly uneasy sitting with Kimiko, yet there were few other places; being seen together off-campus seemed preferable to being seen on it.

"Mr. Will, you look very nice today, I — "

"'Will!'"

"Sumimasen." She smiled and lowered her head as she repositioned herself in Joe's straight-backed booth opposite me. "I think I'll have the fish special like last month," she said while looking beyond the miniature Christmas tree on the far end of the counter. Adorned with a string of tiny light bulbs, it flickered in colors of bright red, blue, green, and white, adding a homey atmosphere to the establishment's austere no-nonsense look. The '$5.95 Joe's Special Cheeseburgur Plate' sign right above it caught my eye.

"Mabel." I gestured for her attention. Joe was out ill with the flu, and the poor woman was trying to juggle both counter and booth orders herself. Moreover, a previous night's snowfall had turned Springvale into a white wonderland, and a light flurry from inside the tiny vestibule was blown in with another entering customer. Kimiko removed her scarf, and I mine. Whether Joe had listened to Petey's beef about the inside temperature earlier that fall, I didn't know; the place was now routinely overheated. "Mabel!" I hollered, and this sign of impatience grabbed the attention of a rowdy bunch in her direction. Mabel didn't look back; they did.

"You think we'll go to Montreal after Christmas? We take my car like I asked." Kimiko wanted to meet some visiting Japanese figure skater at an ice show. Said her father knew the skater's father or something — I don't know. My mind was more on the sleeping arrangements, and I pondered over how to broach the subject, which was unsettling for me at least. Kimiko couldn't see the rowdies, who were still gawking at us, and I grew apprehensive. She could see that in my eyes. Their gawking reminded me of Saigon street urchins and assorted back-alley street toughs I had encountered while on R & R, but these three guys looked a hell of a lot more menacing. I had seen two of them from time to time and never liked their look.

"What's matter? You liked my idea before, no? Something no good now?" Her crescent-shaped eyes, now soft and mournful, cast a dour look in the direction of the flickering tree. Enhanced by their soft, dreamy look, they beckoned me with a kaleidoscope of promises. At that moment, she looked almost beautiful, no matter what Mark had said after they'd first met. The orange pastel of her blouse's collar complemented the hint of the facial foundation she wore high on her cheekbones; it immediately reminded me of the Asian model repeatedly featured on glossy fashion magazine covers. Though I never read them, except at the dentist's or doctor's office or supermarket checkout line, the resemblance was uncanny, and I would half-mumble something about it, to which she always responded with a puzzled look. Around Orientals, it was often hard for me to tell what they were thinking.

"Yes — I mean, no — uh, that is, the idea's fine, Kimiko." Her face broke out in an elusive smile as she moistened her lips, and I adjusted the blinds at our window. "Let's eat." The guys were getting to me; I was hot and uncomfortable already. I tried to ignore them.

The smallest guy had fed the jukebox some coins, and the sound of America's perennial favorite Christmas song filled the air. My apprehension lessened — why I'm not sure. Maybe it was because tough guys don't listen to Bing Crosby's White Christmas, I said to myself, and I tried to focus on the upcoming trip with Kimiko and Joe's greasy 'Special Cheeseburgur' plate.

She practiced her origami skills with our tissue napkins while we continued to discuss the trip. During the meal, the three guys had quieted down; nevertheless, you could hear their steady generic profanity, and I wondered how much of it she comprehended, if any. In her world, I knew that all were held accountable, morally responsible, for the outrages of a few. Here, even inclusive of cultural relativism, I thought the idea repulsive that she could ever somehow yoke me to this bunch of assholes. I added ketchup to my leftover fries.

"Better we be going?" she asked and reached for her scarf and pocketbook.

I nodded in agreement, concurrently holding two polarized sentiments: one about her still hilariously unidiomatic speech (her written English was appreciably more polished); the other about the still-present problem awaiting us in the parking lot. (They were outside and appeared to be tampering with Kimiko's car.) I got scared; Kimiko sensed it.

"What's matter?" she asked, brushing back her hair and buttoning her coat.

I didn't say anything as I stood up, just adjusted the blinds again and continued studying them from the booth. Still there. Kimiko then understood, as did the few others who remained inside. Mabel, who'd never seemed to like me, maybe thought I was a cheap tipper — whatever — came over. She exuded the look of a waitress, battle-worn from over twenty years of counter wars, at least ten of them at Joe's: pencil tucked behind ear; always-present gum; coffee-stained apron.

"Want me to give a call to state police barracks? Hines? Leopold? It'll be a while before they can get here. I know they're troublemakers. Why don't you two sit down and have another coffee? Don't worry about your car. I know who they are." She had stopped addressing me as "Hon."

"Thanks, Mabel. But I'll handle it." I hadn't the foggiest idea how and absent-mindedly started for the door followed by a hesitant Kimiko. Mabel reminded me we hadn't paid (I probably hadn't even left a tip), and Kimiko quickly took care of it. I intuited I was walking straight into trouble, and memories of being told by my battalion commander right before the heat of battle to "Just do it!" flashed before me. We strode out the vestibule in what seemed like one stride. Perhaps I was overreacting? But there was no such luck. The goons were waiting.

I stepped out into the snow-speckled parking lot, Kimiko clutching my arm. "Oooh, what have we here? … He's a professor at the college … Folks here say you was in the Navy, teach … So, what is it you profess, Professor? … Everyone knows Navy's filled with faggots…."

Kimiko nervously handed over her car keys.

"What's this? Got you a 'sugar momma'? Hear Mercedes got shitty windshield wipers," the largest of the three sneered. Besides Walt Patterson, he was the biggest man I'd ever seen in Springvale. He leaned over, twisted back the wiper in his huge hand, and smirked. "Aw, will you look at that?"

"Where d'ya get a car like this on your salary, huh?" the little goon squealed. "Gigolo-geek gift from a gook? We've been seeing you two lately all kootchie-koo." They all laughed.

"Look, we don't want any trouble. Wh-Wh-Why don't you just let us alone?" I said, praying my voice wouldn't crack any more, and strode toward the driver's door, leaving behind a trembling and bewildered Kimiko.

"Not so fast, geek." A tattooed hand slammed down on my shoulder and spun me around in the snow like a kid's old-fashioned top. It was the big guy.

Not exactly sure what happened next. Something of a blur. My civilian reflex reverted to a military one. Couldn't have lasted much more than a minute, tops.

Rage inside my guts exploded. I think I distracted him, jumped up, and smashed my elbow straight down into his collar bone — it takes something like only five psi to break it — and head-butted him. He tottered. I grabbed his collar and rammed him — headfirst — into the side window of the Mercedes. I thought new car windows, especially those of expensive models, were supposed to be constructed of Plexiglas or something, materials that don't easily break. But the glass splintered into a concave spider web-like design, and his face was a bloody mess. The smaller (though still bigger-than-average) goon was already on me, furiously flailing away with both fists. One smashed into my eye. I went to kick him in the groin; he dodged, making me miss wildly, and I wound up kicking the side mirror instead while ripping open my pants and slashing my leg. Part of the mirror went flying at Kimiko. She screamed. Again, the smaller goon rushed in. I caught him with a straight finger jab to the eyeballs. He shrieked. A stiff-arm jab to the Adam's apple polished him off. I thought I broke a thumb. All the while, the little guy had taken it in, safely standing on top of the vestibule steps. I looked up at him. He scampered back inside, even more scared than I. The huge goon moaned, struggled to get up, then staggered backward into another car and back onto the pavement. I wasn't finished with him yet. I rushed over and, like a punter given the signal while crouched before the goalposts with the clock ticking down, kicked his football of a head. Blood flew out his mouth along with a couple of teeth and what looked like a piece of tongue. Blotches of blood splattered all over, leaving bright crimson stains in the snow. Kimiko jerked a hand over her mouth to squelch a scream. Nothing came out. One of Joe's patrons bent over and puked his lunch over the newspaper box. Sirens wailed in the distance.

My legs started to buckle; my testicles were in my throat. I was utterly drained and staggered into Kimiko, who wore a 'this-isn't-happening-to-me' look. She did her best to steady me against her car. Spittle dribbled down my chin.

"I called Deputy Leopold at police barracks. That's him coming now," said Mabel.

Her customers stood there, gawking like kids at a schoolyard rumble during recess, the little goon still hiding, probably in the toilet. Somehow, I made it to the driver's side, struggled to get in, and started up the engine. I glanced at Kimiko, now in the passenger's seat and still spaced-out, floored the accelerator, spinning the car in the snow, and swerved out of Joe's lot and onto the road.

***

"I oughta read you your rights and run you in right now. Self-defense, maybe, but with excessive force," said Little Leopard the next day at the minister's home. "You messed them up, 'specially Tiny, pretty good. He's bumbling around Plymouth with a brace around that horse neck right now. I'd keep an eye out for him if I was you. He's a bad character."

I added nothing to what I had already told him. He studied my reaction and waited for a response. Still, I said nothing. He edged closer and continued to glare, hoping I'd crack. I could smell his breath. I returned the stare. It was getting to be a contest, like between two kids at a school showdown. Leopold would lean over, as far as he could on his toes, in a futile bid to stretch out his approximate five-foot, seven-inch frame. In public, even while off duty, he always wore thick-heeled boots. I would've laughed if I hadn't been a participant in what had happened. Truth be told, however, I was afraid of the incident getting back to Swenson.

"OK, then, that does it. I'll wrap up my report at the office. I know where to get you," he said, walking out the door. But he abruptly stopped, stood motionless, then spun around, pointed his finger at me, and froze. "You, I'm going to keep my own eye on you."

The thing is, he could've eyed me all he wanted. No problem. He wasn't inclined to make a problem. I had heard, circuitously, or "through channels," as Mark would put it, that he never finished his report, or at least hadn't forwarded it. Both Hines and Leopold had had run-ins with all three hoodlums, but it was rumored that Leopold had botched a potential pedophile conviction against the huge goon, an ex-professional wrestler, and he'd gotten off on a technicality. It had embarrassed the sergeant. Two of the three had spent time at the state prison, and Leopold was now champing at the bit to amend his previous goof-up and, by at least pinning on the goon the weak yet additional charge of willful damage to a motor vehicle, restore himself to the good graces of his boss. Perhaps he felt they got what was coming to them.

Nonetheless, it was far from over. SOB Joe hollered for restitution for damages to his window after part of the Mercedes' side mirror broke it, though he knew the guys and was ecstatic over what had happened to them. After all, business was business, but when word got back to all his militia customers — and it got around fast — like a weasel, he backpedaled, saying he was 'only joking.' Unfortunately, it was worse with Kimiko.

For, difficult as it may have been for my American mind to fathom, Kimiko was embarrassed, had 'lost face,' and, as if that weren't enigmatic enough, was angry over damages to her beloved Mercedes (a college graduation gift from her father), as though I were somehow to blame, for Chrissakes. First, she worried about being interrogated by Leopold, then about everything getting back to campus, and finally about her family, particularly her father, getting wind of it. I didn't know it at the time, but she schemed to alter the auto insurance claims report to remove any hint of violence and make it look like a 'pure' accident. Besides, she mused, how could we now drive to Montreal? What would she tell the few students who remained on campus? Over the next few days, she avoided being seen with me all banged up. I tried to remain empathetic; it was difficult.

The goons, particularly the ex-wrestler, could be gunning for me. I "packed heat," my old Colt .45 accompanied me everywhere, even to school. I didn't know, and honestly much less cared, about gun restrictions and kept the Colt loaded and out of sight, even from Kimiko. I continued to ponder what would happen if news got back to Rodgers, let alone the college president, both away on vacation. For sure, life had taken on a decided twist since I had left Wedgemont.

The landlord had actually given up egging me on to attend his church services and now didn't so much as bother to welcome me downstairs to be with his family nor say so much as "Merry Christmas." With Mark away and Kimiko probably nursing her Mercedes and busy saving face (you would've thought she, not I, had sucked up the blows), I spent Christmas Day alone. Well, not exactly. William Blake was my holiday company. I pored over his verse. I was especially fond of "For the Sexes" and was preparing a presentation scheduled at a conference during the spring semester. I had tried to regale Mr. Mercotti with Mr. Blake to no avail. Every time I burst out with a few lines, Mark would become lost in a mental fog. The futility of this endeavor became evident; I dropped further attempts to poeticize him. Some men are not made for poetry, even for listening to it. I had tried my hand at verse while an undergraduate and remained something of a poetaster, however.

Late next morning, I started for the library for further minor research. From the periphery of my vision, I caught sight of the minister hiding behind his living room curtains, a decided look of resigned disgust in his eye, as I kick-started the motorcycle into a rumbling roar and slowly proceeded to what little there was of downtown Springvale. The two-room library, if you could call it that, resembled more of an oversized closet; it would serve just fine, however, since it had an Internet hook-up and updated encyclopedias. I dared not show my still puffed-up face on campus.

My interest in the UFO phenomenon and related issues had subsided. Between classes and Kimiko, and martial arts in the college gym and sideline research at the next-door library, my focus had rechanneled into what most of society would describe as "practical pursuits."

While browsing the Internet, an article grabbed my attention, leading to another, and I found myself sucked into a story about a covert CIA-Pentagon brainwashing project involving pharmaceuticals like 'proethyl something' — I'm not positive of the nomenclature. The report alleged that the Pentagon, at the behest of the CIA, had begun a series of ultra-secret experiments on their troops in Vietnam. Psychotropic drugs were purportedly used synergistically with long-distance manipulated audio frequencies to stimulate chemical changes in the neural pathways leading to the brain to create a kind of modern-day myrmidon. If it sounds technical, I suppose it is. I hadn't the requisite background to ascertain what was techno-babble and what wasn't, yet certain elements rang true. Among others, an Army lieutenant colonel, long since retired, was quoted in a deathbed confession. Indeed, I had heard about him through a veterans' advocacy committee; mainstream media had all but ignored the news. There was more. Details of the confession jolted me back….

I remembered lying on a cot in a sweltering hospital tent jerry-rigged to an M-106A1 mortar carrier. Rat-ta-tat-tat of machine-gun fire erupted in sickening synchronization with mortar explosions. The reverberations shook the ground under my cot; they were advancing nearer to the tent. I got a whiff of CS gas, then of death in the taste of hot blood trickling into my mouth, and then I sensed it in the air, in the clouds visible through the crack in the tent opening, in the wailing and the moans of the dismembered yet breathing soldier lying next to me, the stump of his knee crawling with flies. A guy stood over me. I lay there half-conscious. He murmured something to another guy about a weird-sounding drug. That was funny. I never recalled seeing either of them before; they weren't attached to our medical unit. My last conscious thought was of being injected with long needles — one behind my ear.

"Sweet Jesus! If it ain't The Man himself."

I shot up and fell backward and almost out of my chair. The loosely holstered Colt .45 flew out from my coat and went flying on the library rug. Two dark hands, small yet powerful, had clasped my shoulder from behind, the fingers digging into my flesh. Reflexively, my hand jerked back, grabbing his thumb, and reinjuring my own. I would've tried to break his —

"Leroy! Never sneak up behind me like that again!"

"Ahhh. Just testing your reflexes, Champ." Leroy's boy, Josh, stood behind the magazine rack, chewing gum, smirking.

"My reflexes are fine. You scared the mother — out of me." We searched for the weapon. Simultaneously, some kid with a pimple for a nose watching us from a distance blurted out something to the effect, "Mommy, that big man over there with the funny purple eye got a gun."

A hush fell over the room. The kid frowned and then sneered at Josh. Perhaps they knew each other. I quickly limped over to retrieve it, being careful not to reinjure my leg. The librarian, an old semi-sclerotic schoolmarm, unexpectedly startled back into life, overheard the kid, and scurried over. She examined us through thick, black granny glasses as if we were a couple of intrusive Springvale misfits invading her private domain. I was sure she'd blab it to the town hall. We made for the door.

Once outside, Leroy stood in front of me man-to-man. Although I towered over him, he would always hold his ground like some playground schoolboy zealously protecting his turf. He stood with arms akimbo, as was his habit, as though he were back in the ring in his native New York City waiting for the opening bell. Josh stood behind him and to the side.

"OK, let me have it. C'mon. Heard it from the guys at Jimmy's range; now I want to hear it from you," he exclaimed while spitting out a wad of chewing tobacco.

"Now, Leroy. Look, there's not that much to tell. You heard it all already."

"'Not that much to tell'? 'Not that much to tell'? Aw, c'mon, Will. Let's have the details. How'd he hit you? Let me have a look at that hand." It was wrapped up; he grabbed for it. I jerked it back, not quite fast enough, and let out a yelp. "Sorry."

Josh tittered.

"What you laughin' 'bout, boy?" Leroy growled. "Get back and wait in the car!"

Josh hesitated.

"You want a smack?"

Josh turned toward the road, head down, gangly hands dangling at his sides.

"Tha's better." Leroy watched him and shook his head. "Man, that kid."

"As I told you...."

Leroy spat again. His tone suddenly changed; his voice lowered. "Will, maybe you don't know. I've had a confrontation with one of 'em."

"With Tiny and his gang?"

He nodded. A look of resignation came over him, and I saw the hurt. "We've known each other since — when? Labor Day? You've been over the house several times. You know my family, but not the other folks here, Will. You may think you do." He paused; his eyes narrowed. "You don't."

He shook off the snow encrusted on his boot. "Man, the way some town folk look at you, you and your woman. A few of them even been talkin' lately. You know what they've been sayin' 'bout you."

"Can't help whom people look at or what they say," I said sarcastically. "You of all people here ought to realize that. There's a dissertation I read about race hatred — "

"Don't you lecture me on no race hatred! Think I don't know all 'bout that stuff? Think you're the only one who's ever read any academic stuff 'bout that? Think I don't see it, from a distance, up close, ev'ry month? Ev'ry week?"

His face then softened; he glanced down, knocking his boots against the library steps; then he looked up, his eyes searching mine. I wanted to tell him something but just managed an insipid "Yeah."

He had taken a job here, I knew, to get away from the "shit and the slime," as he once put it, of New York City streets. Whether he and his family would stay, especially his wife, I wondered from time to time.

"You know, I wanted to thank you for standing up to those guys."

I laughed to myself over what choice I had had. "What for?"

"Think I owe you, man; we all owe you…." His voice went hollow.

"You don't owe me anything. Nobody does."

Josh honked on the car horn. "Damn kid," Leroy muttered. "See you at Jimmy's at next week's meeting, huh?" He turned in the direction of the car, paused, and turned around again. "Thanks anyway."

And I watched him walk away….

As soon as I could, I e-mailed Mark details of the article I'd read. He phoned, excited and half-paranoid, saying, "Don't ever again relay your interest in that information over a computer hook-up like that." When I phoned him about the confession and name of the lieutenant colonel, the line suddenly went silent. There was a long pause. Then he said in all earnestness: "Remember the time, earlier in the year, late spring at Central Cafe, with that punk and his girlfriend? Remember what I told you about when the time comes and about trust?"

I said I did.

"Remind yourself, Bill. Remind yourself."

***

Back at militia headquarters, Jimmy's barn was abuzz with excitement over the fight. Like all good stories, it would get better with time. Though I had taken on only two men — as if that wasn't enough — the number soon escalated to three. Throwing in the little guy, it should've been two-and-a-half. With an intensity almost matching that of my attackers, members would individually hit me with the inevitable questions: "How did they hit you?" "How did you hit them?" "What brought it on?" And "How" — not if — "did the Little Leopard try to intimidate you?" What I had been reluctant to divulge, Leroy had gleefully taken upon himself to fill in, as if he had had a front-row seat at the Friday night fights: "He's built to be a bruiser, and his neck size shows you that, man; he'll take a good shot to the head. "He's…." Try as I did to soft-pedal the incident, which only served to magnify my image in their eyes, the story only grew, and I was acutely aware of developing a potential reputation as a wild, flying-fisted professor. Even though the news wasn't published, by New Year's, word of the knockout brawl at the diner had spread to every homestead in Springvale. Worse yet, a canard was bruited about how I had fought to "save and protect" Kimiko, a story, I speculate, that buried itself into her brain.

Except for Swenson's small contingent of international students, though, word of the brawl hadn't gotten back to the semi-secluded campus. I hoped that any recall of it would fade by the start of class mid-month. Kimiko had gone and blabbed everything to the international students. Apparently, that an older prof had deigned to endanger himself the way I had for her, a mere grad student, enhanced her stature in their eyes. In part, thanks to the canard, I went from pariah to hero. Now that the battle wounds were less visible, she no longer avoided our being seen together in public. It reminded me of veterans: everyone likes to be around unscathed war heroes (like in the movies) but come back home blinded or with a missing limb, and people cringe and look the other way. I theorized I no longer represented the battle-scarred soldier to her way of thinking. When we had earlier talked about going out, she had been oh-so-polite and otherwise equivocal ("You'd better be inside your home and take easy." "Don't worry much for me; please study for now your research"); the cultural schism divided us at times, and I thought about what we were destined for.

I was in the student center on my way to my office when I came upon Kimiko's clique....

"Vaht do you tink is going on between de two of dem? ... Have you seen his eye? The poor bastard ... Yes, I know he lives off-campus at some clergyman's house ... So why talk about them behind their backs? Why don't you ask them, Wolfgang, since you so damn nosey? ... I'm not nosey, vy I don't — Vaht? Vaht is it? Vaht's de matter? Oh, it's — it's Dr. Vahtson. How do you doing today, Professor?"

"Doing just fine, thank you. Any of you seen Kimiko — I mean Ms. Tanimoto?"

One of them smirked, saw me notice, and immediately stopped. "Oh, she should be here soon. Take a seat, please. Coffee?"

"All right, thank you." I grabbed a chair. Three of them rose simultaneously for the coffee. Embarrassed, they gawked at one another, smiled, then sat down, not quite sure what to do next. Then one of them again rose and hurried to the counter.

"I admire your treatise in Modern Literary Research on Baptiste Molière," said one of Kimiko's girlfriends.

"Thank you. By the way, it's 'Jean-Baptiste Poquelin,' better known as 'Molière.' Just 'Molière.'"

"Oh, sorry." She giggled.

"Where did you see it?"

"Ve vere researching at de library," the German chimed in.

"That's interesting. Our library doesn't carry MLR," I said with a tinge of the sardonic.

"Well, uh, it must have been an extra copy that someone brought in from outside," said the woman.

"I see." I didn't want to embarrass them further. Almost all of them were from wealthy and, above all, had generous parents; the president let everyone know, quite summarily, that they especially were to be treated "with due and proper respect."

"May we change the subject?" said one of the men anxiously. "I hear that you were a martial arts expert trained in Southeastern Asia, Vietnam," he continued, staring at my still-discolored eye. Then, the tone and tempo of the conversation took off. Abruptly, they pelted me with all sorts of questions about my past, quickly becoming more intimate, presumably their curiosity having been whetted by Kimiko. Unlike my American students (who didn't ask about the war, and to whom I didn't volunteer information, America just wanting to put it behind her), they were different.

"Vahs de American role imperialist like de Bertrand Russell's International Vahr Crimes Tribunal said?"

"What did you do during the war?"

"How do you feel about missing comrades?"

"About yourself...?"

They fell silent.

"War is never all right nor, maybe, ever all wrong. If that doesn't make any sense, it's because there is no sense to make out of it. It's legalized murder sanctioned by governments. We were young and gullible, and many of us believed in what our leaders told us. None of them, our leaders, tasted their own sweat or blood in those goddamned jungles. It's not like you see in Hollywood movies. It's guts and blood — for real — and guys accidentally shot from behind and dying in each other's arms; sometimes the last word ever to fall from their lips was their first, "Mama." When I was there — I look back sometimes, like in a dream, and see the faces of fallen comrades, faces fading with time yet still here inside of me. They look back at me, and they are silent. Silent and searching, searching for something or someone that was once part of their existence. The search goes on for eternity, and then, like in a dream upon awakening, they fade away. Yet I know they are still inside of me — always." I stared at the floor and started to choke up. "I'm not particularly proud of some of the things I did."

"We understand," somebody whispered.

Shit, how could they understand?

"You can look up now. Here. Coffee."

"Thank you."

The center was nearly deserted. Like Kimiko, this coterie would be staying through the holidays, most of them as foreign nationals not having anywhere to go. The double-floored building, now devoid of the raucous and often profane sounds of youth, took on a perverse and melancholy mood right before New Year's, as though it were somehow alive or, perhaps more fittingly, dead, and I wished to be elsewhere. I did not want to think of the war, so I drank more coffee, as if, pray to the gods, coffee could transubstantiate into whiskey and dull the simmering rage, now half-awakened, within. The war was a lie; our leaders were a lie; I was the biggest lie of all. The coffee went down hard.

"Hey, there's our dean," one of them said.

We saw him at the cash register attempting to retrieve loose change, fumbling with coffee cup in one hand and a handkerchief tucked into his pants in the other, spilling coffee on himself, backing up and bumping into a little girl, then looking like he didn't know how to apologize, ever-conscious of his status. It was unusual, his being disheveled. Not like him. He was always so much in control. I turned away. But it was too late. He had already spotted me and started walking in our direction.

"Season's greetings," he said with an anemic smile. "You all look in fine fettle." Some of the students half-rose, bumping into chairs and one another; some of them remained seated; all looked at one another, not knowing what to do. I almost jumped up myself, a reflex of my military days when the commander would walk in.

"Uhm, may I have a word with you over here, please?" he asked.

I walked over.

"I do say, we haven't seen each other in quite some time, have we? How's the target shooting, by the way?"

"Splendid."

"I see, well then, very good." He fidgeted with his coffee cup and adjusted his glasses. "There's just one other issue I wish to address. It's Ms. Tanimoto. I hear that she has quite taken it upon herself, with all her effort and time she's put in, to claim the Lit'rature Department almost as her own." He paused, then hastily emphasized, "Including professors within the Department. As such, perhaps one would want to consider keeping one's distance. Know what I mean?"

"I think so."

"When she first became a TA, it was my decision to assign her elsewhere; she all but implored me, however, to be assigned to your department shortly after September. In fact, truly, she bordered on the intransigent." Then he leaned over and added in a notch above a whisper, "It has been said at the president's office that her father is considering making a rather significant contribution to the college endowment at the time of her graduation. We wouldn't want to get her sidetracked and thus jeopardize this in any way."

"Heavens, no."

He looked at my eye, started to say something, then caught himself. Something told me he sensed it was too personal, the kind of thing you inquire about only with friends or perhaps with solid acquaintances, and he thought better of it. He always kept things formal.

"Ah-hum. Well, I think I shall be going." He adjusted his glasses and tucked his ubiquitous pipe inside his suit pocket. "Do finish your research for that spring presentation, Dr. Watson. Surely, you'll forward a splendid performance. I know we can depend on you. Incident'ly, keeping up with E.A. Stuart's recent research on Blake? Or is keeping up with her already considered praxis in your field?"

"Surely." I lied. Really, reading Stuart's Blakean criticism was de rigueur. I didn't think much of and had not bothered to study her recent research, however. As an academic, one dared not admit it.

He started for the exit, then, as an afterthought, with that anemic smile, added, "Of course, if you're ever by my office, just 'pop in,' as the expression is bandied about here, for a little chat."

"Why, of course." I watched him walk away, and I walked back toward the group.

"Ahh, Professor Watson," Kimiko said breathlessly as she came running in, gently dusting off several snowflakes from her coat collar. Seeing the other students, she abruptly halted, then slightly bowed, as if the others almost expected her to. Some of them pretended not to look.

I muttered a half-assed inquiry about her well-being.

"No so good. I thought I saw one of them, one of the three goon, as you say, downtown."

I moved to comfort her, noticed the students, and pulled back. "In that case, don't leave campus." She nodded. "Look, I'm late. Mark and I'll pick you up tomorrow at 20:30 hours — I mean 8:30, so we can be on time to the Grange," I said and headed homeward.

***

Springvale's Harpers Grange stood just outside town and had hosted the New Year's Dance as far back as old-timers could remember. The area was known for its old New England Yankee die-hard traditions, such as the Harpers Grange Dance. The community was a hard-working one year-round; this was their night to unwind. Inside the hall, within earshot, I could make out the usual banter.

"If milk prices don't rise up by summer, the husband and me might have to sell off some acreage again to those damn developers down in Manchester to stay afloat, Mike," said an elderly woman.

"Milk prices, nothing. It's the rising price of feed that's going to be the death of us all," retorted another farmer.

"You folks just better forget that cow talk for now and come over next week for a look at the brand-new New Year's Jeep specials on my lot," shouted Mike Richards over the rising din coming from the six-piece band warming up nearby.

"And who's here?" somebody shouted.

"Mark, Will, and Kimiko — I can never get your name straight — good to see you could all get here. Telling you, you can't beat those old Dodges, eh, Mark?" said Mike, trying to maintain his stance in the jostle of the crowd. Mark beamed at the compliment; Kimiko's Mercedes was still in the repair shop.

Virtually the entire town, or at least all the non-deadbeats, were there all dressed up in their finest outfits, one of the few days of the year other than Sundays that they did so. Bright-blue balloons and red-sequined party banners hung from the Grange rafters. Loud laughter and the chinking of drinking glasses mixed with the sound of the band's lead singer wailing out an all-but-forgotten cowboy tune. One of the old farmers, already drunk, in an apparent bid to crown himself country music's next heartthrob sensation, tried to hop on stage, slipped, and fell back, banging his head on the beer keg and busted the spigot, dousing everybody on the spot. We snaked our way through the packed, rowdy crowd the best we could, I pumping my hands along the way, Kimiko clinging to my arm and smiling, Mark, the would-be 'Good Time Charley' looking like he was really above it all.

My injured eye still caught sidelong looks and invited muffled whispers. Whereas I caught admiring glances up close and poor-bastard stares from afar, Mark made the ladies' heads swivel at all distances. No sooner were we seated next to Leroy and Petey and their spouses, several of the braver, unattached womenfolk, young and old, pretty and others not so blessed by Providence, asked Mark out on the dance floor. Mark graciously obliged several times, even going so far as to thank each one profusely, then settled down during the band's intermission.

Petey took another snort of beer, wiping his lips with his shirtsleeve. "Will you look at that?" he said, holding his wife's hand while pointing with a cigar in the other, to a fellow, at a distance, yet noticeable to us all. "Why do they always have to be so in-your-face? Don't you just hate faggots, Mark?" His wife tittered. Petey looked back at her and smiled, patting her hand. Some revelers impatiently began tooting out loud, cacophonous blasts on their party horns; the drunken farmer again had to be restrained from crawling atop the music stage. Inside the old cavernous wood building, sound echoed off the rafters; we could barely hear one another.

"I said, 'How do you like partying with chocolate boy?'" It was Larry, suddenly, in an alcoholic stupor, sneering at Leroy.

Leroy sprang up, ready to pounce like a cat, his wife flashing a worried glare. Sensing trouble, Richards, who happened to be nearby, grabbed Larry's arm, hard, and shoved him on his way, reminding him of his administrative suspension since the shooting range incident. "Filthy nig — " Larry managed to mumble and stumbled on his way, spilling beer all over his shirtsleeve from the mug he held and not bothering to look back, as though blundering through a dream. Mark, out of embarrassment or sympathy or pity or what-have-you, put his arm around Leroy's shoulder, said something in his ear, and rocked him to and fro like a big brother. Leroy managed a toothy grin; his wife wore a what-in-hell-are-we-doing-here look.

I felt Kimiko's hand squeeze mine. She didn't look at me. The band returned to play, and I pulled her out from behind our table and onto the dance floor. As if Larry had never showed up, Leroy was now all smiles and gave me a thumbs-up signal. Except for his wife, everybody laughed and partied on.

We swayed to the slow, gentle late-night rhythm, now sensual, though it wasn't supposed to be, and I pulled Kimiko against me, two bodies moving as one. Some firecrackers went off behind the stage. Momentarily frightened, she clutched me tighter, then didn't let up. She buried her face against my shoulder; strands of her midnight-black hair touched my cheeks, and I caught the slightest trace of the smell of lilac. The fragrance, soft music, and hard drink wore on my semi-conscious thoughts drifting away, and for a moment, I tasted the lilac and breathed in her essence. Dancing stars seemed to be revolving around her radiating face. Her radiance transported me to a dimension ethereal....

"Asshole! Watch where you're stepping!" an old lady hollered above sleepy country music turned rock-and-roll lively. She looked down at her feet, then glowered up at me. Kimiko didn't appear to notice or at least, atypically, didn't care. I moved to rejoin the others.

"What's matter? Something wrong?" she purred.

"No, no. What in the world makes you say that? Let's sit down. Now. That's all." I fumbled around trying to pick up and hide behind an empty chair, almost knocking it over. I hadn't realized it; she'd gotten me aroused.

"But why? Why do you go away from me? You don't like me now, Will?"

"Yes, I mean, no; that is, I do not not like you, meaning, yes, I do. Like you, that is. I desire, that is, like you very, very much, Kimiko. Believe me."

She turned her head to one side and viewed me from the corner of one eye. Some of the guys at the table saw us; Petey then yelled out, "Will you look at that, folks. Will's having such a good time with himself now he's slogging over the chairs, leaving behind his China doll to dance with herself. Hey, Will! Stop doting tonight on your boyfriend Johnny Walker and start concentrating on your girl-friend — or are you already hiding your trouser snake?" Except for Leroy's wife, who retained her hangdog look, they all keeled over in laughter.

Thus, we carried on throughout the night, my "China doll" and me, and Mark and my militia cohorts, secret comrades-in-arms now more than mere boon companions, I having spent so much time with them, truly as much as I could. Though I thought the cadre tight-knit and trustworthy, on occasion I had suspicions, if that's the word. I overheard from time to time what sounded like trifling to-dos in snippets of hushed conversation between Petey and Mike over things like the procurement and storage at Jimmy's compound of the notorious so-called stub ("cop killer") ammunition and related matters.

"Sheez, I think I'm ssh-through for the night. Let's punch out, hon." Walt Patterson, drunk, stood up, threw his huge arm over his little wife like a bear protecting her cub, then staggered back into her, almost knocking over the empty beer and whiskey bottles strewn on top of our table. It was well into the New Year. The crowd had dwindled; the band had packed and gone, and all that was suggestive of the earlier evening revelry was the old drunken farmer now spread-eagled on the stage among shrunken, lifeless balloons and confetti, his mouth open wide and snoring, his face a mask of whiskey-sotted bliss.

"Iz time to go," someone said.

Much to my surprise, Kimiko offered no resistance to my suggestion to sleep over at my place, and like a bastard, I schemed on how to get rid of Mark, my best friend and the one who'd chauffeured us out to the Grange, to begin with. Yet he was observant of the situation, and Walter's wife, at once looking pitifully at her utterly soused husband, offered overnight accommodations to Mark in exchange for his somehow lugging the beast back into their home. Kimiko and I left in Mark's '88 Dodge.

"You have no reason to be afraid of me, Will." Kimiko giggled through her fingertips as she leaned over toward me behind the steering wheel. I could detect the faintest trace of whiskey lingering on her breath. "So, what do you try to hide from me tonight at the dance floor? Why you try to hide?" I put my free arm around her, pulling her close, cuddling her, gently kissing her forehead. Her eyes, gentle and resembling those of a doe, locked on to mine. I swerved the Dodge purposefully, pretending to avoid a tractor partly hidden in a snowbank piled high to make extra room for entrance to one of the town's granaries, and she was pushed even closer into me.

"So that's what you think? I'm hiding something, eh? Maybe I can show you later." I pushed down on the accelerator.

When we arrived at the house, dawn was creeping along the southern edge of the White Mountains veiled in the early-morning mist. The minister was already stirring, judging from the lights downstairs. Kimiko and I made our way up the private stairway to the top floor, and I reflected upon what the killjoy's evening celebration must have been like.

Inside I eased myself onto the rock-hard bed, Kimiko lay beside me, and I contemplated whether to uncork another of my cheap bottles of red wine (with a full-time job, I had graduated to barely more expensive brands), then decided against it. I gazed out the window, the eastern glimmer now getting more pronounced, then at nature's distant tableau of snow whirling in the barren cornfields, swirling and whirling, whirling, swirling.... Round her, snowy Whirlwinds roar'd/Freezing her Veil, the mundane shell/I rent the veil where the Dead dwell. I started to recite aloud. "When weary Man enters his Cave/He meets his Saviour in the Grave/Some find a Female Garment there — "

"And some a Male, woben with care."

"Lest the Sexual Garments sweet — "

"Should grow a debouring, Winding sheet."

"One Dies! Alas! the living and dead!"

"One is slain! and one is fled!"

"In vainglory, hatcht and nurst — "

"By doubles spectres, self accurst."

"Blake, 1802."

"Blake, 1800. 'To the Sexes.'"

"Hmph. Since when did you become the expert?"

She smiled and licked her lips. "Since I have you for my teacher."

"I think that poem essentially shows the dichotomy inherent in all living crea-
tures; that we, as celestial beings, or more precisely, in a mundane or earth-bound
attempt to attain this 'outer' celestial beingness, sometime fall short in our striving
to do so, hence the 'doubles spectres, self accurst.'"

"No," she slowly began, "I don't think so. More than dichotomy, mere inheritance paradigm." She opened her ever-present dictionary. "That's along E.A. Stuart's argument, could be. Rather it goes beyond dichotomy inheritance to being
bordering on symbolizing the polarity of our being, our soul, or our spiritual nature, with our physical one as both-sexed being. You said not, before your beginning line, that the speaker is her-map-ro-die-tee, like the offspring of A-prodite
and Her-mees."

And so, she lectured on in this vein, and I realized that Kimiko held as great an
insight, or at least a feeling, into the metaphysics of it as I did, if not more so. Since
my own student days, I had sensed how society's twisted expectations, and those
of the academy, dictated that educators, or so-called superior ones, at any rate,
would always lord it over everybody else, but I never confessed this to Kimiko.

I shut off the nightstand lamp. Kimiko gave up the sexy-looking silver choker
she'd worn all night and put it in my hands. Outside, the snowy whirlwinds did
indeed roar; inside, it grew hot. And steamy....

"See here. I want a word with you — now," the minister said in uncompro-
mising bluntness the next day. I had tried to be quiet with Kimiko, evidently to
no avail, for he babbled something about kids, presumably his own, being exposed
to "so much licentiousness expressed with loud, uttermost abandon." It would be
"professionally judicious to look for tenancy elsewhere," he intoned in measured
incantations, as though behind the pulpit. You would've thought from the way he
described me that I was Lucifer incarnate. He continued to blabber on about how
much his home, indeed the entire neighborhood, would be oh-so-much-better-off
without such a "motorcycling, gun-toting, street-tough senior citizen stud."

Chapter 5

On the shifting stage of economic affairs, things were starting to look up again, at least nationally. The holiday shopping season was an especially vibrant one; this was parlayed into a much-needed shot in the arm for the stock exchange, which, in turn, seemed to kick-start the economic engine humming again. Dairy prices rose momentarily, a boon for the local farmers; people's purse strings were a little fatter. Regional ski resort revenues held their ground, and the maple syrup season appeared to be off to a good start. Of course, that the NBA season was in full swing and that the Super Bowl was coming up always helped. For many Americans, zonked out in a never-ending sports stupor, nothing else would've mattered anyhow. Even the militia issue subsided. With the fragile fabric of overseas stock exchanges, the markets, though not strong, stabilized. Overseas oil was still plentiful. Precious metals prices remained steady. Except for the Middle East, political tensions appeared to ease. In all, it looked like Happy Days were coming back again.

Mark thought differently. At Joe's Diner a couple of weekends later, he was lecturing all who would listen. To his mind, all this was "the calm before the hurricane," for "that's how it would happen." People would be lulled into a false sense of complacency, he maintained; an "uptick in the economy could do it every time." I thought his argument pedestrian; he saw it as "right on the money." Then, too, we discussed our other usual topics like the national militia issue and UFOs. The two of us were seated hunched over cups of coffee in the first booth next to the vestibule late Saturday morning.

"Nothing's out of the ordinary, Mark. Hell, you're still doing OK peddling your computers. You see anybody around here" — I pointed my coffee spoon at nobody in particular — "about to bury themselves in fall-out shelters?"

He took a sip of coffee, paused, and cracked a thin smile. "That's not the point, and you know it. Why do you think the FBI and BAFT are coming down on our militia brothers, especially out West? Hmm? Why? You think that what happened at last week's showdowns in Wyoming and Montana and — what was it? Idaho, too? — was any accident? Militia-instigated?"

"Well, I don't know."

"You 'don't know'? Let me tell you; they weren't. The White House and CIA are testing the waters."

"What do you mean?"

"I mean, they're gauging public opinion as to how far they can go, how much the public will tolerate by way of a crackdown. Elections aren't that far away, even the Republicans are getting in on the act. Look at Reischner from New Jersey. Now he's siding with the president on a militia crackdown and a suspension of 'stub' ammo sales — and he snake-slithered his way into the Senate on NRA backing!" Mark's crescendo startled the early lunchtime crowd now beginning to swell. Mabel glanced sideways at us; Joe appeared not to notice.

"Easy, buddy," I said. He was given to such occasional outbursts, and by now, I considered myself accustomed to his polemical repertoire.

Mark fingered and fumbled with our salt shaker. Next, he held his hand out and then stroked the two-day growth of stubble along the rigid edges of his chin. He observed me for what seemed to be damned near an entire minute. "OK, OK." He quieted down. Momentarily. The conversation somehow slid off in the direction of our Southeast Asian experiences and UFOs there during the war.

"Think it was the fall of '73. US Air Force Chief of Staff General George Brown himself said that UFOs were seen up and around the DMZ at night in the late 60s, but the military never referred to them as UFOs, only 'enemy helicopters.' Funny thing is, you know, the North Vietnamese didn't have any helicopters," I said. Mark peered out from behind the Venetian blinds at the parking lot and toward the church steeple at the far end of Springvale's snow-swept village commons and softly smiled.

I continued, "Brown said that they were only seen at night around the DMZ, in the late '60s, but I told you about my sightings: daytime, far from the DMZ, well into the '70s. When I reported it, I was told to keep my mouth shut, especially after the Intelligence Briefing Team to the Commander-in-Chief of the US Pacific Fleet interrogated me."

"I know," he murmured, almost tenderly.

"Huh?"

"Oh, I mean, uh — nothing." He quickly looked away while fidgeting with the salt shaker and then hurriedly took another sip of coffee. "Hey! Think you can refill the tank here a little, Mabel?"

My gut impulse was to find out what he knew. At that instant, I wanted to reach out, grab him — shake the truth out of him. Then I thought better of it. Yet what exactly did he know? How? He adroitly redirected the thrust of the conversation from that of my war perspective to that of a global one. He began, slowly, as if warming up to some august proclamation.

"UN Secretary-General U Thant, a few years before Brown's announcement, tried to focus on UFOs in the Outer Space Affairs Committee of the UN. '67, '68, '69. I tell you the CIA and Pentagon brass were scared shitless Washington would lose preeminent investigative oversight into the phenomenon to the Reds and their Third World sympathizers in New York." He wiped his lips. "The public never heard the rest."

Mark's secretiveness could irk me at times, no doubt. Yet mostly, he could get to me whenever an available woman was around — he had an uncanny knack of wedging himself in between, leaving me to pick up the pieces. The closer Kimiko and I got, the more he insinuated himself into the relationship, a not-so-hidden burr in what many would consider the unlikeliest of places. Charming when it suited him to be so, he could project a dyspeptic disposition — as with Kimiko shortly after Swenson's classes resumed.

***

Late one wintry Saturday afternoon, we were inside the garage of my new apartment. I was working on Kimiko's Mercedes, tinkering with this and that. The two of them were far off to one side. Over the racket from the radio, I could barely hear them. The tension gradually escalated.

"Mr. Mark, you don't have to accuse me of — "

"I'm not accusing you of anything — "

"Ahh, but you said it before — "

"That's because you implied the Liberty Militia has no business in Springvale. That it's a bunch of country misfits, weird rednecks fixated on guns."

"But that's not true!" By now, Kimiko was visibly upset and quickly made her way back to my side. Mark stood there, goofy-like, though in a sense, apparently pleased with himself. I started to say something to him, then realized that the more I thought about it, perhaps there was some truth to what he had said, so I motioned to Kimiko to sit down while I got her some coffee. The incident would've been forgotten in a day or two, yet it was indicative of my relations with him, especially when there was an attractive woman who'd come to know us both.

***

"Christ, did you see this morning's headlines? Catch last night's news broadcasts? Some goddamned militias down South are calling for a march with loaded weapons on Washington around Presidents' Day. Look, I have to get to Western Civ, so I don't have time to talk to you. Read USA Today's cover story. Goddamned militia freaks gone crazy. President ought to round 'em up — every last one of those bastards."

Monday morning. Two blubbery co-eds. I had driven to the campus library and had heard it on my new car's radio — well, new used car. An upsurge in militia activity had shocked everyone out of New England hibernation. Jesus, even college kids are talking about it, I thought to myself. Rumors were flying. This had to affect us back at Old Jimmy's headquarters. It wouldn't be long till I found out. However, what really caught my attention that morning was the seemingly unrelated story buried between post-Super Bowl homilies and assorted celebrity piffle. More evidence was leaking out about the Israelis' nuclear weapons — and their purported willingness to use them on the Arabs. Worldwide markets, especially those involving oil, started to unravel again. This time America didn't appear to be immune. I sensed I'd better rush over to Old Jimmy's, skipping my appointment with Kimiko.

I pulled up near the barn. The usual mix of pickup trucks, modified Jeeps, snowmobiles, and ATVs were in the lot. Everyone had gone inside. I smelled something big going on. Members should have been at work. I walked through the back entrance and made my way to the rear of the congregation. Nobody noticed. An aura of electricity hovered in the air.

"I'm telling you, boys, we'd better be watchin' our backs!" said Mike. "Just got word from other patriots out West and Will's buddy, Mercotti, who I wish was here today — and this is supposed to be confidential — that things are heating up for us — fast."

"What things, Mike?"

"Increased surveillance, for one. Maybe even somebody even trying to start something, blame it on us. We can be expecting Hines and his yelping puppy to pay us a visit soon, real soon."

"Damn those two guys, and especially Kevin!"

"No, sir! We can't get in their crosshairs. Hines's going to be pressed from state police headquarters in Concord to — oh, didn't see you, Will."

Twenty or so cadre pivoted around. "Have a seat.... Where was I? Like I was saying, heat's on. Let's not get burned, boys. When Walt makes it here from Laconia, we're going to be assigning everybody to a cell to streamline communications, for starters. Codes and passwords later."

Could this have been it? For the first time since meeting them all last year, I sensed — no, saw — the face of fear. No bragging prattle about what they'd do to defang Trooper Leopold, the Little Leopard, no tough-guy talk about 'blowing away' corrupt, slimy Concord and Washington politicos. We mingled and wondered if the noose was beginning to tighten, if the chessboard, which was our America, was now metamorphosing into a hidden quagmire ready to ensnare us all.

Early next morning, Kimiko was at my apartment entrance. It wasn't like her not to plan a stopover, but she didn't as much as phone. I was still in pajamas; she was pounding on the door. Hardly awake, I stumbled over some leftover wine bottles making my way to open the door. Her face was pressed against the windowpane, both hands in double-fisted grip, jiggling the doorknob, rattling the windows.

"Open! Hurry!"

"I'm coming. There. What is it?"

She threw her arms around me and held on tight. "Ahh, Will. I'm scared, scared for us, but 'specially you!"

"What is it? What happened?"

"I overhear in the office Dean Rodgers over the phone say that the president wants to — "

"President in Washington?"

"No! Swenson president! He wants to know when and who from Liberty Militia comes to campus. Supposed to keep as secret. Will, I'm scared. President's going to know about you. Your job here...." She bowed her head and laid it on my shoulder.

"Well, the Brit-shit knows about my affiliation already," I confessed. "Nothing that can be done about that now." Neither of us spoke.

Finally, she looked up. Tears were welling in her eyes. "What's going to happen to you? Can't you quit, only quit the militia?"

I knew she was well-intentioned. Neither did I have to ponder my answer. "No, no, I cannot. Nor would I ever. You see, when I went off to the war, silly or nonsensical as it may sound, I believed I was fighting for things like freedom of choice, freedom to believe in and associate with whomever you want. We have broken no laws, harmed no one. What you ask of me, dear Kimiko is what I cannot ask of myself; it's something I cannot and never could do. My involvement in the militia? It's the revelation — the reflection — of the truth of who and what I am as I walk down the path that life has laid out before me."

"But I can't think of you to get hurt." And she broke into gentle sobbing.

A few days later, I thought about what she had said while driving home at night and listening to the radio. All week TV and radio talk shows had zeroed in on the militia issue now exploding like a long-delayed time bomb. Most callers came down behind the government; they cried out for suppression. Beneath the hue and cry for legal restrictions, many of them sounded like they were searching for scapegoats. I hadn't driven very far along the ice-encrusted main road leading into central Springvale; snow piled high along the roadside twinkled, reflecting the rays of the brilliant full moon glimmering overhead. The car sputtered. I worried about its reliability. Then, suddenly, the talk show I was tuned to went dead. Next, an unidentified woman announced that an emergency message was to be broadcast from the White House. It was the solemn voice of the president.

"Good evening, my fellow Americans. As you well know, these past several weeks have been turbulent ones for the peoples of many nations, yet particularly for us Americans here at home. Many well-knit organizations, scattered throughout our great nation, yet particularly those headquartered out in the great West, have attempted to usurp the rule of law and have sought to sow disharmony, discord, and utter disaster in the states in which they are situated. I am principally referring to members of various so-called people's militias. They have attempted to unbalance and uproot the very foundation of civilized society: respect for the law. You have heard of the several coordinated shootouts during the past several weeks. No man, no organization, no so-called people's militia is above the law. And the law we will maintain. As your duly-elected president, I have hereby signed an Executive Order to restore order and respect for the law, effective immediately. As such, I have ordered the following temporary measures: one, all sales of private firearms are suspended; two, all distribution and sales of firearm ammunition are suspended; three, marches, demonstrations, or other large-scale public protest gatherings of more than twenty-five people are suspended. Additional restrictions may be forthcoming as deemed necessary. If, in fact, you are in support of these temporary measures — and I stress that they are just that, temporary — you are strongly encouraged to relay your support to your elected government officials. More information will be given to you in the days ahead. Although some may view this development as unfortunate, it is necessary to restore order and respect for the rule of law and bring back safety and security to our nation's law-abiding citizenry. God bless you, and God bless the United States of America."

"Restore law and order"? "Bring back safety and security"? The platitudes echoed in my ears. The words turned rancid and churned in my stomach. Springvale's neatly arrayed farmhouses with their empty verandas and recently snowplowed driveways leading to austere-looking mailboxes lining both sides of the road — flew past like shadows in a dream. Don't remember finding my way home that night. Somehow, I did. All that I vividly recall was meeting the cadre the following weekend over by Jimmy's barn, near the rundown lean-to which once served as Jimmy's cattle-feeding station abutting the highway.

"Hines and Leopold'll be here shortly," said Commander Mike Richards to his full formation. "I've taken the liberty to call for a meeting out here instead of at headquarters this morning. Sorry for the inconvenience. Don't want to appear too accommodating to Hines and Leopold. But remember: We've no axe to grind.

Not yet, anyways. Don't volunteer any information. Let the command chew the fat. Be mindful of our last assembly. Liberty and integrity."

"Liberty and integrity," resonated the cadre.

"Looks like them there now!" someone shouted.

"Yeah, but look! Coming in an unmarked vehicle," shouted another.

Tension thickened with the swirling gales kicking up and spewing tiny ice crystals over the snow-blanketed pasture, the crystals biting our faces. If you gazed into those faces, you would've seen a creeping mixture of worry and fear. Yet there was determination as well. Mike. Walt. Leroy. Pierre. Alfonso. Little Mike, plus forty-odd others: all determined to stand up straight till the end. I was proud to stand among them that day.

"OK, men. Here they come," said Richards. "Supposed to be only Hines and the Leopard."

Three — not two — men exited a plain black sedan. Sergeant Hines, in uniform, made his way over, his boots crunching the ice as he walked, followed by an unidentified Hispanic male in civilian garb, then Leopold in full state police regalia. They stood foursquare in front of us as though forming a firing squad.

"Howdy, boys," said Hines, dipping the brim of his hat. The unidentified man edged closer to him; Leopold jutted out his jaw and leaned back on his boot heels. "This here is Agent Bobby Ramirez from the FBI. He'll be here for the time being to monitor the situation. Guess Mike told you why we're here." He paused and spat off to one side. "President's signed an emergency order. Don't have to remind you what it says." Hines wavered and gazed at the barbed wire fence marking the edge of Jimmy's pasture. "Look, fellas, I know most of yous; we grew up together. Our kids go to school together. Don't make this harder on me than it already is. Appreciate it that you've left your weapons home." He looked up again, partly to shield his eyes from the sun, partly to buy time perhaps, as if by doing so he could imagine himself somewhere else, and this all wouldn't be happening. I'll never know. His voice then quivered.

"I've not come here today in front of you looking for a confrontation. If everybody keeps a level head, we can all get over this together.... About your storage of ammunition. The governor says — "

"The governor's got no authority in this matter!" came a voice from the rear. Don't remember who it was, though it could've been any one of us; it was a shared sentiment.

Leopold inched forward; his eyes got big. "Oh, but you're so wrong about that. I'm afraid he does. He — "

"Shut up! Like I was saying, as a state police representative of the governor's office, I'm going to have to examine your ammo cache. Soon. You know of the other restrictions," Hines broke in.

The Little Leopard slunk back to his former position; Ramirez continued to stand in his, steely-eyed and ramrod straight. Hines's placation aside, the militia heard the countdown to the confrontation clock ticking.

As though that weren't enough, the following week, Swenson's president and the dean, apparently in an effort to look good to the board of trustees, called a college-wide meeting over the escalating national crisis. I wasn't sure of their agenda; rumors were being bruited about among the faculty, but Kimiko said she had heard it would entail a general attempt to demonize the Liberty Militia. In the name of civic obligation, of course.

She and I wiggled our way from the rear to the middle of the packed crowd in the granite-walled auditorium. The crowd of several hundred had taken on a circus-like atmosphere. Kimiko led the way. Whenever we got separated, our first inclination was to clasp hands; then, we would catch ourselves. The president and the dean were already milling about onstage. I took a closer look. Between them was Bobby Ramirez.

Dean Rodgers approached the microphone. "Please be seated, everyone." He cleared his throat while adjusting his bow tie. "I do believe you're aware of the reason for this assembly. I have the delightful pleasure of introducing to you today our distinguished guest from the Bureau of Alcohol, Tobacco, and Firearms, Agent Robert — er, I mean Bobby — Hernandez." A mixed chorus of cheers and catcalls went up. Kimiko glanced my way, pulled my hand into her coat pocket, and squeezed it.

"No BAFT in Springvale!" a couple of co-eds screamed.

They were drowned out by a multitude of other voices. "Shut the hell up!"

"Hernandez" — whatever he called himself that day — stared out into the auditorium, looking tired and drawn.

Rodgers called for order. "Mr. Hernandez has requested that I, speaking on behalf of the president and the board of trustees of Swenson, relay the following requests: that you immediately inform us if you've witnessed any sightings or even overheard any discussions about the caching — I mean hiding — of ammunition or firearms in Springvale and surrounding communities. This applies particularly to our own homegrown Liberty Militia. Mr. Hernandez shall be in close contact with us. The same applies to word of any armed demonstration against the president's Executive Order. You may remain anonymous; all responses shall be held in the strictest confidentiality." He hesitated and then smirked. "Appropriate compensation shall be offered for any salient information effecting an arrest."

Silence crept over the hall. A few of the faculty and assorted staff members looked at one another in disbelief. Kimiko coolly surveyed the room from wall to wall, eyed me, and bit her lip. She tugged on my collar, gently pulling me toward her, and whispered, "I'll be with you, Will." Ramirez-Hernandez remained seated, occasionally turning to chat with the president; the dean droned on about the nobility of ratting on fellow citizens in the duty of high civic-mindedness. Outside the huge arch-shaped stained-glass windows, there lingered signs of early spring. Days were growing longer; icicles were melting. At the entrance to the hall, a huge snowman, one which always reminded me of one my sister and I had built as kids, stood noticeably shrunken since being constructed over the term break. Water droplets, merging into tiny trickles, streaked down the multicolored windowpanes as I continued to think of her.

***

Over the next several days, I also thought a lot about old relations: Army buddies and commanders, professors, employers, Steve, Maria, Julie, even Sheila, from whom I hadn't heard. They all lingered heavily, faces filtered through the prism of the recesses of memory. I thought of how a personal crisis would precipitate that in us. This latest crisis, though, was truly national and fast becoming global. The national press was still free, or so it appeared; overseas reports critical of the president's alarming declaration of near-martial law were still disseminated here. Americans and foreigners alike wondered for how much longer. Quickly, the American ethos was turning sour as the economy nosedived, followed by that of the rest of the industrialized world. Mark mentioned that this would entirely unravel US military alliances; it didn't take much insight to realize that. Several Arab states attacked a portion of Israel, though the situation didn't explode into all-out warfare. Closer to home, the media portrayed vigilante groups as hell-bent on scapegoating after they reportedly burned alive dozens of Mexicans on the US side of the border. All this transmogrified into a multihued mosaic of sweeping paranoia. It didn't take long for it to seep into the streets of quintessentially American Springvale — and Joe's Diner.

"Little Leopard's got a new boss-man to report to for the time being, anyhow," said Joe. "Some Spanish fellow, probably from Washington, maybe Boston. They were probing me for information about you people, 'cept her." He nodded toward Kimiko, in between wringing out his mop and badmouthing his waitress. We sat at the far end of the diner: Kimiko, Mark, several other militiamen, and me. "Why should I protect you guys? What's the — Christ, will you get those customers, Mabel? What has Liberty Militia ever done for Springvale? Huh?" He flicked the ash from his cigarette tip into the mop bucket. "Ha! Bust up some wrestling thug and his sidekick punks and now bring in the feds to this cow pasture." Kimiko even sniffed out the sarcasm. Petey appeared about to say something and then pulled back. The command hierarchy had repeatedly warned us about getting sucked into a public confrontation. Lately, we had been living by negatives. We had to. Still, it became too much for Petey.

"You listen to me, you fat fuck."

"What did you call me, Corporal?"

"You heard the first time. Who the hell do you think steered business to you and your sister all these years? And who helped you dodge the Vietnam draft?" Joe winced. Some of the others, upon hearing the revelations for the first time, sat transfixed in a hybrid state between entrancement and disgust. Joe bit on his upper lip and shook his head. "And while you're at it, you can thank Will here for finally cleaning house of those three hooligans instead of trying to pin your two-bit repair bill on him."

I wished Petey would keep my name out of it. Like the chickens local farmers housed, folks were still clucking over the incident, and I became acutely aware of the garlicky scent of boiling spaghetti sauce now dripping over the sides of the stainless-steel vat and pointed it out to Joe in a bid to break the tension. "Thank you, Will," he spluttered, almost obediently trudging toward the stove and fumbling with the switch. The others looked on as though in a trance, not quite knowing what to do or say next. Joe was but one town resident. Militia members, including women auxiliaries, observed with quiet alarm the simmering suspicion townsfolk regarded us with. Increasingly, we turned to one another.

Kimiko by now had been all but living over at my place, at least on weekends. We tried to keep our relationship from evolving into the focus of Swenson's attention. (I cared nothing about what Springvale thought of it.) She told the others back at the campus that she had a weekend job, which her entire dorm knew was a lie, given the silver spigot to her father's money pot. Yet nobody seemed to begrudge this; Kimiko never exuded the impression of being purse-proud and treated virtually everyone who ever met her with utmost humility and respect, though on occasion, she could be sly when it suited her. And Mark — for a while, we didn't see much of each other; he was busy, so he said, with his job. With the national crisis deepening, he now drove up from Connecticut more often, and I'd have the two of them over to my house almost every weekend. They became recurrent players in my life, and Mark's pointed admonitions steadily won over the ear of the Liberty Militia.

Mark and I hiked out to Babson's Ravine off Route 25 to meet up with Mike, Walt, Petey, and several other hardcore members. It was early in the day, and the crisp late-winter air bit into the nostrils. We trod the still snow-covered footpath leading from the highway through the woods up to the first waterfall. Mark hadn't been wearing the requisite footwear, only worn-out jogging shoes, and he cursed the leftover patches of mud and snow as if it were nature's cruel insult to him personally. When we got to the base of the falls, I offered a swig of hot brandy and gestured to him to sit on a dry log to keep warm, for he was by then in a cranky mood. We would wait there for the others. Meanwhile, we talked of trifles.

"I hear them now," I said.

"Who brought her?" Mark said upon sighting one of the women auxiliary members.

"It's OK; she's been a long-time organizer. Trust her as well as any of the men," said Walt.

"Hmm."

Mark hesitated. "Well, then, here's what we're up against in addition to this." He held up a news story alleging citizens "overwhelmingly in favor" of the militia suppression. "I've got it on an inside source in intelligence: the president's planning further crackdowns now that he's tested the waters and received little opposition. Could be a so-called terrorist attack set up by federal agents. Agents could start invoking Title 18 U.S.C. Section 922, 924 hand over fist. Prepare to meet only in cells of five members at a time, each cell with a password to contact another. I know you started this, but we've got to get serious about it. Only Mike and Walter should have the complete listing: segmented oversight, similar to MI, but not the same. Nobody, but nobody, talks to the feds alone. Speak nothing over the phone; write nothing on the computer you wouldn't repeat to the world. Watch your backs; keep an eye out for strangers. Decide between yourselves if patriots keep their guns at home. That, though, may all become moot soon. Oh, and another thing. That Ramirez guy? Well, as you probably know, that's an alias. But he works for Militia Watch Task Force, FBI. Don't tell him the time of day." He went on about rumors of a coup by the Joint Chiefs of Staff. "Doubt it will happen, though. Current leadership is pretty gutless. Politicians first; warriors second, if that. And with the volatility in the Middle East, they won't take matters into their own hands." We all looked at one another.

For a drawn-out moment, all one heard was the thunderous roar of the waterfall and the raucous flittering of a blue jay and what looked like a seasonally premature robin in a territorial dispute over the top of the falls. We knew things were getting worse fast. The wind changed direction. Spray from the falls touched our faces. With it, I felt the pristine hand of nature against the cruel backdrop of the raw stench of humans and their intrigues. Finally, Mike mentioned how he and Petey would come out to the falls as kids and dare each other to jump.

"You know, it became something of a place, almost sacred-like, like where you'd walk in a cemetery where your kinfolk are buried, but this place … this place is for the living," Mike said. I thought I saw something of a wistful tear. Petey watched him kneel to dip in his hand at the edge of the deep blue-green pool and smiled. It was as if the falls mirrored the steadfastness of Mike and Petey's long-enduring friendship. The others felt it as well. It was a scene I'd always remember.

We trudged down to the highway. It had unexpectedly gotten colder; a gentle snowfall began descending on the rolling landscape. We approached our vehicles, parked along both sides of the road. Someone yelled out something about traffic tickets under everybody's windshield wipers, now half-buried in snow. The wind started blowing snowflakes in our faces from all directions.

Petey snatched up and held out his ticket in one hand while squeezing a cigar stub in the other. "Will ya look at this? Courtesy of our beloved Trooper Leopold. 'Illegal Parking' my ass! Jeeze, how'd he know we were here? Thought this place out of his jurisdiction."

Everyone else agreed. "Goddamned Leopard!" shrieked the woman as she smashed her fist into the hood of her truck. "Sonafabitch is looking for trouble!"

Chapter 6

The authorities continued to whip up anti-militia frenzy. In subsequent weeks harassment from all sides intensified: from Leopold (presumably on orders from Ramirez-Hernandez), townsfolk, Swenson's administration, even students. That both the collegiate Right and Left would consider an obscure and motley group of local veterans and farmers exercising their Second Amendment rights as the "enemy" I would've thought hilarious — until I started receiving unsigned and threatening notes under my office door from the Conservative Club and the Trotskyite Revolutionary Party.

I resumed carrying the Colt .45 to school and, in fact, everywhere. This time Kimiko knew about it, as did the colleague with whom I shared the office, though I tried to hide it from her. The old witch was a senior prof who appeared to have it in for me no matter how hard I tried to be nice to her. She seemed to be in full concert with the president's edict on firearms (we never actually discussed it) and perhaps felt threatened personally by the presence of the handgun. I couldn't be sure. She wouldn't discuss that subject either, try as I would to broach it. As spring daylight lengthened, my collegial patience shortened. The stalemate couldn't continue; of this, I was sure. There was still no law against private possession of firearms purchased prior to the Executive Order, on campus or off. But she heavily intimated notifying "the officials" of the weapon, which I later kept secured in my car. She continued to rant and fume that I was "a potential threat to the peace and order of all civilized, law-abiding Americans." The fact that I was obeying the existing laws made no difference to her, and I ceased trying to advance the position.

Others in Liberty Militia fared no better. Alfonso's truck tires were slashed, his daughter threatened at school with warnings that "communists and ungrateful wops had better clear out of New Hampshire" and there'd be "hell for you to pay for your old man's troublemaking." Little Mike's mailbox was demolished; he said his local bank loan application was rejected after previously being accepted. "Bastards wouldn't even give me a good reason; they just said I could file a complaint, half-daring me to bother." Petey said his barn windows had been broken, several of his maple sugar trees axed, and that he was getting harassing phone calls at all hours of the night, sometimes practically every hour. Now ethnic barbs stung even Larry's ears: "Kill dumb-assed Polacks!" Worse yet was the toll on Leroy and his family.

Leroy's wife, never crazy about leaving New York for a 'cow town,' grew increasingly disenchanted with rural northern New England life. She incessantly badgered him about relocating, and I once accidentally overheard her say, "We'd better get outta this racist cracker cow-shit town if you want to still call us a family. Can't take no mo' of these honkie rednecked hicks." Leroy was fixated on making a go of it, however. He remained in a quandary over how, often asking me for guidance. I hardly perceived myself as a socially well-adjusted role model, yet he was importunate, and I reluctantly capitulated. We had been meeting alone, usually behind the Grange, before get-togethers with our cell of cadre.

"Man, I dunno what to do in my life, Will. Family's fallin' apart. Ev'ry time wife and me try and talk…." His voice trailed off. He spat out a tobacco plug to one side, leered at the lump, shook his head, and added, "Gotta stop this, gettin' to be 'n 'diction…. Our boy's havin' problems in school. Kids are really givin' 'im a hard time in class, even in sports. Been demoted from team captain." He scanned the horizon. "'Cause of me and the militia."

I tried to console him the best I could. I rested my hand on his shoulder, muttered a few inanities, measuring his response. Sometimes a man just needs the feel of another's steady hand to stiffen his spine, and I sensed Leroy needed another attentive masculine soul. This partially worked; he was still crestfallen, though. We made our way out from the rear of the Grange and hurried to hook up with the other cell members. "But I ain't quittin' Liberty," he said, eyes narrowing. "Dudn't matter what she says."

***

My job was going well (I was voted runner-up for the fall semester Outstanding Teacher Award — and good thing, too; winning is usually the kiss of death in academia for newly appointed profs), but rumors about Kimiko and me snowballed. The word spread that I was merely using Kimiko for her purse strings. I'm sure people saw us off campus occasionally holding hands as well as seeing me at times behind the wheel of her Mercedes — alone. It didn't irk Kimiko, but more surprisingly, Dean Rodgers was cordial as ever, occasionally stopping me in the halls to "wish you the jolly best with the upcoming presentation on Blake." I suspected he had an inkling by then of my romantic relationship, having known all along of my militia connection, but he never let on. I became suspicious about his ostensible indifference. Then I got caught (literally) on campus in broad daylight holding Kimiko's and my underwear.

It was just before Composition and Rhetoric class. I was running to my car in the main parking lot perpendicular to the library, holding an armful of recently washed clothes from the campus laundry, when I slipped and fell backward in the early-spring slush. Kimiko's roommate and pals were stepping out of the library.

"Are you all right?" she asked.

"Yes, fine, thank you."

"You don't look it." I fumbled with the laundry, just then realizing it contained Kimiko's unusual-colored underpants with their unique, eye-catching arabesque design.

"Well, well. And whose are these?" one of the pals asked and held up the panties for the others to gawk at. "Anybody's we know?" She twirled the panties overhead. "Or are you just practicing a little cross-dressing on the side, Professor?" The parking lot exploded in shrieks of laughter.

"Aw, c'mon. Don't take it all so seriously. We won't tell anyone, will we, girls?" another said. They nodded in mock agreement.

I was left lying in the slush to collect my clothes and wits, what few I had left. How the hell was I to know Kimiko had put her underwear into my wash for Chrissakes? I scooped up the now-bespattered laundry, dumped it in the car, and headed for class. Campus was soon atwitter. It wasn't long before the old witch back at the office heard about the incident and tried to blackmail me with it, suggesting that the dean would find it "interesting." (She would never speak directly about anything.) Our long-overdue showdown. Vulgar. Quick. Decisive. Call me shameless, yet I had rifled through her mail one day. I had suspected her of carrying on an affair behind her husband's back; her mail proved as much. I lost my temper (the first time in years), spat out a sexual vulgarity I'll not repeat, and, careful to repeat her own term in a mocking tone, said that her husband might find my discovery "interesting." The gray-haired prof remained speechless, too dumbstruck to proffer any meaningful rejoinder. With her, I was yakked out myself. She never threatened me again. Of course, in retrospect, I could've been far more circumspect, but I was at my wit's end. The 'incident' could've undoubtedly affected my career. Instead, a voice in my heart cried out that bigger, more momentous things were now sucking us into the vortex of history.

***

America's social fabric was being shredded while the nation disintegrated against the whirlwind of international affairs. The stock market plunged further. Cyber attacks against US computer networks became commonplace; this, in turn, precipitated further market gyrations. Oil prices seesawed. Worse, race riots were reportedly erupting like long-festering pustules, not only in cities coast-to-coast but in hitherto quiescent suburbs. Living in the boondocks, I didn't experience this; however, media reports of out-of-control riots were broadcast almost daily. And our Fourth Amendment right against illegal search and seizure was fast being whittled away.

On a recent trip to Mark's place, I was routinely stopped twice by local and state authorities, my vehicle searched. I wasn't transporting my handgun, although, amazingly, it was still legal to do so. Mark said Washington wanted it that way for the time being so that it could incrementally trump up additional restrictions and further usurp the Constitution in the guise of public safety later. Some people's tempers would flare; a few would resort to violence; Washington would be handed a mob-sanctioned impetus to come down harder still. Even the underlying threads of small farming communities were becoming unraveled.

The two tiny local banks "temporarily" closed the following Monday. Some area establishments put a moratorium on credit card purchases: disruptions in the payment process, it was said. Growing lines at the gas pumps became a reality. Store prices of essential commodities began to soar; in cities, it was worse. Schools were still in session; kids were increasingly staying home or just not bothering to slog to class. Many parents were too worried about their own day-to-day problems to notice. Some residents who weren't farmers had their work hours cut back or were laid off altogether. Supermarkets were still well-stocked; fewer folks had extra money to buy goods other than essentials. The only smiling souls in town were the preachers. Simmering panic had driven people to dig in their pockets and offer Sunday donations more than they ordinarily would, perhaps in the hope that Providence would look down and bless them in accordance with how much they now sacrificed. Economic disruptions didn't impede paid attendance at regional sporting events, however, they increased. Sponsors took in more money than ever, one of them boasted. As a result, admission prices at several key events were raised; fans gladly ponied up the difference. Some sort of pro wrestling show featuring Tiny as one of its gladiators pitched tent for the weekend in a makeshift arena at one of the regional Granges. Every performance sold out early.

Kimiko and I took to scaling back our expenditures. Not that we were ever big spenders, but people with money, or at least those giving off an impression of having lots of it, were becoming targets, in some respects even more so than the Liberty Militia. Militia members were at least thought of as homegrown working folk, except for me and a few others. Of course, unlike in Wedgemont, there weren't that many wealthy people here. The Mercedes stood out as my purple eye had; we began driving my old car more, hers less, and then we kept the Mercedes locked in my apartment garage. A few of the students weren't so discreet. One got beat up especially badly by locals, enraged that someone need not be as provident in life as they. Tensions between college and community rose; fewer students were seen strolling on the streets off-campus, particularly alone and after dark. Townspeople liked it that way; they looked at them as spoiled interlopers, kids who had never had to work a day in their lives. In reality, this wasn't so, but it mattered little; it was popular sentiment, and the town clung to it ever more tenaciously. Because their own children could now afford Swenson even less, folks grew angrier all the more, as if the wealthy students were personally responsible for the souring plight of the surrounding community. Even though the same students poured much of their parents' cold cash into town businesses, local folks, like indignant welfare recipients, accepted it begrudgingly. Through it all, I sensed things would only get worse, and Kimiko and I grew more protective of each other in our own ways.

Increasing campus chaos and her family's recent and expressed concern over her safety drew us together in a last-minute meeting behind our department headquarters right before spring break. Economic upheaval was forcing some students to think seriously of withdrawing. She appeared seemingly out of nowhere, bubbling and bouncing into the little garden not yet in bloom. From one of the rust-ridden chairs the department kept out all winter for smoke breaks, I rose to greet her. A sharp gust unexpectedly blew up. I gestured for us to go inside, then thought it better to remain outside for more privacy. As she approached, I saw she was wearing a chic purple-pastel one-shoulder chiffon jersey halter dress with a matching handbag. She looked as if she had jumped off the cover of a high-fashion magazine at the supermarket checkout counter.

"Sorry I'm late." She licked her lips. "I didn't think you'd be — "

"Kimiko. Look, we have to talk."

"Yes, I know. I told my father that I was fine. No problem."

"Good. But something else." I looked away, noticed the nearby tiny cherry buds ready to burst, and thought of where I had been this time last year in Wedgemont. "Look, things are bad and getting worse. You can't go hopping and bopping around campus, let alone off, dressed like that. People, even if they don't act like it, are petty; they pretend to admire wealth in others, yet in reality despise them for it. Or at least for showing it."

"What? What you expect me to do? Walk around in public dressed like American girls? No makeup, no look, no style, no clotes, only shirt and pants, maybe dungarees? Been there. Seen that. No thanks."

"Don't mean it that way. I mean, you must be more discreet. The circumstances, the times, demand it."

"So now you my teacher and my father, could be?" We burst out laughing; this time, she had the last word.

"I brought you memo from Rodgers-san. Copied it from office. Not yet final. Don't tell."

Kimiko was developing into quite the campus snoop. She had taken on inter-organizational duties in addition to her TA ones. For a moment, I contemplated the small, smudged paper and reflected upon what somber secret it held. I nodded; she handed it over.

"To all our devoted faculty and staff —

This semester has been a most difficult one. By virtue of the burgeoning national and international crisis, some of our students' parents intend to withdraw their children if circumstances worsen. Parents have notified me personally of this dire intent. Correspondingly, the unfortunate development translates itself into an evolving financial exigency. As a result, the college administration, with the full support of the Board of Trustees, has been forced to execute the following measures:

If deemed necessary by the Office of the president, faculty and staff layoffs will commence in accordance with employment seniority insofar as feasible. Contracts shall remain valid through the academic year, terminating July 31st, barring any unforeseen calamity.

Please do accept my heartfelt apologies over this most unexpected and tragic turn of events.

Cordially,

A. Rodgers, Ph.D.

Dean of Academic Affairs"

At the bottom and to the side was the barely legible handwritten inscription: "Cf. Hernandez 1st."

We looked at each other. Nothing had to be said. In my peripheral vision, I saw the witch-prof watching from our second-story office window.

***

Mark came up the next weekend like usual. Said he had some documents to show the militia. Kimiko and I drove down at night to pick him up at the Manchester bus terminal. Understandably, he didn't want to transport his handgun in the old Dodge through Massachusetts with its added gun restrictions because of increased police roadside surveillance and harassment; rather, he wanted to target shoot and had preferred to leave the weapon with me. (The authorities still weren't boarding public buses.) We considered the prudence of continuing to pop off shots at the range; he chided me over my "reluctance to exercise constitutional rights to keep those rights," for "why the hell did you fight in Vietnam?" Then, half-joking, half-serious, as if he were my drill sergeant, he added, "Grow some balls, for God's sake." The remark perplexed Kimiko, ever curious over our idioms. I had my hands full and fidgeting trying to explain it during a private moment at the terminal.

The three of us pulled back on Interstate 93 heading north and crossed the Merrimack River, Mark's shirtsleeve loudly flapping in the wind outside the window as we cruised past small farmhouses lit like phosphorescent dots in the distance. He spat out the window. I observed Kimiko's disapproving look in the rearview mirror while I weaved in and out of slower-moving traffic.

"What's the rush?" he asked, leaning back, trying to get comfortable.

"Nothing. Just that we saw what could've been a start-up roadblock south of Bow. Thought perhaps we could pass it before it's assembled."

"Hmph." He smiled. "Be seeing plenty more, soon. I — " Mark and Kimiko bounced around in their seats while I gripped the steering column, slowing to avoid what looked like a man exiting a Jeep, his buddies staring, one hollering to slow down. "I got some papers for you. Have it that the Federal Emergency Management Agency and the Attorney General are urging the president to ban private possession of any and all ammunition. NRA Executive Board's got wind of it and can't seem to project a united front in response. Their own president's now too bloody timid." I slowed down further; the man came into better view: a soldier, the Jeep a military one, National Guard. Mark lurched forward for a clearer look as if to inspect the roadside warriors personally. "What the — ?"

I tapped the brake, jerking the car to a stop. Emergency vehicle headlights threw flashes of alternating red and blue light reflecting off surrounding road signs, then seemingly bouncing off nearby trees. Amid the confusion, radio messages crackled and reverberated over the heads of the soldiers with M-16s and flak jackets, now shining flashlights and peering randomly into passing vehicles, then into every other one. We could barely discern the messages. Broken. Garbled.

"Alpha Company ... two possible suspects, maybe three ... what did you say? ... over and —... unconfirmed bioterrorist attack south of Montreal — repeat: that's unconfirmed ... roger ... suspects headed inside border, possibly for Boston area ... we do not have a visual...."

Two guardsmen from the rear walked by. Mark and I both noticed that, contrary to well-publicized regulations, neither wore identifying insignia or name tags. Abruptly, ahead and to our right, several teens were dragged from their car. The kids were laughing; one looked like he was sneering and sounding off to the guardsmen. A soldier smashed his rifle butt into the kid's face; the kid staggered and fell face-first into the pavement. Somebody in another car kept screaming obscenities at the soldiers to stop. They ran over and beat the protester with their flashlights. Other passengers in the vehicle begged them to stop. Kimiko went to yell something out the window. Mark threw his hand over her mouth. The battered kid lay on the pavement, writhing and screaming curses at his tormenters, blood streaking down his face and forming a small, cherry-colored splatter on his shirt collar now visible in the flashing blue and red emergency headlights. The apparent leader of the guardsmen hollered something to the others; they hurriedly fanned out toward the motorists stalled on the road. Some soldiers headed toward us.

"Get going now. Turn off the lights. Go, go, go," Mark said.

"You crazy? What for?"

"Floor it!"

I slammed the accelerator. We stalled, tires spinning and screeching against the asphalt. Then we blasted out from behind the truck in front of us, Mark and Kimiko lurching forward, and raced out onto the open stretch of road. We roared down the interstate in a maelstrom of chaos, the soldiers too taken aback to react immediately.

"Turn your lights and radio on and get off at the Bow exit. Take the back roads. Didn't get our license or a good look. Never get us. Besides, they're concentrating on the southbound lane."

I did as he demanded, Kimiko still seated in the rear, horrified.

"WBXZ, Boston. We have a special bulletin: An unconfirmed biological terrorist attack is believed to have taken place in Sherbrooke, Quebec, approximately ninety miles east of Montreal. A carload of suspects is thought to be traveling south across the US-Canadian border. The FBI is investigating. Also at this hour, the president has ordered all privately-owned ammunition for firearms to be brought to local or state police for safe storage; violators risk forfeiture without receipt. Additional details will follow."

"I'm sorry, Bill. Heard about a probable edict on ammo before it was announced. Wouldn't ya know? Don't have to repeal the Second Amendment. All you have to do is ban ammo, so we can use our guns like clubs. Wanted to bring up several bricks of .357s in my bag to cache."

I slammed on the brakes, swerving to avoid smashing into the guardrail. "Goddammit, Mark! You placed all of us in jeopardy tonight. Could've been shot back there."

He nodded, said nothing, and stretched out his arm, gripping my shoulder with that powerful hand, almost as if he had then become a surrogate driver. He examined my face. I intuited an ever-deepening mystery in his. I gazed out the window. In distant pastures along the edge of a waterhole, cattle were hunkered down for the night under an open-air lean-to. Kimiko squeezed my hand. Sourcing my faith in the core of my soul, I found an empty moment. Life was spinning out of control. I turned around, staring back into the nothingness of the road, wondering what evolving realities the gods had chosen for us. The radio announcer apologized for interrupting the NHL game: Arab states had invaded northern Israel.

To my and Mark's surprise, when we got back to Springvale, Kimiko didn't whimper or cringe; neither did she whine over being placed in jeopardy by Mark's subterfuge. Later I asked her about it. She replied, "My father taught us in life to have and live by a code. If you know your friend made some kind of honest judgment mistake, you stand by him. I, too, saw beatings. And I stand by the two of you. Remember this." Her fingertips brushed against mine. I knew again that her mere touch could quietly sear my soul.

Chapter 7

"This is a live announcement from CNN. US Mid-East troops have been put on Threat Condition Delta, the highest alert status. Fighting between Israelis and Arabs appears to be contained in the northern sector near the Lebanese border. This is unconfirmed. The president will make an announcement shortly. Now we're working on a direct feed to the White House. We are going live to the White House Rose Garden. Here is — ladies and gentlemen, the president of the United States."

" — a beautiful spring day here in Washington, but while birds sing here, blood is being shed in the streets of the Middle East. As you know, fighting has broken out between Israeli and Arab commandos in the northern section of Israel. I have spoken with both the Israeli Prime Minister and several Arab leaders. To date, violence, though at fever-pitch level, has been contained to this area. Be assured that we — I personally — are doing everything humanly possible to effect an immediate ceasefire. In the meantime, I have ordered the Secretary of Defense to put all our troops in the region on Delta readiness state of alert, that is, maximum alert status. I will keep you informed of any breakthroughs as they develop. Yet no one should misconstrue our resolve to stand by our long-time ally and friend, Israel. In consultation with the Secretary of Defense and the Joint Chiefs of Staff, the Selective Service has been ordered to initiate call-up procedures if a general mobilization is warranted. As your duly-elected president, I have also placed several large metropolitan areas under curfew until further notice. With that, I bid you good afternoon and God's blessings."

Mark, Kimiko, and I were inside the unheated student center. Heating oil deliveries had been halted or were at best sporadic. Though well into spring, days could be damned chilly in this part of the country; nights, far worse. Too, trash had been piling up. The college, already in dire financial straits, had laid off half of its custodians. To our right, we overheard two students, whom I recognized from the soccer team.

"Why in the hell do we have to listen to all this crap? The NBA playoff commentary was coming up, for Christ's sakes!"

"You telling me? Why are the games always being interrupted?"

I wondered if I wasn't living inside some giant circus.

One of the women from our library staff entered. "Professor Watson, do you have change for five dollars? The cashiers said they ran out of small change. Something about the banks closing early and the cafeteria not being able to get sufficient change to operate."

"Here's your dollar. Forget any change. Coffee's on me."

"Oh, thank you. You're so kind."

I watched her get the coffee and return; she contemplated whether to keep her gloves on indoors. Kimiko and Mark were heavily absorbed in the news broadcast.

"I can't fathom this layoff notice from Dean Rodgers. Can you believe it?" The librarian shook her head.

"What did you expect?" I said. "You saw his earlier admonition."

"His what? Oh, I know, but I thought educational personnel weren't supposed to be let go, that we were different."

"How so? Did you think we're special? Show-business performers?" I hadn't meant to be sarcastic; nevertheless, the poor dreamer became visibly upset, and I let her sputter on.

"I just thought that we're supposed to be different, professionals in a profession."

I had been in a nasty mood and couldn't take any more of her prattle. I gestured to Kimiko and Mark for us to leave. The staff was beginning to sweat. As long as they only read about things in the papers, it was no big deal. But see a notice with their names on it, and it sinks home. Her remarks were typical of dreamers, especially academic ones.

More than inconvenience and unemployment were taking place. When the three of us got back to my apartment, I noticed there had been somebody inside. "You two stay here!" I yelled and ran downstairs to the superintendent's apartment; the old fellow was already expecting me and poured himself another shot of whiskey.

"I'm sorry. They were here not more than an hour ago. Said they didn't need a search warrant," he said, steadying himself against a corner of his kitchen table, tottering under the weight of his bloated belly.

"Who was here?"

"That pipsqueak of a state cop Leopold and some FBI guy, looked like a Puerto Rican or something."

"What did they want?"

"Didn't say. I'm sorry. Had to let them in. Hear now they got a right to seize and search at will," he drawled, wiping off the whiskey trickling from his mouth with the back of his hand. "Guess the president's culled and voided the Third Amendment. Better check to see if nothin's missing. You ain't hidin' no guns upstairs, are you?"

I hurried back up the stairway. Kimiko and Mark knew something was amiss; it looked like Mark was already blaming her in part, for what I didn't know, though lately, they had been getting along better. Kimiko was sitting fretfully on the edge of the sofa, Mark looming over her. Spring sunlight poured through the kitchen window and seemed to cast a surreal, almost halo-like effect over her. She was not quite focused on him nor eyeing me, and my first recollection was of her the previous fall sitting demurely in the English department's lounge when we'd met.

"Why, why you look at me like that?"

"Like, like what?" Mark stammered and backed off.

"You think I had something to do with items in Mr. Will's room remiss?"

"No, I'm sorry. I didn't mean to imply…." Mark turned away from both of us and looked out the window at the crocuses and assorted hyacinths lining the apartment complex entrance. He appeared genuinely remorseful, and I neither pressed home the incident nor returned to it later. I chalked it up to irritability over his employment troubles and tried my best to put the memory behind us. (Kimiko wasn't as merciful. Later that evening when we were alone, she chided me on my perceived "reluctance to stand by your woman who stands by you!" Again, I felt hemmed in the middle and torn between taking sides.)

Despite searching as hard as we could, I couldn't find anything missing or seriously tampered with. "Let me sweep the place for hidden electronic devices," whispered Mark. "I can get the equipment in a day or two." I dismissed his offer as unnecessary. Between the break-in and Kimiko's and Mark's new spat, I was wrung out like a worn-out dishrag, and I struggled to put the day behind me. It turned out to be an insignificant prelude to the following evening's events.

The Springvale Board of Selectmen convened an all-out emergency town meeting at the regional high school to deal with the tightening crisis. Paranoia was trickling in everywhere. Old-timers said it must've been the first emergency roll call since Crazyman Wilson torched the old town hall. Except for the head selectman, service on the board was strictly voluntary; none of them could ever be singled out for overwork. All of the militia would attend, as would Troopers Hines and Leopold, even members of the college community, including Dean Rodgers. The crowd numbered several hundred. Unexpectedly, Ramirez-Hernandez was also there — and at least two unidentified aides.

The head selectman bellowed over the din of his increasingly edgy townsfolk. "Hear ye! Hear ye!" The overhead ceiling lights seemed to sway slightly in rhythm with the board's calls for order. "Hear ye!" he continued to wail in language as timeworn as the table behind him that the board had set atop the desolate stage. The auditorium was also unheated; it looked like the school couldn't afford anything other than decrepit furniture left behind from the days of the pioneers. Sounds of the gavel smashing against the frail lectern, perched precariously on stage, echoed throughout the assembly walls. "Order, please! Order! Order, Goddammit!"

I glimpsed at Kimiko and Mark, who had adamantly decided to come with me, then surveyed the crowd fidgeting in their seats. Some of them shuffled and squirmed and blew on their hands to keep warm. The night was unseasonably cold. You could see the air shoot out from our mouths and noses. Big Walt, Mike, and Petey seemed to create an oddly protective cordon around Sergeant Hines standing on the opposite side of the room from Trooper Leopold, Ramirez-Hernandez, and the new tagalongs. Leroy and his boy, Josh, mingled the best they could within a circle of the town's older women harbored alongside the auditorium windows. Josh caught sight of us, and the two of them snaked their way through the throng to be with us. The room began to take on an air of simmering panic. What smelled like stinking cat urine came my way, from where I'll never know.

"I said, 'Hear ye!' or whatever the heck I said to you it was!" The head selectman gripped the lectern and then launched into a lecture about why we were there. From his demeanor, you'd think the old sodbuster thought himself star professor at Swenson.

"Why are we here?" he asked.

"To get you anointed to another term in office?" a shout came from the rear. The room erupted in a spasm of nervous laughter.

"Ha, ha. Isn't that funny?" one of the other board members said. "Go on, have your little fun now. We've got serious stuff to consider here tonight."

The head selectman released his grip on the lectern and held up his hands in a bid for quiet. "All right now. Let's get down to talk shop." He paused, scanning the crowd, and waited for them to control themselves. "Let the board tell you tonight that we're in big trouble here in the Granite State. But we're lucky; we've got food and, above all, each other. Not like from what I hear what's going on in some big cities down south of here like Washington, Atlanta, even Boston. Folks, they're already slaughtering each other in the streets over gas, food — or just because somebody looks different." Again, he paused, this time for the words to penetrate our consciousness.

"Yeah, I hear it's some wild, fucking niggers," came a murmur from the middle of the pack. It sounded like Larry. Many in the crowd jeered.

"We have to pull together, rely on each other, help each other, work with each other, each and every one of us," said the sole female board member. "I mean it." She turned toward the head selectman, now returning to speak from behind his lectern.

"OK, you've heard the board. Let's get down to details. No — we'll take questions later, Garwith." The assembly twittered; Kimiko wondered what was so funny. No matter how many years they had heard the old boy's name, it was still amusing. "First, the board believes we here in Springvale ought to declare ourselves weapons-free." A single groan went up. "We need to be sanctioned by the governor's crisis management task force that we're in compliance with the president's Executive Order."

"What the hell for?" screamed Petey. Other militia members, even a few of the other townspeople, joined in. "The Order pertains to ammo, not weapons, you idiot!"

"Err, I know. But if we're certified to be weapons-free, we may qualify for additional emergency state funding."

A collective groan rose from the audience. Many openly voiced objections, stating that no such municipal funding was realistically available — for any community. Trooper Leopold rushed forward to hog the floor.

"If we consider what the head selectman suggests, we can lead the way for Carroll County. Concord is bound to notice, if we all come clean — "

"Who says we're dirty?" somebody hollered.

"Come clean with the authorities; it's not too much to ask. Just surrender arms and ammo to local officials," Leopold shot back.

There were some hisses and catcalls. Yet others nodded in agreement. Sergeant Hines, ironically enough seated in the thick of Liberty Militia members, couldn't take any more and jumped up. "Now you listen to me, Leopold! You know the president's Order and the governor's announcement don't call for any such thing. What's more, you're out of line. You've no authority to request any damn thing!" He continued to stand, shaking.

"Oh, that's where you're so wrong, Sergeant." Leopold pivoted to face his entire audience. "The Bureau of Alcohol, Firearms, and Tobacco, an arm under direct presidential authority, sees it differently."

The Little Leopard turned in his new master's direction, as though begging approval, and smirked. Ramirez-Hernandez still stood in the shadows (literally) at the edge of the auditorium. Gaunt and drawn, silhouetted under the ceiling lights, he reminded me of one of the zombies in a recent horror film. Near chaos burst out. Mark shook his head. The head selectman bolted to the front of the stage to regain the floor.

"All right, all right. Listen to me. We can come back to that later. Another thing we ought to consider: an emergency tax to cover unforeseen expenses brought about by the national crisis. I'm talking funds for unexpected manure drainage, uncompleted bridge repair, removal of trash piling up near Logman's Road — "

"Whaddya, nuts? Damn-near half of us are out of work, Miles. Where do you think we're going to get the money?" came a shout from the rear.

"I know, I know. But we've got problems we've got to attend to…."

Off to one side, an old woman staggered forward. "Look, the mill rate is set once a year. You know there's no provision in the town bylaws to change that. As it is, I can't even make do on what my louse of a husband left me with — nothing!" The depth of discontent started to swell. Springvale was swimming against the tide.

"We ought to at least consider it," the head selectman shot back.

"Fuck you!" screamed the woman.

The meeting disintegrated into a cauldron of confusion. Sporadic pockets of pent-up rage boiled over at nothing and nobody in particular. The board shouted for everyone to be calm. Patient. Considerate. A fist went flying where Dean Rodgers sat as though in a stupor. The dean shot out from his chair, suddenly jolted into reality. He scurried off to one side. Women shrieked. Combatants rushed each other, cursing, yet were just as quickly yanked apart by several on-lookers and trundled outside. Mark gestured to Kimiko and me for the three of us to leave.

***

I could walk away from the torn expectations of the town, expectations blasted apart that night at the school auditorium, yet I remained helpless in the struggle with my rematerializing Vietnam ghosts. I had gone several weeks without a conscious recurrence, but the next afternoon they hit with full force. I had gone to take a nap on the living room sofa; Kimiko and Mark had apparently reconciled and were talking in hushed tones in the next room. I must've sounded like a lunatic; Kimiko rushed over and kneeled at my side.

"What? What is it?" She gently put her hand on my forehead, then rose to go to the kitchen and returned with a wet hand towel for my face, which was dripping sweat. She had witnessed similar episodes, though this one was by far the worst for her. "You try to relax." She dabbed the towel to my forehead and continued holding my hand.

I dreamt of lying limp on that musty Army cot in that boiling jungle — and of the needle inserted behind my ear. This time I remembered, hazily though, of peering through the tent opening and contemplating — almost identifying with, of being — an image of a small, silvery-gray UFO hovering, silently, barely above the tree line.

"Hmph. Bet you never got service like that in 'Nam, eh, Billy Boy?" Mark stood over me, grinning.

"I had that dream again, Mark. This time there was a UFO — right outside the tent where I lay after I got hit outside Loc Ninh, the time when the major bled to death lying next to me." I was embarrassed but continued. "This sounds crazy. There was the number sixty-seven. Some kind of significance to it. I experienced it synesthetically. Like I could taste it, feel it."

The grin faded; his face transformed into a mask of brooding intensity. "A memory repressed like that can cut you worst of all, and you wouldn't even know it, like staggering in the dark right before the dawn."

"What kind of gibberish is that?" I demanded.

"You take it easy now, Will." Kimiko pushed me back and loosened my shirt button.

"Here." Mark stooped over and began massaging me behind my ear at the exact site of my injection. It felt good. Kimiko's touch was gentle; Mark's was powerful. Call it what you may, camaraderie between veterans, what have you, but at that moment, his hand was the more reassuring. "Do you remember? Evil is as evil does."

Now, what's that supposed to mean? I thought to myself.

"Bill?"

"Yes, Mark."

"I wanted for you to — no, nothing."

And I drifted back to sleep....

Mark was up early the next day as usual. His boss had suggested he take a month-long 'hiatus' from work, he said, in hopes that business would pick up after that. I had slept the entire afternoon and evening, while Kimiko had already gone to class — what was left of the crumbling curriculum at Swenson.

People prayed conditions wouldn't get worse, that they'd at least level off. But when global oil supplies trickled, so did other basic services like mail delivery. As finger-pointing intensified, searching for scapegoats did as well. Because the oil crisis originated in the Mid-East, Arab-Americans and Jews served just fine. Panic began seeping in, particularly in cities. Everything became rationed. Now that the oil spigot had all but been turned off, gas pump lines stretched farther; then there came days with no gas at all. A strange thing happened, too. Trying to protect the pumps at night, attendants would 'ride shotgun.' But presidential edict outlawed ammo purchase and possession. Employees would stand watch with guns and no bullets, presumably. At times it worked; at times it didn't. Thieves never knew who had loaded weapons. Establishment and residential break-ins soared. Many people were glad they hadn't turned over their ammo; those who had cursed the authorities and then themselves. Then things really nosedived: even pro sports team schedules became disrupted. It all had a domino effect.

Now that Mark had secretly brought up a sizeable quantity of .357 ammo, we'd have to cache it. Fast. We thought it wise to restrict knowledge to only a few in the militia. We'd team up with Leroy before heading out to hook up with Mike and Walt. When we dropped off Kimiko at the college, I discovered that my class later in the day would be canceled for lack of students. We were running late. I careened my car in the direction of Leroy's home.

"What are you going to do?" Mark asked over the news broadcast blaring from the radio.

"About students dropping out? About my job?"

"Uh-huh."

"I don't know, Mark. I don't know. Guess I'm good till August."

He leaned out the window and tried to spit out against the on-rushing wind. "You really believe that, don't you?"

I was tempted to egg him on, as though now he would divine my future, yet was able to bite my tongue. We drove to Leroy's in silence, Mark clutching the ammo like a half-starved mongrel guarding the last remaining bone in the world.

I veered the vehicle onto Leroy's driveway, hopped out, and walked to the front entrance to meet the figure heading toward it.

"What do you want?" It was Mrs. Morton behind the screen door.

Leroy rushed forward from behind. "Thas' no way to greet our man."

"Your 'man,' huh?" she intoned sarcastically. Leroy brushed her aside, greeted Mark, and jumped in the car, as if he couldn't run away fast enough. His wife remained, sneering from the doorway, wearing her omnipresent apron and hang-dog snarl.

"Whew!" was all Leroy could manage between his home and our rendezvous with Mike and Walt near the deserted bridge over Babson's Creek. The two of them appeared in the distance at the far end of the abutment; I slowed down the car, keeping an eye out for uninvited visitors, half-expecting Leopard and Ramirez-Hernandez to fly out from behind one of the clusters of white birches lining the rock wall alongside the road.

"Aw right," roared Mike. "We have to move fast."

Without so much as a greeting, after parking, we bolted down the footpath, still mushy from recent spring rains, leading into the scrub brush at the base of one of the area's monadnocks. I could never quite get over how Mark, whenever hiking, would still look for hidden mines and tripwires. Soon we came to the far end of a lonely granite ledge with a freshly dug mound of earth, partly disguised by a moist clump of birch and pine tree branches and assorted rotting leaves and ferns. At the bottom of the shallow pit lay a huge plain steel box with some ammo already visible in it.

Mike gestured to Mark to cache the prospective treasure. Walt grabbed a shovel, seemingly from nowhere, and began burying the bullets. "Don't have to remind you how appreciated this is, Mark," Walt said. The others nodded in agreement. "You know, you always reminded me of Rock Hudson in A Farewell to Arms," he continued between shovelfuls.

"Yeah, but he was queer!" cut in Leroy.

"Uh, I didn't mean it in any way like that," Walt shot back. "No offense given."

"None taken," said Mark, wiping the mud from his shoes.

"You'd never know that by looking at him in those love scenes with Jennifer Jones," Walt went on. "Makes you wonder who's really normal." The rustling of birds nearby warned us nightfall was approaching.

Mike tamped down the dirt with his feet. "Maybe this could be our own Farewell to Arms," he said, nervously scanning the tree line of the horizon fading fast under encroaching twilight. "Sssh! What the hell was that?" We all froze. I swore

I heard my heart beat; you could taste our paranoia. "There!" A large buck stood in the distance. Mike shook his head. "Let's get out of here."

When we got to the road, Walt remarked he thought he had just seen Petey drive by behind the wheel of a brand-new truck. "Not possible," said Mike. "I'd know who in Springvale would get a new truck, remember? Besides, where would Petey get the money?" Walt scratched his head, shoehorned his mammoth frame behind the wheel of his own ramshackle Jeep, followed immediately by Mike.

Leroy, Mark, and I quietly pulled into Springvale after dusk. At a farmhouse just over the town line, civilian and military vehicles, emergency lights flashing, were parked in the middle and on both sides of the road, partially blocking traffic. We could hear shouting yet couldn't quite make out what was being said. We coasted to a near-stop. Men in ski masks, camouflage fatigues, and flak jackets, carrying semi-automatics were scurrying in all directions. A few of them wore gas masks. It looked as though they were being directed by several others dressed in plain, black outfits with white lettering on their backs. A lone siren screamed from behind the adjacent cow pasture. We inched forward....

"What are you doing? Leave us alone — please! We didn't do nothing wrong. We always obeyed — followed the law.... Look, I'm a veteran.... For God's sake, man, don't take us away from our children. Please! We only tried to — "

The siren drowned out their cries for mercy. An agent began manhandling a middle-aged woman. He turned around. On the back of his jacket was written 'AFT.' Another man, presumably her husband, hysterical, screamed, "Get your hands off her!"

A crowd of their neighbors began to form. The agent tried to drag the woman into the vehicle whose siren had now been turned off. She was too strong. Leroy started chuckling. Another agent stepped in to subdue her.

"Please, please, I'm begging you, don't take my wife!" Their two teenage children, watching from their veranda steps, horrified, rushed to their mother's side. A third agent, off to one side, jumped in and cut them down with a stream of savage blows to their heads from his rifle butt. The husband again shrieked. The third agent gleefully shot pepper spray into his face. The farmer choked, keeled over, and fell face-first to the ground. Several agents ran forward to stomp him, bloodlust in their eyes.

"Look! There's Leopard and Ramirez," said Leroy.

It became too much for the swelling crowd of disgusted onlookers.

"Stop it!"

"Fuck you fuckers!"

"Are we going to just stand here?"

They strained forward. The agents were getting nervous. Two or three raised their weapons in the air as though readying to fire.

"Goddamned Nazis!"

A tear gas canister went off; the cloud drifted our way. The crowd's desperate cries grew louder.

"Quick, roll up the windows," cried Leroy, spilling his coffee cup and scalding Mark. Mark howled as Leroy struggled with the window handle. A rock smashed into our rear window.

"Get outta here!" Mark hollered, clutching his arm. I threw the car into reverse gear, slammed the accelerator, and promptly plowed into a government emergency vehicle, caving in its side. A hubcap went spinning off into the darkness. Leroy almost went flying out the door. Mark looked out. "Oh, shit."

"Sonofabitch! You!" The agent who had been beating on the kids stumbled out from the undamaged side, bleeding, and staggered out in front of us, his handgun drawn. A shot rang out, exploding our windshield. Flying glass bit into Mark's face.

We choked over the mix of tear gas, our own mucous, and Leroy's chewing tobacco spewing forth. I slammed the brakes repeatedly before finding the gas pedal. The agent looked like he was aiming for a second shot. We slammed him.

When Mark and I finally returned to my place after dropping off Leroy, Kimiko was already waiting outside in the late-evening cool spring drizzle. She stood alone in the dark by the driveway, hugging herself with her glitzy overcoat, more befitting an evening in Paris than here in Palooka. She eyed the damaged car, Mark's bleeding face, and my lesser injuries. She gasped in disbelief. "What — what happened? Did you take an accident? I was so worried."

"No, not really an accident," I said, shaking my head and stumbling toward her.

She put her arm around me, pulling me into her. I softly stroked her hair and kissed the top of her head. Mark took it all in from a distance, leaning against the shattered windshield, perhaps wondering what measured promises the future held.

Once inside, we mapped out our strategy to deal with the evening's events. As it turned out, Mark didn't need medical attention, only sleep. We didn't know if the agent we steamrolled was still alive. And even if he had not survived long enough to identify the car, the blown-out front window would give us away. We were fairly confident, however, given the darkness, the tear gas, and the chaos, that nobody had gotten a good look at us. Besides, they now had their hands full with a slew of other residents. We'd wash the car and have the windshield replaced secretly by a militia comrade, and we soon discovered that the farm family had been initially confronted for hoarding not weapons and ammo but gasoline. Everybody sensed more searches and seizures were imminent.

Kimiko approached me late in the evening after Mark had gone to sleep. Her hesitation indicated a heightened sense of urgency. "Sit," she said. "Please." She added nothing, only stared down at the living room rug, fingering a tiny porcelain puppy-shaped knickknack, her favorite charm.

My stomach started to knot. I knew enough about Kimiko by then to realize that her actions signaled a cultivated response of reluctance not yet articulated. Were she to speak immediately, I would have gladly listened. But I sensed what was coming.

She struggled to begin….

"My father, again, called. This time he wants of me to return — immediately. At least for now. So that I must do. I booked a flight tomorrow night. I'm sorry."

"I see."

"Used to be when I was little, living and growing up outside Osaka, often I wondered of what kind of man someday I'd meet. No, I didn't want a rich man, nor even a handsome one. I wanted a man with heart, a man with a heart which beats of love which endures, in times of joy and in times of sorrow. It's not about family or about position; it's about heart. Family may betray, position may vanish like morning mist over these White Mountain peaks; pure heart beats on forever. It's true we are divided by cultures set apart by many kilometers and by many customs. Yet I believe you are that man, for what does culture matter when two hearts will beat as one?"

"But I never thought you — "

"Sshh." She put a finger to my mouth. "Don't you cry for us. My heart for you will always be. Hanaretakunai."

"What is that supposed to mean?"

"Never mind, Will, never mind." She wet her lips.

I felt her warm breath and then the throbbing of her pulse. She was one woman hard to let go, harder to keep. "I will be gone only short time."

In the morning, I called the college to report in sick, not that there were many students staying behind to teach anyway. Kimiko and I drove the Mercedes down to Boston's Logan Airport amid increased roadblocks and harassment later in the day; the vehicle would have to be left behind with me. In my gut, I tried to say goodbye with no pain, no regrets. She said it would be only for a "short time." Still, I tried. Against the backdrop of a world sliding into chaos, the best we could do was promise to stay in touch.

When I returned well past midnight, Mark was waiting in the doorway, still unshaven, adjusting his ponytail: "Is she really gone?"

"Uh-hmph."

"Really?"

"Really."

"There's more news — bad news. Liberty headquarters at Jimmy's barn burned to the ground. Too late to do anything now. Talked to the guys, and we decided to go out to Jimmy's later, day after tomorrow. Your dean called, though, saying he wants to see you in his office before classes first thing in the morning."

"About?"

"Didn't say."

"I see."

The night would drag on.

Chapter 8

At dawn, I rose to drive to the college, leaving Mark behind. That I only had the Mercedes made me feel conspicuous. The spacious campus square emerged in front of me, now almost barren like spring flowers without petals. The gate guard shack was deserted. Though barely sun-up, a few students were already in front of their dorm, feverishly packing their vehicles as if a bomb were about to detonate. I rolled into the faculty parking lot. The witch-prof happened to pull up alongside me. We didn't say anything, and I trudged through the lot and on toward the administration building.

Alone, the dean was milling about in his secretary's room adjacent to his own. He appeared to have been working throughout the night: unshaven, bouffant hairstyle disheveled, bow tie slightly askew.

"Oh, there you are. Well, don't just stand there. Come in," he said and continued piling up folders. "Be with you in a bloody moment."

His secretary's desk was almost cleared. I had heard that she was now on payroll part-time. He bellowed out a disgusted "Umph," fumbled while trying to adjust his bow tie, then violently jerked it off and threw it on the floor while spewing out some barely audible obscenity. Oddly, he next sat in his secretary's chair. "Sit!" The early-morning rays seemed to annoy him. He gazed out the office window and then hurried over to adjust the shades.

"You phoned last night?"

"Indeed. It's about Ms. Tanimoto — again. Incident'ly, rarely do we entertain a situation like this. I've taken the liberty to call you in because you appear at times to be her, uh, mentor. It's her father. He wants her back immediately. Need I spell out to you how this could derail prospects of any appreciable contribution to the endowment fund if she were not to complete the academic year?"

"I thought she had already left."

"Well, I believe her automobile is sitting outside. Only bloody Mercedes in Springvale that I've ever come across."

"I see."

"Plan to see her anytime soon?"

"I wasn't counting on it."

"Look, the financial health of the college is quite ill. I don't have to tell you how immeasurably appreciative the college president and board of trustees would be if … I think you follow where I'm going with this." He paused. "Well?"

"Yes, yes, why, of course. I'll see if I can't work something out."

He cracked an icy smile. "Splendid." What smile he had manufactured then vanished as he leaned forward, gawking out over his glasses. "I should hope you'd prove more adept at perhaps convincing Ms. Tanimoto to stay here than you were in Boston with your presentation on Blake. In any case, please see what you can do. Do remember, Dr. Watson, that your first year here is probationary. Very probationary." He asked if I had anything to add, and I replied in the negative. "Then that'll be all."

I sat there remembering the Blake presentation and how some prig from Harvard had joyfully exposed me to everybody, catching me with my pants down after pointing out my misquotes from memory of several minor verses, and then I looked out over the dean's head toward the window and contemplated the Mercedes, dumbstruck over my stupidity.

"I said, that will be all."

Though still early, I went to my first class of four students (no one showed up for the second) and later schemed to find out when the dean would be out so I could drive Kimiko's car back home undetected. It proved to be no difficult task, and by mid-afternoon, I was at my apartment front door to be greeted by Mark in an especially buoyant mood.

"Well, your car's fixed," he said, beaming and leaning hard against the doorframe as if holding it up. "One of our boys from Liberty. We even repainted the hood."

"Good."

"Say, what did your boss want?"

"He wants Kimiko to return, or, rather, thinks she never left — "

"She's not coming back, is she?" he sputtered, almost breathlessly.

"Easy, Mark. He just wanted her to complete her academic year. Figures that way her old man will cough up big bucks for the college trust fund. That's all."

"That's all?"

"That's all."

Mark kept smiling; his eyes took on a joy of their own. "We can go hook up with the boys tomorrow."

"I know. You already said as such last night," I replied and went inside.

Come daybreak; only reveille was missing. Mike all but commanded us to be up on time "to shit, shower, and shave," and Mark and I quickly walked out the door into pouring rain to pick up Leroy on the way to rendezvous at Petey's farm, which was serving as temporary headquarters. We spoke little on the ride over. Images of Kimiko flashed in front of me.

"All right, guys!" Leroy shouted, smiling from his porch steps as I eased into the driveway.

I motioned to Mark to remain behind as I bolted through the rain for the main entrance. Leroy advanced to the front of his doorway to greet me, still grinning. Mrs. Morton was just as quick to position herself between her husband and me as I approached. She stared out from behind the porch screen, angry, sneering.

"What do you want?"

"Well, for starters, a chance to get out of this rain."

"Who told you to come back here? We don't care if you get yoreself drenched in no rain or not. Why'nt you go back where'n you come from?"

The increasing steady force of the raindrops stunned my skin. I tried to pull the upper half of my jacket over my head. "Mrs. Morton, we just came to pick up Leroy." I thought I caught a glimpse of Josh, hiding behind the living room curtain, and turned around to observe Mark, face pressed against the car window, features barely perceptible through the foggy glass.

It got to be too much for her husband. Leroy pushed her out of the way and motioned for me to enter.

"Don't you shove on me like that! Yo' hear me?" She jiggered her stance like a prizefighter trying to balance himself and strained against the screen door, now more than ever determined to keep me shut out, yet Leroy was just as defiant. "Stop it! Stop it! Why you messin' around with these white backwoods cowboys instead of stayin' wit' and protectin' me and yore own family? Why?" She continued to shriek, her eyes blazing.

Leroy shoved his wife backward against the wall, squeezing himself in between her and the screen door and then out onto their porch steps. He swung around to look back, rain streaking down his face.

"Come back, Leroy! Come back! Please, Leroy, please!" she wailed and then sobbed.

By the time we sighted Petey's silo in the distance on the edge of the region's piedmont, the storm's fury had subsided, but not the one brewing inside the three of us over the attack on Liberty headquarters. Then, too, eating away at Leroy's sanity was his family's quandary, and again Mark played the soothing big brother, nurturing him with inane palliatives like "We're with you, brother" and the militia's back-up motto: "Liberty and Integrity." It appeared to work.

"Let's get moving inside the barn, guys. You know, BAFT and the FBI could be lurking around here someplace." It was Petey standing before his semi-dilapidated farmhouse, greeting and directing traffic with a cigar clutched in his hand and dressed, as usual, like a Bible salesman. He would alternately peer through a pair of cheap binoculars, scanning the edge of his greening pasture glistening after the rainstorm, while corralling stray members. "Never know if those bastards could be spying on us themselves right now. C'mon, let's get moving."

Mark, Leroy, and I made a beeline along the shoulder of the road for the rickety barn entrance, slowing down only occasionally to greet others. The command hierarchy sensed the formation was risky, maybe even foolhardy; however, they knew an all-out muster, including female auxiliaries, was imperative now that headquarters was torched.

The air was rife with anticipation inside Petey's run-down cow palace. Members were busy in spirited conversation not only about the destruction of Jimmy's barn but also over the continually developing national and global crisis. Standing by the entrance, Mike and Walt called for order. Mike cleared his throat. "All right, men — and, uh, ladies, too. Get comfortable."

A few of the women went to sit down on the cold, damp dirt floor and were quick to jump up. Some of the men sniggered. Uncharacteristically hidden in a corner, Larry stepped forward, pulled apart a bale of stale hay, and began spreading clumps over the dirt. "Us Polacks enjoy gracious living too, you know. Kapeesch?"

One of the older women raised her hand in a timid bid for Mike's attention as though reliving elementary school days. "What do we do about the old man's barn, Mike?"

"Dunno."

A collective sigh of disapproval went up, particularly from the men. "We can worry about Jimmy's barn later. In the meantime, we'd better think about caching guns and ammo with cell leaders. We can do it here. Petey's always trustworthy."

Petey appeared to twitch. I took a sudden cell phone call from Kimmy. She was excited. She was coming back and already waiting to be picked up at the Manchester bus terminal. Her flight had been repeatedly postponed and finally canceled, as had others.

The meeting dragged on. Nothing of significance unfolded, or maybe I only convinced

myself of it. The assembly dickered over the method and means to cache assorted ordnance. I was excited to see Kimiko again and had a hard time convincing Leroy and Mark to leave early to pick her up, especially Mark. He and I would drive down to get her. It was as if she had never left. "Just when I thought she'd be...." he started whispering to Leroy as we made our way back to the barn entrance, yet he let his voice trail off while tightening his lips and lowering his head, not realizing I'd overheard him. Leroy managed a faint grin at the remark, then tried to aim clear before spitting out a wad of tobacco, but he almost hit one of the women. She instinctively knew it wasn't intentional and pretended not to notice.

"Hanaretakunai," I muttered to myself. Leroy and Mark looked at me like I was crazy.

Chapter 9

The three of us safely navigated our return to Springvale, arriving well past midnight. Something about this 'cow-shit town,' as Leroy's wife had put it, its aura reminiscent of old steadfast Yankee values fast rotting away against the backdrop of contemporary nationwide rootlessness, gnawed at my spirit and anchored me to her bosom. I hardly ever felt that way about Wedgemont, indeed all of Fairfield County. The white-collars there maintained a closer relationship with their portfolio managers than with their own kids. Here I wanted to put down roots, grow old alongside its "rednecked hicks." Perhaps with the escalating tensions, I had been deluding myself all along; the community was transforming itself into another Wedgemont, albeit with less money but with far more honest working folk. I still wanted to belong. I thought more of how Kimiko would or could fit in the US and of her apparent detachment from her Japanese homeland — seemingly standing strong against the swelling tide of global meltdown.

She lay down, uncharacteristically disheveled and not even having brushed her teeth, nudged herself next to me, pushing away an empty bottle of Chateau Margaux on the bed (fatter paychecks had fine-tuned my heightened sensibility for finer wines), and wrapped an arm around my waist. Mark, ever-awake, was in the tiny room next door, which Kimiko had absurdly labeled "the research library," poring over NRA bulletins and documents from Liberty Militia and sister organizations. Exhausted, I slipped into a dead man's slumber.

"Why to you accuse me of something like that! Never I said that about ammo militia or did that before. Always I have best interests of Mr. Will beside my heart. Always I take care of him. Put him first. Make cup of his favorite hot tea. And for you too. Sew dur-tee socks. Help with research. Go — "

"Keep your voice down. You'll wake him up. He's had a shitty night."

"You speak words louder than me. It's you, Mr. Mark, that's turning up audible volume. And I, too — we all have the shitty night, like you say. You need —
"

"That's not my point; that's not the issue I pressed home with you. You have to be discreet about what comes out of your mouth. How many times has Bill told you that? And you're not doing it. Not always, at any rate. And you — "

"You are the one not discreet at time. Look it you. You have no one to look out for and no woman to look for you in return. So you — "

"You're hitting me personally. I've told you, that's my business. You — oh, sorry, Bill. Didn't see ya."

"Gomen nasai, Will."

They were at it. Again. They had been getting along. So it appeared. But hibernating resentments like a long-festering pustule had awakened once more. I studied Mark's face.

"Sorry 'bout the disruption, Bill. Kimiko and me were just having a little difference of opinion. 'Bout nothing, really. Right, Kimiko?"

She wouldn't look straight on at either of us and continued to study the floor. "I make you both some green tea," she mumbled, and then shuffled toward the kitchen door.

"Look, Mike Richards asked me to accompany him this morning to his church. Thought I'd party along. Probably do me some good. Better be going."

"You?" Mark smirked.

I nodded and turned to get away from them both. From behind me, his hand clutched my shoulder. Hard. "Look, I said I was sorry," he said, almost trembling. He thrust up both of his hands momentarily to put his arms around me as if to pull me into him, then froze, arms dangling awkwardly at his sides. It looked like he had a tear in his eye. Kimiko stood watching from behind the kitchen stove. I grabbed my jacket and went for the doorway.

Once outside, I stood contemplating this diminutive dwelling. Metaphysically something had changed. Intensely. One's spirit could sense an effortless breath descending upon the little shelter housing three disparate souls, each with myriad dreams, and in one magic, fleeting moment, all hearts beat synchronously with the greater cosmic heart of the universe. Enchanted whispers sounded a soft plea for reconciliation, and for a moment, all was at peace.

***

Mike was already waiting for me. As we rumbled over icy backwoods roads to Sunday service, he largely remained silent and somber behind the wheel, saying little of militias, Ramirez-Hernandez, the plummeting economy. He did grumble something about Petey unexpectedly getting a new Jeep — but not from his lot, and then to my surprise, said that the minister was my old landlord. I laughed nervously. He jerked on the steering wheel, swerving us to the side, avoiding a possum lying splattered on the roadside, guts frozen into the ice. Mike curled his lip at the sight. He was a combat veteran; I thought things like that would never faze him.

We rolled into the parking lot. Exquisitely manicured hedges supporting a light canopy of fresh snow surrounded the church entrance. Several snowmobiles and ATVs were parked neatly off to the side. A dozen or more of the faithful were milling about. I got out and almost slipped in the hard slush while looking up at the imposing white steeple slicing the sky overhead. Though I had driven by before, the huge edifice appeared to be disproportionate to the number of sinners residing in the surrounding communities.

Springvale Church (of which Protestant denomination I knew not, hardly being able to distinguish a Lutheran from Lucifer) had been an outpost of refuge to kindred spirits of colonial Yankees and their descendants for almost two centuries, overseeing baptisms, weddings, funerals, and all mundane matters of the soul. Mike and his parents and his parents' parents, and probably those before them, had trodden these same steps, like so many other families in town, and I marveled at the generational continuity. You could make out the snow-covered church boneyard, where his ancestors were buried, lying sleepily in the distance. I glanced over at him leaning against his side of the Jeep and wondered if he, too, would one day lie there beside them all. He nodded to some of the ladies. Blasting winds slapped our faces. Everybody hurried inside.

I hadn't seen the inside of a church in many years since attending a colleague's wedding. Almost forgot what it looked like. Weak sunlight poured through simple multihued stained-glass windows, gazing almost pitifully over the congregation. One of them, a semblance of Jesus and the Virgin Mary, seemed to transfix and momentarily put a spell on Mike as we passed by. A plain and unadorned wooden

cross hung at the end of the hall behind the preacher's pulpit in front of the mahogany pews, offering little in the way of comfort, and I silently chuckled that here
I wouldn't be sitting comfortably in one of those more recently built movie theater
complexes in Manchester Kimiko and I frequented. Old Glory and the Granite
State flag stood at attention at opposite ends of the building. Mabel, off from the
diner for the day, was there with another elderly woman, and I spotted Sergeant
Hines with his wife and their litter. A voice in front called for order.

"Your attention, please."

Mike and I were seated in the back. I was already half-praying the landlord-
minister wouldn't notice me, though I sensed he would.

"If you would open your hymn book, let's sing our opening hymn, 'How Excellent Is Thy Name,' Number 125. All rise, please."

The congregation rose as one and fumbled through their hymnals, then slowly
warmed up to an off-key "How excellent is Thy name, O Lord; How excellent is
Thy name…," each parishioner warbling out a different tune on practically every
line. The cacophony reverberated throughout the hall. Hines's youngest boy took
note, sniggered, and promptly caught a lightning behind-the-head swat from the
no-nonsense sergeant. The kid yowled. The service slid on after its inauspicious
start-up. The smell of melting candle wax filled my nostrils. I was dragged back to
a fellow soldier's memorial service in Vietnam ….

"'Because he loves me,' says the Lord, 'I will rescue him: I will rescue him; I
will protect him, for he acknowledges my name. He will call upon me, and I will
answer him; I will be with him in trouble, I will deliver him and honor him. With
long life will I satisfy him and show him my salvation…. for he who believeth in
me shall have everlasting life and shall never die…"

"Watch it! Watch the rear, motherfucker! Keep your head down, for Chrissakes! No, don't take his fucking arm with us! Look at it! You a fucking retard,
Watson? What good can it ever do the lieutenant in ya — duck! Get your fucking
ass over to the chopper now!"

"Jesus, Bill. You're shaking. Hands are sweating!"

"And now for weekly announcements. In case you haven't heard" — the dap-
per landlord- minister cleared his throat from behind the pulpit — "Boston has
been placed under martial law since last night."

A loud gasp echoed throughout the hall.

"Didn't know if you all had heard yet. Entrance to and exit out of the city has been virtually sealed off. It's in lock-down. A series of bombs were reportedly detonated by terrorists or hostile Mid-East governments."

Another gasp went up.

"Maybe this could've been divulged at a different place and time, yet I wanted to address it in today's sermon. Additionally, in case you also haven't heard, I'd like you to meet the gentleman on my right from the Massachusetts mosque, Imam" — I couldn't make out the name — "who's an honored guest from the diocese's interfaith initiative born in response to the accelerating international crisis. Please stand, Imam."

A loud murmur shot up to the ceiling. Not all approved of their liberal minister's 'initiative.' "Fucking raghead!" somebody spluttered in the rear. Some shook their heads; others simply stared disbelievingly. Mike wore a dead man's mask. The man was "the first Muslim cleric in over one hundred and eighty years to ever set foot inside here!" an elderly woman whispered in a sacrosanct tone. The wind shrieked, rattling the stained windows as if the Devil himself were outside trying to snake into the sanctuary. The air grew heavier with the burning candle wax.

Another hymn was sung by the tone-deaf assembly while the tiny imam humbly grabbed the trembling arm of an aged and semi-senile parishioner, mumbling and stumbling, and delicately led him to his seat. The sergeant's kid kept his mouth shut. Offering plates were passed around, and I plopped in a couple of bucks, not having noticed how much others had relieved themselves of, and Mike gave me a 'you-cheap-SOB' look. (I wasn't a member of the congregation, for crying out loud.) Overhead, even the multicolored glass image of Jesus and Mary seemed to stare in silent disapproval.

The minister stood up, leaning over and gripping his podium.

"The title of today's sermon is 'Do Not Be Anxious.' Let us not be anxious over what awaits us around the next corner in this life. For who knows what lies in store for us today, let alone tomorrow? Only the heavenly Father. It is written in Matthew 6:33: 'But seek first his kingdom and his righteousness, and all these things will be given to you as well. Therefore, do not worry about tomorrow, for tomorrow will worry about itself. Each day has enough trouble of its own.'" Chuckles resounded as a refrain along with collective "Amen's." "For in this world we are but dust and shadows."

"Dust and shadows," somebody repeated.

Without warning, a middle-aged man dressed like a deer hunter burst through the rear doors, inviting in an arctic blast. "I've got some bad news! The Waltons, Johnsons, and Fleishmanns are still missing from that sports event in Boston and presumed dead in a bombing and chemical attack that's left hundreds, if not thousands, dead." Mike fingered the keys to his Jeep. More icy blasts blew in and with them an unholy fear. The minister raised his arms in a bid to calm everyone.

The gentle-voiced imam stood up to face us. "As it is forever quoted in the Final Sermon in the Quran, 'Even as the fingers of the two hands are equal, so are human beings to one another. No one has any right, nor any preference to claim over another. You are brothers.'" His voice cracked. "Muslim, Christian, Jew. Descendants of Abraham all. We all pray to the same God in holy heaven above, and I am here today to pray with you for our salvation and the salvation of our beloved nation. May God protect her and her people in her hour of greatest need. In God, in Allah's, holy name." He bowed in our direction.

Several women and many men had collapsed on their knees to pray and were weeping softly. Others threw arms around one another, moaning and crying. An inkling of terror that seemed to move in synchronization with the shadows of flickering candlelight silhouetted against the walls crept into the collective consciousness of the assembly. Parishioners looked up at the luminescent Jesus and Mary and toward the preacher, even the imam, for some earthly consolation, a fervent sign of hope. I surveyed the scene. Incredibly, this 'fucking raghead' had ingratiated himself into the bosom of many in the crowd. Outside, the satanic winds were screaming from all directions. We thought the glass would shatter. And the doors remained open.

Chapter 10

"But I'm not so sure that Jackson's 'The Lottery' is in any real way a metaphor for the Holocaust. The character Mrs. Hutchinson doesn't appear to have any resemblance to ..."

"Get him out of this open rice paddy, Watson! What the hell is the matter with you? I gave you an order! Oh, my God! I'm shot! Shot in my chest. Jesus, help me, Bill ...."

"Dissertation deadline is May 15th. And, no, I don't think that a Reader-Response critique is apropos of Faulkner's 'Rose for Emily' under the circumstances. An adumbration of the first critic's analysis leads one to the following ...."

"Give the poor sonofabitch 'iz last rites. In this stinking hell-hole, he earned it ...."

"That's it, stick that needle right there, right behind his ear ...."

"William, I love you ...."

"In the name of the Father, the Son, and the Holy Ghost ...."

"Professore, Bookie — she's always start jelping as sooon as joo pool eento de driveway ...."

"May God receive you with open arms and grant you eternal rest ...."

"Petey says Ramirez and Leopold are scouring the area for ammo caches...."

"Project Sixty-seven; he won't remember any of it...."

"You're not my brother. You're a baby-killer!"

"Professor Watson. Professor Watson! When is our assignment due?"

"Huh?"

"Are you all right?"

"Ugh, yes." My elbow slipped over the edge of the lectern, pushing me off balance. "You were saying something about the Holocaust?"

"No time for a repetition of her analysis. We're out of class time," came a retort from the rear.

"We are?" I looked around the classroom. Few students had returned to Swenson after its president and Dean Rodgers had called for an unprecedented one-week hiatus. Now humbled, they sat bundled up in scarves and gloves and fidgeting, almost spastic, trying to keep warm in our unheated room. Save the administration building, the heat had been cut off because of dwindling oil supplies. A few months earlier, the campus, awash in the frivolities of youth and their parents' money, had resembled a miniature version of Princeton or Yale; overnight, it looked like something out of the Third World.

A husky male voice burst forth from the rear of the classroom: "Tyrone, I keep telling you, you're not transferring to any Division I school for your basketball career. It's over, man. Can't you see? Even the NBA has canceled some of its remaining games. The country's doomed. Better just go back and practice in the 'hood."

"You shut up! You just shut the hell up! I'm transferring this summer! America's going to climb out of this hole. To believe otherwise is a waste of the promise of who we are as Americans." Tyrone leaped at his philosopher-tormentor. Chairs were knocked over. Co-eds shrieked and squirmed. The male students looked on aghast, as though Swenson were too prestigious for anything like this to happen on campus. Tyrone threw a haymaker, missed wildly, lost his balance, and fell face-forward, crashing full force into the glass bookcase aligning the wall. Glass splattered over the floor. Tyrone's opponent went to punch him but slipped and was himself cut when landing on the floor.

I disabled Tyrone with a wrestler's headlock, and two muscular student-athletes I occasionally trained with in the school weight room managed to subdue his antagonist. I had never had an all-out fight in any class, except when I'd taught hand-to-hand combat to two slightly drunken Green Berets in 'Nam, and the memory of the fiasco brought tears of laughter to my eyes.

"You two hold him down for now," I ordered. The brawl, seemingly erupting over nothing, fast subsided, and soon the two raging scholar-beasts were shaking both their hands and bloody heads as though in wonder at what the hell had happened.

"No need to report anything to anybody," I said, half in nervous response to diffuse the tension and half in an attempt to head off administrative meddling. "It'll do nobody any good. I'll take care of the bookcase. Both of you get back to the dorm and put ice on those cuts, though you boys look pretty good to me." They cracked a wisp of a smile.

A co-ed, one of the more masculine and tough-talking feminists in the department, drew close to me, shaking. "Everyone's gotten so tense. I've never seen things happening like this before. My younger brother's been contacted by the Selective Service. Guards have taken over from the campus police and are being posted everywhere. There're rumors that the school's going to close down." Our eyes locked. In hers was abysmal fear. "I'm scared, Mr. Watson," and she put her trembling arms around me.

"I know," I whispered in her ear, softly kissing her forehead, "I know," apprehending that the words, my touch, were hardly enough. In another time, another place, the scene played out would be fecund grounds in academia to invite an immediate asinine sexual harassment investigation, but this was a different day. She was my student, damn it all. I hugged her preciously.

With the evaporation of tension and after cleaning up, I hurried toward the parking lot, passing by the latrines emitting a foul stench, reminding me that some maintenance workers were staying away. Rubbish was piling up, and faculty and students were told to make good use of extra toilet plungers bought in response to worsening developments. The women's latrine smelled worse, and I wondered if it wasn't some natural disinclination on their part to partake in such indelicate chores. That I had experienced unimaginatively far more sordid things in Southeast Asia than the intensifying malodor of human ordure was an understatement, yet it gave me no satisfaction in the soul to witness a new and soft generation depressed over prolonged exposure to nature's functions in the raw. I hopped down the stairwell leading to the lot. Fine, easy rain was blowing into the spacious and increasingly dirty vestibule.

"Whoa ... Hold it right there."

Some cornpone facsimile of a guardsman recently posted at the door entrance grabbed my arm and spun me around. "Let's see some ID." A youth of pimply complexion, short and of weak stature, he was relishing his role as government overseer. "You know the rules by now, big boy." He remained sneering and eye-balling me.

"I thought your rules were to check people coming in, not going out." I think my tone hinted at a tinge of the defiant, for his eyes narrowed, and he closed in and looked up at me, evincing something of a short man's complex.

"Rules are to do what you're told, dude."

I could have crushed him on the spot, notwithstanding his sidearm, but thought better of it, bit my lip, and backed off, ever-mindful of my position at the college. I dutifully handed over the ID. This appeared to appease him, and he eased into a sardonic half-smile.

"Thas better, Mr. Wadzun. You should know better by now than to question government authority, 'specially at your age," he said, shoving the card back into my hand. "Well, you be goin' now, yer hear. G'wan, git." He folded his arms over his chest.

I must have stood my ground momentarily too long for the whim of his newly designated authority because he shoved me through the door into the icy drizzle, and I almost stumbled down the stairs. I wheeled around. Raging, ready to pounce, I glared back up at him. The little snot-ass stood blocking the doorway, leering and sneering, daring the devil in me.

Witnesses to the stand-off were gathering under the rain at the edge of the vestibule as their passage remained obstructed by little Napoleon. It was a haunting reminder of my time in uniform when assorted goofballs I knew were given guns. I got in the car, disgusted, and drove off.

Mark presumably returned to work in Connecticut, Kimiko, to concentrating on graduate studies at Swenson more in an attempt, I divined, to divert creeping apprehension over her family's growing woes in Japan than toward completing degree requirements. Nationally and regionally, presidential and gubernatorial proclamations became more frequent, with Washington zeroing in on 'terrorist-leaning' Mid-Eastern countries and installing expanded curfews in major Ameri-can cities and Concord fingering, well, anybody from motorcycle gang members to 'political agitators' like Liberty Militia. The chemical attack in Boston proved false, not so the bombings. Springvale itself simmered. A presentiment of unstop-pable disaster crept over her greening hills.

***

"Whole friggin' town's fallin' apart." Leroy had phoned to remind me of this on my way to class. "Bridge over Babson's Creek almost washed out. Gotta be takin' a damned detour just to get Josh to school. Town hall's saying there's no money 'n no mo' money comin' in from the state to fix anythin'. Whole town's fallin' apart," he said again, as though repetition would ameliorate the mess or protect us from stirring an awakening nightmare. His voice grew excited.

"There's an emergency town hall meeting tonight at seven, Leroy. Unprecedented, old-timers are saying …. OK, you can pick me up at half-past…. Stop! Don't talk about that over a cell phone," I reminded him.

On our drive over to the town hall later that day, a sullen Leroy started in on the issue seething in his veins. While he attempted to mask his inner tumult, I nevertheless sensed his hurt. A hidden pothole jolted him out of his meditative state.

"Dunno, Will, what I'm gonna do. Wife's threatenin' to leave me. Wants to take Josh back to New York, tha' slimy pit. Him 'n me, we've grown so distant lately. Doesn't want to do anythin' together anymore. Not even spar, way we used to. Iz like I don't even know 'im or her anymore — while livin' under the same roof ta boot. Ya know" — he observed me with a mist welling up in his eye and bit on his lip — "just like me 'n my ol' man." He suddenly turned his gaze away and stared out the window. There was a long pause.

Half out of my own conflicting remembrances giving birth to a compelling sentiment to say something, though I had a Ph.D. in English, I found my mouth fumbling for words.

"Sometimes that's what happens between a father and his son. In the darkness of this world we can't see clearly. We can't seem to touch the other's soul in a loving bond, but only after the death of one of us does the darkness clear. Someday, he'll look back and see you clearly; he'll remember that you did your best for him. That you loved him as I know you do. Listen to your inner voice. Let it guide you. It'll never let you down. You'll know what you have to do. Listen to it. Only you can walk the path set out for you. Yet, in doing so, you'll not walk it alone. Your life is only yours. Live it as only you can and must. If you do this, come one fine day, at that moment of truth, you'll know you chose the right path. We're here."

As I went to step out of the vehicle, he sat there, slouched over the steering wheel for what felt like the longest time, staring out over the dashboard and contemplating an unsettled future. Then in the gentlest of voices through clenched jaws, he simply said, "Thank you, brother. I'll 'member that."

A faint gust of wind, barely perceptible, blew in the noxious stench of rotting garbage piled up off to the side exit of the building. It was slightly before seven; scores of townsfolk were filing in the narrow, mismatching entrance built after Crazyman Wilson had burned it down decades earlier. Inside, the air was laden with the anxiety of a community at the crossroads. An early-spring warm spell had hit the region; indoors, the hall was already growing hot and stuffy. And edgy.

"Your attention, please. Meeting will come to order. I said, meeting will come to order, dammit!" shouted the head selectman. Sounds of gavels exploding onstage resounded through the hall. Behind rickety tables adjoined like matchsticks sat the town's three selectmen begging the raucous crowd for order. Most of the Liberty Militia, at least those living in town, were there. An overhead wall light flickered intermittently, casting a morbid pallor over the assembly, while ceiling fans beat on lazily. Beads of sweat began trickling down my jaw. The tense-faced head selectman stood up and shouted over the congregation for a moment of silence in memory of those residents snuffed out by the Boston bombings. Obscenities rang out amid the silence.

"All right. This emergency meeting is now called to order," bellowed the head selectman again. "We're gathered here today in yet another call to deal with the crisis resulting in a breakdown of town services." A chorus of aahs and amens rose up. "Like cows trudging straight back to the barn at sunset, let me come straight to it. Town's broke. The board's calling for" — he paused to clear his throat, then continued in a louder voice — "an emergency tax levy." Folks stood goggling at one another. Stupefied. Some of them appeared not to know exactly what 'levy' meant in the context used and sought an explanation from others. Silence crept in like a nervous cat. The head selectman fidgeted. If his audience had been restless beforehand, the invocation of a 'tax levy' was the conduit that ignited the seething rage. The place exploded.

"Whadya mean, more tax levied, Miles? Like we told you before, damned near half the town's unemployed or about to be. And you talking about more taxes?" shouted a militia comrade.

"There's no provision in the town bylaws to levy taxes unilaterally — and the board knows it," yammered another, one of the women auxiliary members.

"The government's cutting back on Social Security benefits for Ch-Ch-Chrissakes; retirees in town can't make it on what they're getting as it is," stammered an old farmer.

"My mother has to sell off more acreage to those blood-sucking developers in Boston to make ends meet — and for how long?" chimed in a teenager.

The raucous refrain intensified.

The selectmen grew pale behind their tables. Something was hurled in their direction. Then something else. The crowd, morphing into a mob, surged forward. Leroy, face oozing sweat, mouthed words inaudible over the riotous crescendo. He tugged at my shirt, motioning for us to leave. The head selectman stood waving his arms over his head, pleading for order. A broken wooden chair leg struck him in the head, and he slumped over. Standing in the core of the swelling human tide, we were pushed forward, and I lost my footing. Leroy lunged forward and steadied me from the side. Scuffling broke out. Women screamed. Gunshots went off, resounding throughout the hall.

Sergeant Hines, in plainclothes, had fired to restore a semblance of sanity to the spreading madness. The gun smoke wafted my way. The mob quieted. Those surrounding the sergeant parted from him as though directed by magical incantation.

"Now listen up. This meeting is over. Y'all go home now, y'hear. C'mon. Let's get goin'." He waved the firearm overhead. Grumbling lingered in the rear. He pivoted to face any continuing confrontation. The hall became still. Hines motioned with his head for all to exit. Onstage the head selectman, recovered and relieved, fidgeted like a high school boy attacking a balky bra strap after the big prom. Not trying to push their own luck any longer, the remaining unscathed selectmen scurried to the backstage door. Almost before it had even begun, the meeting was over. Soaked in sweat, Leroy and I hurried for the side exit.

Like before, garbage-rot permeated the outside lot. Maggots crawled around the exit. Townspeople exiting the building froze. A huge low-flying helicopter roared by directly overhead, punctuating the quiet of the night. The nearby "swoosh, swoosh, swoosh" got louder, then faded behind the hilly pastures. The sounds bounced around deep inside my head.

***

Over the next few days, as temperatures rose, so did tempers. Increased military activity became evident. Helicopters flew by routinely. Government militiamen were becoming part of everyday activities and, whether authorized or not, insinuated themselves more into our private lives, even in a cow town like Springvale. We were still able to travel freely, unlike in big cities, where curfews were tightened. While oil production plummeted, gas prices skyrocketed at the pumps. Rationing was intensified. Guardsmen were placed at the pumps. Allegations of corruption in the form of payoffs to them to look the other way when rationing became rife. Fights broke out at the pumps and even at the food shelves, which had more relaxed restrictions. Indeed, there were several shootings. Yet policy toward guns and ammo was conflicting. Mark maintained it was deliberate. That way, he theorized, authorities could better cherry-pick whom they wanted to be charged. Though no longer meeting en masse, no Liberty Militia member had been charged that we knew of — yet. If chaos came creeping upon Springvale, it crashed down like a tsunami on rest of the country and the world.

World energy markets reeled. Oil supplies dwindled, at least the ones that remained available, pushing foreign armies to yearn for a fight. Dissension within CIA and National Security Council ranks over their intelligence assessments ruptured into public disagreements. Rumors abounded of imminent defections or resignations of the Joint Chiefs over pressure to get involved overseas; this, in turn, led to another assessment: difficulty in determining fact from its manipulation. Presumably, the US press was still uncensored; it became impossible to tell. The president made repeated proclamations about the 'terrorist-leaning' Mid-Eastern countries trying to attack us with multiplying 'sleeper cells'; few Americans remained convinced but rather believed his administration was rationalizing a power grab for foreign oil spigots. Honest beliefs became harder to delve into; paranoia among citizens deepened along with the unemployment lines.

Along with most professional sports schedules, and even the NCAA basketball tournament, Hollywood's Oscar night was abruptly canceled. It all left millions of celebrity-crazed Americans yowling for their tinsel fix. They begged for an escape from breathing in the nightmare. For many, it grew difficult to separate Hollywood virtual reality from real reality. Waking up to face a new day became increasingly painful.

People craved new and bigger heroes. Washington, perhaps even more so than Hollywood, was ever-eager to oblige. Or was there ever any real difference between the two? An internationally beloved hip-hop star was tragically killed in an entertainment industry feud. You would have thought Christ himself had been crucified all over again. The president took it upon himself personally to merge with our celebrity-gods at the funeral to plead on national TV for the hipster's countrymen to "lay differences aside, put the common good above that of the individual, and join hands as one people, one nation, to forge ahead, rise up and above the dire international situation." Or something like that. Coast-to-coast worship led by the president for the slain rapper. It led me to question evolving national realities myself — and common homestead realities shared between Kimiko and me....

Chapter 11

"Why is Mr. Mark not calling lately?"

"I thought he was coming up this weekend."

"I see." Ensconced in her favorite chair, her hands on her knees, Kimiko looked down mournfully. A deep, pensive gaze settled over and melted on her face, lit up by late-afternoon sunshine struggling through the kitchen lace curtains. "I see." She continued to look at the floor. "Sometime I wonder about him."

"'Sometime I wonder about him,' eh? What are you trying to say?"

She hesitated. "Why — what does he feel with you? It seem that he has some — how you say it?— core experience with you, almost like you two share common bond of two beings from another lifetime. You two share some kind of code, could be? Can't put my finger at it."

"Heh, heh. Better see Rodgers tomorrow to change your major to philosophy."

"Do not make joke of it." She slapped my hand, and then cradled it in hers. "About you, I worry, Will. Again, last night, that Night Demon come to us to share our bed. You scream in your jungle nightmare. But this time you cry out for Mercotti-san to save you. And something else. You speak of, scream of, something about needles and UFOs. What's secret? Why can't you tell me?"

I think there was a protracted silence. Not sure. I was too rocked from the words, encapsulated by the essence of the moment. Her words percolated in my mind.

"I can't say. I don't know what it is. I don't know. Maybe I'm too scared. Too scared of yesterday to live life today. Maybe I was never the man you thought I was all along. I'm sorry, Kimmy."

"No. Don't say that." She pressed a finger against my lip and then brushed away a tear from my eye. "You very special man, my only one. Only you," she purred, then wet her lips as a thick strand of her hair, the texture of black velvet, which always reminded me of the angel hair on my parents' Christmas tree, fell against my face. "I think I'm pregnant." She leaned forward, pressing her body into mine, and whispered, "Aishimasu, Will."

At that instant, the image of the afterglow of her face etched itself in the recesses of my mind. She leaned over me and sparked a thrilling magnetism within me with the indelibility of her kiss. Crystallizing moments of effervescent enchantment....

***

Back at Swenson, the spring term ground on. By Springvale standards, I was charmed: I still got paid. Sheila, from another lifetime, would be breathless. But, much to the disconsolation of the dean, my second scheduled presentation on William Blake was canceled owing to the shifting chaos. The country was collapsing, let alone the college and its host community, and the prig's life still orbited around academic presentations. I pretended to be undisturbed by his ostensible detachment from core realities and managed to stay clear of him. But it wasn't to be for long.

"I request your presence in my office, Dr. Watson," he said. I fell in step right behind him as I marched into the chamber for the first time in several weeks. Still dimly lit, the Tiffany lamp had been replaced by one with a more modern techno-design, looking weirdly out of place. Except for the little light, it felt like stepping into my battalion commander's office, though, strangely, this time as a peer rather than subordinate.

"Condolences over the Blake cancellation," he said. "I know you would have delivered it artfully." I nodded. "That's not what I called you in for, however. It's more indelicate, matters of mutual concern. It's about Ms. Tanimoto or, more apropos, her father's pledge to Swenson's endowment. It's all become problematic. He promised to make good on his pledge by now. We hear his business is in trouble."

"How do you know that?"

"My job at this time, Professor Watson, entails more than, shall we say, concern over literary seminars. You mean you didn't know of his situation?"

"I don't see her because of her daddy's long pockets."

"We have to do something to reverse the impasse."

"About 'we': I don't see there's any 'we' here."

"Then let me be more blunt. The president and I are aware of your little liaison, yet remain willing to overlook any such indiscretion in lieu of your, uhm, cooperation in the matter."

"What do you expect from me? To fly to Osaka, grab him by his kimono and turn him upside down to shake the yen free from his pants' pockets?"

"Don't get flippant with me, sir! I'll remind you that fucking one's department graduate teaching assistant is quite against college policy. Swenson's not Berkeley, Watson." He paused to let the message settle in. "You've quite a war record, so I hear — though few in academia care about such things — and are quite talented with your fists for an elderly gent. We heard about that little brawl of yours at Joe's greasy spoon around the holidays and your subsequent run-in with the campus militiaman. You do seem to have something of a problem with authority, hmm?" He paused. "You don't much care for me, do you? That much, I understand. Not that many are fond of me around here; that comes with the position. And that position demands immediate attention be paid to the college coffers."

He curled his mustache, tapped his fingers on his desk, as was his habit, and noted sarcastically, "Well, we have to do something. One quite ought to emphasize the utter gravity of the situation. The future of Swenson is at stake and, if I may be so impertinent, yours as well. We've never been in such a precarious financial position — ever. How well the college and the country can ride this thing out remains to be seen. You know, Dr. Watson, I must admit my first impression during your interview was a good one — and in a sense still is; however, to be just as frank, you weren't my first candidate choice. For sure, though, you're one of the most well-liked teachers we've ever had here. That said, I'm running late."

He leaned over toward me on his elbows and continued in a voice above a whisper: "Do remind yourself, Mr. Watson, of my recommendation. Do I make myself" — he paused, for some reason, looked up at the ceiling, then lowered his head and peered out over his glasses as he steadied his eyes on mine — "understood?"

"Perfectly."

"Splendid. Then I expect we shall remain cognizant of dovetailing expectations with our Ms. Tanimoto."

Robilas or Rodgers — the smell of collegial prigs bore down and wore on my consciousness, along with Mark's upcoming visit with its teasing promise of more secret disclosures and Kimmy's purported pregnancy. That Rodgers strained to pimp me became all the more amusing: Kimmy's father's business was kaput. And perhaps I did have a problem with authority.

***

It's been said few things are more tiresome than old veterans swapping bygone war stories and basking in their afterglow. On some intangible, microcosmic level Liberty Militia served as the pulse of leftover battle-scarred sensibilities of aging northern New England vets galvanized into action by the surging global crisis. The members had sensed what we were up against. A rendezvous of my cell was called for by Commander Richards and his deputy, Big Walt. Leroy, Petey, and the two leaders would travel individually to one of Old Jimmy's untorched barns on Springvale's outskirts. Mark, together with me, would drive out later. If travel arrangements intimated excessive circumspection, paranoia seemed the better part of valor.

"You know, I recall a story about a sergeant before a battle outside Da Nang likening his squad to jumpy rabbits when they learned recon hadn't cleared their advance. They were all massacred — including the sergeant. Is Liberty Militia marching down the same warpath?" Silhouetted against a full moon, Mark brushed back his ponytail. We steadied ourselves as we straddled a rusty barbed-wire fence encircling Jimmy's pasture and then walked through the muck while tiptoeing around piles of half-frozen smelly cow dung. The stench of pig shit coming from a distant pen was far worse. In the distance, a lonely white-tailed buck heard us and dashed over a borderline rock wall into the vast anonymity of the field's adjoining forest.

"What are you getting at?" I demanded.

"I was wondering…" His voice trailed off. A helicopter roared by to our right as a chilly gust blew the scent of Mark's cheap skin lotion my way. He then chose to remain silent on the topic of Liberty Militia, but not on UFOs.

"You know," he started, "don't know if you know, but there's been a wave of UFO sightings over the Capitol. Air Force and the Joint Chiefs are denying it, but — "

"No, I don't know," I interrupted half-sarcastically. His august proclamations, at times laden with a unique touch for enhancing the secretive, could scratch under the skin.

"What's the matter?" he countered. "Christ, any time I talk UFOs as of late, it's like you have some living nightmare about them."

"Now, how the hell did you know that?" I had him cornered. Thought I was going to unravel a long-hidden secret at last. He stammered but managed to spit out that Kimiko had told him so back at the house when I'd been out. He had me sandbagged. Again.

The outline of the small adjoining barn appeared over the horizon, its shiny metal covering atop the silo reflecting the moonlight. I laughed quietly as we came upon the charcoal remains of the larger razed structure, pondering what little refuge the isolated crumbling building could offer us. Mark appeared not to notice. We could make out several vehicles parked haphazardly and soon heard men's muffled voices pulsating with apprehension inside the ancient structure. Unknown to all, the meeting would catapult the demon spirit into motion. Words exchanged would freeze our fate and alter our destiny forever.

"Liberty and integrity."

"Liberty and integrity" came the echo from inside the crumbling barn. Light from kerosene lamps, slightly swaying from the wind blowing through cracks in the dilapidated foyer, cast eerie silhouettes that danced on the walls. The fluttering of wings, perhaps a vigilant barn owl rudely startled, came from the rafters. I must have winced at the stench of barn animal excrement seemingly everywhere, for a nervous Petey Hinson smirked and spat out, "City boy still, eh?"

"What do you have for us, Mark?" inquired Mike impatiently as he positioned himself atop an old bale of hay. His voice hinted at an apprehension as of yet unarticulated.

"Think this may be it; we could be headed for a showdown, boys." The rest of us looked at him, then at one another. "NRA has pretty much disbanded, too much infighting between the hierarchy to present any united front on gun rights, and I have it from Army contacts that militia members out West are about to be rounded up on charges of possessing supposedly superfluous armaments."

"Shit," mumbled Big Walt.

"That's right!" Mark shot back. "Listen" — he paused — "it'd be a good idea to centralize caching of all leftover weapons and ammo — immediately. Maybe give only knowledge of the location to Mike and Walt as commander and deputy commander, respectively, like need-to-know access to compartmentalized or segmented information in the military. Of course, as I'm not an official member, that's up to you. Now, in the international arena, media reports are censoring it, but Egypt has denied any responsibility for the attack on Israel and the ones on our oil refineries in Texas. Elements in the White House and the CIA are laying out plans for a retaliatory low-level tactical nuclear strike; the Chairman of the Joint Chiefs is said to be ready to resign over it. Looks like other DoD resignations are imminent. Some — "

"One minute," interrupted Mike. "We can get to any censored national news later. Been doing some digging of my own on local developments. Let me state from the get-go that Sergeant Hines has been relieved of jurisdictional command here because he's been perceived as too soft. He's been reassigned to shuffling papers in Concord state headquarters. Leopold has been appointed in his place, presumably by Hernandez, if that's his name. And that dean of yours, Bill, over at Swenson's been meeting regularly with them." How Richards knew of Rodgers' comings and goings while I didn't piqued my curiosity, and for an instant, I thought of myself as another airhead academic. Big Walt again muttered another obscenity.

"Yeah, I know," responded Mike to Walt's cursing. "And both Leopold and Hernandez have been to local libraries and bookstores checking on who's been reading up on what, and to sporting goods stores to pressure owners to rat on customers' weapons and ammo purchase habits since last year." Mike turned directly to Mark and let loose his bombshell: "I have reason to believe they're preparing a round-up, not only of guns and ammo — but of the Liberty Militia itself."

Leroy, unusually silent, froze while chewing his tobacco. The fluttering of the barn owl, or whatever it was, became obvious once again.

"That bastard Leopold!" shot out Petey Hinson. "Just like the traitor. God, I just pray to Jesus Christ himself that we'll be all right." He shook his head and jammed his fist into a nearby half-rotted barn beam. Any harder, and it would have collapsed the building. Overhead a singular lantern swung wildly as a result of Petey's outburst.

"So, what's your battle plan?" Mark began tentatively while addressing nobody in particular. "Stash the remaining arms and ammunition, destroy the purchase documents? You could do a break-in at the store for any hard-paper print-outs, and I can advise you how to erase any computer records. Computers are my business, remember?" He flashed that movie-star smile that would have softened the heart of Satan. "Of course, there's the problem of the government's computerized files; that can be dealt with as well, however. They're not as hack-proof as you might think, believe me. But the big thing to remember is that even New Hampshire has its fair share of snooping guardsmen and is infested with civilian informants."

Petey flinched. "First, we have to secure all firearms and ammo," Petey said. "I'm up to the task and willing to take the risk. Anything to keep Liberty's legacy secure from state or federal agents. Concord or Washington. Doesn't matter." One of Old Jimmy's hunting dogs could be heard yelping from the direction of his house.

"Noble gesture, Petey," somebody said.

"There's a potential glitch, however," Petey continued. "We've got my brother-in-law staying with us since his business was wiped out in the crisis. Fucking liberal! Can't be trusted. Listens to every phone conversation and eyeballs everything I do. Swear to Christ he'd like to peek at you inside the shitter. Some secret faggot or something. But — "

"I might be able to manage it," Leroy chimed in. "There's 'n ol' shed in back of my prop'ty. Petey, you 'n me could dig unner it. Dudn't know for sure, but should be big 'nuff."

"You OK with that, Leroy?" said Petey, leaning back against the wounded beam post. "I mean, you sure? Don't have to, you know. It'd be dangerous, but as long as no one else knows about it...."

"Sure. It'd be for Liberty Militia; it'd be for the liberty of 'merica. Besides, we could put tha' new Jeep of yours ta good use luggin' the stuff." Petey squirmed and laughed nervously.

"Let Walt and me think it over," Mike said. "But if it's all right with you, Leroy...."

The barking started up again, louder, then louder still with the incessant racket of others joining in the canine chorus. "Something could be going on. Maybe we'd better wrap things up. By the way" — Mike turned to address me — "remember the imam who visited my church earlier in the winter? Been carted off by the feds." "Not in the news, but happening to a whole bunch of them in Detroit," Mark jumped in. "Something to do with American-based Muslims' sympathies for that distribution of pathogens and the resulting epidemic on the border. The media kept it quiet for...." The rest became inaudible as Leroy grabbed my sleeve and shunted me aside.

"Will, need you to take Josh again for a day hike durin' the weekend. Have to talk to the wife alone 'bout what we're gonna do. Sensed it was comin' to this. Seems to be willin' to talk to you more 'n he does to me anyways." He continued hesitatingly. "Maybe ya can let me in on anythin' he knows 'bout what she's schemin' to do. Think ya can help a brother out? Y'know, Will, you're the only real friend I got here. Don't let me down."

I smiled, at least, I think I did.

***

As the weekend crept closer, so did the attendant troubles — in multitudes. Not that I could differentiate any longer between weekends and working weekdays; there was scarcely any work to do at the college anymore. Classes were sporadic, though I still picked up a paycheck — half of what it had been earlier in the term — made little difference. Commercially prepared food and supplies of basic necessities shriveled. The economic system barely functioned. The dean kept riding me about 'Mr. Tanimoto's promised pledge,' and journeying downtown, let alone anywhere outside of Springvale, could be trekking through a minefield. Assaults and break-ins, especially at commercial establishments, became more commonplace. Guardsmen did what they could to maintain order. Futilely. Perhaps there weren't enough of them. I shuddered to think of the eruption and panic in the cities. The media all downplayed it. I carried a well-hidden lethal martial arts device whenever I ventured downtown, even to Joe's Diner. The novelty of its misleadingly benign design was truly amazing, and I would slide into a titter from time to time over how deceptively innocuous it was. It could kill a man within seconds. I grew worried that I would have to use it.

With snoopy and unpredictable guardsmen everywhere, I dared not pack the Colt .45. In contrast to the handgun's lethal steel and what it represented as the ultimate arbiter during the social upheaval, a gentle Kimmy would routinely send me off to class with a line from William Blake: "For you now must 'hold infinity in the palm of your hand' — not gun," as if the survivalist choice was guns or poetry. I failed to find the admonition amusing after attacks increased in frequency and viciousness, especially one that week against an elderly neighbor. While walking home, she was mercilessly set upon and clubbed by presumably local thugs. Hadn't so much as money or valuables on her person — the SOBs. The outrage hit home. Senseless violence was always imminent, and I guarded Kimmy zealously. Her family kept pressing her to return to Japan, yet the worldwide crisis had now rendered ordinary international travel a pipe dream.

While Kimmy and I became as close as lips and teeth, the level of relationship Mark and I shared deepened to one of combat brothers catalyzed by the enveloping miasma of political developments swirling uncontrollably. His uncanny sense for continued concealment of military secrets could pluck an unsympathetic chord, yet I came to rely on him more in a myriad of ways, as he did me. I remained clueless about where this was all headed at the time; in a sense, it didn't matter. As during the fall, he came up often from his job in Connecticut, in part, I surmised because, with the economic dysfunction, he was relegated to part-time employment and had no other place to visit or activity to accomplish. He served as Kimmy's bodyguard while I was at Swenson or otherwise occupied; for that, I remained immensely grateful.

By Easter, he had grown to be something of a familiar figure in Springvale and, in his inimitable manner, projected the aura of a man who at once could be counted on but not disrespected. Mark's subtle and confident peremptory ego proved attractive to both women and men alike, while his striking good looks would unfailingly attract the ladies. Even as intractable a teen as Josh Morton had relished his company, and I suspected his father subconsciously wished his boy to spend more time with this modern-day Adonis than with one uninspiring liberal arts professor. Yet I had relented at our recent barn rendezvous to Leroy's request, as I always did, and Josh was again at my house door that gray, dismal weekend.

"Konnichiwa," said Kimmy, upon spotting Josh's lanky physique ambling toward the front door. She bowed slightly at the hip, and I found it odd she would do so to an overgrown yet still young adolescent, given her extended stay in the US, her kneejerk reaction notwithstanding. "No shee long time. How have you been? Come in. Excuse me now. On phone with family."

"Hey, big fella. Now will you look at this?" Mark violently lurched forward and wildly seized Josh's bicep, exposing it for all to leer at before the embarrassed teen could react. "Lookin' like a winner! Been training with your dad we see, hmm?"

"Nawh." Like a bug pinned under a microscope, the lad twitched and twittered while he stood staring at the entrance door.

"All right. We'd better be going," I interjected, recalling my own awkward days of youth. "Getting late for hiking. Ready, Mark?" I furtively squeezed Kimmy's hand, gave her a weak peck on the cheek and an insipid good-bye, a graying prof still acting like a geeky teenager too timid to express public affection.

The three of us took off in the direction of Babson's Creek. What little was spoken was of that and this, things of no real consequence, uttered neither with excitement nor conviction, for I sensed reserve in Josh's voice because of his worsening family affairs. By the time we arrived at the base of the creek, owing to Mark's gift for soothing the ruffled feathers of others, Josh had lowered his defenses and was talking animatedly, at times with a distinctive maturity beyond the ordinary expectations of his years.

"Are you convinced the Islamic Alliance has held true to their word that they had nothing to do with the sabotage of the Texas oil fields or the slaughter at Haifa?" Josh ignored me to look intently in the direction of Mark, slightly winded from our short ascent up the muddy mountain trail. "Deny, deny, deny. It's said that's been their stratagem since the ascension of their new leader."

Mark chortled. "Since when have you started using words like 'ascension' and 'stratagem' at your grade level, Shakespeare?"

"Contrary to what you may read in the media or hear, we're not all a bunch of semi-illiterates with our thumbs stuck up our ass in the public school system these days," Josh shot back defiantly, sneering.

"Whoa! Hear that, Billy Boy? Should we be impressed with this young lad or what? Chip off Dad's block, eh?"

"C'mon! You know full well that my dad was never any scholastic whiz. Can't read the ingredients off a Cracker Jack box. Just because he's not here, don't rub it into the guy."

"OK, kiddo." Mark slapped the kid upside the head. Josh grinned, knowing he'd gotten the better of a man more than twice his age. "You know we respect him."

We came upon the first rapids. Late-afternoon sunlight hit the water as it crashed down over the rocks and into the streambed swollen from recent spring rains, creating a churning mosaic of silvery white. Upstream lay Josh's favorite spot, the most tranquil of Babson Rapids. We would rest there.

"My dogs are killing me," said Mark as he squatted on a wet log and caught the gentle spray of water roaring over the rock face. Josh appeared puzzled by the expression. "What is it? Don't get it? Bill, maybe this boy's not as smart as we thought he was." Mark giggled.

"Easy on our young champ."

"So, what's cooking at home, Josh?" Mark asked. While on the surface, the words were uttered with an air of flippancy, Josh divined their subterranean intent. He paused to look down at his muddy boots, kicked a rock into the creek, and began tentatively.

"You mean you want to know if my folks are splitting up and if we're staying in Springvale?"

"No, I, uh — well, all right. What's happening?"

"Not sure. They're probably fighting about it as we speak. Suspect that's why my dad wanted me to hang out with you two guys today, huh?" He threw a side glance my way. Mark tittered; I probably did as well. "My mom seems determined to return to New York, taking me with her, leaving him behind to wallow in this 'redneck cow-shit town,' as she puts it. But that's their problem, I guess. So I don't know 'What's happening?'" He looked away from us, his eyes welling with tears.

"I'm sorry," said Mark.

"Nothing to be sorry about. 'And that's the way it is,' as that TV newscaster used to say back in your dinosaur days."

Silence weighed in. All that was heard was the wind whistling through the treetops.

"Still sorry anyways," Mark finally broke in, partnered with keen embarrassment. He looked more crestfallen than Josh, and if not for the solemnity the revelation occasioned, I would have laughed. "I know how it feels to be disengaged from one's parents, especially one's father," he continued, hanging his head.

"My dad, he doesn't care."

"You might not realize it now, but he cares for you, Josh. Believe me, he does. I tell you I know it — in my heart," I said.

"My father doesn't give a shit about me!"

I slammed him into a tree, bouncing his skull off the trunk with a distinct thud. He froze, horrified. "Don't speak of your old man that way! One day today's fog will clear; then, you'll see that he loves you. Loved you all along. Always did." He braced himself against a rock, trembling. "I'm sorry."

Nobody made a sound — neither mouth nor movement. And so, we remained there nestled in our respective perches like three dodos, lost in the sound of the churning waters echoing in our heads, the ravine our eternal confidant and refuge.

"Starting to rain," Mark broke in finally while getting up, though it already had been drizzling for several minutes. "Better be going. Devoured enough truth for one day." He eked out the slimmest of smiles and threw out a twisted look at me and then at Josh, who remained seated as though frozen into his muddy roost. "Whaddya say, kiddo?" he asked gently, putting a self-assuring hand on the boy's shoulder. "Whatever's going to happen is going to happen. We can't alter fate. Let's not choke on it."

Mark stood there, powerful, hulking over him. The boy, outwardly paralyzed, gazed up into the skies out past the clamoring gorge, alive with the reborn wonders of spring and into the infinite. In the next instant, I caught a fleeting glimpse of a hawk soaring over the swaying treetops arching over the ravine, and in some inexplicable way, it made me wonder what I'd be doing with my life if I were back at Wedgemont in Maria's house. "We'd better be heading back," I said.

Back at the Morton's, Leroy was nowhere in sight. His wife rushed to the door to reclaim their son with her usual hangdog look. She seemed flustered, almost disoriented. "C'mon in, boy," she snapped in a matronly tone while throwing a custodial arm around Josh and edging herself in between him and his surrogate dads for the day.

"Josh had a great time," I said.

"Oh, he did, did he?" She continued wearing her usual hostile expression no matter what we said.

"Boy's gonna be a winner!" Mark blurted out inauspiciously.

"Tssh," she snarled. Mark appeared as much at ease as the pope at an abortion rally. She turned to close the door, eyed us still blocking the doorway, and then swiveled around to confront us. "Well, what do ya want?"

"We'd like to see Leroy." I contemplated whether to slap her or bust out laughing, then grinned to diffuse the tension. She saw through it.

"What 'bout? He ain't home!"

Josh stood gawking and taking it all in from behind his mother.

I grew suspicious; noise came from inside. "Then who else is home?"

"What you mean 'who's home'? I said he ain't here," she responded indignantly. Leroy appeared suddenly behind her, agitated. She tried to slam the door. Leroy straight-armed his fist into it, as though returning to Golden Gloves competition, infuriating her. "Why you wanna hang with honkies? Why? 'Cause they educated and you ain't? Y'know y'kin go back to New York and be with brothers a'gin. These people not gonna do nothin' for us. What white people ever do for you, dumb nigger?"

Leroy let loose with a vicious backhand, bouncing his wife off the doorsill with a ferocious 'thunk.' Josh winced but stayed back. She staggered, punch-drunk-like, then fell again onto the doorsill but managed to regain her footing and slide up against the door wearing a welt and a defiant grin, giving the impression they had done this dance before. "White folks' nigger."

I tired of her Afro-racist rant. Thoughts of Police Chief Bull Conners blocking off doorways to black Americans during the Civil Rights era, police dogs and high-pressure water hoses, Martin Luther King, Jr., and Malcolm X all danced in my head. Try as I did to remain empathetic; it wasn't easy. Leroy, unshaken and sure of himself in the rightness of his response, never uttered a word. Didn't have to. We knew to call upon him later. Mark was already halfway across the lawn when I turned to follow.

Hiking home under starless skies, we heard the wailing of sirens from the direction of downtown Springvale. By the time we arrived at my doorstep, excited voices over mobile loudspeakers had chimed in and reverberated over the rolling hills, ordering all indoors to await emergency government broadcasts. Kimmy was waiting nervously under the glare of the porch light.

"Where you've been? Waited too long. Too much worry. Hurry inside. Come on, hurry, will you? Why drag feet?" She got behind Mark and me and gently pushed us inside while staring over her shoulder into the dark as if searching for a ghost lurking under the veranda steps. "Announcement came all this afternoon." She pointed to the TV set, then disappeared into the kitchen, yet instantly returned carrying her tiny tea tray. A printed message glided over the bottom of the screen: "This is a previously taped announcement from the Pentagon War Room from the United States Army Chief of Staff...." Then came the authoritative voice of a dour uniformed officer seated behind an oversized and plain desk. The United States flag was featured prominently to his side.

"Good evening, ladies and gentlemen, fellow citizens of the United States. On behalf of the president, I hereby inform you that, as I speak, your military, under orders from your government, is engaged in low-level and regionally contained hostile actions focused in the Middle East. This action is designed to contain recent developments in that area and in our own country, namely terrorism, sabotage of oil pipelines, and sowing of extreme violence and discord. These recent developments are a scourge to all Americans and freedom-loving peoples everywhere. They cannot and will not be tolerated. Effective Monday, tomorrow, all able-bodied males ages eighteen to twenty-seven, excluding those currently enrolled full-time in bona fide post-secondary educational institutions, are now ordered to report ASAP to their local Selective Service Centers. Specific instructions will follow this message on a state-by-state basis. Your cooperation in these matters, and in all national and state matters pursuant to this nationwide emergency announcement, is ordered effective immediately under penalty of law. Further notices from this office will be forthcoming. There is no reason for panic. The situation remains under control under the direction of your United States military forces. God bless our fighting troops; God bless you; God bless our United States of America."

Mark and I sat silently, mesmerized, sipping on Kimmy's tea. Later we would argue over why that particular admonition and subsequent ones had emanated from the general's 'War Room' and not the Oval Office.

"Mr. Leroy, he called. Said that matter spoken of between him and Petey-san at Jimmy's barn is under control. Said you would understand. Must keep discreet over public phone line, hmm?"

"Thank you."

"No problem. Oh, almost forget. Dean Rodgers-san, he called. Wants to know how you are doing with the problem he said you two discussed in office." Reverently cradling her teacup, Kimmy softly blew away its steaming vapor. She looked distant. "But what problem you have with him? You never spoke of problem."

"Nothing, really. It's nothing at all." Along with the tea, the sheer simplicity of the remark must have absorbed any nascent curiosity of hers because soon it was glossed over by the ensuing newscasts. Not so with me. He had now started badgering me about 'the problem' in my own home. The confrontation clock ticked on for me....

... as it did for others. Over the following days, we witnessed the guardsmen appear at doorsteps unannounced and force their way in, searching for youths who hadn't heeded the general's Selective Service proclamation and anything else deemed 'of interest.' They grew bolder in brutality and intent. They came to our schools; they came to our neighbors; they came to our homes. Trooper Leopold came with them — or with Special Agent Ramirez-Hernandez. The bastards. A few objected forcibly to the intruders and were beaten on the spot or presumably hauled away to the makeshift detention centers rumored to be hurriedly built in remote areas. This detail was again supplied by Mark, its accuracy impossible to ascertain. Government warnings were broadcast daily now, increasingly from military rather than civilian offices. Paranoia edged yet upward a notch; few in Springvale spoke openly of growing repression with the exception of a few 'hotheads' from Liberty Militia. And those at Swenson College....

"Agent Hernandez, come here and take a look at this."

I was watching at a distance from inside our dirty, barely functioning student center. It was Trooper Leopold strutting around from table to table, nightstick in hand, inspecting student IDs and records, looking for anyone running afoul of the recent government edict on conscription. The college had a decent share of part-time students. Ostensibly, he was looking for the part-timers passing themselves off as full-time. It was doubtful the college would cooperate fully and risk even more student withdrawals; in fact, scuttlebutt had it the administration quietly cultivated Hernandez' acquiescence to look the other way in exchange for cooperation on the other, still more pressing matters. Perhaps there was a secret agreement between Hernandez and Rodgers. According to Kimmy, the registrar most likely had altered records to make the difference in status virtually indecipherable, save for the 'secret file.' Of course, if true, it would constitute an egregious violation in and of itself, but it was either that or shut down the store. How much longer Swenson could hold out was anybody's guess. Besides, rumors abounded that other schools, from Harvard to Podunk community colleges, were up to the same ruse. It all engendered scathing campus resentment for the authorities, usually muted, though not always.

"Get your hands off of her!" said a student inside the campus center.

"Steady, sonny." It was Trooper Leopold.

"Don't you 'sonny' me, you son of a bitch!"

"Now, don't go and do something you're bound to regret." Leopold had backed off a tad yet sustained his glare directed at the young man, as was his wont. Other students mingling on the floor, maybe a dozen of them, feigned nonchalance, fearing too strong a reaction on their part would bring uninvited scrutiny into their own affairs. Hernandez, leaving nothing to chance, turned his back to his subordinate with handgun holstered but at the ready and with cool detachment took in the room, waiting for signs of mobilizing opposition. Not that it could have mattered much: more armed guardsmen were standing at the doors. "College ID and newly issued government PDIF. Now. Put your hands on the table where I can see them, son…. C'mon, move! You're wasting my partner's and my time."

"Fuck you and your asshole partner — or is it your partner's asshole? Or both your fucking assholes? Big little man with a badge. I — we don't have to take this shit anymore. We're getting out of here. Let's go, Maria." The student, clean-cut and good-looking, jumped to his feet, accidentally spilling his coffee on the trooper's trousers. Leopold looked aghast at the stain, then glanced around the center to assure himself he had an audience, and in one final split second, jerked his stick overhead and smashed it down with a loud crack full force over the arm that had besmirched his uniform. The kid collapsed to the floor, writhing in silent agony like a dismembered snake. His girl sat bug-eyed, paralyzed with horror; the onlookers appeared sickened. Even Hernandez recoiled. There wasn't a speck of blood, yet we knew he was hurt. Bad. The arm, in short sleeves, looked broken.

"Don't ever question my authority again, uh, son," the trooper, teeth bared, snarled, half at the figure still prostrate in front of him and half for the others to hear. "Now, are we going to see those documents?" he shouted to all except his would-be confronter, still squirming on the pavement.

The Little Leopard had spotted me from the edge of his eye. And he grinned.

***

Late next morning, Kimmy anxiously called from school, saying she was coming home early with "something big to share." Mark had convinced me to prepare a hermetically sealed pathogen-free and fully-stocked 'Doomsday' room in the un-used apartment basement "just in case," as many Israelis had done in the Persian Gulf War. We were in the living room, downing an early beer and discussing sur-vivalist home preparations when she ran through the door. She must have been surprised to see him still there because she gingerly broached the "something big" topic by taking me aside to say that Rodgers had accosted her in the TAs' room over her father's aborted pledge. He had also complimented me to her on my fine work, welcomed my return again in the fall — yet had secretly approved my dis-missal notice. The latter revelation, she confided, though didn't say how she had come across surreptitiously. Kimmy was always adroit at that. She handed me a photostatic copy of the dismissal.

"He is very good at back-stabbing, no? Koumon. Like in Greek mythology, he is the Janus-face man. And then he still expect my father's fortune to go to Swen-son? I see. But my father's business is dead as — how you say?— hangnail."

Mark, feigning preoccupation, reflexively cupped his mouth to squelch a guf-faw. 'Hangnail' may have been hilarious; the rest was not. So I'd been shit-canned. The fact struck Mark belatedly, and he immediately proffered condolences.

Within the hour, I was racing across the campus square, now long overgrown with unmowed grass and strewn with trash. Fighter jets streaked overhead toward the Atlantic to the east.

I jolted past the public latrines at the administration building entrance. Curiously, the stench didn't overpower passersby like before. Maybe it had something to do with senior staff offices being situated nearby, I thought — perks of power — to be able to insulate yourself from the reek of human dung.

I scrambled up the clean, swept stairs. At the top of the staircase, the secretary, witnessing my frenzied advance, stepped forward to intercept me. "Whoa…. Stop right there! You can't go into his office just like that! What the devil's gotten into you? He's inside with…."

I bolted through the door. Rodgers shot to his feet. "Oh, Professor Watson, it's you. You'll excuse me, but I'm in consultation with Ms. —"

"I know who she is."

"Do you need any further assistance in there, Dr. Rodgers?" inquired the secretary in a near-reverent tone.

"No, no… uh, that's quite all right. Everything's fine, thank you. You may exit. Oh — and close the door behind you, please."

"Yes, sir."

"So, Dr. Watson, what brings you rushing in here with such utter impetuosity, hmm?" He locked his arms over his chest, leaning back against the chair while peeking over his glasses, then fidgeted with his bow tie. "If this is about the issue we last discussed in private, rest assured, I've full confidence in you; however, my immediate attention must be given to" — he gestured to his visitor — "and —"

"Cut your bullshit, Adam. It's not becoming of a man with integrity. As if you ever had any."

"Uh — I'll think I'll be going now," the young woman stammered, then violently lunged for her valise and ran.

"Wait — " Like a worn-out statue suddenly animated, Rodgers lifted his hand in an anemic gesture for her to stay, as though the woman could tender protection in the standoff. He shifted his eyes nervously toward mine. "So, what do I owe the honor, the courtesy of your — "

"Sit down and shut up."

" — your visita-tation?"

"Sit down!"

While fumbling for his chair, he stumbled into it.

"I'm tired of your pimping, Rodgers. It's gone on long enough."

"'Pimping'? 'Pimping'? Now see here, what in a bloody day makes you say that?"

"You've been raking me and Kimmy — Ms. Tanimoto — over the bonfire too long to shake loose her old man's money tree. His business empire has gone belly-up."

"'Belly-up'?"

"He's broke."

"'Broke'?" he repeated, still stunned, not altogether comprehending the magnitude of the news.

"That's right."

"Well, I'm sorry if I…."

"It's over, Dean. And I guess I am too, hmm?"

"Wha-What do you mean?"

"This." I hurled the dismissal notice in his face.

"'This'? What's this?" Slowly, his fingers unraveled the crumpled sheet. "Where'd you get this?" he demanded.

"Doesn't really matter any longer, does it?"

"Yes, well, it's…. Oh, drat." The poor SOB collapsed over the desk, burying his head in his hands, almost crunching his glasses and knocking his omnipresent pipe to the floor. I turned to leave. Suddenly, I noticed a never-seen-before bald spot peeking out from behind his bouffant hairdo and almost laughed.

The young woman had left the door open. A small crowd, including the president, stood gawking. The secretary, smothering a smile, approached. "Way to go, Will! Such a splendid performance," she whispered in a mocking tone. I knew that in all probability my career was over. Certainly, at Swenson. Most likely elsewhere. Finished. And I didn't give a damn.

But Kimmy did. We dickered over selling her beloved Mercedes, long concealed from public view and over 'the Janus-face man.' She was glad somebody at long last had stood up to this pompous poof and told him off (Rodgers was despised by all on campus), yet she fretted I would inflame him even more so and sabotage any possibility of the dismissal being overturned. (Rumors floated that the president thought the office incident hilarious.) The thorn of vengeance had rooted itself in Kimmy's heart, nurtured by the dean's calculated treachery. "Koumon!" she spat out, remaining silent-tongued but unembarrassed when queried as to its meaning and revealing fractured glimpses of a hidden side of her character I had never experienced.

"That man." She sat staring at the floor. "He has audacity — and no code."

"Uh-huh."

"Hear of this before dismissal?"

"Of what?"

"Of him trying to chop down my father's money tree for Swenson?"

"First time."

"I see…. Koumon."

***

Soon matters of immediacy would pull me back to the present, and I found myself back at Joe's Diner in my favorite booth seated alongside Mark and opposite Leroy with the usual, albeit dwindling, lunchtime crowd.

"You don't have to get involved with this stashing and caching of Liberty's arms and ammo, Leroy," Mark said. "You're not in the militia hierarchy." He paused. "You thought out the risks?"

"It's for — "

"It's for this; it's for that. Leroy, just think about it first. Think about it thoroughly."

"I have."

Leroy's steadfastness of purpose stood solid. Suddenly, Mark and I noticed his face light up. Amid the clamor of the TV, tuned in to emergency broadcasts, and Mabel barking customers' orders to Joe working the grill, striding toward the cash register was a long-unseen yet familiar figure: Larry. "Easy now," Mark blurted out to Leroy. Leroy tensed up, readying for the worst. Larry, in turn, spotted us and strode toward our booth, smiling. Leroy still braced himself.

"Hello, fellows. How's Liberty?"

"You know, ol' liberty and integrity," Mark mumbled, barely audible.

"'Liberty and integrity,' huh?"

"Yeah, liberty and integrity."

"I see." Larry stared straight-on at Leroy. "How you doing, Leroy?"

Leroy remained stuck in his booth and his silence. Larry saw it was no use.

"Just trying to be friendly, fellows." Larry grinned. "Well, guess I better be going, seeing y'all not very conversational this fine mornin', eh?"

"Guess you better be." Behind Larry, manifesting like a phantom, stood Sergeant Hines. Larry turned around. He didn't wait for a second request.

"Morning, Sergeant," I said. "Have a seat."

"I'd avoid him," the sergeant said, with a reverential nod to Larry walking out of the vestibule, as Hines eased his frame into the booth alongside Leroy. "And I'd avoid Leopold, too, if I was you."

"What do you mean?"

"Look, I know I shouldn't be saying this, but Leopold has taken over effective command of the region — "

"That right? We didn't know."

" — and he's up to no good."

"How's that?"

"He's up to no good," the sergeant repeated, deflecting the inquiry. He eyed me. "You know, I never did care much for professors after my first and only year in college out of the Navy."

"Well, we're not all that bad."

"Think so?" The sergeant lapsed into an abbreviated smile. "Covered up your excessive-force assault of Tiny here at the diner around the holidays for you, Watson. Wasn't Leopold, you know. Tiny's a bum." The smile deepened. "Just for your information."

"Thanks. I suspected that."

"I know you did." The suggestiveness of the remark intrigued me.

Protracted silence crept over our booth like early-morning clouds over the nearby White Mountains. There we sat. Like four dummies. Leroy cradled his coffee cup in ebony-hued hands, deftly breathing in its aroma; Mark tugged at his gold earring, perched his chin in the palm of his hand, and gazed out the window at the incoming drizzle. And I looked at Sergeant Hines biting into his lip, unblinking, staring into the empty section of the tabletop in front of him as I thought how stupid we must have looked....

The sergeant came alive. "Leroy." He leaned back so as to look at him full-square. "You've got a good son there in Josh. He stood up to my boy's bully at school." He paused. "Wish that my kid had stood up for himself, though." He snorted. "Shhh...." Leroy nodded. "You know, I, uh, I.... Look, I know you men might not believe this, but I just want you to know that I think, well, I think that what Liberty Militia is doing — has done — is pretty damned good for the community, instilling patriotic values 'n all. I know that we've had our differences in the past, but you've got to consider my position as local badge man. It ain't easy, that is, to straddle both sides of the farm's fence, if you know what I mean."

"Much appreciated," uttered Mark. And I thought his remark odd since Mark wasn't even an official member. Leroy continued sipping on his coffee, more to wet his lips than to drink.

"There's something else I want you boys to know." The trooper's voice grew clear and strong. "There's reason to believe — I've reason to believe — Leopold might be trying to initiate some stakeout, some setup, of your militia, most likely with the FBI. I'm telling you this on the q.t." (I must've smirked, for they all looked up and at me. Hadn't heard that expression in a long time. Seemed odd coming from him.) "Watson?"

"Nothing."

"Well, I'm telling you honestly, sincerely: Watch your back! He's up to something, he is."

"OK, thanks." It happened to be Mark. Again. (Is it that Leroy and I lack graciousness? I thought to myself.) "We'll keep that in mind, won't we, fellas?" Leroy and I nodded as Leroy motioned Mabel over for a refill. "Good."

"Well, then, that's a wrap. Got to get back to headquarters in Concord. Paper shuffler now. Leopold's our new badge boy." He smirked. The sergeant threw his legs into the aisle in front of Mabel, who was clearly annoyed as she hunched over our booth, coffee pot in hand. "And by the way, let's keep in touch on this one." His voice echoed a certain earnestness. "You take care of Josh, Leroy, ya hear?" We watched him amble down the aisle, not in any rush to assume his new responsibilities in Concord. Dodging customers at the cash register, he headed toward the exit, tipped his hat to Joe, mopping up a ketchup stain, and made his way out the door.

"Shit," Mark muttered.

"Something's coming down on us. Sense it in my craw, like my granddaddy used to say," said Leroy. Fumbling with his coffee cup, he pointed to the fence line at the edge of the town commons, where a lone moose and her calf stood grazing in the distance under a wisp of a cloud. They had been seen in the spot regularly during the spring, and he nonchalantly mentioned how remarkable it was they had not yet been shot. I first thought the remark callous, but considering how often he spoke of 'the slimy shoot-'em-up streets of the Bronx' where he had lived, soon thought otherwise and wondered how much his life had changed, as had my own, since moving to Springvale. He would often speak, titter really, of how, upon first coming up to New Hampshire, his wife and Josh had mistaken a moose for a deer, yet secretly confessed to Mark and me that he, too, had been guilty of worse Big City Boy gaffes. Though I hadn't realized it earlier, we had grown close, perhaps too much so, and, once again, he and Mark served as the brothers I'd never had. If you'd observed Leroy and me, you'd intuit nothing in common: neither race nor physique, education nor upbringing. Didn't matter. As with Mark and me, our future had been thrust upon us by unforgiving circumstances, our destinies now interlocked forever. For the longest time, I studied Leroy's eyes, tired and bereft of emotion, and a foreboding inside me, couldn't say precisely why or what, told me tomorrow the devil was ready to dance.

Mark, edgy, was fidgeting with his gold earring with one hand, stained coffee spoon in the other. "You fellas paying attention to that?" He signaled to the TV above Joe's cash register, remarking that there appeared to be a split in US foreign policy, mispronouncing 'schism' as 'chism.' A National Emergency News Bulletin was streaming across the bottom of the screen: "Egypt's dictator likely toppled in military coup.... US breaking with UK in strategy to address rising tensions in Middle East.... US government divided? State Department and Department of Defense apparently at odds over recent developments.... Congress being called into emergency session…. White House appealing for calm and cooperation among all parties involved…. Live announcement from Washington to air shortly." News reporters armed with microphones and cameras were shown rushing across the White House lawn.

Joe, still gripping his mop while leaning across the cash register, leered into the set, unblinking, then coolly surveyed oblivious customers and shook his head, mumbling something about "folks won't give a shit about what's happening unless somebody takes one in their own backyard, maybe not even then. Jesus Christ." Mark smirked.

A local station affiliate next zoomed in on an ongoing Harvard University Square riot. Dozens of student demonstrators were being clubbed and tear-gassed by guardsmen, precisely over what, it was impossible to determine since the scene had grabbed the attention of the diner's patrons, who drowned out the reporters' commentary with their wisecracking about Swenson students.

"Ha! They should do that to our local college brats!"

"You mean 'rats'?"

"No, I mean brats — er, bratty rats." They roared.

I mulled over their 'jokes.' But not for long. I sprang from the booth and all but ran to confront them. The creeps squirmed in their seats and grew pale. They knew I taught at the college. Mark, shaken, was just as quick to follow. He twisted my arm behind my back and violently shoved me back into my seat.

"Never saw you like that. What's gotten into you, anyways?" Leroy, too, tensed up, bug-eyed.

"Listen, no one talks about my students like that…. OK, sorry. Then, second thought, I'm not." The three of us sat there, grinning. We looked back at the loudmouths. They saw us and made a line for the exit, grousing about "gun and run Liberty Militia cowboys," and hurried out to the parking lot. The sweet smell of Joe's special baklava dish that he often cooked up that time of day, ridiculously exotic for a cow town like Springvale, wafted our way. Mark's nostrils flared, and he beckoned Mabel for a slice. Over a misty horizon, the moose and her calf had vanished.

Leroy's empty eyes came alive. He stuck his tongue under his lower lip, puffing out his lower jaw: "I wanna — how d'ya say it?— cache the militia's ammo 'n arms. Git it done wit'. We gotta keep the stuff safe, y'know. No more time to waste. I take responsibility. I'll git it done wit' Petey immediately. He wants it stashed over at his place. Like you always say, Will, gotta do what ya gotta do, right? Matter of 'merican freedom — our freedom!— bein' at stake. I gotta get goin' over to Petey's."

Mark and I could see that to argue further was no use. He was determined to soldier on. It was a measure of the texture of the man's soul. My gut feeling of potential peril aside, we knew arguing with mule-headed Leroy to be like proselytizing the pope to become Buddhist. Leroy looked away and over to where the moose had been; Mark jabbed his fork into the precious baklava, jammed a piece into his mouth, and gulped it down, hardly bothering to chew, evoking in me the fondest memories of Buckie, my neighbor's dog in Wedgemont. More urgent news alerts streamed across the TV, and then came the hollow voice of one of the American Navy's four-star admirals, half-dead, from the Pentagon Situation Room. "My fellow Americans, we are faced with a growing crisis of extreme magnitude…." The alert was drowned out by the laughter and bustle of Joe's customers. Mark strained to listen. Leroy left a tip on the table, as he always did, no Cheap Charley he, though like almost everybody in Springvale now was damned near broke as a joke, and got up to leave.

"I gotta get me some of dat!" he exclaimed upon inspecting a hot-looking busty patron, not much older than a teenager, swiveling her hips as she jiggled past our booth. He grinned a long, overdue grin.

I gotta get me some of dat!

Vintage Leroy. The words danced inside my head. Loud, strong, robust, they bellowed forth from a man still vibrantly alive, alive with multiple passions and righteous conviction of the still-proud soldier marching off into tomorrow's battle he knows not of. He had moxie all right. And a lot of tire tread left in him. For they would be the last words we heard uttered from our brother's lips. The last time we would ever see him alive. In some crazy, phantasmagorical sense, I prayed we could've intervened that day against events, fate, call it what you will. All of us. It wasn't to be.

I would savor our shared memories and rue those never to be.

Chapter 12

Realities on campus and at home were evolving satisfactorily given what others were enduring. There were still some classes and guardsmen. Trooper Leopold and Agent Ramirez-Hernandez continued to be sighted on campus, even Sundays. My nightmares of 'Nam abated somewhat, along with their shared glimpses of needles, UFOs — and the number sixty-seven. Mark tried hard to get along with Kimmy, in her first trimester and fretting over her family's wellbeing in Japan, particularly during the springtime hanami (cherry blossom viewing time). Indeed, you'd scarcely even know by her looks and demeanor that she was with child. Mine. Yet I hardly considered myself a would-be father and felt guilty over the indifference. The guilt I kept to myself. Or at least I tried. She seemed to accept that — or at least pretended to. I tried to avoid the topic. Our bedroom fires now flickered hot — and cool.

Dean Rodgers kept prying into Kimmy's father's finances. Perhaps they embodied a final, flickering ember of hope for the college's own. It irked us no end, but now that she was back in the household and there was another mouth to feed and soon would be another besides my own, the poof's sniffing snout had to be kept muzzled. Delicately. He would soon request I "pop in" his office to listen to his usual calibrated rhetoric skillfully sculpted and laboriously prepped, passing off as a "little chat." He did his bloody Brit best to gloss over our confrontation in his office earlier in the semester, humiliating as it was, and I felt the concomitant urge to do likewise. Luckily, I wasn't shit-canned on the spot. My intended dismissal had been put on hold. A "most egregious misunderstanding," according to the president. I had to tiptoe still. After all, Rodgers did remain our frontline "college commander." But we both knew he needed me to work Kimmy.

"Do come in, Dr. Watson. And close the door behind you, please. Thank you. Be seated and do make yourself comfortable. This is singular in nature, nothing combinatorial."

"Nothing 'combinatorial'?"

He motioned for me to sit and didn't play bingo in addressing matters. There was no pretense anymore about dancing around Kimmy's and my 'relationship,' not even by his own choice of words, ever sculpted. "It has come to the attention of this office that Ms. Tanimoto has encountered some academic challenges in Professor Lane's class, some difficulties perhaps, to be a tad more forthright, eh?" Drumming his desk with his fingers and twirling his mustache, he eyed me coolly, though I figured he could barely discern my profile, as dimly lit as he still kept the room. The teacher in question was the witch-prof. "Any personal insight into the issue at hand, Professor?"

"Huh? I mean, ugh, I hadn't any real clue, really."

"Hmm. As her, uhm, mentor, I thought you might. Well, one must consider potential implications to any, shall we say, obstacles which might emerge with her possibly failing Dorothy's — I mean Dr. Lane's — class." He was still holding on for a reversal of fortune for Kimmy's dad.

"First time I heard of it. Really."

His tone grew impatient, almost desperate. "Do what you can, whatever that could be, to see she gets through this one. Tutor her; encourage her — anything, just as long as she makes it through the term. Remember: the administration remains committed in trying to do what is, uhm, functionally feasible to bring you back in the fall." How this was to be, with things collapsing, was ludicrous. I tried to sit with a poker face.

"I'll see what I can do."

"Good, good! Please do." He beamed over the edge of his glasses. "Anything you'd desire to add?"

"No, not really."

"Very well then. Oh, the door on your way out."

"Pleasure's been all mine."

"So hasn't it been mine, Professor Watson, so hasn't it been mine." In the darkness, he eked out the tiniest smile, Mona Lisa-like.

I walked over to the office I continued to share with the witch-prof for any further 'insight,' detesting as ever to speak with her. She was already in, arranging mountains of texts and monographs, an accumulation that all but burst out of its tiny confines. She eyed me immediately. With the usual contempt.

"So, you've seen the dean, I take it, Watson. We both know what this is all about, don't we?" she spewed out.

"Look, you've had it in for me since the day we met in September. Can't we just call it a truce? I — "

"What makes you say that? That I've 'had it in' for you? Why, how could any self-respecting academic have it in for a militia, gun-toting, Second Amendment loony — with the hots for the department's graduate assistant, half his age at that?"

"Yeah, well, speaking of her — "

"Speaking of her, everyone knows her English is truly not all that up to snuff. Wasn't for her father, probably wouldn't even have been admitted. The Oxford shit's been coming down on me to 'see what one can do to entertain any possibility of Ms. Tanimoto's passing this spring.' Enough to make me puke, the bloody bastard. No one can stand him. Thought that administrative pressuring of faculty to pass a student was against school policy, but we know I don't have tenure, and complaining about the pompous clown to the Faculty Senate...."

"Do what you think is right."

"Sure, and say good-bye to returning in the fall. A Ph.D. from Cambridge couldn't find work now as a part-time janitor here — anywhere — with the state the economy's in."

***

"Konnichiwa. Where have you been? I thought already classes over on campus. Come, come in. Let me take jacket. Here. Some green tea on table. Be comfortable. Mr. Mark went to store. He said he had to buy rest of items to tight-seal basement room for emergency, as you about earlier talked." She entered the kitchen.

I sat down at the table and the tea. "Kimmy, I hear that you're not doing all that well — failing?— Professor Lane's literature survey class. Is it true?" There was no response. "I said, 'Is it true?'"

She crept, cat-like, into the living room, eyes downcast and fixated on the floor. "Why? What makes you think that?" she said through tightening lips as she eased herself onto the sofa.

"Because Rodgers and Lane said as much."

"Hmm…." She looked up, though not directly toward me, and bit her lip.

"Well?"

Her head lowered; she uttered a faint "Sumimasen" and "I'm sorry, Will. I'm sorry."

"Why didn't you tell me?"

"I do not want you to be upset," she whispered, fidgeting with her hair. "My performance as student reflects on you as my teacher, yes?"

I said nothing and retreated into the kitchen to get us dinner. I returned, and we sat down to a meal of cold chicken and warm beer. The underlying universal male-female dynamic routinely elevated itself to that of a singular dimension; our East-West cultural divide at times emerged to be a chasm. Our cultural equation could balance out to be lopsided at times.

"Konya daite," she purred.

***

A day or two later, I got a mysterious phone call from a woman whose voice I'd heard before yet couldn't place. She told me to look inside my mailbox. I went outside and discovered a typed note in a plain envelope directing me to come to the rear of the town library parking lot at 5:30 p.m. the next day — alone. I told neither Kimmy nor Mark.

I drove out from the house late that afternoon, scarcely knowing what to expect. Riding horses, kept by local farmers for wealthy out-of-towners, were already drifting toward their stables as I sped by greening pastures neatly aligned alongside still-barren uncultivated fields. One horse I always saw was limping alone on the muddy path leading to the crumbling barn, victim of a local hooligan and his pellet gun. For discharging the weapon in the commission of this offense, he was hauled off by guardsmen and hadn't been heard from since. A strong spring gust blew through the mane of the wounded filly, reminding me how Sheila's hair would similarly flounce in the wind, and I reminisced how in our marriage we had been sleeping in the same bed but dreaming different dreams. I wondered if the same would befall Kimmy and me. A crow cawing overhead jolted me out of the daydream, and I found myself pulling into the library parking lot.

I stepped out of the vehicle and surveyed the scene. Tense. Except for my car and a lone auto I knew belonged to the librarian, the lot was empty. The frigid spring air expanded my lungs, energizing my nervous spirit. Though I had never noticed before, the tiny library, white paint peeling and also a victim, though from floundering town finances, appeared dreary, almost depressing, erected against the backdrop of equally rundown buildings dotting the town commons. Nearby forsythia bushes about to burst into brilliant yellow were the vantage point's sole redeeming sight. My thoughts wandered off to my hometown of Wedgemont, Sheila, Julie, Vietnam....

A hand seemingly from nowhere touched my shoulder. Springing around, I found myself staring straight into the piercing eyes of Sergeant Joe Hines — and almost pissing in my pants. I prided myself on a veteran's residual instinct for survival yet was caught unawares. I had to remind myself once again I had been Specialist Fifth Class Will Watson — John Rambo, never. Hines, in civilian clothes and appearing fully in the winter of his career, didn't volunteer a word; he gestured me to follow him inside. The woman's voice had been his wife's.

Except for a couple of teens and the librarian, the semi-senile retired schoolmarm, the place was unheated and deserted. The sergeant led me to a corner behind a bookshelf, suddenly pivoting around to size me up. He remained silent, somber, and a bit flummoxed.

"Why?"

He stood motionless and then looked out the window. "This is between you and me on the q.t. Got it, Watson?"

"Sure."

Hines turned around and leaned toward me, his voice wavering and remaining soft. "Like I told you before at Joe's, I suspected that Leopold could be up to something, trying to put something on the Liberty Militia. Now I have little doubt. Meets with FBI Agent Ramirez, if that's the name, behind Petey Hinson's barn every Tuesday and Friday night around dusk. 'Course Petey's in on it. Meets with both of them. Sort of a stinking threesome." The sergeant snorted; his jaws clenched. "I'd never have believed it. Leopold, yes; Petey, never." His head shook; his eyes twitched, the confession grim and grueling. "How, how could it be? Leopold's a snake, but Petey...."

"I know."

"If anybody back at Concord headquarters knows of me telling you this, I'm finished. In fact, could be worse. Whole lot worse." He spoke of what and how he knew of Springvale's 'stinking' ménage à trois. "How do you think Petey could afford his new vehicle in these times? On his maple syrup proceeds? Ratted on all of you and got paid for it." Finally, he told me of the dissension boiling within New Hampshire State Police ranks over pressure from above to spy on and crack down on ordinary working folks, a sentiment already shared among Carroll County residents. "That's a wrap. I'll be in touch."

"Sure."

The sergeant spoke softly: "Watson, just want you to know that I think you're a helluva — " He stopped in mid-thought. I never inquired why.

That Petey Hinson was an informant....

Senior militia hierarchy had to be told immediately. But both Mike Richards and Deputy Commander Big Walt were out of town and not scheduled to return for at least a day. I called Leroy's home with no luck, then drove over to discover it locked up. By then, it was late in the day; nothing more could be done until the next, and I headed home in a spring downpour, deciding to hold off on informing Kimmy until after contacting Leroy or Mike and Walt.

By sunup, none of the three had come home, and Mark and I drove out to Joe's Diner for coffee and the slim hope of meeting any of them. After nursing the brew and a headache from sleeplessness, I started for the exit. In the half-lit vestibule was silhouetted a mammoth frame: Walt Patterson's. Upon hearing my revelation, he said Richards might not be back for a couple of days and that he alone would stake out Petey's place that night with binoculars. His tone, blasé as it was, made me suspicious.

"What do you make of it?" I said to him.

"Of what?"

"Of Petey's treachery."

"It's a surprise?" he asked rhetorically, arching an eyebrow.

"Whatever became of the Liberty Militia's motto of 'Liberty and Integrity'?"

"Hmph! Know what I first noticed about you last fall, Watson? That you're a man of your word, of principle, of 'Liberty and Integrity,' an idealist. But you know what?" He pressed two bulbous fingers together on his meaty hand and jabbed them into my shoulder. "People say that they love idealists but in reality, despise them. Sticking to principles only gets you killed quicker."

I said nothing.

"I'll check out Petey's barn tonight," he repeated. "Leroy's the most vulnerable. He has to be notified immediately. Have to recache the weapons and ammo, but if he already cached the stuff at Petey's, don't see what we can do to unfuck it all now." That much was obvious; Mark and I nodded in acknowledgment and looked at each other incredulously. "I can't get over to Leroy's now. You two head over there ASAP."

I'd be late or miss my morning class. Didn't matter. Mark and I jumped in my vehicle and raced over to Leroy's. His wife was already waiting for us in the doorway, as if by premonition.

She greeted us, absent a better word, with a junkyard dog's snarl, lips curled back, glaring white choppers gnashing. "What you two want? He ain't here!" In a second, she would confirm our lurking fear. "He be just dragged away by that snake-pig Leopold and that Spanish-lookin' FBI agen' guy. Said they wanted to interrogate him back in Concord 'bout your goddamn Liberty Militia guns 'n bullets."

Mark began to speak with a thin voice, hesitatingly. "Mrs. Morton, we're determined to do whatever's necessary to see him back safely, get whatever legal representation's necessary — "

"Ha! What's you gonna do to save his black ass now, white fella? This all you white folks' fault to begin wit'. He never should've got involved wit' you guys 'n you militia!"

I started to counterclaim and just as abruptly stopped, for I sensed that I was talking to a child. A timid Josh, looking weak and worn out, appeared behind his mother. "Either Leopold or the FBI agent say when he'd be back?" I asked.

"No, i-ther didn't say nothin' 'bout that!" she said, sarcastically mimicking my pronunciation.

"Don't worry, Josh," Mark said, intervening. "We'll do what we can to get Leroy — I mean your dad — back. We'll get on it right away."

Words intended to reassure didn't hit their mark. Josh, almost trembling, stood behind his mother, looking for the first time like a boy instead of a man. I wanted to throw my arms around him; the she-beast stood between us.

"Guess we're finished here, Bill."

"Guess ya are, too," she snapped, "'n none too soon. Dudn't want you aroun' here in the firs' place. 'N jus' remember, jus' because you take Josh out for hikin' 'n stuff doesn't make you his daddy. His daddy's in jail — 'cause of you!" Josh winced.

***

Over the next several days, Richards would call for an all-out emergency formation. Kimmy began worrying incessantly over the Mortons ("What becomes now of Leroy-san? For his wife and Josh? Kuso!"), regularly making reference to the lad as though he were our own son.

Mark busied himself with stocking up the hermetically sealed emergency 'war room' in the basement. He was all but finished as a computer salesman, and now at my own job, I only pretended to work since the campus was semi-deserted. Work became problematic as electronic communications were unreliable; the World Wide Web was more down than up; cell and landline phones fared little better. Old-fashioned technology, mechanical typewriters, and the like had made a comeback on campus. Rodgers, Leopold, Ramirez-Hernandez had never left.

News of both national and worldwide riots over vanishing food and fuel supplies cascaded over the airwaves. As predominantly agricultural workers, most local residents continued to be insulated from food deficits, but not so from other spiraling shortages. Perhaps townsfolk had been to the wishing well one time too many. Across the land, the authorities tightened the noose. Rumors of makeshift detention camps, hastily built in response to erupting domestic disturbances, proliferated. The whoosh-whoosh-whoosh of overhead helicopter gunships and the wailing of sirens could be heard at any hour, even in a hick town like Springvale, destinations and missions impossible to tell.

If media outlets like CNN and assorted websites, purportedly yet uncensored, were to be believed, day-to-day affairs in foreign countries were worse. From Springvale's surrounding valleys to the megacities of Boston, New York, London, Moscow, Beijing, Tokyo — the masses slogged on, onward against the relentless winds of history, now whispering not promises but presentiments to be contemplated only in the pulsating shadows of tomorrow.

Chapter 13

"Liberty and integrity."

"Liberty and integrity!"

"All right now. All boots front and center — now! Let's get right to it. As Liberty Militia commander in the great Granite State of New Hampshire, this formation, fittingly at Old Jimmy's where we all started, is now officially convened. Me and Walt called this meeting, gentlemen and, er, ladies too, in response to recent developments. As you all know by now, we've been targeted by the FBI, state police, Army National Guard, and God-only-knows who else." Collective snickering rose up from the assembly, more to relieve simmering tensions than to react to Richards' feeble stab at humor. "Mr. Leroy Morton, loyal Liberty soldier and American patriot, was apprehended by Trooper Leopold and that FBI agent and interrogated in Concord over caching our Liberty weapons and ammo."

Members, squirming, looked at each other. From the rear echoed an anonymous shout, "Give that soldier a twenty-one-gun salute, if I could, though I'm glad I didn't hand over all my guns and bullets." Members, more than two score, and including Mark, murmured their assent to both counts.

"Men, ladies, we're all under attack, goddammit! We — "

"Just a minute, Walt." Richards was determined to hold the floor. "Let's address Leroy now. I can tell y'all now 'cause it's not classified anymore. Everything was supposed to be cached at Leroy's place initially. At the last moment, it was moved to Petey's." He swung around to confront Hinson, who was clutching his always-present cigar and sporting a visible eye tic. Petey was present, yet Leroy had been hauled away. A pebble had been tossed in a cosmic pool of collective consciousness; the revelation hit members in successive ripples of awareness. It was one pork chop of a discloser too big to swallow. Members stood by, stupefied.

"This wh-what you brought us here for?" stammered Petey. Blood drained from his face, presenting a deathly pallor. He had been thrust ineluctably and without exit onto the horror movie set of his own production. "Brought me here in front of everybody to sandbag me?"

"You sandbagged yourself, you sonofabitch!" screamed Richards. "How, how could you, Petey? For, for what? A goddamned new Jeep? Ratted on and sold out your brothers to Leopold and the FBI? You think…." Childhood memories like jumping with Petey off Babson's Ravine falls must have weighed too heavily on his heart, for Richards keeled over in a stupor and tumbled backward onto one of Old Jimmy's milking stools. It was out in the open now; the rupture was complete.

"I didn't mean for it to happen this way," sobbed Petey. "Swear to Jesus Christ I didn't, Mikey. It just — it just got out of control. Leopold started flashing cash in my face, just a little at first. I got hooked, then he said if I didn't dance faster with him and the government, he'd turn me in to you guys. I'm — I'm sorry…." He tottered. Next, he fell forward. Holding his head in his hands, he almost banged it against a protruding barn beam and then collapsed on his knees, shaking. Mark glanced at me and then continued like everyone else to stare at Petey, frozen in time, still kneeling and sobbing, as if begging Holy God to snatch him up and away, plant him in another lifetime, or return him to earlier days with Mike, and the nightmare would be over.

Richards, steadying himself on his stool as though to brace for the aftershock, leaned toward Hinson. "And what about Leroy, Petey?" Hinson rocked to and fro on his knees. "I said, 'What about Leroy?'!"

"Wh-What about him?"

"Don't play me. He's dead." The revelation exploded throughout the assembly. The catalytic moment seized the attention of all. "You and Leopold beat and killed him inside the interrogation unit at Concord, 'cept you made it look like he hanged himself."

"I didn't touch him, Mikey! Swear I didn't. It was Leopold's idea to rough 'im up. Leroy started mouthing off to him. You know Leopold. Tries to be the big man inside a boy's boots. Nobody meant it to turn out the way it did…. Oh, my God, my God…." Hinson, now almost prostrate, continued his rocking on the ground.

Richards couldn't endure it anymore. He jumped to his feet and rushed Petey. "I'm going to smoke the dog piss out of you!" Several members dashed over to intercept the furious advance of the former Marine. They held him face-down in the dirt, and he lay wildly flailing his arms over his head and cursing the childhood days he'd spent with the man while yet a boy.

"Look, I have to run to the shitter. I'm gonna throw up," uttered Hinson in one decibel above a whisper as he clutched his gut. No one wanted to be vomited upon. He bolted toward the barn outhouse unobstructed. A piercing gunshot reverberated throughout the farmstead. The throng rushed the scene. Petey must have retained a hidden handgun he hadn't cached. Before them on the outhouse floor lay the body on its back, twitching, yet surely devoid of life. Part of Petey's head had been blasted away in a manner of which I'll spare the details. In that maelstrom of chaos that moments earlier had preceded his death in that shattered brain, he must have known his future lay already behind him. A red streamlet started pooling off to one side. His cigar sat propped up between his legs like an erect, grotesque penis. One of the women fainted; in a corner Alfonso vomited up what remained of his dinner.

Upon seeing the body, Mike stood transfixed. He then collapsed. The hatred he had shown moments ago was now replaced by an inexorable sadness which had overtaken him, possessed him really, and he showed a softened, boyish image of himself to suggest that this was all a sick dream twisted awry, one from which he would soon awake, and he and Petey would find themselves swimming once again in Babson's Ravine. "Petey, Petey, Petey," he cried softly as he knelt by the body and tenderly stroked a bloodstained hand. "Where did it all go so wrong?" Mark, standing alongside Richards, took everything into the essence of his soul. Much out of rhetorical character, he tried to put it poetically, "What we do to others in this life in the evening of our days returns to haunt us with the dawn of the next." Little did I realize at the moment how this remark about the lives of others would foreshadow events in his own.

The morning of Hinson's funeral, militia members debated whether to attend. But not for long. Most thought his death tragic, though not brought on by anyone other than himself. As Liberty Militia's homegrown traitor, he had betrayed and endangered all — and Leroy Morton lay dead because of his treachery. Mark and Kimmy declined to attend, but Mark believed that Petey at least had departed from this Earth by way of an honorable exit. Possibly representing an atavistic throwback to her Japanese heritage, Kimmy thought the same. I decided to go by myself as an onlooker rather than a participant.

In the distance overlooking a grassy knoll, lay the burial site. It belonged to Springvale Church, whose Sunday service I had attended earlier in mid-winter with Commander Mike Richards. For whatever reason, this was one service where he would not be present. A three-vehicle motorcade crawled toward the open pit. A hard, cold rain began to pound a relentless pitapat against the aluminum canopy shielding the grave as if befitting Petey's violent end. A half-dozen or so people set foot from a limousine and plain sedan following the hearse. They encircled the gravesite, lingering for several minutes. From my location, I heard a tender voice, presumably the minister's, as the body was lowered into the pit, "He maketh me to line down in green pastures, He leadeth me beside the still waters, He restoreth my soul...."

My mind wandered off and over Springvale's green, rippling hills and her lush valleys with their roiling springs swollen from the season's rainfall, resplendent with springtime's eternal gift of life overpowering this fleeting farewell. I thought of what Petey's and Mike's boyhood days must have been like in this pristine place, their joys and passions, shared fears and tears. Later in life, Petey exited the world's stage the way we all enter: alone. And scared. And I thought that it all wouldn't matter what Petey had accomplished on his brief sojourn through this world as a loving and beloved father, husband, and friend. As it was written so many centuries ago, "The evil that men do lives after them; the good is oft interred with their bones." And indeed, so it was with Petey Boney Hinson. For now, he would be remembered as Springvale's own Benedict Arnold.

***

Leroy Morton's death was different. It had catalyzed the militia. Members were seething with rage. They sensed it a matter of days before they, too, were rounded up and hauled off in the event authorities decided to widen the noose and lasso more members. Some called for armed insurrection; itching for a fight, they had not handed over all their private firearms and ammunition. Though surely outnumbered, outgunned by the authorities' 'real' militia, we were well-armed and organized. Besides, the authorities were stretched thin in the hinterlands. They had grown weary of their duties and were tiring of confronting their fellow citizens, with a few exceptions like Trooper Leopold, who upon confrontation was galvanized to seek out more. A strategic fissure between Richards and Patterson became more visible over how the cadre ought to protect themselves if necessary. There developed an anti-Richards' faction that considered him weak and ineffectual. Hidden ripples of desperation undulated during informal militia get-togethers. If anger abounded within militia confines, it detonated among local townsfolk. More residents grew recalcitrant, increasingly mouthing off to guardsmen. And reaping the consequences. The federal government broadcast emergency plans to institute a national biometric ID card and asset forfeiture program. Not that the locals had anything left over to cough up. Open revolt and insurrection escalated in cities. Government responded with even greater oppressive countermeasures.

Morton's inquest concluded that he 'beyond doubt' had died by self-inflicted hanging. With Sergeant Hines communicating inside information, this was known to be a lie. You'd have thought Hines himself now a full-fledged Liberty member, disillusioned as he was with his new 'badge boy' duties. Hometown ties had rooted and overtaken oath-bound responsibilities. He evolved into an invaluable inside contact.

Leroy's funeral had to be delayed. His wife wanted the body buried in New York in the family plot; the government had begun restricting travel. Panic was spreading. People were trying to escape the big cities for the countryside. To hide where and to do what was difficult to determine. Lawlessness became the norm. Law enforcement was fast losing control. City residents who just lost their food for the day to gangs of marauding thugs were considered lucky. Outright rape, mutilation, and murder in open streets were growing common. In some other countries, it was reported to be worse. Precisely how it was hard to fathom. I worried constantly about Mark, and especially Kimmy and the baby. At home, I became aware that she was developing more matronly instincts, however subdued. And insights....

"Try to feel the baby here." She took and placed my hand over her stomach. "Go on. Try. Well, what is feeling?"

"I don't feel anything. Honestly."

"Sekinin totte! I knew you say that! Maybe because you neb-er experience having a full family before, could be?"

"What are you insinuating by that?" I'm not sure Kimmy understood the word, but she understood the question.

"Sorry. I don't mean it that way."

"Then what way did you mean it?"

"Maybe because it's you don't have family tie when we first met." She paused and then added the afterthought, "Like so many Americans, they living with, by, of, and for themself. How you say? Loner. Lone Wolf. Few friend, family, let alone family value. No human community. No sense of belonging to anybody or anything utter than themself. Maybe that's why you so close to Mercotti-san and Liberty Militia. It's like family for you. They your family you didn't have. No brother. No relationship with sister. Parents long dead. As Japanese say, you're now orphan. I think of my own family in Japan, and now I can't be with them anymore during this terrible time. Don't know what's going to happen to them. But you have Mr. Mark and the militia."

"You don't have to — " Suddenly, it occurred to me. She was right. Caught with my pants down and my soul exposed, I tried to worm my way out of facing the reality of certain truths in life. "Ha! Ha! Got us on that one, you did." I might have muttered something else. Don't know. Just mumbled and stumbled. "To change the subject, if we may, Leroy's funeral, or at least what to do with his body, among other things, are going to be discussed at that emergency town meeting tomorrow. We'd all better be going." She had a faraway look. I next heard a cell phone ring and Mark approaching the doorway.

"The covered bridge over Clawson Creek is all but washed out. We'd better leave early tomorrow if we can't drive over it on the way to the emergency meeting at town hall. Might have to wade through the creek to get there. Not deep, but it'll be cold. Better wear those fishing boots. You, too, Kimmy," he said. It was the first time I remembered that he had ever publicly considered her sensibilities, however slightly, in front of me. She was still too far gone to take notice. He caught her indifference, was slightly ruffled by it, then walked away to avoid any further tinge of embarrassment. I let the matter sleep.

Chapter 14

Dawn broke strong and clear, heralding a promising day. I headed over to the semi-deserted campus more for coffee and to snoop around than to work. The college reflected a ghostly aura. Ubiquitous sprouting weeds and uncut grass had overgrown alongside the buildings, projecting the appearance of a botanical garden in the making rather than a miniature Ivy League school it once resembled. Ramirez-Hernandez was gone, as were almost all students except for Swenson's international contingent, foreign travel all but suspended. Guardsmen were missing except for the pimply, cornpone snot-ass I'd had the run-in with earlier that winter. Like the Little Leopard, he strutted around snot-ass as ever. Rodgers hadn't noticed me; he was too absorbed in feverishly clipping away at overshooting shrubbery with a pair of gargantuan hedge clippers mismatched with his effeminate physique, a sight I never thought I'd behold. He still reported in for whatever leftover duties he could conjure up, as did the witch-prof. I wasn't as fortunate at avoiding her gaze ("Oh, it's you — again"). She had but one or two students in classes and would fully conduct them anyway, so determined she was to "be a self-respecting academic" in hopes that the dean took notice come prospective contract renewal for the fall. Three students showed up for my class that morning. Canceled it anyway. More compelling things to do. Nightfall came quickly that day.

The sun dipped beneath the horizon behind our house. "C'mon, let's get crackin'," exclaimed Mark. "Town meeting's scheduled for 20:30."

Mark, Kimmy, and I piled into my car, and I sped toward downtown. "Yes, that's what I expected," said Mark. He pointed ahead to multiple vehicles backed up in front of the decrepit covered bridge spanning Clawson Creek. "Slow down. Looks like we'll have to hoof it through the creek after all, just like I said. Good thing you brought those boots, Will. Oh, now, will you look at that?" Ahead, inside the bridge sat a blubbery farmer atop his ATV wedged precariously between shattered wooden planks. In the creeping darkness, a small throng of onlookers was gathering off to one side, gawking at his predicament.

"Get out of there now, dickhead!" yelled a grandmotherly-looking woman at the entrance.

"I can't, Hon'. I'm stuck. Help."

"Told you not to attempt it, you fat dumb ass. C'mon, kids. Let's walk the creek. Let Uncle Dickhead here figure it out for himself." The crowd laughed. If the incident was any indication of things to come at the town hall, it'd be a rough night ahead.

Kimmy and Mark hopped over the road guardrail and slid down the embankment to the creek, slip-sloshing in the only fishing boots, oversized, I had to lend them. Behind the distant mountain ridgeline, rays of an emerging full moon twinkled on the surface of the rushing waters. "You are too cold, Will, without boots," she said, offering to share one of the oversized boots and her hand with me to halve my misery. "Domo," I said. And I reflected on how her seemingly goofy traditional Japanese graciousness must have been unfathomable to Mark's modern American mindset. She and Mark waded in ten feet ahead of me, physically; emotionally, she may as well have been between Mars and Jupiter. In the past day or two, our spirits had slipped into a distant coma; Mark sensed that as well. I took her hand anyway. He smirked. "Come, come with me, Will," she said.

Velvety shadows crept over the mist rising from the churning waters; an early night owl hovered and hooted in the frigid wind whistling through the treetops. Townsfolk, many holding hands, edged their way through the bone-achingly cold water and toward the town hall, each pondering a jumbled foreboding and optimism over what lay ahead that night inside its aging walls. On the way to the entrance, we trekked over an open pasture as if on a minefield; it was laden with piles of fresh cow manure plopped everywhere. None had thought flashlights necessary; we used the moonlight, strong and bright now, to dance around the dung. Several of the older, fatter, or otherwise less agile townspeople, pants still soaked and clinging to their legs, got hung up maneuvering over the fence line's barbed wire and tore their clothing while cursing their fate over this homegrown obstacle course. It would now be a round-trip for all, the evening's obstacles just beginning.

Locals began gathering aimlessly around the entrance, the overhead outdoor light flickering, seemingly in concert with the assembly's intermittent emotions running from forced optimism to despair. The edgy clamor of the crowd, as if readying for what was coming inside, revolved around Hinson's and Morton's deaths and Crazyman Wilson's curse of burning down the town hall over taxes. I kept my pain and pity for Morton to myself. Talk about what people should do ping-ponged from resistance to staying the course and adhering to whatever the town council might suggest. "All Springvale citizens inside! Now!" shouted a selectman from inside the lobby. Residents, a few hundred strong, entered in single file as though marching into a battlefield.

It was unheated inside and musty, befitting the building's recent less frequent usage. A minister, one that I didn't recognize, stood on the auditorium platform overlooking nervous faces. "Now that everybody's settled, let's have a brief invocation to beseech God's blessing — "

"What the hell for? I don't — "

"To invoke the blessing of the Holy Father, that's 'what the hell for,' sir!"

"So, who elected you our overseer and lord? You know damned well, preacher, that the region's not countenancing any obligatory prayer invocations anymore at public meetings."

A chorus of hisses and catcalls shot up to the ceiling.

"Shut the hell up and let us pray, you liberal shithead! Why don't you go back to New York — Greenwich Village or wherever it is you're from." The congregation howled its agreement.

"Better yet, I'd send you back to old communist Russia if I could, atheist bastard. You don't belong here. This is still a Christian country, or at least county. You ACLU leftist loon types make me sick. Coming in here from the cities and tryin' to take over and all. Change our ways and customs going back to our colonial forefathers' generations before your folks even set foot on these shores, you spaghetti-noodle wop you."

The minister appeared to nod in agreement.

"Yeah, who says this region's not cunt'nancing no more oblig'tory prayer? Think you're some hot-shot intellectual or sumpthin'?" yowled another.

"All right, all right. That's enough. Just y'all simmer down now." The voice was one of only two selectmen present sitting alongside the minister on stage. The head selectman was out sick.

This is how it kicked off. Bitter. Acrimonious. Divisive. Like usual. Mark shook his head and sniggered; Kimmy remained frozen-faced, not knowing how to react or just wasn't concerned.

Abruptly, all eyes narrowed in the direction of a hulking and drenched figure barging through the entrance. He stopped in mid-stride for a moment while perusing faces in the crowd, the contour of his massive frame silhouetted against the dim-lit lobby. It was 'Uncle Dickhead.' He was livid. He made a beeline for his wife or girlfriend or whatever she was to him, shoving others out of the way, blubber bouncing, cussing the day she was born.

"Now you hold it right there, Johnny!" ordered the other selectman. "I said, 'Hold it!'" The farmer stopped, coming to his senses. "That's better. Now let's get down to business."

The selectman paused, clearly nervous. He surveyed all of us from one side of the room to the other. He was patently apprehensive and groping for something to diffuse the bubbling tensions. It looked like he was trying to marshal his courage in a face-off with the school bully during recess. Seconds slid by.... No response. His audience grew agitated.

"Well?" somebody said.

"Ah, I've got good news for you. We on the council have decided on a definite no to any emergency tax hikes. No tax increase whatsoever." He paused again to let the revelation seep in, in hopes of earning a momentary reprieve, perhaps wishing like Petey Hinson, he could be magically teleported to someplace else. The revelation only earned the poor SOB added scorn.

"Stepped in this cow shit before. Council doesn't have authority to unilaterally raise up taxes. Nothing in town charter or bylaws 'bout that," some woman insisted.

"OK, OK." His tone immediately grew conciliatory. "What the council suggests is volunteering to help reconstruct Springvale's collapsing infrastructure because no emergency monies are coming at the fed or state levels — period. Some of you had to wade Clawson Creek today to get here, right? We're poor and broke as a church rat."

"That's church mouse, Shakespeare," an elderly gent shouted out sarcastically.

"You don't have to insult me like that, goddammit!"

"Sorry, it's just that we're scared, Stanley. Everybody is."

"I know. But we have to stick together. Stay strong…. We need the old covered bridge repaired and up and running right away. There're all sorts of things. There's a volunteer signup sheet to fill out during the break. Mike? Tony? Alfonso? Dave? You, too, Rebecca. You've got big, strapping boys who could help out. What about the rest of you?" Townsfolk murmured an insipid assent. "Other items on tonight's agenda involve the latest developments which you've all heard: the tragic deaths of Petey Hinson and Leroy Morton." The other selectman cut in with something about asking for volunteers immediately. "Ah, all right. Instead of waiting for the break, let's have a show of hands now for volunteers." No hands went up. "I said, 'Let's have a show of hands.'" Two people begrudgingly raised theirs, timidly scanning the room for reinforcement. The selectman's rage grew inversely commensurate with time's passage.

"Where's the money from Washington? I — " someone hollered.

The selectman exploded. "There is no money from the government! What the hell is the matter with you people, anyhow? Goddammit! We are broke! On our own! Nobody from Washington or Concord is coming to save our ass! They can't even protect their own! Don't you realize that they're raping and killing each other right now in the damned cities, and nobody's doing — or can do — anything about it? They've lost control. It's anarchy in the streets. Now everybody, let's get our goddamned heads out of our asses, and let's pull together now!" The room echoed his outburst, fell silent, and then came alive with shouts of, "I'll pitch in for…." "You can count on me to…." And so the refrain rolled on. Mark smiled.

An attractive woman walked onto the stage and whispered in the selectman's ear. He looked back at her, shook his head, and turned around to face us. "I've some troubling news. Something's happened to our longtime resident state trooper, Kevin Leopold."

"Like what?" somebody asked.

"Yeah, what?" another repeated.

"What the hell now?" came a third inquiry.

"He's dead."

The room grew sullen. Silent.

"Sergeant Hines, who's not here today, as you can see, is investigating. Leopold's dead."

"Dead?" his audience whispered in disbelief, looking at one another aghast. Reactions were mixed. To some, the trooper was the local face of 'the law,' to others, he was a petty tyrant.

"You'll be informed as soon as we get details," said the selectman. "We're dying even here." He tried to go on but choked.

I pondered who 'we' were.

He scoured the audience again, struggling. "All right, let's get on with it. What else was on the agenda?"

"The other deaths. Those of Hinson and Leroy Morton," said the other selectman.

"Yes, Mr. Morton and Petey. As you know, I, I — lost my train of thought again. Where was I?"

"'Bout Morton and Hinson," repeated the other selectman.

"Yes, Morton and Hinson. As almost y'all know by now, Petey Hinson, "Boney," as he was also known, was born and raised here and a founding member of Liberty Militia. He ended his life by his own hand — or should I say .38 Special?— over allegations of spying on its members for payoffs from the state police and FBI."

"No 'allegations' of any sort. A traitor, simple and pure," someone blurted out.

"Look, I'm trying to be diplomatic. Man's dead."

"Save that diplomacy talk for the bastards down in Washington who got us trapped in this manure pit," said one of the militia's female members.

"All right, Sandy. Then let's go to Leroy Morton. He hanged himself at Concord State Police headquarters after being interrogated for burying the Liberty's weapons' stockpile."

"Didn't hang himself! Murdered by our so-called public service law enforcement agents!" yelled a militia member.

"I don't want to speculate on what happened to Mr. Morton."

With the mention of the name again, a loud, painful "Ooowh" rose from the rear. It was Leroy's wife with Josh. They hadn't been noticed. The audience parted, and they stood out like evangelists at an abortion rally. She looked heavily sedated, dopey; Josh appeared reed-like and lifeless.

The selectman took notice, muttered condolences, and cleared his throat. "Didn't expect Mrs. Morton to be here. Although newcomers to town, Mr. and Mrs. Morton and their son, Joshua, came from New York, Bronx I'm told, to start a new — "

"Leroy!" she wailed.

"To start a new life here for — "

"Arghh…. Leroy! Leroy!"

"Ugh, better get right to it. We need to bury the body. She wants it done in New York, but the town hall's been notified that main arteries leading in and out of all major cities have been sealed off. She doesn't seem to understand."

It was odd hearing him refer to her in the third-person, as though she were back in New York and not here with us. The ceiling light flickered; Kimmy squeezed my hand.

"Where's the body?" a woman hollered.

"It's, it's here."

"Well, where?" she said, irritated.

"Right behind the curtains backstage."

The audience gasped.

"So what the hell did you expect? We had to keep him here. As she's his next-of-kin, we needed her permission to bury him, but she's in no condition to render consent, and the boy's still a minor. Other family members can't get up here to get him. We're working with our legal counsel to override and get him buried here."

Mrs. Morton retained a modicum of mental strength to comprehend the go-ings-on. Josh was faring little better. As if the selectman had slapped her face with his revelations, she awoke from her stupor, agitated, angry, and screaming hyster-ically, and rushed the stage, taking the entire assembly unawares. She leaped upon the stage and tore aside the curtain, exposing the closed casket. "Leroy! Leroy! Leroy!" she sobbed, draping herself over the plain, unadorned box with such force that the thud of her head smashing into the wood resounded throughout the auditorium. She appeared to be knocked semi-conscious from the impact, and blood trickled from her nose and the corner of her mouth. "Leroy, Leroy, I love you! Don't leave us!" It was too much for Josh; he ran to her side, one arm slung around his mother, the other atop the box containing his father's fallen figure, and cried out for him.

"Daddy! Daddy! Come back to me, Dad, come back! I love you, Daddy!"

The audience, many moved to tears, could barely contain themselves.

"Leroy! Don't leave us like this! You can't do nuthin' like this to us, Leroy. You can't! Answer me! Oh, Holy Jesus, this is not happenin'. Please, please, God, bring 'im back to us!" Some looked away; some stood there transfixed, as if spiritually impaled by the scene unfolding onstage. The selectmen, their heads hanging, didn't know what to do. Each time the lead selectman went to speak, words hardened in his throat.

The minister approached the casket to put his arms around Leroy's wife and tried gently to shuttle her away onto a nearby chair. "Don't touch me!" she screeched. He backed off and attempted to do the same with Josh, kneeling and sobbing. "Leave 'im alone!" She had collapsed to her knees and began crawling to the chair unattended, then hoisted herself into the seat while brushing away the tears, blood, mucous, and spittle that had started to pool at the corners of her mouth.

"Come sit down next to your mother, son," the minister said softly as he hastily fumbled with another chair to align it with Mrs. Morton's. "Here. That's better. Now try to comfort your mother." Josh embraced her, and she violently threw her arms around her son and rocked him to and fro as she must have done when he was her baby. And it was as if he still were.

A solitary teardrop trickled down Kimmy's cheek; Mark tried to mask his emotions by coughing nervously. Townsfolk, emotionally spent, needed to recover their sensibilities; the Mortons maybe never would. One of the selectmen quietly called for an interlude of a few minutes to soothe things over. Some of us headed outside for a smoke or fresh air. A lone siren was heard faintly in the distance, as was the familiar "swoosh-swoosh-swoosh" of a helicopter closer to downtown. It wasn't long before everyone was called back in.

"Since we're here today, let's have a word or two in memory of Leroy Morton," said the selectman. "We'll probably not be together again soon as we are here today. It's fitting that we publicly acknowledge his passing since private funeral arrangements are undecided. Who would like to speak?" Nobody answered.

"How about you, Will?" said Alfonso. "You were his best buddy."

"Who, me?"

"Yes, how about it, Will?" others piped in. "You're a speaker." It took a minute to collect my thoughts, clear my throat. "We're waiting...."

"An American. Above all, that's who, that's what Leroy Morton was. Oh, yes, beloved husband, father, militia loyalist, veteran, boxer, friend; he was all these things, but first, and always, an American to his dying breath. What does that mean, to be an American? As he lies here now in his coffin, death having kissed his lips and silenced his laughter, his voice, forever, we remember him for what he stood for, like the granite rock from which our state's nickname is derived. He stood for protecting and providing for his family as husband and father in the direst of times; in the face of encroaching government tyranny, he stood for liberty, ultimately giving his life for it, for the right to keep and bear arms to protect that family. As the sun goes to sleep in the west for those blessed with a full life, he was cut down in the high noon of his. He stood for Old Glory and the best of what she embodies and always has.

"Turn around and take a look at her standing lonely and still in the back of this room. Take a look at her. I said turn around and take a look at her, dammit! You see, just as I did, he fought this nation's thankless war in Vietnam. We talked about it. Many times. And like me in the end he was not truly fighting for that flag. What we were fighting for — give me a moment because sometimes the pain is too much.... What we were fighting for were towns like this! Small towns of America, towns of her plains, of her valleys, of her seashores, of her mountains, towns that enshrine the embodiment of the very best this land, this nation, has to offer. But sometimes, not all of these towns lived up to their essential decency; they let people like him down because of the color of their skin, the look of their faces. Men like him fought, bled, and died in rice paddies a world away, and, if they didn't die, came back here to places where they could not, they would not, be treated like Americans, could not be served at a lunch counter, a barber shop, a bus stop. But he, and others like him, stood for and fought for these towns anyway.

That's what they did for towns like ours. Always remember this: as the sun rises here in New England and sets in California, it is in the heartland in towns like Springvale where we find the pulsating eternal lifeblood of America — and this is what men like Leroy Morton have stood up and died for! Now we bestow upon him our final farewell; now he joins the ethereal realm of sacred dust, the ultimate destiny of us all.

"Lastly, he stood by me as a friend. Forever faithful. He once called me the only true friend he had here in his adopted hometown. For that, I am eternally grateful and proud to be called his friend. And for that, I salute you, my friend. This is where he fought his last fight; this is where we're going to finish and win it for him — and ourselves! There was, there is, no more faithful American."

There was a prolonged silence. Then the place exploded. People went crazy. A man rushed over to me, a local I'd seen from time to time, quivering, tears streaming down his face, and grabbed me. "I want to thank you for those words, sir. I'll 'member them to my own dying breath!"

Chapter 15

"How you doing, Watson?" Guess you've heard by now — from Mike Richards or your buddy Mercotti — that Trooper Leopold's been murdered. Rope-strangled behind his garage. Looked like something of a professional hit, too. No standout suspects — yet."

It was Sergeant Joe Hines in plainclothes. He stepped out of his vehicle. He had driven out alone to my place early in the morning, ostensibly to stay in touch with Liberty Militia members as he had said he would.

"'Murdered'?" I said. "No! Really? Hadn't heard. Just heard he'd died. What the hell happened? Any leads?"

"Nothing solid. I'm not personally in on the investigation, but from what I've heard and been told, looks like a Mafia-type job, a professional hit. Killer didn't leave behind any DNA. No prints, nothing, except for the ropes like some memento; otherwise, he processed the scene clean. Even covered up his footprints, probably wearing plastic bootie covers, they tell me." He looked down at his own shoes. They were always shined. He didn't appear perturbed.

"My sympathies. I know you two worked together as partners for years."

"Don't be. Sympathetic, that is. Although I won't say he had it coming to him, certainly nothing like this, he was always…. Well, you know how he got to be, especially in later years. Hate to say it, but I suppose you and other Liberty members won't be all that upset."

"Oh, heavens no. When a law enforcement officer is killed in the line of duty — "

"Cut it out. Don't play me for a fool. We both know how he treated militia members, including you. Tried to slap on you that trumped-up charge of excessive force against Tiny, that bum. Come to think of it, he's being considered a possible suspect in Leopold's murder. Off the record, I can't see how. Too much of a dumbass. Doubt his IQ score adds up to the number of tattoos he has. Stuff about him being a probable suspect is on the q.t." He leaned back over and then against his unmarked cruiser, took a final drag on his cigarette, and tossed it in Kimmy's tiny garden along the edge of the apartment complex. Though barely daybreak, he looked like he had been up and around for some time, maybe all night.

"You said Mark already knew?"

He took off his goofy-looking deer hunting cap, looked away, gingerly fingered the rim, then stared straight at me. "Yes, thought he'd have told you by now."

"Well, uh, he's been away. Yes, away."

"Oh? Really now?"

Mark had been gone, yet not long. I didn't know what to say. I mumbled something, not sure what, and went to change the subject. "How's your boy doing? Is he — "

"State Police hierarchy in Concord managed to keep the murder out of the Free Press in Manchester and The Concord Monitor. TV, radio, miscellaneous online news sources, too — you name it. Has to come out eventually, however. With all that's been going down around here recently — Morton, Hinson, others — now it's hardly even front-page news. Any other time...." He fell silent. So did I.

"Well, my kid's doing OK, I guess," he said. "Schools aren't regularly in session anymore. Same with Swenson, eh?"

"Huh? Uh, yes. Same with Swenson."

He eyed me quizzically. "You got something you want to say to me, Watson?"

"Me? 'Bout, 'bout what?"

"Dunno, Watson. Your lights are on, usually, but sometimes nobody's home."

"No — well, I — I mean we, Liberty Militia — were wondering what happened to FBI Agent Ramirez. He's not in on Leopold's murder investigation, is he? He hasn't — "

"Been recalled back to regional headquarters in Boston indefinitely. More pressing matters there than here in this cow-shit region. Damned near anarchy in Boston."

"And what about Mark? Why did you personally apprise him of the details of Leopold's death?"

"No reason particularly, other than he knows a lot about forensics, even has some experience."

"He does?"

"Well, you tell me. After all, he's your friend. You mean you didn't know that about him?" I said nothing. "Tell me, Watson, what do you know of him?"

"Maybe not a damned thing!" I regretted the outburst immediately. It was too late. I muttered some tripe, hoping he'd change the topic.

"Hmph. Well, say 'Hello' to Kimokee for me. You've got a good woman in her, you do, Watson. Don't take her for granted 'cause they don't make them like that anymore. Not here, at any rate. Maybe not even any longer in China. She's a throwback to that Italian opera — what was it? Madame Butterfly, huh? Protect her. Sexual assaults everywhere now. We can't contain it. Might as well hang on to any weapons you haven't forked over. I don't care any longer. Need all the protection you can muster with all the lawlessness exploding."

At that moment, Kimmy appeared at the window. Reflexively, Hines dipped his cap in her direction, as he'd do to all the ladies. His police radio crackled. "Quiet! … Oh, shit. Another home invasion in Meredith, off Route 25 by Winnipesaukee. I'm off-duty. But I'll take it anyway. Have to run."

"Apprise me when you collar the killer, Sergeant."

He glanced over his shoulder. "Right as rain, Watson, right as rain. Tell you what: you'll be the first to know." He bit into his lip, grinned, got back into his vehicle, slammed the accelerator, and spun off and onto the road.

***

"Been busy the past day or two, Bill?"

"Sure. Like usual, Mark. Why do you ask?"

"Oh, just because."

He continued leaning back in his chair at my kitchen table; Kimmy was out weeding the garden. I caught sight of his face from the corner of my eye. He was unusually quiet — and scrutinized me inquisitively.

"You've got anything to say about the day of the town hall meeting?" he asked.

"Not particularly."

"Sure?"

"What do you mean?"

"What do I mean? I mean, I know who killed Leopold."

"Oh, you do? Who?"

"You," he said. I turned around to face him full-on. At that instant, I must have been more concerned about how I looked to him than how he looked to me, for I lack a vivid memory of his face…. "I know you did it, Bill. Can't really blame you, close as you were to Leroy and all. 'Course everyone knew the Little Leopard was really the Big Snake. Had it coming to him after all, didn't he?" His eyes narrowed. "I said, 'Had it coming to him, didn't he?'"

"I see."

"Yes, I too 'see.' See it all."

"What do you mean?"

"Well, by the trail you left behind at the murder scene."

"What 'trail'?"

"The signature rope knots that you used to garrote him, the special rope knots you were taught in Vietnam. The double sheet bend, and I believe, Prusik knots. Maybe to kill him by way of a rope, the way Leroy was killed. A tit for tat. Or a rope for rope." He laughed. "Got to hand it to you, Bill. You're pretty clever. Sergeant Hines showed me photos. I caught the rope details immediately. Don't worry, though. He doesn't know. Never catch on."

"I see."

He stood up, turned away, and started out of the kitchen, then looked back over his shoulder. "Unless, of course, I was to tell him."

"Of course."

"Have some things to attend to. I'll be in touch. Soon." He brushed back his ponytail. "By the way, my contacts say things are in worse straits than Washington's letting on. Better double-check that the basement room lacks nothing." I watched him stride out of the door. That he would suspect that I had committed a capital crime would undoubtedly create a pustulating psychic barrier between us, but that he would insinuate he might inform the authorities meant our relationship was now problematic indeed. Truth be told, I honestly didn't know what to think.

On her way back inside, Kimmy must've overheard the tail end of the conversation, for she remarked, "What's matter? What's matter, Will? Something wrong? What's it now? What's he say? You shaking. You look like you trapped and frozen inside one of your crazy dreams!" She went toward the kitchen window, softly pulled apart the curtains, and spied Mark's Dodge slowly pulling out from the driveway, Mark looking back out from the window, smiling. And I wondered if he knew his role of interloper between Kimmy and me was finally over.

"What did that man do now to you, Will?" she blurted out indignantly. "You know I can't watch for him — anybody — to hurt you, b-b-but especially him," she stammered in rising anger. "Speak to me!"

With those words, I heard and saw Sheila's voice and face instead of hers. I must've lost it. "Lemme alone!" I spun around and away. Violently. She was just as quick, wrapping her arms around my waist, pulling me into her. "I'm sorry, Kimmy. I'm sorry. Mark's been my best friend. I don't know what to say now. Don't know...." I felt her fingers, her blood and bone, dig into my flesh; they were strong, her spirit stronger. Until that moment, I never realized the power she possessed in this world gone mad.

Perhaps I was "trapped and frozen inside one of my crazy dreams." Maybe we all were. Soon the dream burst into a nightmare. And damned quick.

**

I had started driving out to Swenson campus to check up on Kimmy's friend, as she'd implored me to, and on my class rosters. I hadn't driven far. In the distance were four local thugs attacking a young girl. Like a pack of wild hyenas, they were on top of her. In broad daylight. Practically in the middle of the street. She couldn't have been more than a kid in middle school; in fact, I had seen her around from time to time, as well as her attackers: four older guys, probably in their thirties. Springvale was like that. If you didn't know the name, you at least recognized the face.

"Stop it! Stop it! Please, just let me go! Please! Please! I'm begging you. Arghh...."

"Why, why should we? Ya little bitch! Ya gonna get what's coming to you now! C'mon, hold 'er down, fellas. Don't expect me to do all the work myself, Chrissakes." It appeared to be the leader. "Feels good, doesn't it, bitch? Ha, ha, ha.... Gonna have us some fun now, ain't we boys? Gonna fork and pork you but good, just like we did that other little pig last week."

"Arghh.... God, please make them stop...."

It's not your battle, Watson; it's not your battle.... It's not my battle.... I can't get involved; I can't get involved.... Don't look. Look the other way, dammit! Don't look. I tried not to. I slammed the accelerator....

I pulled up to and got out at the entrance of Swenson's graduate dorm housing the international students, still shaken, my stomach churning. Hardly anyone was around. I hurried past the empty, filthy entrance that emitted a stale, moldy stench, where days earlier militia guardsmen had stood sentinel. Wolfgang, the German who had always been interested in my war experiences, was outdoors sitting on one of the dormitory benches reading, and he bolted toward me to shake my hand.

"How do you doing today, Professor Vahtson? You looks a little, vy, a little...." He let his voice trail off. He laid aside his text, something on the life and times of the German philosopher Ernst Cassirer. "So nice you come to visit here today. Vaht may I do for you, Professor?" I told him I had come out to check up on Kimmy's old roommate. He said that she was fine, taking a nap, and had asked not to be disturbed. Then he inquired about final exams.

"Don't know. I'll ask at the admin building on my way out. Hardly anyone left on campus anyway. Some things are more important than final exams. Like survival. You got enough water and canned goods to eat for now stored in the cafeteria. Fresh produce, too. They've an emergency generator still working there. You're lucky. What you guys need to do now is to protect the women here, Wolfgang. And yourselves."

"Vaht, vaht the hell you talking about, Professor? No vomen are in danger here."

"Listen, it's turned into a hellhole. People are going crazy. You haven't been traveling off-campus. Even a cow town like Springvale's gone crazy. There're marauding gangs that could come here." I put both hands on his shoulders and squeezed him. "Listen to me!" He stood there, astonished. "Come on, let's go to the cafeteria. I'll show you how to fight and what you and the other guys can use as weapons." A few of the other students from Swenson's leftover international contingent heard us, and we all made our way over to the cafeteria, now devoid of workers, while passing by mounds of rotting garbage and the reek of human urine and excrement. "Look, I know the indoor toilets aren't flushing," I said. "Best you stop relieving yourselves out here in the open, though." Some of them sniggered. "I mean it. You'll have disease in no time. Let me show you how to make a communal cat hole. It may be inconvenient, but you'll have to do it if you want to survive."

"Never thought I'd be coming to America to study how to camouflage and cover my shit," said one of them. They laughed nervously in unison; an aura of creeping inevitability had descended upon the campus.

Soon I was bouncing up the stairs of the main administration building. The place was still reasonably clean. The president had been away recently, to where even his executive assistant said he didn't know. Handwritten notices, highlighted for emphasis, were prominently posted at the entrances and exits, beseeching faculty to stay the course and administer final exams to any students who would take them. A disheveled Dean Rodgers remained in his office without his secretary.

"Oh, it's you, Watson. Remember to give your finals if any students show up. And do proffer me some bloody good news about anything, man, although I don't know if I could possibly recognize good news anymore." He fingered his bow tie, making it more askew.

"Well, the possibility of Ms. Tanimoto's father coughing up cash — "

"Oh, drat, drop that, man! We all know it's over, as if to say it ever was going anywhere. He's lucky to enjoy an extra bowl of rice and a bottle of sake, the way things are going. Do get your head out of your ass once and for all, Professor Watson!"

And so that's the way his pimping, his gaseous rhetoric, would forever end: with Kimmy's dad lucky to swallow a few extra mouthfuls of rice and swigs of sake, and with me trying to keep my head out of my ass. I descended from the building, passing by the witch-prof on my way out to Liberty Commander Mike Richards' place on the outskirts of town. She didn't say anything to me. Nor I to her. Just as well. She was out and about, furiously scrounging up what few students remained to take her exams. Diehard till the end.

Branches ripped off from recent storms littered the roadways. At times I had to get out and clear the road the best I could. New Hampshire's birch trees were particularly troublesome to remove, and like some school kid not getting his way, I cursed this new development. Government expenditures were no longer available for routine road-clearing, only for extreme emergency services, and even those had been cut back. I spoke aloud to myself about how much longer Sergeant Hines himself could expect to cash a full-time paycheck. Images of the street rape flickered and wormed their way inside my brain.

Richards in shirtsleeves was out in his front yard, raking debris from the recent storms. I laughed that his employment as a book salesman had never been especially lucrative, given the appearance of his tiny yard and home. Then I thought of my own situation. I stopped laughing. A brisk spring breeze blew away more debris hither and yon, and as I veered into his driveway, I chuckled at the Marine's futile attempts to rein in the wayward mess. He was growing more agitated by the moment. I got out of the vehicle.

"Oh, it's you. 'Bout time. Incidentally, you heard about the Little Leopard by now, I'm sure." Richards leaned up against his rake and then came straight to his real point. "There's developed a split within Liberty. Me and Walt Patterson. Thinks he's officer-in-charge now, he does. Guess it doesn't come as any surprise, does it?"

"Can't say that it does, Mike."

"Yeah, well, he's calling for Liberty to put up armed resistance to the growing anarchy in town, make it some sort of a vigilante militia. I've told everyone that's not what we're about. Never have been."

"Sometimes local justice can be good when government fails."

"He's calling for an all-members' formation. Told him we should at least wait till after the governor's statewide emergency address."

"And?"

"And he pretty much told me to go back and shine my boots."

"Meaning?"

"You can be pretty dense. But then, too, you're a professor. Figures."

"You don't have to insult me like that, Mike."

"Yeah, sorry." He looked away and up into the overcast sky, threatening another deluge. "Meaning he pretty much told me to go to hell; that's what he meant." Lightning struck in the distance; a moment later, a thunderclap exploded. "Hear that? Three seconds away and moving here at just over a thousand feet per second. Bet even you didn't know that. Barely a half-mile away. Blowing our way. Be here in no time."

"What do you intend to do?"

"Well, I was wondering if you could contact some of the members and talk with 'em — future of Liberty's at stake, Bill. Be much appreciated. They respect you. Always have. Maybe even more than they do me." He snorted, again looked up at the clouds, low-hanging, and fast-moving in our direction, and continued. "You know, after losing Leroy, then Petey...."

"What's going to happen to Leroy's remains?"

"Don't know. Have to ask at the town hall. They're in charge." His eyes misted. My own might have as well.

"I know how you feel about all this. I'll see what I can do."

"OK, thanks." He followed me as I returned to my car. "Hey, sorry for being such a wiseass to you. You know, maybe" — he bit into his lip —" maybe it's because you made something out of your life, yet after retirement from the Corps, I never accomplished anything with my own."

"That's not so, Mike, not so."

"'Not so', huh? G'wan now. Get going. Get out of here. Go." His jaws clenched.

I felt a raindrop or two on my arm resting on the window ledge as I turned on the engine and watched him bury his head inside his hands. The poor SOB.

It was getting dark and I was hungry. I wasn't the only one. In a rolling corn-field, part of a larger classic landscape, I spotted a black bear and her cub lolloping behind her, the two of them foraging for food near a cattle-feed stand. And I marveled how, like humans, they can get so lazy and greedy when expecting a handout. It was a panoramic vista: acres of dandelions dotting the hills amid bursting white clover in full bloom. A Thomas Kinkade canvas come to life, emblematic of rural northern New England's regal majesty. I decided to stop by Joe's Diner for a meal of my own, one of his latest 'specials' — whatever.

The winds howled. The oncoming storm developed into an all-out downpour. It almost felt the rain would crack my windshield; the wipers couldn't move fast enough. More trees lay in the road in front of the diner. I entered the half-lighted parking lot; mine was the only vehicle in sight.

"We're — I mean I — was about to close." It was Mabel shouting from the vestibule over the raging storm. "Joe's been out sick, or so he says, the lying bastard. Anything so as not to come out here today and pay off his help. Supposed to give me a ride back, too. Come on in, since you're here. Tell you what: give you a hot meal on the house if you'll offer me a ride home in this mess. Can't beat that now, can you?"

I ran out into the screeching rain and hurried inside. Hadn't stopped by in a week. Business had dropped off. The place was shoddy. Yet I had scarcely eaten all day and wasn't about to complain. Hell, she did say that the meal would be free. I thrashed the excess rain from my jacket and settled down in my favorite booth; Mabel poured me some coffee and went to work on my order. She quickly noticed that I spied a handgun hidden under the cash register. "Didn't think I'd be crazy enough to be out here by myself without a little help from my friends, Smith and Wesson, here, did you? Why, even Hines doesn't care anymore, with all that's been going on. Suspect he now secretly supports decent folks arming themselves. He's got more than he can handle. You call 9-1-1 now and they all but put you on hold. If something happened to me, by the time he'd get here, I'd be dead." She smirked. "Here's your eggs and steak the way you like them: both medium-rare."

"Thanks. Haven't been around lately. What have I missed?" I attacked the steak. Tasted great.

She motioned overhead to the spluttering TV, dying out from continuous use. "Nothing in Carroll County, but I'm sure you know by now the whole country's going straight to hell. One emergency bulletin after the next." She fidgeted with an extra coffee spoon. "Don't know how much longer we can hold out." Her face twisted; then it came alive. "There is a new development, now that I've seen you. Tiny's gone and got himself rebaptized or something. Swear to God! Dumped his two punk sidekicks and started going to church like some holy roller!" She threw up her arms and roared. "Hear he's even trying to get rid of some of his tats with a laser! Was here the other day. Even said he was sorry over what happened to you, at least the damage to your girlfriend's car."

"G'wan!"

"It's true."

The TV announcer grabbed our attention. Something about an emergency broadcast announcement from the governor's executive office. A bulletin streamed across the bottom of the screen stating the NBA Finals were canceled. "I'll start closing up," Mabel said. "You can catch that phony windbag's announcement from Concord later in the week at home."

I dropped her off at her apartment and swerved around toward the town hall. It was getting late. The memory of the street rape gnawed at my brain. Her primordial shrieks echoed inside my head. I hadn't realized it, yet I caught myself sweating and clutching the steering wheel so hard I practically ripped it off the column. Rage left over from the war, Leroy's death, the rape, whatever, was boiling over inside me. Again. I took deep breaths the way Army medics would tell us when we tried to decompress right after a battle. Never seemed to work. Surprisingly, the town hall was still open.

"Any of the selectmen still in?" I asked a clerk. She pointed for me to enter an adjacent room. Sitting behind a desk was one of them whom I had seen prominently at the emergency town meetings.

"Let's see, you're the silver-tongued teacher from the college, right? Mister…"

"Watson, Will Watson."

He rose to extend his hand. "What can I do for you today, professor?" He appeared smaller in stature, almost diminutive, compared to when I had last seen him looming large, illuminated under stage lights, set off by the aura of authority.

"For one thing, I'd like to know what's become of Mr. Morton's remains. He was a dear friend of mine, perhaps my closest in Springvale."

"Ah, yes, Mr. Morton's remains." He shook his head. "Truly a tragedy, eh?" He took a deep breath and then blew it out forcibly, as though to ready himself for some august proclamation. "Yes, well, his wife was utterly distraught over what had happened to him, his suicide, some say foul play. And his boy — "

"His remains."

"Yes, his remains. Well, we had him cremated. Had to. No way could we get the body back to his native New York."

"Who's 'we'?"

"Town council in consultation with the selectmen. We wanted to give them to his widow, the boy's too young, but she was, and we're told still is, too distraught. Practically killed herself. Still might do it, I've been told. Not talking or cooperating with anybody. Only mumbled something about going back to New York."

"So, where is he?" I asked. He pointed to an urn resting peacefully atop a mahogany mantelpiece in the next room. "You serious?"

"Look, I know how it looks, but you have to understand that nothing like this has ever happened here before — it was unprecedented. Ordinarily, we'd hand over the remains to local clergy, but he wasn't a member of any congregation here. What else could we do?" he stammered, then adjusted his glasses about to slide off his nose.

"I see. Well, in that case, since no member of his family is claiming him, I will." I started walking toward the room.

"Now wait a minute! You can't just come in here and do that!"

"Why not?"

"It's not — it's not standard — I don't know. Look, let me talk it over first with the council and other selectmen. I'll let you know. Anything else?"

"Yes. What's next? What's your contingency plan for the town?"

"'Contingency plan'? 'Contingency plan'? How do you mean, sir?"

"I mean, what have you implemented by way of emergency civil defense-type plans in case martial law's declared, food and water rationed, roads blocked off, energy sources disrupted, operability of town emergency loudspeakers — "

"Why, why, we never specifically considered that! Guess we don't have any. But, but the governor's going to make an announcement soon!"

Disgusted, I pivoted around to walk out.

"There's always the churches to lend a helping hand," he squealed as I marched toward the exit. "At least, I think. Oh, and the loudspeakers work just fine!"

And so it was. Springvale's future lay in the hands of bureaucratic nincompoops. It would be every man, woman, and child for themselves.

I went outside. The storm was subsiding, yet not the one inside me. I got in the car and headed home. Some power lines were downed. Streetlights were flickering; many were out altogether. My car had only one headlight working, and in places the road was flooded and hard to see. Had to slow down. Caught sight of one of the local churches in the distance. Its doors were opened wide. Overhead lights and a sea of burning candles illuminated the inside. From my viewpoint outdoors, the place looked like a miniature cathedral lit up under a Christmas tree. There appeared to be a large crowd inside. Unusual, I thought. It was a weekday night. I slowed down more, almost to a crawl. Something odd about the scene, couldn't say what, piqued my interest. I rolled down the window and craned my neck to get a better view. There was a large, animated throng of worshippers inside. Must've been close to two hundred. Upon a closer look, they didn't appear to be engaged in worship services at all. I got out, almost slipped in mud, and approached the entrance. There was a heated discussion, verging on argument. Precisely about what, I couldn't make out. I got closer and decided to step inside.

"As minister of this House of the Lord, let me say to all of you it's always open to His children. You women, and anybody else for that matter, are safe here; nobody's going to hurt you. We don't have any firearms here for protection, but what we have here is the love of the Lord, for they that beseech Him in their hour of greatest need — "

"And why don't we bring in firearms for protection, preacher? Who in almighty hell's going to protect anyone from these gangs of wild jackals, even in Springvale, when they're baying for blood? Who? Better yet, how, you tell me?" cried out an elderly woman from the rear.

"The Bible tells us that we don't need guns when we're — "

"The Bible doesn't say a goddamned thing about guns! Didn't even have any when it was written, Mr. Man-of-the-Cloth!"

The voice dripped sarcasm; it was one of Liberty's lesser-known members. I couldn't remember his name; only recently did he become active in the cause. He trembled when he spoke; face-to-face with a 'man of the cloth,' he wasn't backing off.

"Don't you reference the name of God here in that vile manner, you blasphemer!"

"I'll reference it any damned way I damned well please!"

Several men nearby lunged forward and grabbed at the arm of the 'blasphemer,' violently yanking him aside, demanding he "take a deep breath and try to calm down!"

"How the hell can I calm down after what happened to my neighbor's little girl right here this morning, practically right outside these steps, right in goddamned daylight for everyone and his uncle to gawk at? How?" he screamed, shaking.

"Yes, I've heard she was raped by four thugs," said the minister mildly in a manner intended to diffuse erupting emotions.

"No, she wasn't raped. Darn close to it, however," yelled one woman pushing her way forward from the rear of the audience. I recognized her as one of Liberty's auxiliary members. "And this Magnum is what prevented it!" she hollered, aiming the gun up in the air toward the ceiling for all to see. A collective hush rose throughout the hall, and then there were cries of "Yeah! That's it! Way to go, sister!" Even "I pray you blasted their balls but good!" Desperate outbursts spawned by desperate times. Yet not all concurred. Mumblings of "I hate guns!" and "Gun violence begets more" could be heard. The minister, now flummoxed, appeared at once to resign himself to the futility of pressing his point further. This was one congregation hell-bent on vengeance.

"Didn't have to shoot. Once they saw me, they ran away like some girly-boy facing his angry momma." A chorus of laughter burst forth. "Sergeant Hines is now investigating. Maybe by next month; he's that backed up." Muffled assent and attendant sniggering came from all corners of the assembly. She turned around to face me. "And you, Watson. Saw you take off in your car. Thought you were going to try at least do something about it, Chrissakes." I felt a compulsion to say something, anything. Words died in my throat. "Holy Jesus," she said, shaking her head.

One of the old women hobbled forward. "Yes, local boys, young and old alike, can't seem to keep their penises in their pants!" she exclaimed. "Never could. Gotten out of hand!" she fumed. A polarized reaction, mostly along gender lines, followed. "You said it!" and "Come off it, you crazy old bitch!" and "Just how the hell would you know? Speaking from experience?" Things were snowballing out of control. Another elderly woman standing beside the minister lamented the "disgusting garbage mouths some people have these days when in the house of God." The minister dipped his head slightly in tacit concurrence and made a bid for everyone's attention.

"All right, I know we've all been through a lot lately. Let's just all take a deep breath." Collective sighs of "Amen" went up. We tried to collect ourselves, with varying success. I caught sight of Tiny in a corner the same time he saw me. Barely recognizable. He had trimmed his hair and shaved his stubble, and he now sported a mismatched suit and tie: a complete-enough makeover, the envy of any TV contestant. He nodded in my direction, went to say something, then, thinking better of it, stopped himself in mid-sentence and merely smiled. I mulled over his new look, wondering if it were a ruse to deflect state police suspicion of him in Trooper Leopold's killing.

"As I said, the Lord welcomes all of you with open arms into His holy church. As head minister here, no one shall be turned aside, for, in a sense, this is your real, your ultimate home. Feel welcome. If you feel endangered at home, particularly you women, we've cots, water, sandwiches. I would just like to add, your generous donations would be most welcome as well. God loves a cheerful giver. Book of Corinthians. The more one gives, the more one shall receive."

"Ha! Money-begging as bad as the Catholics, maybe worse," spat out someone in the rear.

"I heard that crack!" shot back the minister. "Heck, it takes money — you know — to pay for these things. I can't steal this stuff and pass it out for free." Many in the throng nodded their agreement. "Many of us still seem to have money left over for sporting events, entertainment; it purifies the spirit to pitch in for neighbors in greater need."

At the mention of sporting events, the ears of a man standing next to me perked up. He leaned over to speak to his companion, scarcely above a whisper: "Heard today that the NBA's canceling the Finals. Of all things. Jesus, I pray to God it's not true. Nothing's like this has ever happened in history. How in God's name are we going to survive?"

It was late now. With that remark, I had heard enough. Had to head home. I still thought of the aborted rape, then of Mark, then of Leroy and Josh. I was concerned about our baby, but in a sense, not that much about Kimmy herself. She had the company of my Colt .45. Along with plenty of ammunition. I headed for the door.

Chapter 16

"Good day to all of you in the Granite State. This is your governor speaking to you from the executive office here in Concord. I have ordered all available New Hampshire TV and radio stations to broadcast this emergency message. I am going to deviate from my earlier prepared script. Let it be stated from the outset that this is a message of preparation, not panic. We are facing perilous times, not only here, but throughout the country, indeed, the world. America is facing her worst crisis since Pearl Harbor. The United States of America is on the verge of all-out warfare. That's right: all-out warfare, principally in the Middle East, yet elsewhere as well. I was told by various sources in Washington not to mention this today. This, in good conscience as a Christian more so than as your governor, I cannot, I will not, do. In recent decades it's been almost anathema to mention the word 'Christian' in public discourse, certainly in public political discourse. I don't care now. Current events demand that I give you a full and complete rendition of the truth, of what we are facing here today at this very moment. For that, I am prepared to face whatever consequences befall me from out-of-state officials. Above all, my first duty, my first obligation, is to serve and to protect you who elected me to this office, not to any politico in our nation's capital.

"I'll be unusually frank with you today. It's been said that politicians will lie, say whatever it takes to get elected. Let me say to you here today that this is one man who's going to give it to you straight. First, the situation, both nationally and internationally, is worse than what you've been led to believe by many federal authorities. Let me repeat: both on the national and global scale, things are worse than what you've been told by many Washington officials. That said, we must leave it to our federal authorities to protect the entire country in the best manner they see fit. Second, as your governor, however, it is my responsibility to protect our citizens here the best way I see fit. As such, I am directing our state National Guard to assist the Office of Emergency Management and State Police to quell the rising tide of lawlessness, particularly in our cities. Over the past several weeks, the wave of violent assaults, including rape and murder, rioting and arson, have sky-rocketed to epic proportions in some areas of the state. Effective tomorrow at mid-night, there will be a midnight-to-6:00 a.m. curfew. Those in violation of the cur-few will be detained; those caught committing violent crimes on our streets at any time risk being shot on sight. It is regrettable to have to institute this drastic meas-ure; most residents of our great state are law-abiding. Unfortunately, a few — yet too many — have chosen to take it upon themselves to exploit current conditions. For anyone who is thinking about taking advantage of the existing situation to commit a crime, think again. Anarchy cannot, will not, be tolerated. All citizens are hereby ordered to obey all directives from state authorities. There will be no second request. Third, we must make collective disaster preparations for ourselves, our families, our neighbors, our communities. Immediately. Preparations are being made statewide to ensure the availability of adequate water and food supplies for all communities. In the meantime, each of you must do their share to stock up on individual provisions and fortify your home as your shelter. Details on how to best do this will be forthcoming. There is no time to waste.

"Please stay tuned to your regional station or channel for further instructions specific to your individual community or county. You know, as your state leader, I never thought I'd have to deliver an announcement such as this. May I take this moment to wish that each and every one of our law-abiding citizens receives the Holy Grace of God. By staying the course together, we can get through this to-gether. New Hampshire always has. God bless you, and God bless these United States of America, especially our beloved New Hampshire."

That Washington was lying about the extent of military involvement overseas came as no new revelation. Since my soldiering days, I had long lost belief in gov-ernment. News reports were rife with inconsistencies and outright contradictions. Few folks paid consistent attention anymore. However, the announcement trans-formed itself into a simmering resentment within Kimmy.

She sat on the living room sofa, brushing aside her hair. And then a tear. "I know now I may neb-er see my family again, my little doggie, Sasha...." She de-scended into gentle sobbing. I had never seen her so moved. I put my arms around her shoulders, gently rocked her side to side, kissed the crown of her head, and whispered simply, "I wish I could vouch for the safety of your family in Japan, though you know I can't, but at least the two of us will pull through this here together. We'll make it." The image of her sobbing froze in my mind.

"What can I do for them?" she wailed and wept, staring at the floor. "Nothing!" I went to comfort her again, then stopped. There was this distance between us. There's pain at times inside every human being that can only be dealt with alone.

I stood up by her side awkwardly. "I'm going out to the Morton's'. Check up on them, at least Josh." Her head still lowered; she appeared to nod in understanding. I made my way toward the door and turned around. She sat there, slumped over, hands stroking her knees, girlish…. I wanted to reach out to her, placate her bitter soul….

Outdoors, the winds gusted. They seemed to dance with the overhead clouds. Birds were out singing in full force. New England springtime splendor once again had burst forth eternal in her prime. It would soon be Memorial Day. Tiny crocuses, alongside lilacs emerging in swirling patterns of vibrant purplish hue and forsythia bushes exploding in brilliant yellow, dotted the landscape. The scent of the lilacs wafted my way. I drifted back to where I had been in Wedgemont this time last year….

Memories of Maria, Buckie, Sheila, Steve's Central Café all bubbled in my brain. How they would ride out the crisis, assuming they could, jabbed at my conscience. Then in my gut. There was the bitter realization I could do nothing for them, not for any of them, and it pained me to admit the fact. In Springvale, we had more than our own hands full.

I started up the car. Most roads were in poor condition from the recent rainfall and lack of maintenance, and I contemplated how, even if, I could make it to the outskirts of town. More than one bridge appeared to be on the cusp of yet another collapse. The thought of being greeted again by Mrs. Morton's signature hangdog snarl instilled reservations in me, but I drove on. The vehicle made crunching sounds as it ran over and mashed the downed tree limbs scattered in the roadways. Few pedestrians were outside; fewer vehicles roamed the roads. No state guardsmen had yet returned to duty. Farmhouses and barnyards rolled by. Except for horses and cattle in greening fields and some deer carcasses hung out to bleed dry, Springvale resembled a ghost town. Joe's Diner even appeared shut down for the day.

When I arrived, I noticed the structural integrity of the tiny bridge leading to her home was compromised. I decided to park and stepped out to wade into the shallow but bitter-cold mountain stream. From a distance, things looked askew. Feet numb, I approached the entrance. The lawn hadn't been cut, but Leroy was never one for home maintenance, I reminded myself. The front door was ajar; the place appeared to have been ransacked. I caught myself, my fist in midair, about to pound on the door, half-expecting her to pounce out from behind, then pounded anyway. Then again. An eerie silence hovered over the doorway. I went inside.

It was dark. I flipped on the light switch; the electricity was off. I cut my hand on the worn-out and jagged edge of the switch. My hand started bleeding. In the hazy light, I could make out that the house had been pillaged. Leftover editions of a Harlem newspaper, evidently one that Mrs. Morton subscribed to here in the hinterlands, fluttered in the breeze coming in from a smashed-out window. Leroy's boxing trophies still adorned the living room mantelpiece. Next to them stood a recent photo of a toothy Josh and another of young Leroy and his wife, cheek-to-cheek, in happier days. Clothes and assorted knickknacks lay strewn on the floor. What appeared to be African statuaries lined the wall; some had been toppled over. The room smelled moldy.

"Is that your car outside?"

I spun around, trembling, pissing in my pants.

"I'm the woman next door. Sorry, didn't mean to spook you."

"You startled me. A little bit at any rate." I worried that she would notice my stained trousers. "Just came by to check up on them."

"They've taken off, that crazy old black bitch and her boy. Said something about New York. House was broken into right after by the gangs. My boyfriend really ought to nail the door shut. Vandals came and took everything they're going to take, though, I suppose. You're a big guy, yet you didn't look like any thug or vandal from outside. Never could figure her out. Wouldn't cozy up to white folk, no matter how hard you tried to be nice to her. Led a pretty lonely life here, she did. What she was doing here, I'll never know. But that husband of hers was a good man, damned good man. Always giving folks a helping hand in the neighborhood, forever doting on his kid. Shame what happened to him, huh? And the boy — witty as a razor he was — and twice as sharp."

"I see. Well, I'd better be going. Nothing I can do to help out now."

"Wish I could be more help. You'd better bandage up that hand. Too bad it had to turn out like this for them. 'Cept for her, they were really good folks. I dunno. Maybe she had her reasons for not liking white people."

"Think so? Maybe." I grabbed at one of the fluttering newspaper pages, pretending to read it, and used it to cover my crotch as I advanced toward the door. "Too bad for her, I know, but I really worry for their son."

"Used to come over and tutor my sister's kid, who's dumber than a box of rocks, in math and in English, too. Spoke like some kind of little professor. If he hadn't been stuck out here in these woods, he could've been headed for Harvard or something."

"Maybe."

On the way home, I stopped at the general store downtown, now open only a few hours daily. Shelves were almost bare. Scarcity of provisions played on people's nerves. Customers cursed the government and then one another over who should get what little remained. A fistfight was about to erupt off to my side over the last jar of peanut butter. I scrambled out of the aisle and went to pay with a credit card. Bank ATMs for dispensing cash had been down; some area banks hadn't opened at all. The cashier tried clumsily to take an imprint of the card with her pencil and paper while holding up irate customers queued up behind me. "Why don't you use cash, knucklehead?" an old woman yawped from the rear. She was soon joined in by a chorus of others. I went to do so, methodically counting what few bills I had but came up short. This time lapse infuriated impatient patrons all the more. Through the window behind the register, I saw an elderly neighbor behaving oddly in the rear lot. I left the items on the counter, other than the few I could afford to pay cash for, and headed outside. "The nerve of some people!" the woman fumed again to all within earshot as I descended the stairs.

The neighbor was pacing aimlessly, as though cornered; she appeared to be in a state of high dudgeon over the presence of a man on the other side of the small, secluded pond next to the rear lot. He was carrying a machete. Other than the three of us, the area was vacant.

"What's the matter?" I asked. She didn't respond. "I said, what is it?"

"It's him, it's him; he's the one."

"Who?"

"The gang leader, that hooligan. I haven't had anything to eat in four days. No money. Social Security checks aren't coming in. And he steals what little food we have. Threatens me and my sister. We called the police, and they said unless he assaults us, they can't afford to send anyone over. There — look! See? He's trying to attack the town swan!"

"Here, take these food items. G'head. Need them more than I do." I turned in the man's direction.

She started to weep. "God bless you, sir. May God bless you. Nobody'll help us. I'm so weak and hungry."

I turned toward the man. "You there! What are you doing?" He pretended not to hear. "I said, 'What are you doing?'" The latter outburst, louder and shriller in intensity, visibly agitated him. He stopped stalking the swan, pivoted around, then hurried toward us, brandishing the machete.

The old woman stood as if locked in a trance, petrified. "Look, you go home and lock yourself in. Let me try to handle this." She remained frozen. "Now, you listen to me, woman. You got food for several days. Go home and lock your doors — now!" I shoved her on her way. He was fast-moving. "Go!" She started to leave, observed his devilish stare as he was now almost upon us, and froze again.

"What have we here? My favorite ol' bitch again. Gotta follow me around. Just can't get enough of me, right, bitch?" She edged backward, nearly tripping on the damp grass, terrified. I stepped in between them. "And what are you? Wait, you're that guy in the car who drove off scared, stupid, and shitless when me and my boys were going to have some fun with that other little bitch the other day, eh?"

"Look, we're not looking for any trouble. The lady here and I were just on our way." I fumbled for her hand while backing off, not taking my eyes off the machete he waved in the air, again pushing her to go. I saw that we were still alone; no one was coming to help. She turned to leave. He went for her. I stepped farther in between them. He stopped.

"Why, I ought to chop off your head here and now, the way I was going to do the swan." He pointed the machete at my head.

The woman was gone. I backed away more. "I wouldn't do that if I were you. You'll rue the day."

"What? 'Woo the day'?" He laughed. "Who the hell you think you are? Some intellectual or something? Teach you to talk like that to me." He moved in closer, the machete poised ever-outward from his straight-armed grip. "I've seen you in town with that Chinese bitch. Think I'll fork and pork her after I finish with you here, you gutless cow — "

He never saw anything. I had motioned toward the swan, deflecting his attention. Hot pepper spray, which I'd kept hidden in an inconspicuous slit in my coat, hit his face full force. He collapsed to his knees, clutching his throat, gasping and gagging, and dropped the machete. I walked over and kicked it away. "Now, were you saying you don't like 'Chinese bitches' and 'gutless cowards'? That's a rhetorical question. You know what that means?" He shook his head. "No? I didn't think so." I started to explain, then decided not to. Went to spray more of the hot stuff in his face. Just for good measure. Then I dragged him by his hair along the pond's edge while looking out for witnesses, his heels violently thrashing and digging into the ground to steady himself, and took him inside a nearby open shed and shut the door. I tied his arms behind his back with my scarf and placed my belt around his neck.

"We'll be here awhile. What's your name?" Mucous and spittle drooled down his chin. "What? Can't hear you. A little louder. You were plenty loudmouthed outside a minute ago."

"J-J-Joey."

"'Joey'? Mine's 'Will,' but you can call me 'Bill,' if it pleases you. My friends do. Anything but 'Silly Willy'; that's what the neighborhood bully used to call me growing up. No need to be formal now, don't you think?" He continued choking and gagging. "You know, a cowboy from Texas in my unit in 'Nam in '73 was named Joey. Funny thing is, though, resemblance between you two ends there. He had a code, principles. What've you got? Know what? I was once told by a resident here that I had principles, too. Told me that that would just get me killed quicker, the way it did Cowboy Joey in 'Nam: skinned alive and dismembered by the Viet Cong. Ever see a friend's body that's been skinned alive and dismembered, Joey?" He shook his head. "No, I didn't think so either. Know what memory of that does to you? How it stays and rots itself away into your brain, your guts, year in, decade out?" I grabbed his hair and twisted back his head to scrutinize his face. "I said, Do you know what that does to you?" He murmured some sort of assent. "Yeah?"

His gagging became a gurgle. His face was changing color. I lightened the grip on the belt. "Cowboy Joey had a code. What's yours? Elvis and Budweiser? Stealing food from near-starving old ladies, raping little girls for 'fun,' and decapitating swans? That's what you been put on this Earth to do with your life, Joey? I said, 'That's what you been put on this Earth to do'?" He started bawling. I forced his head against the floor to muffle the noise.

"You know, an existentialist philosopher once said that 'hell is other people.' You wouldn't know anything about 'existentialism,' would you?" He nodded. "But you would about 'hell being other people.' You see, you're that 'hell,' Joey. For other people. And maybe to yourself. But no more." I looked out the window. The lot was deserted.

"Believe in God, Joey?" I asked. Again, he moved his head; it was impossible to determine the answer. Not that it would matter anyhow. "When I was in 'Nam, especially on night patrol, I'd look up into the night sky and wonder myself. It's been said that we're made in His image. But what's always bothered me about that is, if we're made in His image, how could that apply to something like you? Oh, I know. We're told we're not to judge; only He could do that or is supposed to. Somehow that was always too pat; never made any sense. Know what I mean?" He tried to move, maybe break free. "Don't. It'll only hurt more. Just try to relax. Go with the flow of it. Make it easier on yourself. It'll come quick and painless. Promise."

I looked through the window at the swan, still swimming in circles around the pond, seemingly oblivious of the precarious situation it had faced moments earlier. "Hmph. And to think you wanted to decapitate that. Could that be His image? The image of God? You know, all the time I lived here, I never paid much attention to that swan. Could it be I wasn't paying much attention to God?" I stood fixated by the magnificence of its rhythmic movement in the still waters.

"How old are you, Joey?" He managed to mouth the words "thirty-nine." "'Thirty-nine'? Prime of one's life. And what did you accomplish in those thirty-nine years?" He gurgled and tried to speak. Something. "Never mind. I know. I know in your thirty-nine years you never saw the beauty in this world, the beauty in the faces of those neighborhood little girls you raped for fun or tried to, in the faces of the terrified and hungry women you stole food from for the helluva it, in the image of that sentient creature, frolicking in the pond outside, that you went to slaughter, again for fun. You want to know what, though? I saw nothing of beauty in this world myself for the longest time, Joey. Maybe we're really brothers under the skin after all, eh? Unlike so many of my brothers I left behind in Vietnam, I was given a second chance. They weren't even given that. And so, I'm going to give you that second chance, Joey, aged thirty-nine, homeboy from Springvale, New Hampshire." I stood him up. "Look up and out of this window at the beauty of the swan. It is in giving up your life that the swan there lives eternally. Behold the beauty of the swan, Joey. And now it's time to go ever so gentle into that good night." I reached for that martial arts device I always kept hidden in my pocket....

When I arrived home, Kimmy was already waiting by the door. "Where've been? Been waiting oh-so-long. What's, what's this?" She held up the cut hand. "And this!" She motioned to the blood covering my shoe.

"Must've dripped from my hand. Got cut walking around in the dark at the Morton's." Just then, I realized the blood had saturated the shoe opposite the injured hand. She hadn't caught the discrepancy.

"Let me make it better." She went to the bathroom and returned with gauze and Mercurochrome and attended to the hand.

"How's your day?" I asked.

"Good. And yours?"

"My day? Interesting. Yes, interesting. Definitely got some things accomplished. How's the baby coming?"

"Ahh. Fine." She smiled and wet her lips. "What's happened to Mortons?"

"Abandoned their house and left for New York City."

"And downtown?"

"Not much. Just a near-fight over a jar of Skippy peanut butter at the general store."

"Hmm, not surprised.... Too much blood on your shoe for such small cut."

"Think so? Maybe."

"Mercotti not called yet."

"What? What happened to 'Mercotti-san'?"

"Hmph," she snorted. "Make not joke of it, that koumon." Another TV National Emergency News Bulletin interrupted regularly scheduled programming: a notification that the president was about to announce something big. "Talk. Talk. Talk. Warning. Warning. Warning. Can't keep up with it. Broadcasted all day. Oh, here's letter. From relative?"

What ought to have taken a couple of days for delivery had taken two weeks. It was from my aunt. Hadn't been in touch in years. With some anxiety, I tore open the envelope.

"Dear Billy,

I had considerable difficulty tracking you down. I hope this letter reaches you (the mailman barely works now) and finds you in good fortune. Heaven knows you've had your lack of it in life. I do hope your new job has turned out good, given the fact that it's been the first real one you've had in years. Your mom and dad always favored your sister, but you were always the smart one. (Except for making money). Just to let you know, I hear your ex is not doing all that good with her new boyfriend. Why not contact her? To cheer her up?

I'm making do here since Uncle Joe died. Surviving. Like everyone else during the crisis. Wonder if you think it could lead to World War three? The politicians are saying no, but you know how there lying all the time.

Punchie's doing fine. Our doggy's getting old. Going to be 13 soon. Hope you'd have seen her before leaving Wedgemont. I remember how you'd play with her after you got married and can still see you chasing her in the garden. She misses you. Well, I better be going. Pray for me here, Billy. I'll do the same for you there.

Your auntie,

Betty

P.S. I almost forgot. Your sister told me she's sorry for all the things she called you when you returned home from the army. I'm so sorry the family has broke up. Just wanted to let you know.

P.P.S. You never should have been sent over there to fight in that stupid war, Billy! Look what it did to you."

I contemplated the "P.S." for the longest time.

"Will, Will, what's wrong? What is it?"

The overarching insensitivity didn't cut me, but reading "P.S." did. My eyes welled up. Exhausted, I made my way to bed, wishing I'd wake in the morning to discover that the day had been a dark dream. I, too, again thought of what the war had done to me.

Chapter 17

We never did hear from the Oval Office or from the governor's executive suite — only from hell. Rumors abounded of a coup in Washington, most likely by the Joint Chiefs. News reports became ever more haphazard; it was impossible to tell. Outdoor temperatures ratcheted up a notch or two, as did people's desperation. Springvale became our crucible. It wasn't long before I would receive three cell phone calls in rapid succession that would rip apart my guts and change my life forever.

I considered driving out to Swenson to see how things were going. Decided against it. Had done all I could for the semester. Meanwhile, key Liberty Militia members had been calling for a meeting to discuss convening an all-out formation, absent Mike Richards. "Tired of being stalled and deballed," one of them put it. I declined to meet up with them, welshing on my earlier agreement with Richards. I knew, regardless, that cohorts would make good on their intention. More urgent matters beckoned — like simple survival.

Ordinary household items grew scarcer. Mark did stock the basement room, true, yet the necessity of several additional essential items surfaced. On our porch, I hugged Kimmy goodbye and then drove downtown for more batteries and candles.

I swerved to dodge rotting roadkill starting to pile up in and around central Springvale for lack of Transportation Department funding. Out of a corny sense of civic obligation, several times, I stepped out from the vehicle to kick to the curb broken bones and splattered guts, trying my best to keep any fresh blood from splashing on my shoes and pants. Hell, nobody else was doing anything about it.

When I got downtown, store shelves were almost barren. Procuring simple necessities became akin to trekking through a jungle. Once inside the general store, I lunged for the last remaining batch of flashlight-sized batteries, running shamelessly in the aisle past an old man coveting the same, almost knocking him to the floor. "Sonofabitch, you!" he cried. All of the candles had been sold out. I hurried for a nearby food mart. My phone rang.

"Watson?"

"Yes?"

"This is Hines."

"Oh, what can I do for you, Sergeant?"

"You can't do anything for me, Watson, but I can for you."

"Oh, how's that?"

"It's about your buddy, Mark Mercotti. Heard from him lately? If so, where is he?"

"He called recently to say he somehow made it back to Connecticut and that he'd call back soon — today in fact — about something big."

"He did, eh?" It sounded like he snickered next. "Look, we've lost control of the situation in the region with all of the escalating chaos, but I managed to find time to do some investigation into his background back at headquarters." He cleared his throat. "I don't know what's in store for his future, but he's had one helluva checkered past."

"Wh-Wh-What are you talking about?"

"Well, for starters, he got chaptered out of the Army in the middle of his career."

"Why?"

"Homosexuality."

"What?"

"Personally, I don't care; that's none of my concern. What is, though, is his background while stationed in Vietnam."

"What 'background'?"

"He was in some sort of black ops, something so secret, I can't scratch the surface of it, not even with old contacts inside the intelligence community. Hit a dead end every time…. Watson? Watson? You still there?"

"Huh? Uh, yes, still here."

"Well, just wanted to apprise you, like you'd put it. And one more thing: I'd like you to come in to headquarters soon."

"For what?"

"To answer a few questions."

"About?"

"About your relationship with Trooper Leopold."

"My relationship with Trooper Leopold?"

"Yeah. Should only take a few minutes. Routine stuff."

"I see. I'll come soon."

"When?"

"Tomorrow afternoon."

"Good. See you then. Oh, and Watson."

"What?"

"Let me know when you hear from Mercotti again. Got some questions of my own for him."

"I see."

"By the way, there's been another homicide recently in your area."

"Really?"

"Didn't hear about it?"

"Not a thing. What happened?"

"Happened behind the general store, over by the pond. Can't say anything other than that."

"Closing in with any leads?"

"You kidding? We're so backed up here at headquarters. Like I said, we've lost control. Besides, Leopold's getting first priority. He was one of our own. Of sorts."

"Hmm."

"You know, you and Mercotti were — how can I say?— quite a team."

"Yes, perhaps we were at that. 'Quite a team.'"

I stood outside the store, transfixed. My head was spinning. I tried to collect myself and got back into the car.

I turned over the engine and slowly headed for the food mart. State guardsmen were still not posted to enforce the governor's curfew; it was said they were more needed in the cities. Townsfolk were queued up off to the side of an ATM in front of one of the local banks, which appeared closed. Scuffling broke out. My car edged slowly toward the mart; roads hadn't been cleared of debris for days. I worried about Kimmy and stepped out to use the town's sole public phone; my cell battery was dying.

"Forget about it!" someone shouted. "Gangs busted it so no one could call 9-1-1 if their personal phones don't work, as if anyone's going to respond anyway."

What Sergeant Hines had just told me reverberated in my brain. I looked at the phone, busted, then at the town center in the distance, and contemplated what had become of Springvale.

It was getting late. I didn't want to leave Kimmy alone for long and thought about returning home but was determined to get the candles. Fighter jets streaked overhead, heading south as cattle bawled in a far-off barnyard. The phone rang. I pulled off to the side.

"Bill? Mark."

"Mark? Worried about you. You all right?"

"Well, I'm doing best I can. Now you better listen up, Bill, and listen good. There's not much time left. I — "

"'Not much time left'? Not much time left for what?"

"I'll explain everything. But you have to listen to me, Bill. Listen carefully. What I'm about to say to you will shake you to your core. Remember that time last spring at the cafe in downtown Wedgemont when we were talking about AVCs — I mean UFOs — and I told you there'd come a time for you to know certain things and to trust me?"

"Wondered about it every day since."

"Well, that time has come."

My heart started pounding. I leaned over and braced myself against the steering column. "G'wan."

"What you thought was real in your life is not. I — "

"What are you talking about? If this is your — "

"Shut up and just listen! After your actions on the battlefield near Loc Ninh, you were being put up for the MOH. It got quashed before it ever got to the desk of Secretary of Defense Laird. Had to be. You couldn't afford to be made a hero and put in the limelight. You see, you were part of an ultra-secret CIA-run project to mold a new super-soldier — Project Sixty-Seven. I know because I oversaw part of it. Many were screened, few were chosen. You were chosen during your first tour — by me. Don't ask me why. I had personal reasons....

"Mainly, it consisted of administering mind-altering drugs, psychotropics, usually with needles when the subject was unconscious and enhanced electromagnetic frequencies to the brain via cranial implants. The last phase of the program was set up as a result of the experiences of UFO abductees. UFO researcher Budd Hopkins was the first to write of missing time lapses experienced by them in '81. CIA and elements within DoD knew of this years earlier. Your implant — that's right, you have one in your head right now as we speak — was designed after those found in alien abductees by Project Sixty-Seven. And you always wondered why Colonel Johnson at the VA was suddenly forced to stop treating your headaches. Had to. Wasn't cooperating with her superiors to back off from conducting further tests over the implant. The government couldn't prevent alien abductions. What agents did to you, however, was shameful. That could have been prevented. I know — because I could've stopped them. I'm sorry, Bill. I've tried to make it up to you...." His voice started to crack.

"Until I requested deactivation of your implant, you'd been monitored by our Uncle Sam and the CIA. So has my contact with you. But it doesn't matter now for us anymore with everything falling apart — it's all over. Global events which are unfolding now have already happened. Don't ask me to explain. I don't fully understand myself. Makes no sense, logically. It's all founded upon above-top-secret studies into future events based largely on Einstein's theories involving time. The government tried to intervene to prevent these future events from coming to pass but failed.

"You'll recall Air Force General Brown was very concerned at the time over UFOs. He was neither the only high-ranking official then nor today. They've been monitoring us for a long time, especially since our development of atomic weaponry. In fact, it's thought by some that they're monitoring what's happening with the intention of inheriting the Earth, for want of a better word, after this is over, with some kind of hybrids resulting from breeding ETs and humans. Build a new civilization. I don't know.

"You remember lying injured next to that M-106A1 carrier outside of Loc Ninh and seeing a UFO, then reporting it to the IBT?"

"The Intelligence Briefing Team?"

"That's right. You were told to keep your mouth shut. It was believed you had some sort of contact with it. Why? Not known for sure. I have no time to get into that now. Now there's not much time left for any of us. We're bitched. Get home and get into the sealed basement shelter I built for the two of you."

"Wh-What about you?"

"Me?" There was a long pause. "Time is running out. This is it. This will most likely be the last time we ever hear each other's voices, Bill. But don't worry about me. I'll deal with my loneliness. You just remember to take care of yourself and Kimmy and your baby. That we're human is an illusion, Bill. Remember the true essence of who and what we are ultimately in our brief journey on this Earth."

"And what is that?"

"Ashes and dust."

Springvale's sirens started wailing in the distance and then, just as abruptly, died out. I sat slumped over the steering wheel, clutching the phone, shaking. I can't recall what I did next. Then, for whatever reason, I remember looking out from the car window and over in the direction of the pond behind the general store.

"Get moving, Mac! You're blocking traffic." It was a woman's voice, rough, coming from behind. I tried to collect my wits. I remembered about the candles and turned on the ignition, moving slowly toward the food mart and sitting behind the wheel, dazed, as though locked more in a dream than rooted in reality. Somehow, I made it to the storefront and stumbled through the door. The place was in chaos.

"Damn it all! Get out of my way! Give it to me!..."

"Let me have that last can of baby formula. Please, mister. We don't have enough to feed our kids...."

"What! What! You want ten bucks for this goddamned loaf of bread?..."

"Give me that, or I'll knock your goddamned teeth out. And I don't care if you are a woman...."

"Sorry, Bill. Candles sold out."

I started for the exit, turned around to observe the seething chaos, and walked through the door and onto the stairs leading up to the building. The afternoon sun, now strong overhead and getting more so by the day, cast shadows over the town as if to presage what would fall upon it. I stepped down the stairs and into the parking lot. My phone rang. Again. Thought it would be Kimmy. It was Sheila.

"William? William? I've had such a hard time getting through."

"Sheila? Well, I know my payments have no longer been — "

"It's not about that! It's about us! Those things don't matter anymore! Time is short. They say the East Coast is under imminent attack."

"Who says that?"

"News bulletins."

"They do?"

"Yes. I called — I called to say, to say" — her voice choked — "to say that I love you, William. I need to tell you that before anything happens, before it's too late. That's all that matters now." She started sobbing.

"Oh, Sheila..." My voice quavered.

"He never meant anything to me, Will."

"Who?"

"My new boyfriend, the one I was engaged to."

"I see."

"I only went with him for his money, his brand-new flashy sports car and fancy clothes, to patronize the highest-priced restaurants. Used him for his wealth. Thought it would make me into something special, something high-class. Only made me into the town fool. I'm so, so ashamed."

"Sheila?"

"You're the only one I ever loved, William. Only you. And I gave it all away for something I thought would be better. That wasn't real; it was all an illusion.

To put it poetically, as you were fond of doing when we were at Wedgemont High, it was like a night shadow that evaporates with the coming of daybreak, like I awakened from a dream."

"You don't have to say that. Don't beat yourself up."

"Yet that's the truth of it. Will, remember when we first made love in the old apple orchard? You always thought that it was your rival at Wedgemont, Billy Harbeck, who was my first one. It was never him; it was you. And I threw you away. William, William, forgive me for what I did to you."

"You don't have to ask my forgiveness. It's all right, Sheila, it's all right. And I love you, too. Always did."

"Oh God, thank you, William, thank you. And William?"

"Yes?"

"Remember me." She sobbed.

The sound of a huge explosion came blasting through her phone. The transmission went dead. Fate had plucked her into eternity.

I staggered and almost fell over into a dumpster at the corner of the parking lot, then leaned against it, bracing myself. Thought I might be teetering over the edge. My stomach churned. I was about to vomit up more of this sliver of reality than I could hold down. In the recesses of my mind echoed the stentorian voice of my platoon sergeant right after battle, "Get a hold of yourself! Now's not the time to lose it!" I had to get back to Kimmy. I tried to phone her; my phone went dead. I heard something in the distance closing in. I looked up. A low-flying military chopper soared by directly overhead. Next, a faraway explosion resounded over the mountain ridgeline. In the distance, church bells tolled; that was another alarm for residents to take immediate shelter. There came the feeble sound of the town hall's faltering emergency loudspeaker system — didn't work during the most important crisis in the two-hundred-year-plus history of Springvale. It reminded me of the pipsqueak selectman's boast during my recent town hall visit, and I laughed.

Off to my right, scrambling out of the bushes, came a middle-aged couple. They were dickering over payment for sexual services. The thought of this happening at a time like this hit me as hilarious, but prostitution had started flourishing. "Women will sell their bodies, men their souls," I muttered to myself. Even in Springvale. I might have laughed and cried at the same time.

The tolling of church bells got louder, as if growing more desperate. Down the street, coming toward me stood the pipsqueak of a selectman atop the platform of a pickup truck, shouting into a bullhorn, "The United States is under attack! Get into your homes — now! This is an emergency. This is not a drill. Repeat. The United States is under attack. Seek immediate shelter!" Cattle started bellowing and ducks squawked by the town pond. People ran out from nearby buildings and the store, screaming, the contents of their shopping bags spilling and scattering over the parking lot in all directions. Children and the elderly fell and were trampled. Fighting erupted over the contents of shopping bags. Hysteria exploded everywhere. A member of Liberty Militia became involved in a quarrel off to my side over six-packs of Budweiser. "You sonofabitch!" More words were exchanged, punches thrown. His opponent pulled out a knife, then spat in his face. Vengeance oozing out his every pore, the militiaman whipped out a gun and blew away his antagonist not thirty feet in front of me.

Kaleidoscopic patterns of unholy madness.

I jumped into the car and started it up, spinning the wheels on the pavement, and got a whiff of burning rubber. The vehicle lurched forward violently, speeding out and away from the lot as a headlight was busted upon impact against a bridge guardrail....

Kimmy was waiting at the door. "I was so worried. What's happening downtown?"

"The demons of hell have been let loose."

"What? Come, come in." I tossed the batteries on the couch. "You sweating!" She motioned to the television and lowered her head. "It's, it's not good," she said through tightening lips.

The attack on America had come like a hawk swooping down on its prey in the dead of night. CNN and the BBC, alongside other networks, carried conflicting accounts of the unfolding doomsday: waves of escalating violent attacks out West and on the East Coast. Whether they were committed by terrorists or foreign governments wasn't revealed. More notably, war burgeoned in the Middle East, principally between Arab and Jew (but also among Arabs themselves) involving American and other foreign troops. Heads of state, except for our president, were shown being interviewed. Faces of our military brass, grown familiar to the public over the spring, were also markedly absent. A message from the General Secretary of the UN, begging for peace, was rebroadcast.

One of the networks cut away to a live silent broadcast from inside of what looked like the cockpit of a high-altitude US military aircraft. The quivering voice of a news reporter, evidently on land, announced that the plane was on a mission flying over the Eastern seaboard. Why all this was being broadcast was not revealed.

A gargantuan mushroom cloud suddenly appeared below, on the ground. For the first time in her history, the United States of America became the victim of a nuclear assault on her soil. Witnessing the unthinkable. The final Thread of Ultimate Destruction began to unravel and weave itself over and into what had been the American nation, a history, a people, soon to be but a faded memory as footnoted in some galactic history book.

Kimmy stared at me, her jaw slightly dropping, and, without speaking, sank onto the sofa. Network transmissions fizzled. Callous as it may sound, I thought that if there had to be a detonation over an American city, I hoped it was Washington. "We'd better get downstairs and monitor things with the emergency radios," I stammered. "Every moment counts now. Go." I grabbed her arm, gently pushing her down the cellar stairway, thinking I heard the far-off rumblings of a mammoth explosion, and forgetting to take the batteries. Then the electricity went out. And I selfishly realized that because of the mushroom horror came one emerging reality: I wouldn't have to report to state police headquarters after all.

***

We endured the next two weeks huddling in the basement. Over that time, the room seemed to shrink. I, more than Kimmy, grew claustrophobic, yet the shelter served its purpose. Mark had painstakingly put most of the pieces together from his own pocket: food, water, air filtration and sanitation systems, communications equipment, radiation, chemical, and biowarfare protective suits and detection devices… for which we are indebted to him with our lives. I know I couldn't have done it by myself.

Our supreme enemy was boredom — and not knowing with certainty what exactly was going on outside. One can only read for so many hours. Kimmy tried to teach me new card games with meager success; I only understood the idiot's game of war. She fared little better with my tutelage of her in chess. The absence of the extra candles made nighttime particularly hellish. What would seem to be ordinary nights dragged on in perpetuity until, like some benevolent spirit sent from above, daybreak would creep forth through the sealed windows and banish the haunting darkness of the previous evening. Kimmy could brave the lingering darkness; at times, I sensed I'd go crazy. I thought of the implant still inside my head. Constantly. In the stillness of the night, I'd awaken in a cold sweat, staring out the window into the moody nothingness which lay before me, and then, and only briefly, would shine a flashlight at the hands of the wall clock dragging, dragging.... After virtually risking my life to get them, I had forgotten to take the extra batteries downstairs for the flashlight and would routinely curse myself over my idiocy.

More chilling were the constant screams from outside. At least for the first several days. Neither bombs nor radiation, nor chemical warfare engulfed the town; it was a biohazardous attack that plagued the region. We could only imagine the agony of the victims, not being able to see their faces, daring never to go outdoors ourselves. Too, at times it sounded as if some of them were being hunted by others, likewise afflicted, and slaughtered for sport in one sickening, final orgy of violence. There was nothing we could do about it. Soon nights brought eerie silence followed by empty stillness during the days.

The shortwave radio we listened to, another godsend from Mark, received various communications, albeit confusing, of survivors from afar and several as close as Sherbrooke, Quebec, about a hundred miles north. We heard nothing from or about anyone in New Hampshire. After about two weeks, we heard communiqués in French and English from the Sherbrooke region, saying that the worst was over, at least in North America's northeastern sector, and it should be safe to venture outdoors in southern Quebec and northern New England. Mark's biohazardous equipment indicated nothing of immediate danger and I, absent Kimmy, ventured outside at last.

I walked out, wearing the biowarfare and chemical protective suit as a precautionary measure, knowing full well it could still be risky. There were no signs of alarm from any detection device. The direct sunlight, though welcome, hurt my eyes. What I saw wrenched my stomach.

Scores of residents, corpses rotting, though none near the house, littered the landscape in varying degrees of decomposition, many of their faces mirroring their final death throes. Especially bizarre were the eyes — they were opened wide with pupils dilated, almost popping out from the skulls. This gave them the appearance of an 'I-can't-believe-what's-happening-here' look. What was more bizarre were the animals and birds: They appeared to have been unaffected, as though the dispersed pathogen was designed to target humans only. Pending further assurance, I decided not to go near any of them, though after the underground ordeal, my inclination was to pet, hug, and squeeze the domesticated ones. One stray dog, in particular, reminded me of Buckie. I often wondered what happened to her, more so than most people, including members of my own family other than Sheila. I noticed, too, the lonely swan still swimming in the pond.

The town looked strangely surreal; as if it was an elaborate Hollywood movie set. There appeared to be no human survivors. Peace had finally descended. It felt weird that I could go anywhere without restraint, 'rob' the banks if I wanted, though they never had much money. As if it mattered anymore. A few items yet remained in stores; these were for the taking. I caught sight of several packs of assorted batteries in one of them. I started laughing aloud.

Back at the house, Kimmy busied herself with her new survivalist homemaker routine. She seemed to have bounced back from the ordeal with greater buoyancy than I and didn't mention her family or try not to consciously recollect them. I wanted to shelter her for several days from the atrocities that waited outdoors, thinking up all sorts of excuses for her not to go out. Eventually, she would have to behold for herself the product of man's inhumanity to man, bear witness to the ultimate insubstantiality of his character, the hollowness of his soul. Of this, I was certain. It gnawed at my conscience. Repeated leering at the rotting corpses, especially at the children's, engendered a cancerous defense mechanism within me, and I surrendered to blasé numbness upon walking among them, reminiscent of my war experiences. I didn't realize at the time that the macabre scenes were taking their secret toll on me.

I ventured out to Swenson again. Alone. Didn't want Kimmy to see any of her friends dead. Or experience their stench. I knew I'd avoid the international students' dorm myself. As it would be for her, it could be too much for me....

I walked through the main administration building. The bodies of Dean Rodgers and the president were nowhere to be found. Off to my left, not far from where I last saw her alive, lay the witch-prof. Like the others, her eyes were popped open; they seemed to move, follow my every action as if she were still alive. She had a document in hand, clutching it to her bosom. I picked it up: 'Final Grade Roster.' It was meticulously filled out, signed, and dated. She must've made Dean Rodgers proud. Semper Fidelis till the end, she still wouldn't be coming back for the fall semester. I turned away to leave her rotting there. My foot slipped, and it became wedged under her as if to stop me from leaving and continue to torment me in death as she had in life. I leered at her once more. At that moment, I felt a certain shame for both of us. Whatever our differences had been in life, what had they mattered? I hurried back to the car.

On the way back, off to one side at a distance from the main road, I stopped at the entrance to Old Jimmy's farm. Liberty Militia's original signboard, emblazoned on both sides with our motto, By the sword, we seek peace, yet peace only under liberty, lay half-buried in the mud of a shallow pit, as though signifying the militia's makeshift grave. No bodies lay on the ground; they must've been inside. I wouldn't go in. On the horizon, I saw the shooting range, paper targets still flapping in the breeze. Our mantra of 'Liberty and Integrity!' and the welter of gunshots rang out and reverberated in my ears; I could smell the gun smoke; taste the Thanksgiving dinner Kimmy and I had first shared with the cadre inside the barn. Mark's face, his smile ever-luminescent, alongside those of Mike, Big Walt, Petey, Leroy, and the others, appeared before me. Memories of what they meant to me — what we all meant to one another — came bursting forth. I pondered why and how our lives had become entangled in a mutual network of interdependability and what had they mattered. It was just yesterday....

***

Kimmy and I hadn't been the sole survivors in town after all. Somebody else had taken government warnings to heart — or had taken a civil defense course. As if by miracle, a retired farming couple, their own basement sealed airtight and well-

stocked with sundry provisions, had pulled through. They never could comprehend how. They were gentle folk, grateful as hell to have survived and proved to
be trustworthy companions. He would lead me in practical things that, as an academic, I had never paid much attention to in life, like automotive mechanics, plant
cultivation, animal husbandry; his wife instructed Kimmy in the fine art of food
preservation techniques like canning and confecting all kinds of oddball meals,
survivalist knowhow surely to come in handy. Together, we became a sort of
smaller, modern version of the Swiss Family Robinson but stranded on a cow-
dung facsimile of a cosmic blob in New England instead of on a tropical island.

Shortwave radio carried crazy reports, everything from the Battle of Armaged-
don to the Second Coming of Christ in the Mid-East, locust infestations, and
unprecedented tsunamis. Broadcasts alluded to the total collapse of the US. And
pretty much the rest of the world. The holocaust was over. We all debated driving
out to the Sherbrooke area to meet other survivors; gas was plentiful and vehicles
reliable, though road conditions could prove to be a problem. At least there remained no dangerous levels of radioactive, chemical, or biological contaminants.
Kimmy and I both worried over whether the baby would be born healthy.

Most days, I headed out in the town hall pickup truck, the one used by the
diminutive selectman that fateful day, and, covered in facemask, gloves, and protective boots, rounded up as many bodies as I could manage to transport to the
municipal dump on the edge of town. There I burned them. Unsavory yet necessary, I figured I needed to clear them out for at least a half-kilometer radius from
the house to prevent contamination of drinking water. This became my morning
routine. Kimmy called it my ikigai. I never let on to her what I was actually doing;
she had gone through enough.

I deliberated over what Mark used to say of her and then of his parting remark
on the transitoriness of all human life. It made me reflect on my own life and the
fragility of my relationships with Sheila and Kimmy. With Sheila, our lives, inter-
twined, had been tumultuous. She had that hard edge, so ingrained in the fabric
of modern American womanhood. Peel away the leathered surface, though, and
there was a good woman. Kimmy, as an Asian traditionally brought up to defer
and be demure, publicly exuded a soft veneer. At her core, sheltered behind home
doors, she often exhibited a frequent and simmering petulance. Yet I loved them
both.

The Gates of Hell had been unlocked, my psyche torn open wide. Then once again, I slowly realized that the putrefying bodies of Springvale residents, some of whom I knew — and well — were never inessential shells; they had been human beings who had lived, laughed, and loved in what seemed to be a dream within a dream. Perhaps they weren't truly dead but waiting to be called forth to awaken to yet another dream, a dream in which they would exist in peace and harmony. For the reality that they had lived in and had just left seemed almost too horrible to contemplate. And we, the survivors, would march on to blaze a new world, one carved out from the ashes of the past.

***

Not much later in the season, at twilight one fine day, while thinking of Kimmy and the baby and doing nothing special, I walked by the pond downtown. There at the far end by the shed, was the swan. Under intensifying moonlight, its image, reflected in the water, seemed to coruscate on the surface in the afterglow of day. I was in a hurry to return to Kimmy, but for some inexplicable reason, I stopped.

The swan spun around swimming toward me, then stopped at the pond's edge and looked in my direction. In some strange, otherworldly, and ethereal realm, I sensed it was communicating a sacred whisper, a long-hidden revelation, and a shadow-message seeped into my consciousness. A nameless, all-powerful force, one I had never experienced, overwhelmed me, and, collapsing on my knees, I looked up at the sky. For the longest time, I knelt there while a creeping paralysis overtook me. I felt that my heart, pounding inside my chest, was about to explode.

As if from above, I saw myself walking naked in this world and asked God to forgive me for any crimes I had committed during the war at the behest of the American government in the name of democracy. All the shame, the guilt I carried within me for years, decades, came rushing out. I shook violently and wept uncontrollably with such intensity I could barely breathe. My tongue rolled back, and I choked on the spit and mucous pooling inside my mouth. I almost vomited in my throat. Wave after wave of remorse and penitence washed over me and then, abruptly as the convulsions had begun, they ceased.

And I was made whole.

Epilogue

The silence of the night whispered to us as it crept upon the cutting edge of raw human emotion. Having survived indoors for so long, the shattering of our senses impressed upon us a premonition of promises yet to unfold. Springtime evening's transitory magic was as breathless as it was fleeting. The magic of enchanted moments that we tried to grasp somehow eluded us. In but a passing moment, time would seem to freeze itself, and in some unfathomable way, we knew that which had been real was yet an illusion. In only days a lifetime had swept by us. Skies cleared; the nightmare that lingered over us seemingly like an eternal ghost had vanished. It was our time to live and to love once again.

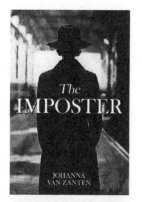
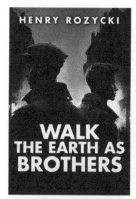

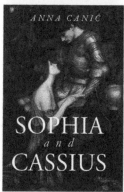

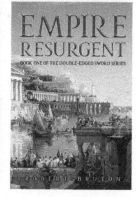